By DON TRAVIS

The Zozobra Incident

Published by DSP PUBLICATIONS
www.dsppublications.com

THE
ZOZOBRA
INCIDENT

A **BJ VINSON** MYSTERY

DON TRAVIS

DSP PUBLICATIONS

Published by

DSP Publications

5032 Capital Circle SW, Suite 2, PMB# 279, Tallahassee, FL 32305-7886 USA
www.dsppublications.com

The Zozobra Incident
© 2016 Don Travis.

Cover Art
© 2016 Maria Fanning.
Cover content is for illustrative purposes only and any person depicted on the cover is a model.

ISBN: 978-1-63477-452-9
Digital ISBN: 978-1-63477-453-6
Library of Congress Control Number: 2016902738
Published November 2016
v. 2.0
First Edition published as The Zozobra Incident & The Bisti Business by Martin Brown Publishers, LLC, 2012.

Printed in the United States of America
∞
This paper meets the requirements of
ANSI/NISO Z39.48-1992 (Permanence of Paper).

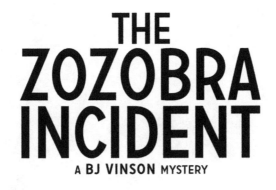

THE
ZOZOBRA
INCIDENT

A **BJ VINSON** MYSTERY

Prologue

South of Santa Fe, New Mexico

THE SANGRE de Cristos to the north and the Jemez Mountains on the west stood like massive, mute sentinels. An unforgiving sun high in the cloudless sky bleached the desert landscape brown and turned Interstate 25 into twin ribbons of glistening black tar. The white four-door Impala barreling down the highway pushed the speed limit—not enough to attract the attention of passing cops but sufficient to clip a few minutes off the hour's drive to Albuquerque.

A blue Mustang convertible closed the distance quickly and then paced the white car. When the Chevy began its long descent down the steep slope of La Bajada into the middle Rio Grande Valley, the Ford muscled past in a burst of speed. Suddenly it swerved right, catching the front fender of the Impala and sending it hurtling toward the sheer drop-off beyond the shoulder.

Chapter 1

SWIMMING THERAPY at the country club had put me behind schedule, so I rode the elevator instead of taking the stairs to the third floor of a downtown landmark building on Fifth and Copper NW. I paused on the landing outside my office to frown at the gold lettering on the door. There was a scratch in the flowing *C* of the sign "B. J. Vinson, Confidential Investigations." I liked that better than "Private Investigator." It had a less sleazy connotation.

I turned the knob and walked inside. "Hazel, somebody scratched—"

My guardian of the outer chamber, Hazel Harris, a plump, gray-haired warden who thought she was my mother, put a halter on my tongue simply by holding up a pudgy white hand. "You're late, BJ. Your first appointment's already here."

"I didn't know I had an appointment. Who is it?"

Her broad mouth compressed into a thin line; her fleshy jowls shook. "Del. He's waiting in your office." Hazel loved me dearly, but she did not approve of my lifestyle. And Del Dahlman was definitely a part of my lifestyle. Or had been.

I blinked. "What does he want?"

A shrug jiggled her matronly frame. "No idea. I met him in the lobby on my way in. He claimed he had an emergency but didn't condescend to share it. 'Confidential' was all he'd say. If you're lucky, it's his law firm's business. Even if it is, you'd do well to show him the door."

"Now, Hazel—"

"Don't flash those apple-green eyes at me, Burleigh J. Vinson. That man's already hurt you enough."

"What do you expect me to do? You said he's in there waiting for me."

"Deal with it."

I opened the door to my inner office, unprepared for the emotional wrench that almost paralyzed me at the sight of the man who had once shared my life. Although Albuquerque is a small-town type of city, I had seen him only occasionally at a distance since our breakup in August of 2005, a month short of one year ago.

"Good to see you, Vince."

Del called me Vince because no one else did. Somehow I found the strength to accept his handshake before dropping into my chair. If he shared my mental turmoil, it wasn't apparent. He wandered the room examining the Gorman and Bierstadt originals and the Russell reproduction. He no doubt recognized them as part of my late father's Western art collection. They'd hung in the house my folks had left me at 5229 Post Oak Drive NW for the three years he shared it with me.

Del settled uninvited into one of the leather chairs opposite my desk. The scent of his aftershave—he still used Brut—wafted across the room and triggered unwanted memories.

"Nice digs." His voice brought me back from the edge. "I was surprised to hear you'd left APD and become a PI. I always heard it was a tough business to break into."

"For a while it looked as though I wouldn't be up to the APD job physically after I was shot, so I left the force. As for being a confidential investigator, it was slow going for a while. But it helps to have cop friends refer business." Del only indulged in small talk when he was nervous, and although that piqued my interest, it wasn't enough to sustain it. "Look, you should take your business elsewhere. I don't care if it is Stone, Martinez, et cetera."

"It's Stone, *Hedges*, Martinez, et cetera. However, I'm not here to throw some of their money at you." He paused, obviously expecting me to ask why he *was* here. I didn't bite. After studying his buffed fingernails a moment, he spoke again. "You must think I'm a shit."

That one, I couldn't pass up. "A *spineless* shit."

"Touché. But we were good for one another, weren't we? It was so perfect we should have known it couldn't last."

"Maybe you can rationalize it that way. I can't."

Del stirred uncomfortably in his chair. The fact he didn't walk out the door told me he was here on a matter of some importance, at least to him. "You know me, I've got to have some action, and I wasn't getting it from you."

"Christ, I nearly died."

Two years ago a bullet had partially severed the artery in my right thigh while I was trying to apprehend an accused murderer, and I almost bled out. I'd been an Albuquerque police detective at the time.

"I know."

"You couldn't put up with the bloody bandages and the festering wound and the poor sap struggling to make it to the bathroom on time."

The reflexive denial in his eyes died. He nodded. "Yeah, that too. I'm not cut out to be a nurse."

"We had a nurse, Dahlman."

"During the day, but not at night." His eyes flicked to mine as he tried to muster a smile. "You've picked up the weight you lost. God, you look good enough to eat. Short-sighted of me, I guess."

"Not really. You'd lose your tan if I showed you my scar."

Bile collected at the base of my throat as I recalled how Del had irrevocably ruptured our relationship by bringing a gay hustler named Emilio Prada into our home. His next words revealed his thoughts were paralleling mine.

"I thought you were just being jealous, but you were more insightful than I was. You saw through Emilio right away."

"He was a gay for pay. Anyone could see that."

"Anyone but me. He rang my bell too much. Besides, he's more gay than straight." Del shook his head as if trying to clear it. "He's a beautiful son of a bitch."

"With 'son of a bitch' being the operative axiom. Is he still around, or has he gone back to Mexico?"

"Around… but not with me. In fact, that's why I'm here."

My left brain kicked in. "He's blackmailing you."

"You always were quick on the uptake."

"So what's the problem? Half the town knows you're gay. Your law partners know, don't they?"

"Yeah, we've used it to our advantage a couple of times. There's some gay money in this town." He scratched his chin. "But knowing it and seeing it splashed across the Internet are two different things."

"Let me guess. He has pictures."

"Some very nice ones. I was quite proud when he first showed them to me."

"And now they've come back to bite you in the ass." I smiled at this quirky turn of fate.

"You may think it's funny, but it's dead serious to me. I need to get them back. Fast."

"So go find him and wring his scrawny neck."

"Not so easy. He's hiding out somewhere. Everything was fine until we broke up, and then he turned nasty."

"What happened?"

Delbert David Dahlman, Esquire, attorney-at-law, flushed a bright, vein-popping red. "He… he moved a woman into my apartment."

I burst out laughing. "Poetic justice."

"Maybe. Anyway, I gave him a choice. Me or her. He chose her and my pictures."

"What's he asking?"

"Five thousand."

"A modest demand. You've given him gifts worth more than that. Like a car, for instance."

"The five grand is only a confidence builder. He'll sell me a few photos for that and then come after me for the big money."

"Crap, man. How could you not see this coming?"

"Love is blind." He tried to recover his aplomb. "Will you help me?"

"Why not let your firm's investigators handle it?"

"I don't want the firm to know. This is in confidence, but I'm up for a full partnership at the end of the year, and this could sink it. I'll pay you. Just help me out of this jam, okay?"

"Damned right you'll pay. I'll bill you like every other client."

After he forked over a hefty retainer check, I started acting like a professional. "Give me Emilio's last known address."

"That would be the Royal Crest, my apartment house."

"Damn. Do you at least have his phone number?"

"I bought him four cell phones, but he couldn't hang on to any of them. Kept losing them. The last time I told him that was enough. I wouldn't foot the bill for another."

"So no phone number."

"Right."

"How was the extortion demand made?"

"I got a note."

"In his handwriting?"

"Hard to tell. It was printed. You know, in block letters. Emilio used to go through the newspaper, so I know he can read English. But I don't know if he can write it."

"Was the demand note sent through the mail?"

"No, it was dropped off at the apartment house."

"With the doorman?" Del had a swanky address.

"We don't have a doorman, but it's a secure facility. It takes a key to get in the front door."

"So it was just left at the front door?"

"It was stuck in my mailbox. Somebody jammed the corner of the envelope under the door of the mailbox. That's where I found it. And before you ask, the boxes are in the front lobby."

"Behind the locked door?"

Del nodded. "I asked the manager if he let anyone in. He said he hadn't and claimed he didn't know anything about the note. I suppose someone could have entered when a tenant went out. Or maybe he sneaked in through the garage when a car was entering or leaving."

"Do you need a key to exit the front door?"

"No, just turn the handle and you're outside."

"Tell me about the people who operate the apartment house. The manager, maintenance people, housekeepers, people like that."

He gave me personal names when he had them and company names when he didn't. I laid the list aside to check out later. "Let me see the note and envelope."

His mouth tightened. He licked his lips. "I don't have them. I was so angry, I tore them up as soon as I read the note. He didn't sign the thing, but it had to be Emilio. Nobody else has those pictures. Hell, just go find him and get them back. You don't need to see the note for that."

I got in a few more questions before he claimed he needed to get back to the office to prepare for court. More likely he wanted to get away because of my irritation at his stupid handling of the demand note. That was all right; I was almost late for a court date of my own.

Later, as I chuckled my way through the metal detector at the district courthouse, the deputies operating the security station must have thought I'd lost my marbles. In fact, during my sworn testimony—authenticating some videotapes I'd taken—I had a sudden image of Del's face as he told his story, and almost snorted aloud.

I would have had a hell of a time explaining to the judge why Wilbur Maple's embezzlement of $100,000 from a charitable trust was funny. Nonetheless, for the remainder of the afternoon, I savored the bittersweet irony of Del's predicament.

Chapter 2

A LITTLE after ten that night, I squeezed my anonymous white 2003 Chevy Impala between two extended-cab pickups in the overflow parking lot across the street from the C&W Palace. The C&W on East Central Avenue was Albuquerque's biggest country-and-western boot-shuffling joint. This was where Del originally met Emilio, so it was a good place to start after a database search failed to turn up current information on him. That was no surprise; the kid probably lived around town with friends and johns.

I pushed through the heavy door and ran into a wall of cigarette smoke, deafening music, and shrill conversation that turned the interior of the nightclub into a health nut's worst nightmare. Bluegrass doesn't go down well with many opera fans, and I was no exception. My parents, both of whom had been teachers, had exposed me to plenty of Offenbach, Mozart, and Verdi, and it took. *The Tales of Hoffmann* and *The Magic Flute* and *La Bohème* had preserved my sanity during the long convalescence after the shooting. A country-western band was a world away from those old masters—maybe even a galaxy or two.

My snakeskin cowboy boots and white Stetson were sufficiently western to allow me to skip the mother-of-pearl studded shirt and tight denim pants. It was a matter of comfort, not snobbery. Cowpoke duds, especially trousers, were too restrictive for my taste.

After buying a vodka rocks at the long bar, I circled the massive barnlike joint, stopping occasionally to talk to acquaintances. The C&W was a hetero place, but there was enough eye contact to spice up the evening, even though I had no intention of making a connection. One slender, athletic guy twirling a pretty coed around the dance floor caught my attention. I invested a few minutes in watching him as I tried to figure out where I'd seen him before. Eventually I gave up and resumed prowling. After an hour of jostling by clumsy drunks and out of control dancers, I was ready to call it a night when—bingo. There he was.

Emilio Prada wasn't making much of an effort to hide. He looked like a million dollars, dancing with a well-stuffed woman who could have been his mother. That roomy bosom was probably where he intended to rest his head for the night. I thought of Emilio as a kid but knew from his Albuquerque Police Department jacket he was twenty-two. He'd come up legally from Durango, Mexico, and had a record for petty stuff—nothing that would get him deported. He didn't seem to be married, and it apparently didn't matter to him which way he swung, just so long as the swing was profitable. I guess that earned him a bi rating.

The handsome shit was dressed all in black, including a ten-gallon hat shoved rakishly back to expose unruly dark curls. A scarlet hatband, a red belt, and a bit of crimson on his alligator boots added the only traces of color to his outfit. On him it was dynamite. He danced easily, confidently, the same way he'd behaved while he was living in Del's room in my house. If Emilio harbored doubts about anything, it wasn't apparent. He counted on charming his way out of any trouble hovering over the horizon.

When the number ended, he gave his partner a hug and a peck on her plump cheek before leading her away through the crowd. I scrambled straight across the dance floor as a twang of guitars and a bang of drums announced the next song. Eluding the grasp of cowgirls bent on dancing—or more likely desperate for a companion for the night—I lost the odd-looking pair for a moment before spotting Emilio holding out a chair for the *mamacita*, like the gentleman he was not. Then he took one of two vacant chairs across from her at a long table filled with Hispanics.

Now, I've got bushels of Latino friends and don't admit to a prejudiced bone in my body, but just as there are whites and then there are whites, there are Hispanics and then there are Hispanics. These guys were the latter. Nonetheless, I took a deep breath and slipped into the vacant chair beside Emilio.

"Hey, man, somebody's already sittin' there," he yelled over the clamor of music and conversation. His calm deserted him for a moment when he recognized me, but he recovered in a flash. "Mr. V. Long time, no see."

"I need to talk to you. Outside."

"Little busy, ya know." He winked at the woman across the table, who looked even flabbier up close. Still, she pushed out her pink, low-cut blouse in all the right places. "Probably gonna have my hands full the rest of the night, ya know what I mean? How 'bout we get together sometime tomorrow?"

"Has to be now."

"Hey, man! You heard the man. Man don't wanna talk to you."

The speaker could have been the dumpy woman's twin except he was younger, even beefier, and sweating liberally. Headed for a heart attack, but not before he could do me irreparable damage. The table went deathly quiet. It was probably my imagination, but this whole side of the barn seemed to fall silent. Judging from the reactions of the others at the table, their leader had just spoken.

"This has nothing to do with you, amigo. I need to talk to Emilio, that's all. He'll be back in five minutes if he behaves himself."

"Cop." The fatty sneered as if the word were a curse. For a heavy man, his voice was ludicrously high-pitched.

"Naw, but he used to be," Emilio said.

I spoke before the big man could react. "Let me see. Jailhouse ink, gang tattoos. I'd guess that Latin cross with a halo on the back of your right hand says Santo Moreno."

A smirk crossed the hood's face as I named one of the city's most violent gangs. "You know that, gringo, then you know better'n to fuck with me. You being an ex-cop and all." He added the last as if I couldn't put the thing together without his help.

"You're wrong. Me being a former cop means I know *how* to fuck with you." I inclined my head to indicate something behind him.

He twisted his thick body around, almost ripping the shirt stretched across his meaty shoulders. Although he could see nothing except a mass of undulating bodies on the dance floor, he bought the idea I had backup.

"Won't always be cops around, asshole."

"Look, jefe, I've got no beef with you. I need to talk to Emilio, and then I'm leaving. We cool?"

Obviously mollified by a show of respect, he leaned back in his chair and swept up a pitcher of beer, lifting it toward me. I declined with a shake of my head.

The thug decided we were cool. "Milio, you go talk to the man."

Risking destruction of the delicate truce we'd worked out, I grabbed Emilio by the shirt collar and dragged him out of his chair.

"Ow, man! Watch it."

"Hey, the cop knows how to treat a *maricón*," someone chortled. "You get through with him, make him wash out his mouth 'fore he come back, okay?"

The remark took the fight out of my quarry. Being labeled a queer by one of the gang told me Emilio wasn't solid with this group. Once outside he twisted out of my grasp.

"All right, cocksucker, what you want with me?"

"What do I want? Right now I'm doing everything I can to keep from beating you within an inch of your miserable life."

"You sore about Del Baby, go see *him*, not me. He come looking for me." Recovering some of his swagger, he leered. "He's a hell of a fuck, ain't he?"

His backbone bruised my knuckles. He doubled over and got rid of the night's load of beer and pretzels.

"Man!" He swiped his mouth with a sleeve and gasped for air. "You… you can't do that. I call the fuzz."

I shoved him back into the bushes lining the building. "You do that, smartass, and they'll arrest you for propositioning me. The next time you mention Del Dahlman, you speak with respect. The man was good to you."

"A'right. Wha' chu wan', man?"

His accent grew stronger. Not the one he used to charm men and women alike, but the patois of the streets that spawned him.

"I want those pictures of you and Del."

He tried to climb back on top of the situation. "They good pictures, man. Hot. You cream lookin' at 'em." He held up a restraining hand as I advanced on him. "'Kay! Okay. If you ain't got none a your own, I give you some. That way you get a good look at Emilio too."

Something wasn't right. If those photographs were his gravy train, Emilio wouldn't surrender them so easily. "No tricks. You pull anything, I'll take my frustration out on your ass."

"That what you want, maybe we can work something out."

I slapped him across the face. In the gloom, only partially eased by sodium-vapor lights mounted atop tall poles in the parking lot, I caught a look of confusion in his eyes. Not anger. Not fear. Emilio's face crinkled with bewilderment. He was an actor. He made his living pretending to be drawn to sexual partners, extolling their prowess and faking concern, but he wasn't *that* good of a thespian. My aggressiveness genuinely perplexed him.

"The pictures, Emilio."

"A'right. I got 'em in the car."

He was recovering now. The barrio lingo was gone. I resolved to watch my step. After all, he was a street tough, and my aura as a former cop carried me only so far.

He headed straight for an electric blue Mustang convertible heavy with gold trim, the muscle car Del had given him. When he reached for something in the backseat, I grabbed his wrist. He understood and waited patiently as I picked up a nylon backpack and made certain there were no weapons inside before handing it over. He pulled out an envelope stuffed with photographs.

The guy had been right; merely shuffling quickly though the graphic images aroused me. As stars of a homoerotic shoot, they made a perfect pair. Emilio's dark good looks played off Del's fair perfection like spring on summer. In appearance each was everyone's ideal man. Even with Emilio in the saddle, the image somehow held.

Yet there was something wrong about them, something off-putting. Was it because they showed Del with another man? I shook my head. I was over that, wasn't I?

"You have any more copies?"

"Naw." He looked longingly at the photos in my hand. Doubtless they were mementos of the best few months of his life.

"I'm going to accept your word on that, Emilio, because if you're lying and they turn up anywhere, I'll come looking for you. Understand? Give me the negatives, and you can go back to your friends."

He shifted his stance. "Can't."

"Why not?"

"Don't have 'em no more. Lost 'em." He backed away as I turned on him. "Hey, man, we can get it on right now, but I can't give you what I ain't got."

I stowed the photos in my jacket pocket and calmly took out a jackknife. Emilio gave me a worried look as I opened the longest blade on the instrument. It probably wasn't the first time he'd been threatened with a knife, but in his business, he had to watch out for his looks. However, it wasn't his person I intended to maim.

He squawked like a strangled gander when the blade punched a hole in the leather of his backseat.

"Not my car!" he wailed. "Don't cut up my car, man. You can't do that." A flick of my wrist ripped the leather a couple of inches. "Ah, man, please."

He probably could have endured my carving up his arms and chest, but this studmobile was his second penis. The only thing he would fight harder to protect was the real thing, and we both knew it.

"Talk." The tip of my knife was still buried in the rich red leather.

"Man, what I gotta do to make you believe me? I ain't got the negatives."

"Who does?"

It was easy to see he considered lying but didn't have the nerve. "Last time I seen 'em was a while back. I showed the pictures to this fella. He got so hot, he slobbered all over them. He wanted a couple, but I wouldn't give them up. They for me, you know. For my own self." There was a plaintive note in his voice.

"So what happened?"

"This guy, he paid me to let him develop some in his... what chu call it? Darkroom."

I pulled the knife out of Emilio's precious leather seat. "So you gave him the film?"

"Just so he could print up a couple of them. And I was right there all the time."

"He returned the negatives?"

The kid nodded and held out a hand, palm up. "Yeah. Put them right here."

"So where are they?"

He shrugged. "Dunno. Next time I looked for them, they wasn't in my backpack no more."

"Who was this man?"

Another shrug. "Just said his name was John." His eyes went wide when I raised the knife again. "But I know where the dude lives. Spent the night with him."

I GLANCED nervously at Emilio sitting silently beside me in the Impala. He was leading us down a meandering road in the remote far Northeast Heights. Lampposts were infrequent. My headlights were the only bright spot in the deep night. Sandia Peak with its corona of blinking, red-tipped TV antennae and the Cibola National Forest crowded us on the east. The Sandia Indian Reservation blocked the way north.

This was one of the ritzy sections well outside of the city limits where front yards were left desert wild, except for cement driveways snaking across the hardpan to anchor the buildings to the roadway. Most of the landscape was vacant, but an occasional rambling house hunkered down beside some dusty road with a name like Black Bear Lane or Calle del Oso. Albuquerqueans were big on bears.

Although it occurred to me that the good-looking creep might be planning something, it was more likely he was simply lost. It was hard enough finding an address out here in the daytime, much less at midnight.

"Shit," he mumbled. "It all looks different."

"You leading me around by the nose?"

"Naw, I swear man. I figured I could find the guy any time I wanted." His teeth gleamed in the faint moonlight as he smiled weakly. "He give me a hundred-dollar tip. But this don't look familiar."

"Okay, you're coming home with me for the night. I'm going to lock you in the basement. We'll try it again tomorrow."

"You can't do that. That's kidnapping or something."

"Maybe so, but that's the way it is."

"Go on down the road. Let's try some more. I got a woman waiting for me, man."

"She's long gone by now. But we'll give it another few minutes."

As we plowed on through the darkness, the first car we'd seen in an hour of wandering the foothills came roaring up on us from the rear. Its sudden appearance made me nervous, but the massive Caddy Escalade roared by in a cloud of dust as I pulled to the side of the road.

"That's him!" Emilio threw a wiry arm toward the windshield. "That's the dude's big fucking tank."

"You sure?"

"Yeah. That's him, I tell you."

"Emilio, if you're lying—"

"I ain't. I swear. Follow the Caddy."

Half a mile farther down the dusty road, the vehicle turned left at an intersection that was invisible until you were practically through it.

"That rock. I remember that rock." Emilio jabbed a finger at a huge boulder on the far side of the roadway. "Yeah, remember that rock." The excitement in his voice convinced me he was on the up-and-up—at least for now.

As my Impala maneuvered the sharp turn, the other vehicle pulled into the driveway of a rambling affair almost as massive as the C&W. I killed my lights and eased down the rough gravel road in time to see a husky, silver-haired man come around the car and open the door for an elaborately coiffed woman. His wife, most likely. The trick with Emilio had merely been a little dessert on the side. This was obviously a prosperous couple returning from a night out.

By the glare of the motion-activated intruder light over the garage, the man seemed somehow familiar. After memorizing his license plate to jot down in my pocket notebook later, I motored past the house and turned on my headlamps. It took another half hour to find our way out of the maze of roads.

When we finally arrived back on Tramway Road, a paved, well-lighted street, I headed straight for the C&W parking lot, using the time to extract details of Emilio's assignation with the mystery man. Misunderstanding, he gave a smirk.

"You get off on that, huh? You know, hearing 'bout me doing it with other dudes."

"In your dreams, asshole. I'm going to get inside that house, and the things you saw are going to prove to me you're not lying. And the details you're going to give me about the man are going to prove to him I know what happened."

"You gonna face the dude down? Hey, man, he give me a big tip. You gonna mess it up for me."

"Tough."

Emilio sulked the rest of the way. Nonetheless, I managed to pry a couple of details about his night with the man out of him. As Emilio crawled out of my car in the parking lot, I handed him a couple of bills.

"There's a leather shop on Fourth and Griegos. They'll repair the cut in your rear seat. You won't even know it was ripped."

I used the rearview mirror to watch him watch me pull out of the parking lot and turn west. All the way down the long hill toward the Rio Grande, I puzzled over how the beautiful, loving acts Del and I had engaged in so many times looked so sordid in the photographs burning a hole in my jacket pocket.

Chapter 3

I RELAXED on a chaise lounge amid the clashing odors of chlorine from the pool and the summer roses climbing the whitewashed adobe walls as I eyed the North Valley Country Club's new lifeguard. Lean, loose-limbed, and broad shouldered, he had the ideal swimmer's build, reminding me somewhat of Del, even though Del was a Teutonic blue-eyed blond, whereas this young man was bronzed and brunet, and his eyes were likely brown. Up close the dark shape on the left pec would probably morph into a small tattoo. Spandex seldom did anything for me, but his thigh-hugging, well-filled trunks were… interesting.

As the place was deserted at this early hour except for the two of us, the lifeguard turned pool boy and policed the area, scooping fallen leaves and debris from the water with one of those baskets mounted on a long aluminum pole. He worked his way to my side and netted a soggy candy wrapper.

"Kids," he observed in a pleasant baritone.

Seized by an unexpected need that was 90 percent loneliness, I did something I had not done in twelve long months—reacted to the good-looking guy. Flustered, I fumbled for the orange juice on a table beside me and overturned my glass.

He knelt to recover the tumbler, holding it up and offering to get me another.

Yep, brown eyes, deep and soulful. Dangerous eyes on one so young. He couldn't be more than twenty. The dark spot above the nipple was a small dragon.

"No, thanks. Nothing left but ice cubes, anyway. But I appreciate your offer, uh…."

"Paul. Paul Barton."

"Paul." I was surprised by the family name. There was a strong Latin look about him. Must be the mother's blood.

"Anytime."

He rose, our eyes locked—and the penny dropped. This was the young man I had seen dancing so energetically at the C&W last night.

He broke first, raking me with his intense gaze. His lips twitched as he zeroed in on a two-inch scar on my inner right thigh. My body looked pretty good except for that purple, puckered blemish. At first I'd been spooked by Del's reaction to the pockmark and tried to hide it from the world. But after putting up with that foolishness for six months, I said to hell with it. The world was full of imperfections, and it could deal with this one too.

"Bullet wound," I said.

"Damn, I'll bet that hurt."

My throat closed up at his casual treatment of the wound. Maybe I wasn't as blasé as I thought. "Like you wouldn't believe. That's why I swim early in the morning. Therapy."

"Swimming's the best exercise in the world," he declared like a true water bug. "And you were really going at it a few minutes ago. Looked pretty good out there."

"Thanks."

As Paul turned back to the pool, a cell phone on a nearby table piped the first line of "Dixie." The conversation was short. He admitted to someone named Jill that he got off work at five but said he'd decided to cool it this evening, turning down what was obviously an offer of some sort. Was it coincidental he was watching me throughout the entire brief conversation?

The image of Paul Barton stayed with me as I peeled off my trunks and showered in the locker room a few minutes later. Then, dressed in Albuquerque casual—leather ankle boots, blue gabardine slacks with a knitted belt, and a yellow silk guayabera—I headed downtown for the office.

ONE OF the best things about a PI license is it gives a person the ability to sit in a cozy office and pluck data right out of thin air. Hazel Harris was a lot better at searching the state's Motor Vehicle Division records on the Internet than I was, but I was unwilling to open myself to rolled eyes and exasperated sighs when she figured out this had to do with Del's case. It took longer, but I got the job done despite the fact this particular database did not permit us to view photographs.

The owner of the gray Caddy Escalade was Richard H. Harding. No wonder the guy looked familiar in the floodlight last night. His picture regularly appeared in both the *Tribune* and the *Journal*, mostly in the society pages. Harding and his wife seemed to attend every benefit and black-tie affair in the state. In the twelve months since moving the company headquarters of Premier Tank & Plating, Inc. to its Albuquerque plant in the South Valley, he'd firmly established himself as one of the city's Four Hundred.

However, recent newspaper articles about Premier's successful petition for the permits necessary to double the size of its local operations were more interesting. The expansion plan had incited a vicious battle. Premier, the Chamber of Commerce, and a docile County Commission stood on one side of the debate. Lined up against them were environmental groups, South Valley farmers concerned about increased usage of river water, an Indian Pueblo anxious over the quality of the effluent released back into the Rio Grande, and a host of other naysayers. In addition, Premier was embroiled in an unresolved labor dispute with a union bent on organizing the plant.

Only vaguely familiar with the details of the imbroglio, I hit the back issues of Albuquerque's daily newspapers to learn more details. The first fact to slap me in the face was that Stone, Hedges, Martinez, et al. represented Harding and his company. And guess who the lead attorney of record was? Delbert David Dahlman, Esquire. But if Del represented Premier, why would Harding try to compromise him? Was his lawyer recommending a course of action the businessman didn't like? This required a consultation with my client.

The Stone, Hedges receptionist faultlessly recited the names of all eight senior partners in a rapid singsong and then passed me to Del's personal secretary—or was it executive assistant by then?—where I encountered a problem. The lady, whom I pictured as a skinny, nose-in-the-air, horse-faced puritan, stated in exaggerated back-east nasal tones that *Mr.* Dahlman was in a deposition and would be unavailable for the next two days. Adopting a tough brusqueness, I informed her this was a matter of vital interest to her boss that required his immediate input. Del obviously had not taken her into his confidence about the blackmail demand, because a sniff of disdain was my reward—although she did condescend to take down my name and number.

I'd short-circuit that stuffy old bag. But dialing Del's cell phone number proved me wrong. The call went to voice mail. I left a somewhat impatient demand that he call me back and hung up.

That left only one course of action. I phoned Premier and was able to get an appointment that very afternoon.

Prior to the meeting with Harding, I made a host of boring phone calls to fill in some blanks about him. One item of gossip was of particular interest: Harding's wife was one of several local women who had recently taken a weeklong Caribbean cruise sponsored by a social club—so she was probably out of town when Emilio got together with her husband.

The drive to Premier led me through a South Broadway barrio crammed with mom-and-pop businesses advertising goods and services in either Spanish or English—and sometimes both—before approaching a miles-long industrial corridor. Shortly before the road climbed a hill overlooking the Isleta Indian Reservation, I came to a tangle of corrugated-metal buildings, water and chemical tanks, and other less recognizable equipment. At the rear of the sprawling Premier facility, a large glass and brick edifice was rising from the desert landscape. When completed it would no doubt house the company's new headquarters. I wondered how the other execs appreciated Welby's Slaughterhouse as their next-door neighbor to the south.

Harding kept me waiting for ten minutes before an attractive secretary escorted me back to his office. Our meeting reinforced last night's impression. He was a big man, towering over my six feet by at least four inches. The hair that had appeared silver in the glare of the intruder light retained a touch of the haystack, a faint yellow. Harding's shoulders and arms were massive. He wore a white silk shirt with sleeves rolled halfway up thick forearms pelted with graying hair. His eyes were an intense blue that no doubt could be grandfatherly kind or mad-dog mean. This executive had clawed his way up through the ranks to the pinnacle of his company. You didn't fool around with a man like that, but I was about to try. I surreptitiously triggered the small tape recorder hanging on my belt.

"What can I do for you, Mr. Vinson?" His heavy voice matched his stocky build. "It isn't often I receive a visit from a private investigator."

"Which is probably the way you like it."

He failed to rise to the invitation for some old-fashioned joshing.

For an instant I questioned Emilio's story. This was the quintessential "man's man" sitting across the broad walnut desk from me. Had the kid latched onto the first car to pass us in the dark on that lonely stretch of road last night? Despite the sudden doubt, I sighed like a man exhausted by life and took the plunge.

"Mr. Harding, I'm here on a delicate matter. We could spar around for a few minutes, but it wouldn't change my mission, so I'll just come out and state it."

"Please do."

"A few weeks ago, you picked up a hustler named Emilio Prada and took him home with you. During the… build-up, shall we say, he shared some photographs with you. You were intrigued, but not for the reason he thought. You recognized the man with him in the photos and wanted copies of the pictures for your own purposes. He allowed you to print two of the more revealing photos. I need to retrieve them."

"I have no idea what you're talking about."

"Sir, if I were not certain of my facts, I wouldn't be sitting here embarrassing both of us."

"You admitted your source was a hustler. Why should you take his word over mine?"

"Because he knows what I'd do to him if he lied to me."

"So he made up a story to get you off his back. I assure you I am a happily married man."

"I've dealt with enough hustlers to know when I'm being hustled. He described you, your Caddy, and your house. He took me there last night."

"Ah, the car we passed on our way home from a party. That proves nothing, Mr. Vinson."

"The tiled foyer to your house leads to a large archway flanked by two temple dogs, beyond which lies the living room. Emilio thought they were lions, but then, what does he know? If you turn to the left, you go down a long hallway to the bedrooms. I doubt you took him to the master bedroom you share with your wife. It was a guest room on the ground floor with pink decor. Emilio described it as 'fairy pink.' As to more personal matters, you have a thick mat of graying hair on your chest and belly and an appendicitis scar. Your—"

"Enough!" Harding's face was glowing, although not from embarrassment. "I won't be blackmailed by some cheap private eye. You try saying those things publicly, and I'll have your license and see you making licenses of another sort up in Santa Fe."

"Don't threaten me with anything short of a shotgun, Mr. Harding. I have no intention of blackmailing you or exposing your secret unless you force me to. All I want are the photographs of Emilio and the man with him. And the negatives."

"Say it out loud, why don't you? You want the photographs of Del Dahlman displaying his attributes for the world to see."

"No, I want the photographs of Del Dahlman engaged in private and personal acts the world wasn't *intended* to see. The same private and personal acts you and Emilio undertook in that pink bedroom."

There was a long silence. "Are there pictures of me? Did the creep sneak a camera into my home?"

"Not to my knowledge. He simply let it be known that some of the pictures had gotten out, and Del wants them back. End of story."

I tensed as the big man stood suddenly. He was twenty years my senior, but he could put up a hell of a fight if that was the way he decided to go. There was little doubt I could take him, but he'd have all the help he'd need from a hundred employees within seconds. But doing battle was not what he had in mind. Harding walked to a file cabinet, removed a small box, and unlocked it with a key. He took out two snapshots and handed them over. They showed Del and Emilio at their most glorious.

"The rest?"

"That's all there are. I only printed those two. That little hustler stood right beside me while I developed them."

"You didn't make more after he left?"

"How? He took the negatives with him."

I held up the photos and took a shot in the dark. "You scanned these into your computer, didn't you?"

Harding flushed but nodded. "Yes."

"Are they backed up anywhere else?"

The big man dry-washed his face and shook his head before firing up his computer and permitting me to delete the photographs. An expert might be able to retrieve them, but this was the best I could do. Then I faced him squarely.

"The negatives?"

His eyes reflected anger. He brushed his hair with a palm that was halfway curled into a fist. I was about at the end of my run. Pretty soon he was going to remember he was a captain of industry and start acting like one. "I already told you your hustler took the negatives with him."

"Did you share these photos with anyone else?"

"Hell no! Why would I do that?"

"All right. I'll accept your word on it."

That snap decision was based on two things: he wouldn't have scanned the two pictures into Photoshop if he had the negatives, and if he'd printed copies from Photoshop, there wasn't anything I could do about it.

Harding sat down behind his desk. "You've had your say, and now I'll have mine. You think you know something about me that could damage my reputation. Do I have to fight you on this?"

"A one-night stand with a male prostitute is not going to hinder your career or destroy your social life. However, if the big world out there learns of your little peccadillo, it won't be from me."

He nodded but wasn't finished. "You're obviously working for Del. That means the pictures have become a problem for him."

"Maybe he just doesn't want them floating around out there. Would you?"

"Should I consider changing law firms?"

"That is something for you and Del to discuss. Of course he might wonder how you obtained the pictures in the first place."

"Does that mean you aren't going to tell him?"

"I'll let him know you had them, but there's no need to explain how you came by them."

He didn't like that but had no control over the matter. I left him tapping his letter opener on the desk blotter, an expression of frustration familiar to me. I switched off the tape recorder as I got into the car.

BACK IN the office, I collected my calls. Nothing from Del. After plopping down behind my desk, I put my feet on top of an open drawer and stared out over the roof of the library toward one of the city's older neighborhoods. A surprising number of trees towered above the rooftops. Albuquerque's ubiquitous Siberian elms, with their long, drain-clogging roots, were the lasting and sometimes nettlesome legacy of a long-dead mayor named Tingley.

Harding had not put up much of a fuss over surrendering the pictures. Of course, he may have scanned them into another computer, but that didn't seem likely. He wanted those pictures out of curiosity or as leverage in case he got crossways with Del in the future. Harding was a man with money, and there seemed little profit in trying to blackmail his own attorney. Even if so inclined, he would have gone after a lot more than $5,000. Something more like the size of Stone, Hedges's fee to Premier, for example. Unless, of course, he was merely probing Del's vulnerability. My client could give me a better idea of that supposition should he ever deign to return my calls.

I heard Charlie Weeks, the retired cop who handled my overload cases on an as-needed basis, come through the outside door and greet Hazel. I allowed them a minute to chat before calling him into my office and updating him on Del's problem. I handed over the list of employees and contract companies of Del's upscale, high-rise apartment house just off Menaul Boulevard in the Uptown area. He agreed to check out the Royal Crest and proved how sharp he was.

"Okay, I'll get right on it." The corners of his mouth lifted slightly, and a twinkle came into his eyes. "And I'll keep Hazel out of it."

I paused before speaking. "Good. And thanks."

"Course, I'll have to figure a way to phony up the time sheets."

I broke out laughing. "Charlie, you know we don't phony up anything. Hazel's gonna know. But it would help if she knew after the fact."

He nodded and turned to leave. "Figured."

I bid the two of them good-bye a few minutes before five o'clock and walked down two flights of stairs, heading for my car. The crush of city, county, state, and federal employees, augmented by those who fed off of them—bankers, lawyers, court reporters, bail bondsmen, and the like—all fleeing Albuquerque's downtown confines at day's end was not unlike a big puddle overflowing. Rivulets rushed in all directions, freely at first before slowing to form new puddles until their pent-up energy was released anew. That was northbound traffic at five that afternoon.

Although my timing was wrong by half an hour, my hunch—more accurately, my hope—paid off. The lifeguard was lingering in front of the old Moroccan-style gates of the North Valley Country Club. Dressed in knee-length khaki walking shorts and a form-fitting polo shirt, Paul looked as fetching as I remembered. He brightened when the car pulled to a halt at the curb. After giving me a broad smile, he hopped into the passenger's seat.

"Hi, Mr. Vinson."

He had gone to the trouble of learning my name. He pulled the seat belt across his torso—and a fine torso it was too.

"Call me BJ or Vince. The Vince comes from Vinson."

"What do most people call you?"

"BJ."

"Okay, then I'll call you Vince. At least when nobody's around."

I smiled to myself. "Where can I drop you?"

He managed a beguiling yet innocent look. "Wherever you're headed is okay by me."

Taking another man to the home Del and I had shared stirred up some residual pain, but it was going to happen eventually, so it might as well be with this wholesome, clean-cut guy. And it turned out I was wrong; he was twenty-one and a senior at the University of New Mexico majoring in journalism.

Chapter 4

AFTER DROPPING Paul at his car in the country club employees' parking lot that evening, I slowly drove to Post Oak Drive. Curiously at peace with my world and myself, I undertook a much longer, transcendent journey over the course of that five-mile drive. I hovered on the cusp of learning something essential about myself—something vague and unformed but vital.

Unlike Del, casual affairs left me physically sated but emotionally lacking. This evening, as I broke a long dry spell with an athletic young man possessed of a great deal of charm, I expected to face a night of self-loathing and despair. Yet, as I turned into my driveway, painting the door to the detached garage with my headlamps, I understood what was struggling to come into the clear light of conscious thought. My body was totally satisfied, and my spirit—my *psyche*—was well nourished.

I sat in the car for a few minutes musing over the evening and trying to determine exactly *why* I felt the way I did. Paul was extremely pleasing to the eye, and the sex was spectacular. But that wasn't enough to explain this afterglow… this euphoria. Was that an overstatement? I shook my head. No. It was appropriate. And sitting there in the darkness, I zeroed in on why. After our incredible union, I noticed no change in his demeanor beyond a subtle relaxing in our club member–club employee status. He was as interested in learning who I was as he was in letting me know who he was. Intelligent. Curious. Respectful. Add that to his physical beauty, and I began to understand my reaction to him. I was smiling broadly as I got out of the Impala. Neither of us had mentioned another assignation, but I damned sure knew one was coming.

Once inside the house, I tried Del's home phone. He didn't answer, and his cell was still going to voice mail, so I settled down in my home office to review a particularly nettlesome case file. I normally refused domestic peep work on principle, but occasionally a disgruntled spouse catches me in a weak moment. Sherry DeVine, a woman I'd known since grade school, had slipped in her request at just such a time.

I knew Jerry DeVine, his habits, and his weaknesses, so it was ridiculously easy to gather proof the guy was running around on his wife. Even so, I had dragged my feet delivering the report, mostly because all three people involved were so screwed up it seemed a shame to deprive them of what little pleasure they'd managed to garner in their dreary lives. Sherry's family money gave her a safety net, but Jerry was hanging in the wind. The gal on whom he'd gambled his meal ticket was even grosser than Sherry, but she must have had something because DeVine met her every Tuesday and Thursday without fail.

I picked up the phone to get that unpleasantness out of the way. Sherry went hysterical in the middle of my verbal report, but she would probably end up forgiving Jerry and holding the entire affair over his head like the Sword of Damocles for the rest of his miserable life. Sherry and Jerry—a match made in hell. Vowing to never again take another domestic job, I stuffed my report and the supporting videos in my briefcase for Hazel to send out tomorrow, along with an invoice.

After that my mind turned once again to Del Dahlman. It bothered me that he hadn't returned my calls, but I knew he wasn't irresponsible, so there had to be a reason. Sooner or later I'd find out what it was, and if I didn't like his excuse, I'd tell him to take his blackmail demand and stuff it.

I had met Del while I was still a police detective. It was 12 April 2002 at 1415 hours. I had been sequestered in a bland gray police interview room with the bland—and at that moment equally gray—son of a prominent Albuquerque businessman accused of breaking and entering, DWI, speeding, reckless endangerment, and being a general pain in the butt, when this blindingly handsome kid barged in.

"Hold it. My name is Del Dahlman, and I'm this man's attorney," he announced.

Convinced this stripling could not possibly be out of law school, I made him haul out three different pieces of ID before he put his foot down. His blond widow's peak shook with indignation. Or was it nervousness?

"Look, Detective... uh...."

"Vinson. B. J. Vinson."

"Maybe I ought to examine your credentials. Now, let's get down to business."

By then, of course, I knew he was twenty-eight—only two years younger than I was—had memorized his name and address, and noted he was with Stone, Hedges, Martinez, Blah, Blah, Blah, the biggest law firm in the state. Also the one with the longest name. In the cop's world, he would soon be labeled "one of the Blahs."

I had worried he'd be a barnburner, but he turned out to be a decent sort. He merely made sure his nincompoop of a client got a fair deal. A month later he represented the suspect in another of my cases, and when our adversarial responsibilities ended, we became close. We moved in together shortly thereafter. He was as fantastic to love as he was to look at.

As I shook off the emotions my reverie had raised, I was shocked by thoughts of Paul Barton flashing through my mind. In need of distraction, I glanced at my desk clock. Although it was almost ten, it wasn't too late for the crowd at the C&W Palace. Things would just be heating up over there. I threw on a windbreaker against the night's chill and headed for the Impala.

I picked up I-25 South and exited at Central Avenue, turning left up the long, steady climb to the heights. Central was once touted as the world's longest main street and had been a stretch of the famous Route 66 before Eisenhower's interstate highway program did it in. Now lined with one-story brick and stucco antique shops, cheap motels, bars, and adult book stores, Central was well past her glory days, but she still put on a flashy show of neon lights by night. Inevitably the morning sun exposed her timeworn wrinkles and sagging frame.

I had intended to use this time to think. Instead I found myself examining the venerable old gal. The impressive campus of Presbyterian Hospital showed signs of recent construction, but then it usually had something underway. The University of New Mexico was a beehive of activity. Apparently some sort of musical performance at Popejoy Hall had ended, and cars were now spilling out of the side streets. The trendy Nob Hill Mall, with its boutiques and outdoor cafés in the Midtown area, drew college students and young adults from every walk of life.

I motored past the sprawling and aging New Mexico State Fairgrounds, where a weekend flea market, in-season horse racing, and daily casino operations attracted gamblers, drunks, touts, and prostitutes of both sexes. Back in the days when I was a street cop, this area and the rabbit run a little farther to the west had dealt me more trouble than anywhere else. I'd pinched more than one thief trying to sell his loot in the flea market. I'd faced down a distraught family man who'd gambled away the mortgage money at the racetrack and was determined to commit suicide by cop in the parking lot, but thank goodness my partner and I talked him out of it.

A few blocks east of the fairgrounds, I pulled into the C&W's parking lot and found a spot directly in front of the joint. I locked the Impala and walked to the front door, mentally preparing myself for the blast of humidity and humanity that would greet me. I wasn't disappointed.

There was no sign of Emilio Prada, but I got butterflies at the unexpected sight of Paul shaking his thing on the dance floor with a petite, enthusiastic cowgirl dressed in buckskin and fringes. Paul was a package of raw sex in chinos, yellow T-shirt, and leather vest.

The Santos Morenos occupied the big table in an area of the club they'd apparently claimed as their own. The sweaty honcho who'd crossed verbal swords with me last night seemed to be giving the group the benefit of his life lessons. It was the same bunch—minus Emilio. What the hell, nothing ventured, nothing gained.

I walked up and greeted the group with false cheer. Everyone stared back blankly except the leader. My gang squad contact down at the station had identified him as Miguel Arrullar, which was ironic since *arrullar* meant to lull or to coo in Spanish. His street name of Puerco was more appropriate. This guy was more apt to grunt like a pig than coo like a dove. The long, lean cat at his right was his main man, another homegrown hood named José Zapata, called Zancón because of his lanky frame and long legs. The dark-chocolate dude to the left answered the description of the Haitian thug, Jacques Costas, commonly called Jackie.

"Damn, you getting to be a habit," Puerco grumbled. "A bad habit."

"Pleased to see you, too, Puerco."

Somebody had a good eye. Arrullar genuinely resembled a pig. Small eyes, broad nostrils, short, bristly beard, and a face as wide as a boar's head. His shoulders were fat and powerful and porcine.

He seemed pleased. "You heard a me, huh?"

"Who hasn't down at the police station?"

"What can we do for the ex-dick who got shot to pieces rousting some poor bastard?" He'd done his homework too.

"Not much." I turned to the others at the table. "How you fellows doing? Don't see Emilio with you tonight."

"Old Milio's working. Got somebody flat on their back by now, but God only knows who." Zancón blurted it all out before Puerco silenced him with a glare.

I nodded. "As far as I can tell, he's always working. If he's breathing, he's figuring out how to fleece his next john. Anybody know where he's crashing?"

"Hard to keep up with Milio," Puerco said. "I see him, I tell him you're looking for him. That oughta make his day."

"Mine too. Well, you guys have a good evening."

"We plan on it, gringo."

That accomplished nothing, unless you consider Emilio being warned I was on the prod as something. Once in the crowd, I paused to look back at the table. Sure enough, the head pig was on a cell phone. That was bad. It was a sign that queer or not, Emilio was gaining a better footing with the Saints.

Reluctantly leaving Paul on the dance floor, I abandoned the raucous noise of the crowded nightclub for the cool air of Albuquerque's emissions-clogged main drag. It dawned on me that sitting in the parking lot might be the best course of action. If Puerco had called Emilio, he probably told him the big bad PI had left. With the coast clear, Emilio might decide to join his friends. My parking spot had an ideal view of the C&W's front door, so I made myself as comfortable as possible and dialed Del's numbers again. Still no answer. I was beginning to worry a little.

As I waited I observed the traffic going in and out of the nightclub. Young, mostly. The men tended to arrive alone or in groups, as did many of the women. People departing, however, were in pairs—a man and a woman. This was a great hookup joint. Sitting by myself in the car, I wished Paul would stroll out of the club alone.

An hour later the lot's harsh lights turned Emilio's blue Mustang a sickly puce as he wheeled down a row of parked vehicles. I was standing behind his car before he climbed out of the driver's seat and paused to stroke the headrest fondly. If the guy had an emotional attachment to anything, it was to his car. He turned and started for the club, recoiling when he saw me.

"Damn, Mr. V, you scared the shit outa me."

"I'll bet I did. You thought I'd already left, didn't you?"

"Dunno what you mean. You catch up with that dude in the big house out in the foothills?"

"Yeah. I don't think you oughta go near him again, if you know what I mean."

"I hear you, man. Pissed, was he? Well, glad that turned out all right."

"You're not off the hook yet, Emilio. He didn't have the negatives. All he had were the two snaps you let him print. So, who else have you shown them to?"

"Nobody, man. Told you that already. I gotta go now. My compadres are waiting for me inside."

"Not so fast. Either hand over the negatives or give me a list of everyone you shared those pictures with."

"I done *told* you, ain't nobody else, and I don't have no negatives."

"This time I won't pay to have your car seats repaired."

"Hey, man, don't cut my car. I'm gonna call a cop."

I reached into my jacket pocket and extracted my cell. "Here, use this. Dial 911."

He waved the phone away. "What I gotta do to make you believe me?" The pouty kid evaporated and the street tough materialized. "But you ain't gonna cut up my car no more. Why's Del so hot for them pictures, anyway?" He gave a smartass smirk. "Or is it you that wants them? You having trouble getting it up without some help? That the problem, Emilio give you all the help you need. Be worth it, man, I promise."

"No way in hell. Right now all I want from you is help figuring this out."

The hustler wore his brains right out on his face; I saw him snap to the situation. "Somebody putting it to Del using them pictures, right? Well, it ain't me."

"I believe you. It's whoever got the negatives from you. All you have to do is tell me who that is."

Perhaps somewhat appeased by my left-handed appeal for assistance, Emilio leaned casually against the Mustang and crossed his arms over his chest. "That's what I like about you 'n' Del. Don't look homo and don't act it, but you sure dig it. Anyway, you being like that, you ain't gonna take nobody down for having a little fun on the side?"

"Not looking to take anyone down except whoever's trying to compromise Del."

"Well, sure, I unnerstand that."

Anxious to get me off his back, Emilio shared details of his sordid life in the months since he'd taken the pics of Del. I made a list of three probably phony names, along with descriptions that might or might not be accurate. "Where did you have the pictures developed?" I asked.

He raised a leg to pry out a pebble stuck in the heel of his boot and then pressed his shirt down where his crossed arms had creased it. "Friend of a friend."

"How many copies did he print?"

"Just one. I was right there all the time. Wanted to see how they come out."

"How did you pay him?"

The kid smiled. "How you think? Old Rory's hot for Emilio, so I give it to him the way he likes it."

"You spend the night?"

"Hell, no. Took care of business and got outa there. And them negatives was right in my backpack. That big dude in the foothills used a couple of them to develop pictures, remember?"

"You're sure you had a negative for each picture?"

"Right on. I made Rory match them up. Didn't want no pictures around I don't know nothing about."

"Rory?"

"Rory Tarleton, the dude who printed them for me."

"How about your buddies in the nightclub? You share the pictures with them?"

His eyes went round. "You crazy, man? No way they into that kinda thing. They see pictures of me like that, they toss my ass out the door and stomp on it. I ain't that stupid."

"You trying to tell me you aren't servicing them once in a while?"

"Hell, no. They skin me alive, I tried that."

"Don't snow me, kid. It's called paying your dues for the protection of the club."

He smiled and smoothed an eyebrow with a long forefinger. "Emilio pays his way, but not like that. He can do some things for the Santos they can't do for their own selves."

"Like what?"

"Just little things. You know, like chores."

"Maybe so, but you better understand one thing, Emilio. Even if they tolerate you, even if they give you a little cover, you're not one of them and never will be. Remember that and get out of town if things go bad."

He shrugged his indifference. "Naw. Emilio's good for them. Like I say, he don't look like no gangster, so he can do stuff for them others can't. He's useful to the Santos."

For a kid up from Mexico, Emilio had a surprising command of the English language. He also had a mixture of accents. At times he sounded damn near like a Southerner. Then the gangster lingo of California would show up. At other times his language was almost cultured. It was like talking to a chameleon. He stood there and changed colors on you. He had probably learned English by watching American movies.

As he brushed past me and headed for the club, I strolled back to my Impala fretting over where the hell Del was. I'd virtually put the rest of my business on hold to accommodate his crisis, and now he'd disappeared.

Chapter 5

DAMNED NEAR two weeks went by before a sleepy, grouchy Del Dahlman answered his home phone one Monday morning. He let out an irritated snort when he recognized my voice.

"Christ, Vince, you know what time it is?"

"Seven o'clock on a bright New Mexico morning. The state fair is about to get underway with countless thousands getting fleeced by a hundred vendors. The Santa Fe Fiesta is hanging right over the horizon for its share, and the International Balloon Fiesta is hungering for whatever's left."

"Such cynicism. The fair and the fiestas are better than a month away, and besides, they're a hell of a boost to our economy. You know that."

"So I do." At least he sounded awake now. "Why are you still abed?"

"Been taking depositions and trying a case in Dallas."

"How do you try cases in Dallas?"

"I'm accredited before the Texas bar. And I'd still be there if the other side hadn't agreed to settle late yesterday afternoon. Got in on the red-eye last night. Or rather, this morning. I was planning on lying in bed until some dumbass woke me up."

"Wouldn't happen if you returned your phone calls. Why don't you stop by my office on your way downtown for a progress report?"

"You got it figured out?"

"No, but you can help me sort through some information."

He agreed, and I hung up, perversely pleased at managing to screw up his day. Minor payback for major sleep lost during our breakup. The meeting with Del meant I'd have to cut my pool therapy short, so I decided to skip it altogether and went straight to the office. Given the two-hour time difference back east, I could get in a couple of phone calls to the Boston PD on another case.

It was a good hour before Hazel was due to arrive, and as much as her mothering got to me, the office was a bleak place without her around, at least in the early morning hours. I managed to get most of my phoning out of the way before a warm, wonderful aroma and the sharp sweetness of something unrecognizable announced the arrival of my client.

Del still looked like an adolescent—great genes, probably—and blessed with a comeliness that transcended male and female. It was a blend of both, I suppose. But for the first time since I'd known him, he had bloodshot eyes—a refreshing reminder he was merely mortal. The aroma he brought with him came from hot, pungent coffee from the deli down the street, and the unidentified stimulus was a warm danish.

He struggled to balance two plastic-lidded cups of steaming coffee and a white bakery bag, barely managing to set them on my desk without dumping everything all over my pale green saxony carpet. I reached for one of the coffees as Del plopped into a chair across from me. Wordlessly he opened the bag and took out a couple of warm cheese danish.

"You look like hell." I took a sip of the brew and laid one of the pastries on a napkin. "Damn, that's good coffee."

"Yeah, well, you look pretty too." He picked up the other cup and took off the lid.

"Speaking of pretty, I don't think Emilio's the one trying to yank your chain."

Del froze with the cup inches from his lips. He put it back on the desk without drinking. "What are you talking about? He's the only one who has the pictures."

"Well, strictly speaking, that's not true."

Del shrank with mortification as I outlined my findings to date, alternating the delicious bits of narrative with tasty bites of pastry. His coffee cooled as he slumped in the chair, taking the verbal body blows without uttering a word until I finished my report.

"Harding?" he asked in a small voice. "Richard Harding of Premier Tank & Plating? How did he get his hands on them?"

"I'll leave that to your powers of deduction. You must have some since you claim to be a lawyer."

"Come on, I'm paying your bills. How did he get them?"

"That's not germane to the investigation. I found them and retrieved them, and that's all that matters."

"Vince, you're enjoying this way too much."

I sobered, or pretended to. "Any reason Harding would want the upper hand with you?"

"None that I know of. I was the lead attorney in his plant-expansion fight. Still represent him in a union matter. He ought to be cheering me on, not distracting me."

"Way I figure it, he glommed onto a couple of the photos when he saw them. For leverage in case you had a disagreement."

Del nodded. "Sounds about right. But he can't do that now, right?"

"I recovered Harding's copies of the pictures and deleted them from his computer. I'm no expert, but so far as I can tell, they're gone. Before we leave Premier, there's one other possibility to discuss."

"What's that?"

"The pictures were locked in Harding's office. What if some of the help rifled his files and handed over copies to the union people?"

"Oh shit!" Del exclaimed. "But wait, wouldn't they just contact me and threaten to reveal the photos?"

"That makes sense, but maybe it's like you said: you validate your vulnerability if you pay the five thousand."

"I don't think so. Demanding money is a patently criminal act. No reputable law firm would be a party to that." He paused before shrugging. "But you never know."

"A law firm doesn't have to be involved. Maybe the union people are doing it on their own."

He dry-washed his face. "So what do we do?"

"I'll phone Harding to see if anyone broke into his computer."

Del seemed to have lost his appetite for the moment, so I confiscated his danish. No use letting it go to waste.

"By the way, assuming Emilio was the only one with the photos was dumb. He had to get the film developed somewhere, didn't he?"

"He could have done that at home."

"Come on, this is Emilio we're talking about. And if he didn't do it, somebody did."

"True."

"And you never considered he'd use the photos as bait for new johns?"

He groaned. "Never crossed my mind. Damn, who else has seen them?"

"Emilio gave me a few names, but I don't know if he gave me all of them. He's pretty active, and having one of Albuquerque's leading attorneys as a satisfied customer isn't hurting his rep any."

"I'll hurt more than his rep if I ever get my hands on the little shit."

"In my book it would be justifiable homicide, but the justice system might take another view. Which brings us to the question of why aren't you returning my calls? If it's not important enough for you to respond, then it's not important enough for me to pursue. Maybe we ought to forget about the whole thing."

Del's lips went tight; his left eye twitched. "We can't do that. Please, Vince. See me through this. I apologize for the phone calls, but like I said, I've been out of town. Working twelve-hour days lately— trying to earn that partnership, you know."

"If this doesn't get cleared up, there probably won't be any partnership."

"There will if you'll keep the lid on this thing long enough."

Acid boiled up out of my stomach. "Is that what this is all about? You want me to keep the lid on things until you get your damned promotion?"

He sagged back in his chair. "No, that's not what I meant. I want this thing resolved, partnership or no partnership. But I need your help to get it done. I'll do a better job of keeping in touch from now on. I promise." He licked dry lips. "Where did you find Emilio?"

"Right where you met him. At the C&W Palace."

He closed his eyes and gave an exasperated sigh. "I hung out there for two days, and there wasn't a sign of him."

"Do you know a character called Rory Tarleton?"

"Who's he?"

"The man who developed the film. I'm going to look him up later this morning. Do you or your firm have anything going with Miguel Arrullar or the Santos Morenos?"

"The gang? Not to my knowledge. It's possible, although improbable. We mostly practice corporate law, but we do a little criminal work. I doubt we'd accept a client like that, though."

"Might not be a client. Maybe one of your clients got robbed or swindled and these guys showed up on the radar screen."

"That could be. Let me check it out, but please don't tell me the Santos have the pictures too."

"Emilio says no. He's trying to get in tight with them for protection, and his being gay or bisexual makes it dicey for him. If he waved those pictures around at those fellows, he'd be out on his ass. Or dead on it."

"Do you think Emilio has any more photos?"

"No, but if he knows who has the negatives, he could print another set. And speaking of those infamous pictures… here." I slid an envelope containing the photographs across the desk to him. He put them in his jacket pocket without examining them.

"And just for the record, I didn't keep any of them or make copies." I paused a beat. "How could you get mixed up with that guy? He's dangerous."

"Aw, Emilio's a little wild, but dangerous?"

"Think about it. He has sex with anybody who'll pay the tab, which is dangerous in a serious way. *And* he's hooking up with some of the deadliest people in this part of the country."

"Emilio's careful. He practiced safe sex, even with me." Del scowled. "As for the other, that's a new development. He was always a loner. Ours was probably the longest relationship he ever had."

"And that worked out well, didn't it?"

He gave me a look. "Put the needle away. I don't need that right now. It looked for a while as if it might last, but he got a yen for a woman, and I needed to have him to myself. When I fought him on that, it ripped things apart. There, does that make you feel any better?"

"I wasn't looking for gratuitous information. How did he take the breakup?"

"Well, he left the apartment mad as hell, if that's what you mean. He thought I ought to let him move that woman into his room permanently and take turns with us. Or," he added distastefully, "have a go at it with both of us at the same time."

"Who was she?"

"Some woman named Estelle Bustamante."

"What do you know about her?"

He shrugged. "Pretty woman about five six or so. Long black hair. Not much else."

"Do you know how to get in touch with her? Have a picture? Anything to help locate her?"

"No, I don't. Wait a minute… I did snap a picture of them one day."

"You took a picture of Emilio and your rival?"

He flushed. "That was before I knew what was going on. I thought she was a relative or something. Anyway, he asked me to take a picture, so I did."

"And you still have it?"

"A copy of it. Yeah… somewhere."

"Good. Dig it out and get it to me. She may not have anything to do with this, but we need to cover the possibility."

"The extortion note wasn't a woman's writing. It was crudely written in what I swear was a man's hand."

"That doesn't mean anything. She could get anyone to write it."

"That's true." Del grimaced. "Damn Emilio. I oughta chase the little twerp out of town."

"Maybe, but not just yet. I might need his help running this thing down. But when you decide it's time, I can tell you exactly how to do it. Threaten to take his car away. He's in love with that Mustang."

"Can't."

"Don't tell me you gave it to him free and clear?"

"Clean title."

"Dumb."

"Love."

"Lust. By the way, you're going to see an expense item of a hundred dollars. That's for the repair of his seat cover. I cut it up a little."

"Christ, if you had to do that, couldn't you at least make him pay for it?"

"Saved me hours of bullshit. I put a knife to his car, and he yakked his head off. As for who pays—I cut, so you pay."

We both flinched as the front office door opened. Hazel did that to us. She stuck her head inside and sniffed. "Oh, it's you."

"And good morning to you too, Hazel." Del attempted a smile.

"Whatever." She withdrew to the outer office, prudently closing the door behind her.

Del was justifiably proud of his ability to charm people, but even he accepted that Hazel Harris was immune to his appeal. After promising to send over the picture of Emilio and Estelle, he cleared out of the place. While Hazel slammed around the outer office, I scooped up pastry crumbs and drained Del's cup. That coffee was good right down to the last tepid drop.

EMILIO'S DIRECTIONS to Rory Tarleton's place had been vague, and the South Valley was not the place for vague. Before locating the address, I had to make a couple of stops to ask after the short dirt road that didn't appear on my city map. The small, sand-colored adobe house was missing large chunks of stucco, which gave it a snaggletooth appearance. Weeds and an occasional tuft of genuine grass sprinkled the dirt yard like a week-old beard. A puke-green Toyota on rims almost blocked the driveway in front of a carport filled with junk. This was obviously a residence, not a place of business.

Banging on the doorframe and peering in windows too dirty to see through produced no results, so I walked around to the backyard. The ten-by-ten frame structure hugging the cinder-block wall at the rear of the property was probably Tarleton's darkroom. When pounding on the door brought no response, I tried the knob.

"Hey!" a voice yelled from inside. "Don't come in here. I'm developing film."

"Mr. Tarleton?" I balanced my tone nicely between authority and amiability. "We need to talk."

"Go 'way."

The nice disappeared. "Either we talk out here, or I come in there."

"You'll ruin the run. Give me five minutes."

I hungered for a smoke to occupy my time as the five minutes stretched into ten and then fifteen, but Del and I had given up tobacco in a burst of healthy living on our first anniversary. In view of the wrecked relationship, I might as well take it up again, but I didn't have any smokes with me. As my mind rounded on that conclusion, the door to the shed rattled.

The man who emerged was a Marine drill sergeant gone to pot. The shoulders were still square but everything else was wrong. His face looked like his front yard: dusty brown and speckled with a hoary stubble. His long, unkempt reddish hair was shot with gray. All of that was easily fixed, but the bulging stomach would take some work. It was an odd belly, gathered right in front like a pregnant woman's in her ninth month. But the gunny's voice was still there.

"Who the hell are you, and whadda you want?"

Resisting the urge to snap to attention, I held out my hand. "B. J. Vinson. I'm a confidential investigator."

He ignored my offer to shake. "What're you doing investigating me?"

"Trying to get to the bottom of a sensitive matter. You know a hustler named Emilio Prada?"

"I know a fella called Emilio. Don't know his last name. So what?" The words were still crisp and straightforward, but the eyes beneath his protruding brows had gone wary.

"Did you develop some film for him?"

"Maybe. But that's between him and me."

"And me. Look, I did four years with the Corps as an MP, so your DI tactics won't work on me. I've thrown too many like you in the brig. Maybe even you."

"Could be. Been there a few times. When was you at MCRD?"

Tarleton referred to the Marine Corps Recruit Depot in San Diego.

"Ninety-two."

"Hell, I coulda been your babysitter."

"Yeah, and I coulda put you in the brig as payback."

"Could be," he said again. "Commissioned or enlisted?"

"A butter bar that turned silver before mustering out."

"Officer material. So, whadda you looking for Emilio for?"

"Not looking for him. Looking for some film he had developed."

A crafty look crossed his face. "Them racy ones of him riding the blond-headed dude."

"Right the first time."

"Ain't got them. Handed them over as soon as they was developed. What I want with filth like that, anyway?"

"Emilio claims he paid for them by giving you a ride."

Tarleton's face turned mottled. "That lying little shithead. I charged him fifty bucks and tossed him and them dirty pictures out as soon as they come off the dryer."

"Why'd he bring them to you? Why not some commercial place? That would cost him a lot less than fifty dollars."

"What kinda private eye are you? A pro'd call the cops in a minute."

"They wouldn't be interested unless minors were involved."

"Maybe so, maybe not. You wanna take a chance like that with the fuzz? So it cost him a little more, but he didn't have no worries with me."

"Question is, did you make a few extra copies for yourself?"

"How? Emilio stood right there and watched me develop the film. He was like a mama hen guarding her brood. I figured the blond dude was his sweetie pie, and he was jealous somebody'd try to horn in. Guess maybe I was wrong."

"What makes you think you were wrong?"

"You poking around for them dirties makes it look like blackmail. The blond dude famous or something?"

"He'd just prefer his image didn't show up where it doesn't belong. You have any trouble with me tossing your place?"

"Fuck no, you can't go poking around in my stuff. Why'd I let you do that?"

"To keep me from going to my buddies down at APD. They likely have a sheet on you, enough to give them something for probable cause. Someone might want to follow up with a visit. So if you'd rather deal with the police…." I left the rest hanging.

He shifted his feet and studied the dirt on the ground, looking uncomfortable.

"Look, all I'm interested in is finding those negatives. I've got a blind eye to anything else."

Tarleton gave it some deep thought before waving his hand toward his darkroom. "Have at it."

It wasn't long before I regretted the devil's bargain with the old Marine. The stuff that turned up might not have qualified as kiddy porn, but some of the girls skirted awfully close to the edge. I went through his darkroom, his house, and the car up on blocks before tackling the rat's nest of the carport. Tarleton came right along behind, using my search as an opportunity to separate his trash into piles. One would go back into the carport, the other to the garbage. I was a filthy mess by the time it was over, but his place looked a sight better than it had an hour ago.

More than a little frustrated, I took my leave and drove straight home. A car parked at the curb in front of the house raised my antenna, but alarm quickly turned to joy. It was Paul's old purple Plymouth coupe. As I pulled into the driveway, he got out sporting an anxious grin.

"I was just about to leave," he said. "Hope you don't mind me dropping by like this. I kept thinking I'd see you at the pool, but you haven't been by. So I wondered if anything was wrong."

My smile was broad and generous, nothing hesitant about it. I was happy beyond my ability to express it that he'd been the one to make the next move.

Realizing he was babbling out of nervousness, I set his mind at ease. "Have a new case that's taking up too much of my time, that's all. I'll be back in the pool as soon as I can."

Paul ducked his head. "So, it's okay? You know, me coming by without an invitation?"

"It's not only okay, it's great. Come on in while I clean up. I look like I've been collecting garbage."

The grin came back. "Well, doing yard work, at least."

Paul Barton was exactly what the proverbial doctor ordered. He whipped up a mean omelet while I showered and shaved for the second time that day. Then he served a surprisingly delicious meal on my mom's everyday china. I ate in my bathrobe as he sat opposite me sporting one of those form-fitting T-shirts he wore so well. This one had a logo reading, "Protect Human Rights—All Human Rights!" Probably not many people realized the rights he was advocating.

Chapter 6

I STRETCHED and resisted the urge to turn over and go back to sleep. My hand brushed the other side of the bed, encountering only an expanse of cool percale. My eyes snapped open and I sat up, surrendering to another stretch and a jaw-cracking yawn. A note on the dresser expressed appreciation of the night we'd shared and said Paul had gone to an early class. It also gave a phone number for future reference.

The next move was mine.

I recalled watching him sleeping beside me last night, amazed at the visceral reaction the image provoked. My stomach fluttered. Was I ready for that kind of emotional attachment?

Time enough to figure that out later. My principal chore this morning was to locate Estelle Bustamante.

When I arrived at the office, Hazel stuck her nose in the air as she handed over an envelope. "Delivered from that man's office this morning."

"Ease up on him. You oughta be happy he's nothing more than a paying client these days. Think of it, Hazel. Del paid your salary this month."

"I'll give it back."

Hazel was aptly named. She reminded me of that sassy maid of the same moniker in the cartoons and TV sitcoms of old, who ruled the fictional Baxter household with a firm hand. Hazel had been my mother's best friend and, like her, a schoolteacher. Until she retired and took over my office, that is. I resigned myself to the fact that the last word in the matter of Del Dahlman would never be mine.

I went into my private office and opened Del's envelope, which evoked a sharp breath. I could see why Del thought Emilio and Estelle might be related. Both had beautiful brown eyes, and it would be easy to take them for brother and sister except for Emilio's possessive arm draped over her shoulders, his hand resting on her right breast. The couple in the photograph was the fulfillment of every mother's dream. Emilio, arguably even better looking than Estelle was, exuded the machismo of a man claiming his woman. The kid projected raw eroticism.

Estelle Bustamante had no phone, at least none listed in her name. I pocketed the picture and headed for the Motor Vehicle Division to look up my old buddy Susie Garcia.

I asked the clerk at the front station to let Susie know I needed a minute of her time. Then I sat down to wait. Susie had been sweet on me ever since the second grade. Her eternal optimism about landing me in the sack stemmed from a junior high incident when we had come within a hair's breadth of "doing it," as we called the ultimate intimacy in those days. I had been the one who pulled back at the last moment, which should have been a clue to my future. At the time all those raging hormones confused the issue.

"Hello, lover. God, you look terrific, you know that?" Her voice startled me.

"I've been described in a lot of ways, but *terrific* is a new one. You're the one who looks great. I'll bet your cheerleader's outfit still fits you to a T."

"Really?" She placed a hand to the back of her head and preened a little. "You must need a favor. Well, come on back, and let's see what we can work out."

Susie managed the MVD office just north of San Mateo and Montgomery NE. She led me to her bland gray government-issue office, slipped gracefully into a chair, and motioned me to a seat across the bland gray government-issue desk. With a dimpled smile, she reached for the photo in my hand.

"Wow! Which one are you hot for? They're both dynamite."

"I know who he is. It's the woman I'm looking for. Her name is Estelle Bustamante."

"Anything else? DOB, address, that sort of thing?"

"Nope. That's why I brought the photo."

She found the information within minutes. The license photo did not do the woman justice, but it was clearly my Estelle Bustamante. After Susie provided an address and looked up vehicle information for me, we verbally jousted for a few minutes, resurrecting school experiences and remembering them differently.

THE BUSTAMANTE woman's home in an early-twentieth-century residential section north of Old Town was one of those tall narrow houses with the foundation in the Spanish culture and the rafters in the

Anglo. The pink stucco probably hid genuine adobe, but the attic window beneath a steeply pitched tin roof came right out of the Midwest. The place was neat and well tended, and I understood why when a plump, darker version of Hazel answered the door, still wiping her hands on the apron around her waist. This was probably Estelle's grandparents' home, and they were people who came out of a world where a family's abode reflected who they were. And these were old-fashioned, neat folks who took pride in themselves.

"Morning, ma'am. My name is Vinson, and I'm looking for Estelle Bustamante."

"Why are you looking for Estelle?" Suspicion and worry did battle on her broad features.

"I'm trying to locate a friend of hers, and I thought she might be helpful."

"What friend?"

"A man named Emilio Prada."

The woman frowned so deeply her eyes became squints. "*That* one. No good. She's finished with him. She can't tell you nothing. You a policeman?"

"No, ma'am. Used to be, but I'm a confidential investigator now. May I speak to her, please?"

"Not here." She spoke in clipped tones. "Work."

"May I ask where she works?"

"She don't want you bothering her at work. Like to get fired if she goes talking about personal things at work. Lawyers don't like people doing that."

"Lawyers? Would that be Stone, Hedges, Martinez?"

"Never heard of them. These are labor lawyers over on San Pedro somewhere, but don't you go bothering her at work. You hear me?"

"Wouldn't dream of it, ma'am. I'll come back and see her this evening… if that's all right."

Flummoxed by a simple, if insincere, courtesy, Estelle's grandmother allowed the corners of her mouth to turn up. "You do that, young man."

Out of sight around the corner, I pulled a yellow-page directory from my trunk. There was only one listing for labor attorneys on San Pedro NE: James, Jamieson & Smith, PA. With the scent of prey in my nostrils, I raced across town to a small, single-story brick building I'd passed a thousand times without noticing the unpretentious sign.

I pulled into a convenience-store parking lot across the street to consider my options. This was definitely a lead worth pursuing. The linkage of Emilio, Estelle, labor lawyers, Harding, and his labor problems was too strong to ignore. And Del's racy photographs neatly squared the circle. I took binoculars from the glove compartment to examine the small building across the street. Its generous windows were well screened by lush foliage with leaves the size of elephant's ears. In fact, that's what the plants were called. Nonetheless, I was able to make out a woman who could have been Estelle seated at a desk in the lobby.

To get a voice for later comparison, I called the firm and watched through the window as she picked up the telephone. I apologized for dialing a wrong number when she answered in the same singsong tones as the Blah receptionist.

I'd just finished an artery-clogging hotdog and a sugary forty-eight-ounce cola from the convenience store when three women exited the James, Jamieson & Smith building shortly after noon. Estelle was sandwiched between two females who towered over her petite figure. All three piled into a middle-aged Ford Taurus. Because Estelle drove, and because the make and model matched the description Susie Garcia had given me, I figured the car was hers. I tagged along behind long enough to confirm the license plate number and then peeled off to take care of a few items at the office.

THE JJS law firm began emptying promptly at five, but Estelle did not emerge and head for her car until almost five thirty. Deciding against waylaying her in a parking lot with an abundance of legal advice readily at hand, I allowed her a block's lead before falling in behind her. She drove directly to a day care center on East Lomas, where she picked up a toddler with black hair. Emilio's kid?

Next she pulled into a Smith's supermarket parking lot and lugged the child inside to do some shopping. Half an hour later, I pressed the Record switch on the tape machine on my belt as she dumped a bag in the trunk of the Taurus.

"Ms. Bustamante?" I softened my voice to avoid frightening her. It didn't work; she jumped as if goaded by a cattle prod. "Sorry, didn't mean to startle you."

"Who… who are you?" She turned to face me, shifting the baby, a boy of about eighteen months, to her left hip. "How do you know my name?"

"My name is B. J. Vinson, and I'm a confidential investigator. I need to ask you some questions about Emilio Prada."

A shadow flitted across her face. The full, pouty lips pulled down into an attractive frown. She had spectacular dewdrop eyes and lustrous black hair that fell below the shoulders. "Oh, him! I haven't seen him in months, and I hope it's a lot longer before I see him again."

"So, you're not involved with him at the moment?" I stared pointedly at the kid. She took my meaning.

"He's not Emilio's. His father went to Iraq." Tears threatened to brim. "And didn't come back."

"Sorry for your loss. That's happening to a lot of good men and women. Do you mind telling me where and when you last saw Emilio?"

As she strapped the boy firmly into a child's car seat, Estelle sketched her recent life with broad strokes. She went into an emotional and physical tailspin when her fiancé was killed in the war. She took to drinking, doing drugs, and running around the countryside, not too particular about the partners she chose. She was aware of Emilio's reputation but didn't really give a damn. When he asked her to move into "his" apartment, it seemed the answer to her prayers.

Del Dahlman came as a shock. She knew right away they were lovers but was too mired in alcohol and marijuana to pull away. That didn't happen even when Emilio offered her to Del. The lawyer's rejection, in its own perverse way, was an even greater blow. But soon after Del threw them out of his place, she woke up to reality and went home to her grandparents, reclaiming her life and her child. She had barely managed to hang on to her job with the law firm, although she had to work like a Trojan for the next six months to rebuild her reputation as a reliable employee.

"When did you see the pictures?"

"What pictures?" The words were reasonable, but the wary look on the woman's face rendered them false.

"Those of Emilio with another man."

The child fussed, distracting both of us for a moment. "I don't know what you mean."

"Estelle, you're not a good liar. Those pictures could be big trouble, and it's my job to recover the prints and the negatives. I intend to do my job. Hopefully I can accomplish that without causing waves, but if I can't, then I'll stir the water."

She straightened from comforting the boy and met my eyes briefly. Then she dropped her chin and blushed. "All right. Yes, I saw them. They were… they were disgusting. I told Emilio to burn them."

"Did he?"

"No. And that's when I came to my senses and saw him for what he was."

"And what was that? A blackmailer?"

She glanced up, startled. "No! A man who prefers other men. I was just a diversion. Someone to dangle in front of his lover to make him jealous."

"That won't wash. He moved out rather than give you up."

"That's what I thought too. But he was just angry because the lawyer made him choose. I don't know how many times I caught him looking at those pictures with a hungry look on his face. It was plain to see he felt he'd made a bad bargain. And then we had our fight, and I left." She shivered. "Thank God it came down to a fight. Otherwise I'd probably still be with him, drinking and doing all kinds of bad things."

"How many of the pictures did you take when you left?"

Her eyes flashed. "None! What would I want with them? They were a matter of shame to me. A reminder Emilio wanted a man instead of me."

"Did you know the man in the pictures with him?"

She colored again. "Of course. It was Mr. Dahlman. I thought he was a nice man, but when he and Milio fought, he said some terrible things. Not only about Milio, but about me too."

"And that made you mad."

"That hurt me. And, yes, it made me mad too."

"So you decided on some revenge."

Estelle shook her head. "No. When Milio and I had our fight, I was grateful to Mr. Dahlman for making me see some things." Her eyes widened. "You… you said something about blackmail. Is Milio blackmailing him?" Then, bright girl that she was, she made another connection. "You think *I'm* trying to blackmail him?"

"Are you?"

"I wouldn't know how," she said. "I don't have the pictures. Never had them. Don't want them. What if my little boy saw them?" She trembled at the thought. "And I don't believe Milio would blackmail anybody either. He does things for money—bad things. But not that. I mean, if he exposed those pictures, they'd show him too, and his macho pride wouldn't allow that."

"Macho pride? You said he preferred a man to you. Where's the macho pride in that?"

"In those pictures, he was…." She paused, stumped. "He was the man, but it was *with* a man. He'd never want anyone to see that."

"Apparently he's been hauling them out and sharing them with men he picked up."

"His fairy friends, you mean? Yes, he would see no harm in that. It would be his way of bragging. But not to anyone else."

"Why? Everyone knows he picks up men."

"Knowing it is one thing. I knew it too, but seeing it is harder to deal with." She shook her head. "No, he would not do that."

"Around the time the two of you broke up, the negatives to the photos went missing. Do you have any idea what happened to them?"

"I didn't know he lost them. He used to keep the photographs and the film in that backpack he carries around sometimes. And before you ask, I didn't take them."

"Do you know how to get in touch with Emilio?"

"I don't know, and I don't want to know."

I asked a personal question to get a measure of the woman. "Since you live with your grandparents, why aren't they taking care of your son?"

Her nostrils flared. "I raise my own child. Nobody else is going to do it. It's hard on me to put him in day care, but it's good for little Luis. He's around other children and learns to deal with them. Besides, *Abuela* keeps him a couple of days a week."

"Thank you, Estelle. I appreciate your candor. If I need to speak to you again, may I call you at your law firm?"

"I guess so."

Driving away slowly, I watched the young mother in the rearview mirror. She went about the business of closing the trunk, checking her child's restraints, and getting into the driver's seat in a completely normal way. Sometimes you can tell a lot about a person who doesn't know she is being watched. There was no deceit, no anxiety in Estelle's body language.

So where did that leave me? The labor dispute still seemed the most likely reason for pressuring Del, but if Estelle was being forthright, how did the pictures come into play? That made me wonder if Emilio knew any of his ex-girlfriend's law partners.

I phoned the office, but as Hazel had nothing pressing, I decided to deny her the opportunity to hand me another case, so I tackled the next name on Prada's list. According to the cross-reference directory in my trunk, one of them, Stephen Sturgis, was a professor at the University of New Mexico with a far Northeast Heights home address. UNM was closer.

I entered the campus at Central Avenue and Stanford, where John Tatschl's bronze of the university's lobo mascot stood in eternal vigilance in front of Johnson Center. As a lifelong history buff, I knew UNM had opened in 1892 with a total of twenty-five students in a Victorian-style building isolated on the desert east of Albuquerque. Now it occupied approximately eight hundred acres totally engulfed by the city's inexorable march to the heights.

A lady in the administration office consulted a directory and sent me to the Department of Communication & Journalism building near the northwest corner of Central Avenue and Yale. Sturgis was a professor in the school of journalism where Paul Barton was a student. Another coincidence?

That's the bad part of this job: it feeds paranoia. We all have some, but it seems a generous dose is virtually a prerequisite for a PI license. Unable to contact the professor, I left my card with a message asking him to phone. Then I spent the remainder of the day attempting to run down more of Emilio's johns.

THE NEXT morning, I sat in my office and reviewed the situation. If Emilio had been straight with me, someone on his list—or someone close to one of those people—had to be the blackmailer. Charlie had not yet gotten back to me about his canvass of the apartment house personnel, but it was really too soon to expect results. With a sigh I picked up the phone and called Richard Harding. He surprised me by taking my call.

"What can I do for you?" His heavy, lumbering voice blasted through the phone. "I hope you're through with that nonsense we discussed last time."

"Not quite. I have a thought I'd like to run by you."

"Run."

"Is it possible to determine if anyone got into your Photoshop files?"

"Someone I don't know about, you mean?"

"Exactly."

"Afraid that's beyond my technical capabilities, but I have someone in the office who should be able to check that for me. What are you thinking?"

"Well, you're in a contest with organized labor, and Del represents you in that matter, if I understand it correctly."

"That's right. You think they're the ones putting the pressure on him?"

"It's a thought. The night cleaning crew likely has access to your office. Do you think a little pilfering is above them?"

"I don't believe anything's above them, but I thought this was a money demand, not someone pressuring Del to lay off."

"True. But it's such a modest demand, it's almost as if someone wants him to pay to validate his vulnerability. Certify the hold they have over him, you might say."

A pause. I assumed Harding was debating which side to come down on. He apparently chose to consider my alternative. "That makes sense. All right, I'll check on it and get back to you."

The next half hour was devoted to my decision-balancing procedure—writing down the pros and cons of each theory about a case and assigning a weighted balance to each. For example, when considering whether to continue my swimming therapy, the fact that it was not always convenient weighed heavily on the negative side, but that is more than offset by the knowledge I will walk with a limp without the exercise.

Right in the middle of analyzing the labor dispute as a possible source of my client's problem, Hazel put through a call to my office, but not before warning it was someone on that "Del Dahlman thing."

"Mr. Vinson, this is Steve Sturgis. I received a message to call you."

"Thanks for getting back to me, Mr. Sturgis. Or is it Professor?"

"How about just plain old Steve?"

"Steve it is. I'm BJ."

"As for calling you back, who could resist the opportunity to respond to a call from a private eye? A shamus."

"Anything but a private dick." Sturgis seemed to get a kick out of that one. "Steve, I have something to discuss with you, but it's sort of sensitive. Perhaps it would be better to meet somewhere."

"My, my. You know how to grab a guy's attention. What do you suggest?"

"Well, you can come to my office, we can meet at the North Valley Country Club, or I'm open to your suggestion."

"The country club is fine with me. I assume they know you there."

"Yes. I'll be in the coffee bar. Is an hour okay?"

"Perfect."

STEVE STURGIS was a distinguished man in his early forties with premature gray hair and an erect, almost military carriage. He projected energy and vitality and competence. If Paul were one of Steve's students, he would be well grounded in his trade. The man inspired confidence. Half a second later, the green-eyed monster punched me in the gut. Had Paul bedded his prof, who was, by the way, eminently beddable? As we took a seat at a table in a far corner of the club's dining room, I shook my head to clear away the thoughts.

"Is something wrong?" he asked.

"Had a thought about another matter I'm handling, and I didn't like it much."

"I see. And what is this case you're working on that involves… or might involve me?"

The waiter interrupted to take our lunch order. I chose the patty melt with green chili and tater tots; Sturgis opted for a grilled salmon steak and a salad with reduced-fat ranch dressing.

"Steve, this is going to touch on something that might be sensitive. It's not an accusation, nor is it meant to embarrass or threaten. I simply need some information on a very delicate case. Do you mind if I tape this conversation? I do that routinely so I can go back and review things afterward."

"Now you have me intrigued. No, I don't mind. Go on."

I spoke into the little machine noting the case number, naming the subject of the interview, and noting the time and date as 1:30 p.m. on Tuesday, July 25, 2006. Then I placed the recorder in the middle of the table. "Professor Sturgis, a month or so ago, you picked up a young Hispanic named Emilio outside of a bar. You took him home, and the two of you engaged in private acts that are your own business and no affair of mine. What *does* concern me are the photos he showed you of himself and another man. I'm trying to recover those pictures and the negatives."

Sturgis glanced at the recorder lying on the table but did not go into denial. He nodded. "All right. That's true. Well, partially true. I allowed myself to be picked up, but the result is the same. And yes, Emilio showed me some photos. He was quite proud of them, actually. I guess he had a right to be. That young man has been favored by nature in just about every way possible. And the photos… uh, helped advance the evening, if you understand my meaning."

"Did he give you any of the snapshots?"

"No. I thought of requesting one, but decided against it."

"Why?"

"I recognized the other man, and since he practices in my brother's law firm, I decided to resist temptation—should it ever present itself."

I sat up straight. "You have a brother with—"

"Stone, Hedges, Martinez, Levisohn, and the rest of them."

"May I ask his name?"

"He's not involved, so I see no harm in it. He's my half brother, actually. Same mother, different fathers. His name is James Addleston."

"Have you mentioned the tête-à-tête with Emilio to him?"

"Absolutely not. While he's aware of my predilection, I don't rub his nose in it. That was a personal and private affair."

"I'll try to respect that."

"Thank you."

"Did Emilio leave anything behind when he took his leave? In the house, perhaps? Or in your car?"

"He drove his own car. He followed me home. And no, he left nothing behind."

"When he came inside, did he bring anything with him, such as a black nylon backpack?"

Sturgis frowned. "Not that I recall. Let's see." He leaned back, examining the club's massive, carved vigas as he considered the question. "He came inside empty-handed. When he showed me the photos, he fished them out of his back pocket. As I recall there were four of them."

"So you saw no negatives."

"No. Just the prints." He lowered his gaze from the ceiling and met my eyes squarely. "Whoa! There's a problem with the pictures, isn't there?" He frowned. "That makes no sense. Everyone knows about Del Dahlman."

"Would you want photos of yourself like that floating around?"

"Ah, I see the problem."

"Please keep this conversation private. There is no need for your brother to learn of this, is there?"

"I don't know. Perhaps I should give him a heads-up on what's going on."

"Up to you, of course, but I prefer you don't. No need to roil the corporate waters at this point. Just for the record, I need to ask a blunt question. Do you have either copies of the photographs in question or negatives of such photographs? Or"—I added to cover all the bases—"do you have such photographs stored in your computer?"

"No, of course not. I do not have them and have never had them in my possession. Beyond"—he covered his bases too—"looking at them with Emilio."

"Do you know of other friends or acquaintances Emilio might have shared the pictures with? Anyone at all?"

He shook his head. "I've seen him around town with other people—men. But I don't know any of them, so I can't help you there."

"Thank you for your candor."

After that, I snapped off the tape recorder and we spent the time discussing how much Albuquerque had changed over the past few years, discovering a few mutual acquaintances as we ate. Then I signed the bill and the professor left after giving a shaky promise to forego speaking to his brother about Del's plight.

The next task, now even more urgent, was to talk to Del again. He suggested a meeting in a neutral corner, so I remained where I was, absently studying the ornate Mexican tinwork adorning the wall sconces and the three chandeliers in the room. The intricate details in those pieces always intrigued me. I often wished I were creative. Over the years I'd tried everything from painting still life to crafting lumpy clay piles that resembled cow pies more than life forms. I love art but stink at creating it.

When Del showed up, he listened to the tape of my interview with Sturgis and was shaken more by this latest development than by anything thus far.

"Jim Addleston is as close to a rival as I have in the firm. He's bright, aggressive, fast on his feet, and ruthless." Del grimaced. "The nature of this thing just changed. Maybe I should warn the partners."

"Your call." I sipped my Virgin Mary. I never drink alcohol while on the job except for nursing one now and then during a late dinner interview. "But let me know what you intend to do. It may affect the way I go about the investigation. Of course, if you decide to come clean, there may be no need for any more poking around."

"Get one thing straight. I want this son of a bitch exposed regardless of what I decide to do."

The next morning, after a quick call to Hazel to let her know he was on the way, Del showed up at my office again. He maneuvered past my office manager, sat in the chair opposite me, and tugged at an earlobe.

"Two days in a row. I'm honored," I said in a flat tone.

"Can it, BJ. There's been a new development. I got another note."

"I hope to hell—"

"Don't worry. I saved it for you this time. As soon as I saw the writing, I knew what it was."

"Was it delivered the same way?"

"No. A messenger brought it to the office."

"I'll need the name of the messenger service."

"I don't have a name. Nobody saw who left it. Our receptionist was called back to the copy room for a moment, and when she returned to the front desk, the envelope was lying right there."

"I'll need her name."

"Hell, Vince, you can't question her. That would expose everything. Besides, I talked to her. She didn't see a thing. I asked around the office, and nobody else did either."

"So the blackmailer was lucky enough to deliver the demand when nobody was at the front desk? Someone's *always* at the front desk, Del."

"That's usually true, unless Belinda steps away for a moment."

"And he just happened to pick that moment? Unlikely."

"I thought about that too. There are glass panels on either side of the big double doors to our suite. Somebody must have watched from over near the elevators until she was called away."

"Anyone notice a loiterer?"

"No one from the office did, and we occupy the entire floor. But I absolutely forbid you to question Belinda."

I made a point of writing the name in my pocket notebook. "That's the receptionist, right?"

"Dammit, Vince, don't go near her. You hear me?"

"Okay, but I'll have Charlie check out her background anyway. Give me the rest of her name."

He fumed a little more but finally provided her last name: Gerard.

"Her fingerprints are probably on the envelope, so I can run them through the system. Who else handled it—and the note?"

"I don't know how many people handled the envelope before I got it, but nobody's touched the paper inside. I used tweezers to extract it."

"Let me see it."

Del pulled two clear plastic sheaths from his attaché case and slid them across the table. He touched one. "These are the instructions for payment of the five thousand." He tapped the other. "That's the envelope it came in."

The blackmailer was getting craftier. The envelope was addressed in handwritten block letters, but the note created by pasting words cut from magazines and newspapers read:

Mail $5,000 in cash to Occupant at 3301 Juan Tabo NE #2223, by Friday. The negatives to two of the juicy pics will be sent by return mail. And call off your private eye or else.

"This could be a break." Del's voice held a hopeful note. "All we have to do is find out who's in apartment 2223, and we've got the guy."

"Too simple. It'll probably turn out to be a UPS or Ship-n-Mail store or something like that. Here's what I want you to do. Mail a nine-by-twelve manila envelope to the address, with a note inside saying the arrangements are unsatisfactory. You need a better guarantee you'll get what you're paying for. Throw in some nonsense about not making any more copies of the photos. Sound confident, but show enough vulnerability so that you don't spook the blackmailer."

"Okay, sounds simple enough. But why a nine-by-twelve?"

"It's easier to keep an eye on a big envelope."

"You're going to be able to do that?"

"With any luck."

"Fine, when do you want me to mail it?"

"Today's Thursday. Tomorrow would be a good day."

"The instructions say payment has to be made by Friday."

"I wouldn't worry about that. The blackmailer will expect a little negotiation. But the delay gives me time to visit the site and get the lay of the land. By then we should know if the demand note and envelope reveal anything about our friend." I paused before adding, "Look, make up your mind. This thing is going to come out into the open. And that's not all bad. When it does, this bum loses his leverage over you. We'll get him, but I can't guarantee the pictures won't show up first."

"Well, we know one thing for certain. This payment is to validate the blackmailer's advantage. He's only promising to return two of the photos. If I pay the five thousand, he'll come back for a hell of a lot more."

I spent the next hour with a man who was more nearly the tough, determined Del I had known and loved. It was almost like old times, when we had shared meals at our favorite restaurant, the Maria Teresa, located in a former residence built in the seventeen hundreds near Old Town. The place was supposed to be inhabited by a couple of ghosts, and more than one diner had claimed to have been surprised by spectral images. As much as we hoped for and anticipated such an event, no wraith was ever so bold as to reveal himself to us. I shuddered involuntarily as I remembered how it all came to an end.

The excruciating pain. The bitter taste and sharp smell of sweat and blood and fear when the bullet struck my right thigh. The terror of descending into hell as I writhed on a gurney. The paralyzing fear of soaring heavenward when they hoisted me into the ambulance. I woke in the ICU with carpet-to-carpet cops pacing the hallway outside. My captain was there, the lieutenant as well. Even the desk sergeant, with whom I hadn't exactly been on friendly terms. But the ranks close when a cop goes down.

My partner, Detective Eugene Enriquez, hovered at the foot of the bed. I opened my mouth and spoke in a shaky, barely recognizable voice.

"Did you get Williams?" Nestor Williams was the killer we'd been chasing.

"Nope, you did," he said. "Got him a second before he winged you. Probably saved your own life. He'd have nailed you for sure if you hadn't ruined his aim with a chunk of lead to his chest."

As things began to go out of focus, I spotted a tall figure standing against the wall. The swelling in my heart vied with the throbbing in my thigh. The pain won; I passed out.

When consciousness returned, Del was still there, only now he was sitting patiently in a chair beside my bed. It must have been the middle of the night because he was uncharacteristically disheveled. The faint lamp glow turned his stubble into gleaming gold. Over the next few weeks, I often found him hovering near as I fought to beat the odds and reclaim my life. My life with him.

He did his best, caring and concerned and supportive during my fierce struggle, but when I left the hospital and needed his assistance,

Del shut down. His love—and I harbored no doubt it had been real—withered beneath his fear of my pain and suffering. It ended irrevocably when he brought Emilio into our home.

The camaraderie that had been building over the course of the last hour evaporated, leaving me chilled. Del gave me a peculiar look; he must have sensed my change of mood.

Shortly thereafter we walked over to the Albuquerque Police Department. I wanted a full set of his fingerprints for elimination purposes, and those guys were the experts in that kind of thing. One of my friends accommodated us, and then I put the fingerprint card, together with the glassine sheets containing the envelope and ransom instructions, into my attaché case.

Since cops tend to go on the record when crimes are committed, my best resources for examining and testing the blackmail note were of no value to me at the moment. Even approaching my ex-partner, Gene Enriquez, would put him on the spot, so I planned to go to a private lab for a forensic examination.

I said good-bye to Del and went straight home, where the situation changed abruptly. Lying right on top of the rest of my mail was an envelope with my name printed across it in large block letters. No postal worker had shoved it through the mail slot in my door; this had been hand delivered, just like Del's. The message inside was simple and direct.

Stop working for that queer Dahlman or die!

Chapter 7

STILL STEAMING over some thug believing he could intimidate me, the next morning I handed over the blackmailer's envelopes and notes, along with Del's fingerprint card, to Gloria McInnes. She looked down her thin-bridged nose at me like an English blue blood. She wasn't. She was born and raised in the little community of Algodones, north of Albuquerque, and was as common as shoe leather. I often wondered at the ribald jokes she must have endured after fifteen years of working in a place called K-Y Lab. The joint was named after its founders, Sol King and Jacob Young, not the water-soluble gel that prompted erotic reactions in countless giggling teenagers and horny young adults. I asked her to print me too, because I'd handled the envelope before tumbling to what it was. I wanted her to test the documents for whatever forensic evidence they might contain.

"Hmm." She ran a casual eye over the crude death threat. "Somebody's getting personal."

"Yeah, and that was his mistake. I'm going to get the bastard."

"And I'll bet you do. Okay, BJ, I'll run a prelim for you, but I'll need forty-eight hours. Of course, if I pick up DNA, I'll need some extra time, but I'll give you what I can Monday afternoon."

"I need it a little quicker."

"Saturday's the best I can do."

"Didn't know you were open on Saturday."

"Just for you, sweetheart. Give me until about six o'clock that afternoon, okay?"

With that promise I set off for 3301 Juan Tabo Boulevard NE, which was, indeed, a Ship-n-Mail store in a strip mall of the kind architects call decorated sheds. There I ran into a stone wall. The thin-chested teenage clerk refused—under penalty of law, he claimed—to reveal any information about the box holder. There was nothing to do but plan on spending Saturday hunkered down in the parking lot to wait for someone to pick up Del's envelope.

Stymied for the moment, I headed for the country club. On the way I used the hands-free phone to call Charlie and ask him to check out Belinda Gerard. He had nothing to report on the Royal Crest yet but said he was working on it.

The summer day was chilled by the monsoon system that usually arrived in July or August to deliver a fair portion of our nine and a half inches of annual rainfall. As the thunder and lightning cooperated by hovering to the west over Mt. Taylor, one of the Navajos' four sacred mountains, I braved the elements and swam for a while, hoping Paul would show up to relieve the youth occupying the lifeguard's chair. He didn't.

On my way out, I paused to view the mural in the club's foyer. Done in a primitive style, it portrayed the founding of the Villa de Alburquerque in 1706. It took us over 150 years to lose the first *r* in the city's name. The dark earth tones of the mural failed to work their usual magic. My spirit remained troubled.

That changed later that evening when Paul answered my phone call to his dorm and agreed to come over. He showed up at my place around nine, and my heart clogged my throat as I watched him bound up the steps and follow me into the house. In the foyer I turned, forcing him to stop in the narrow entryway. Caught unawares, he almost ran into me but managed to stop just inches away. I cupped his head in my hand and pulled him forward. In my thirty-odd years, I've kissed a lot of people, but this was different. Touching Paul seemed to awaken nerve endings that had long lain dormant. My lips came alive with sensations I don't normally associate with a kiss and transmitted this revelation to every part of my body.

He moaned and wrapped me in his arms. A long minute later, when we broke apart, we stood eye to eye, studying one another. My mouth formed one set of words while my viscera cried out for another.

"How about a drink?"

He leaned his forehead against mine. "One," he answered simply. "Scotch rocks."

One. Was that a self-imposed limit, or did it imply an urge to get on to other things? I rested a hand on his hip as we moved into the den. He sat on a stool on one side of the small bar while, after fixing our drinks, I stood resting my arms on the top a moment before suggesting we move to more comfortable chairs.

As anxious as I was to get physical, I soon found myself lost in the history of this engaging young man. His father died of tuberculosis when he was still a child, and his mother worked hard to keep a roof over their heads in Albuquerque's South Valley, sometimes coming home from one job clerking in a novelty store to change clothes and go waitress in a nearby café. Paul had pitched in, finding odd jobs after school and mowing lawns every summer as much as he could. His list of part-time jobs was truly amazing.

As he talked I found myself growing more comfortable with the boy… man. The urge to touch and feel and experience marvelous sensations remained, but my interest in Paul Barton grew as he revealed more and more of himself. He'd fallen in with a tough crowd, some of them relatives, and was heading down the wrong path when something happened to bring him to his senses. He and two buddies rolled a man in an alley one afternoon. The guy was drunk to the point he couldn't defend himself as Paul's companions beat him bloody. For no reason. For something to do.

Even though he didn't lay a hand on the man, Paul was so shocked, he quit hanging around with gang members and started visiting boys' clubs and the school gym, where he discovered a love for swimming.

When he paused in his story, I moved over to sit beside him on the couch. "When did you discover you were gay?"

He turned to look at me. "Is that what I am?"

"Well… I—"

He broke out laughing, wrinkling his nose a bit as he did so. "Yeah, the evidence so far points that way. Maybe we should explore that theme a little more."

"Great idea." My heart swelled so much I was afraid it would split in two.

"I brought an overnight bag… just in case."

"I think you might just need it."

Later, as his head hit the mattress, his charming passive-aggressive manner dissolved and he became a tiger. Or maybe the dragon tattooed above his left nipple.

SATURDAY MORNING, in order to secure a favorable parking place, I arrived at the strip mall well before the scheduled delivery by the post office. The Ship-n-Mail's plate glass window gave a clear view of the bank of mailboxes inside. After buying a book of stamps in order to affix the location of box 2223 in my mind, I returned to the car, counted off rows and columns, and zeroed in on the target. Then I walked to a nearby Starbucks to kill time and pad my waistline.

Some investigators don't like the windows of their surveillance cars heavily tinted, claiming this makes them even more visible. Around Albuquerque it seems like the glass in every third car was darker than the legal limit, so mine were tinted enough to assure few people would spot me lingering for what might turn out to be hours.

I closed down the stakeout shortly before Ship-n-Mail was scheduled to lock its doors for the day. So far no one had even gone near the box. The clerk was a different thin-chested teenager this afternoon, so I tried to brazen it out, claiming to have forgotten my key and asking him to check my mail. The high school kid caught himself in time to ask for ID. When I declined, he inadvertently gave me the information anyway. The box was empty. That left a couple of possibilities. Either the delivery from the postal service had been delayed—possible, although unlikely—or this was a pigeon drop, a way station with instructions to forward the mail to another location.

Hauling out my investigator's ID, I banked on that singularly unimpressive scrap of paper, which totally lacked the legal authority to compel cooperation from anyone, to show the clerk.

"Private eye," he observed nervously. "Never met one before."

"Most people haven't, son. I need the name and address of the box holder for 2223."

"That's… that's confidential information."

"That's okay, I'm a confidential investigator."

He scratched a pimple on his cheek. "It doesn't work that way, does it? I mean, that license isn't like a badge or anything. Uh, is it?"

"It's authorization by the State of New Mexico to engage in confidential inquiries." This kid didn't take pressure well, so I applied some more. "That information is key to a very important case."

"Uh… sorry, mister, they're real strict about that here. I think it's something in the law." He threw out this last tidbit like a lifeline.

"All right, give me your name for my official report. You know, as being uncooperative."

The guy may have been a geek, but he stood his ground. "William Mackson."

Stifling a weary sigh, I grimaced. "Look, just so I don't have to claim you stonewalled me, check the record and tell me one thing?"

"What's that?"

"Are there any special instructions for the box?"

"Like what?"

"Like forwarding the mail, for example."

Young Billy disappeared around the bank of mailboxes for a moment. When he returned he cleared his throat nervously. "There's standing instructions to mail the contents to... uh, somewhere else."

"I need that address, Billy. This could be a matter of life or death."

For a moment it looked as if that approach had scored, but then Mackson gave a wobbly shake of his head. "Sorry, sir, I can't help you. Are you really going to put my name in there? You know, in the report?"

"On the first line."

"Do you have to? I mean, I wish you wouldn't."

"Sorry, son, I can't help you."

Muttering beneath my breath, I returned to the car and dialed Del's cell number.

He did his cursing aloud. "What do we do now?"

"Wait for the blackmailer to respond to your letter. In the meantime, I'm headed for the lab to see if they picked up anything from the notes and envelopes."

"Notes? Envelopes?"

"Oh, yeah. I forgot to tell you. I got a warning to steer clear of you and your smutty pictures."

"You got a threat?"

"Yeah. A death threat, no less."

"Maybe we ought to think this thing through a little more carefully."

I tried to take advantage of the doubt in his voice. "We can always go to the police. In fact, that's a good idea. This thing is bound to come out into the open sooner or later. We've worked our way through practically every social stratum in town."

"I'm not ready for that yet."

"Okay, you're the boss. I'll try to find Emilio again and lean on him some more. Not going to be easy finding the little shit this time. I gotta get going if I want to catch Gloria McInnes over at K-Y Lab by six."

Del chuckled. "That name always grabs me."

"Yeah, and I know where."

The trip, which required bucking the reduced weekend rush-hour traffic coming out of Kirtland AFB and Sandia Labs, wasn't worth it. Gloria handed me back the blackmailer's notes and envelopes with a grimace.

"Nothing, BJ. No strange fingerprints on the notes. The envelopes had a couple that are probably from messengers since they weren't on the notes inside. I printed them and ran them through the database, but no hits. There was no saliva on the glue sealing the envelope or the paste gluing the letters and words to the paper. So there's no stray DNA to test. Really, there's nothing except a few traces of a powder that probably came from surgical gloves. The envelopes are of cheap quality, as is the paper. Sorry, my friend."

"Well, you tried. But this guy's too careful. Do a formal report, including all the fingerprints, just in case, and send me a bill, will you? Pay yourself something extra for working the weekend for me."

AFTER EMILIO failed to show up at the C&W that night, a friendly cop put out the word.

A cruiser spotted Emilio's distinctive Mustang on Sunday morning, and it was still parked in front of a West Central motel by the time I got there. The motel office was locked, so I settled down to wait. Half an hour dragged by before Emilio emerged from a room with a tall, thin, middle-aged man in tow. The lovebirds laughed and giggled their way to his car and roared out of the parking lot. I was afraid they were heading for a bar, but Emilio dropped his companion off in the Cottonwood Mall parking lot on North Coors and roared away, leaving the obviously enchanted john standing on the pavement gazing longingly after him.

I exited the lot in a more sedate manner but had to step on it in order to keep Emilio in sight. Fortunately he came to his senses before either of us garnered a speeding ticket, slowing as he hit the congested commercial area near the I-40 interchange. He continued south and turned off Coors onto one of the residential streets in a neighborhood of small cinder-block homes.

The Mustang turned into a driveway to one of these, coming to a halt in front of a converted garage. He got out of the car and disappeared inside.

So this was the lion's den. Or rather the coyote's lair. I got out of my car and politely knocked, enjoying the dismay that puckered Emilio's features when he answered the door.

Chapter 8

WHEN EMILIO denied sharing the photographs with anyone else, I used threats and intimidation to haul his butt to my home. No harm done; he already knew where I lived.

The house my father built was in a settled neighborhood of 1950s contemporary cross-gabled homes. Most had stone foundations and red brick walls with tall windows and white trim; ours was green. The house was symmetrical, fronted by a wide, low-ceilinged porch enclosed by a stone balustrade crowned with a wooden railing. Square, tapered pedestals supported a heavy roof at the corners and on either side of the concrete steps. Pale shrub roses and English Legends lined the front of the house while Heirlooms bordered the driveway running up the west side to the detached garage. I know this because, as a kid, I helped Mom plant every one of them. Schoolteacher that she was, she made sure I knew what I was planting.

Unusual for Albuquerque at the time, the house had a basement that Dad always intended to finish as a game room, but which ended up as storage space. Now it became a makeshift jail when I took Emilio by surprise and locked the sturdy door behind him.

Then I mowed and trimmed the lawn and cleaned the kitchen while he fermented a little. The lady who came once a week to tidy the house was due tomorrow, but the work drained some nervous energy and tamped down my urge to throttle Emilio Prada. He finally quit pounding on the door, electing to poke out one of the tiny basement windows instead. Although it was too small for him to slither through, he gave it a damn good try. When he gave up the effort, I drove to a hardware store on North Fourth for glass and putty, and put him to work repairing the damage.

The job finished, Emilio faced me with a small putty knife in his hand. He considered coming after me, but in the end he tossed the blade aside and spread his hands in a plea.

"I dunno what you want from me!"

"I want the name of the man or woman who took the negatives. I want to know who's trying to blackmail Del and threatening me."

His large eyes flickered. "Threatening you? Hey, man, it ain't me."

"Didn't think it was. But you know who it is, and you're going to tell me."

He pounded a palm with his fist in frustration. For one moment the street tough had showed his face before hiding behind the male prostitute again. "I told you about everybody."

"You didn't tell me about Estelle."

Obviously surprised, he recovered quickly. "I thought you meant men. You talked to Estelle?"

"You bet. Was that your kid in the car with her?"

His jaw muscles clenched. "Kid? Oh, you mean the little guy? Naw. I didn't even know her when she had him. What'd she say?"

"That you were a low-down snake in the grass and she never wanted to see you again. Showing her pictures of you and Del wasn't very bright."

"Guess not, but I thought it'd spice things up some." He tried out a half smile. "I look pretty good in them pictures, huh?"

"Maybe so, but sticking it to Del probably wouldn't do anything for a woman except maybe turn her off."

"Not all of them. Turns some of them on like you wouldn't believe. But not Estelle, I guess." Emilio suddenly stripped off his shirt and squared his shoulders. He was huskier than he looked. "Let's get down to what you really want so you can take me back home. I need some rest."

I managed to react by the time he had his trousers halfway over his slender hips. "I won't touch you, Emilio. I don't want anything from you except what's locked up in that thick skull. Names, man, names. And get dressed."

He grinned. "You like Emilio, don't you? Go ahead, won't hurt nothing to admit it."

"You're not my type." Damn, the fucker was handsome right down to his toes. And by now that's about all that remained hidden from view.

"Come on," he cajoled. As a professional he no doubt recognized desire lurking amid the revulsion.

I walked up the steps. "When you decide to cooperate, give me a call."

"Hey, man, wait." I turned to find him stuffing himself into his pants. "You in big trouble, you know. You can't lock me down here. That's kidnapping. You made a mistake, Mr. Private Investigator. And it's gonna cost you a bundle. I might even complain about criminal stuff. This is *way* worse than carving up my car seat. Big time. Federal stuff."

Hands on my hips, I stared down at him. "Play it that way if you want. But you'd better leave town as soon as you file the complaint. Maybe even leave the state. You won't be able to pick up a john without the cops riding your ass. It won't take long for word to get around that you're poison. In a week all you'll be able to score will be street pickups on East Central. By the end of the month, you won't even be able to do that. Every time you exceed the speed limit, they'll give you a ticket. Every time you leave a bar, you'll get pulled over. How long do you think it'll take them to nail you for DWI? They'll impound that pretty car of yours and sell it at auction to pay your fines. That's what's waiting for you."

"You fulla shit! You can't do that. You ain't no cop no more."

"How do you think I found you today? I put out a call, and a blue-and-white spotted your Mustang at the motel. So I just waited and followed you and your sugar daddy. All I have to do is let the cops know you're preying on rich men, and you're through."

Emilio wilted. "A'right! You let me go, and we'll call it quits."

"No way. We're going upstairs, have some coffee, and talk like men. You're going to root around in your memory and come up with some more names. And this time don't leave out the women."

"Didn't show them to no women except for Estelle."

He turned civil as we sat at the dinette table, nursing cups of hot coffee. And I have to admit, he made an effort. Emilio was able to describe a few more men, but he didn't know their names. Finally he came to the crux of the matter.

"If you got threatened, don't that mean you already talked to the dude who's trying to get to old Del?"

"Either that, or it's someone who heard about my inquiries. Let's look at this from another direction. Why did you keep the pictures in your backpack? Why not leave them home?"

He flashed a self-conscious smile. "I liked to take them out and look at them sometimes. Old Del and me, we looked pretty good together. He's a prime cut of beef too, you know."

"But why the negatives? Why not put them away someplace safe?"

"Dunno. They was in that envelope with the snaps, so I just left them there."

"Who had access to your backpack?"

Another shrug. "Anybody, I guess. I kept it on the back floorboard of the Mustang mostly."

"With the top down, right?"

"Well, sure. That's what a convertible's for. I keep it down anytime it ain't raining."

"Why not lock the bag in the trunk?"

"I do sometimes. But when I'm in a hurry, I just toss it in the backseat."

Emilio had no inkling of the real value of those photographs. Of course that did not mean there wasn't something locked up in his head that could help my investigation. But if he had such a tidbit tucked away, I was unable to extract it, despite spending another hour questioning him. I finally wrapped it up when hostility began battling with exhaustion. By then he'd given me two more names to check out.

I stood and poked him on the shoulder, bringing his head up from his folded arms. "Okay, I'll take you home now."

"About time." The street tough was back. "Still might turn you in."

"Be my guest. But right now, get your butt in gear before I decide to let you walk home."

He shot up out of the chair. "Let's go."

As we approached the front hallway, he rubbed his eyes. "You ain't never gonna find this dude. Not from asking me questions, you ain't."

"Oh, I'll find him all right. If not from one of your pickups, then we'll get him through the post-office box he rented."

He halted in his tracks. The purr of a motor caught my attention—Something crashed against the picture window in the living room. "What the hell—?"

The sound of breaking glass. A muffled *whump*. The unseen motor revved. Tires screeched on the asphalt. I hit the front door in time to glimpse the tail end of a red pickup disappear around the corner. But I had little time to think about that. A curtain of hungry orange flames eating at my veranda demanded immediate attention. I vaulted over the end of the porch to the driveway and scooped soil from a rose bed. It required three trips to smother the fire. There didn't appear to be any real damage, but both the porch and front window frame would need fresh paint, and the brick wall would require a good scrubbing. The shattered remains of a bottle and a scrap of cloth not totally consumed by the flames marked it as a Molotov cocktail.

As I stood congratulating myself for long ago replacing common screens on my windows with steel-wire mesh, which had prevented the bottle from breaking the window glass, I realized Emilio had vanished.

Sirens!

Old Mrs. Wardlow across the street must have called the fire station a couple of blocks down the road. Damnation. I'd have to hang around and explain things, and probably answer some awkward questions for the cops who would follow. In the meantime Emilio was in the wind. I wondered if the assailant had known the kid was in the house with me. If so, that changed the dynamics of the thing. Both of us could be targets, so I needed to talk to him again.

By the time I finished downplaying the event to the firemen and street cops who showed up, an anonymous brown Ford sedan pulled to the curb and disgorged Gene Enriquez.

"You okay?" Gene, my old APD partner, stopped at the foot of the steps where we'd congregated.

"Yeah, fine. How come you're here?"

"I heard the call and recognized the address."

"Come on inside, and I'll fill you in."

The patrolmen who'd just heard me claim the Molotov cocktail was a kid's prank looked as if they wanted to join us, but Gene sent them to canvass the neighborhood for possible witnesses. I suggested they start with the white brick across the way. Mrs. Wardlow saw everything that went down on the street.

I poured Gene a cup of hot coffee and gave him a piece of the story, figuring he was due *something* now that violence had broken out.

He listened without interrupting until I finished and then asked a few questions of his own. At length he leaned back and sighed. "So, Dahlman's still screwing with you, huh?"

I had no secrets from Gene. He understood the place Del had held in my life; he also knew the details of the rupture between us. "Yeah, you might say that. Although this is a straight business deal."

"And this kid's the same bozo who split up the two of you last year?"

"You can imagine the embarrassment that caused Del."

"Not enough. Not near enough. So, where are you on the investigation?"

Half an hour later, a restored gunmetal-gray '63 Ford Fairlane with green flames emblazoned on the hood eased into the driveway. Emilio ailed out of the front passenger's seat as José Zapata, the thug called ncón, eased out of the driver's side and ate up the distance to the nt door with his long stride. He was well named, that one. Long and y described him perfectly. So Emilio had called on the Santos to haul ome. I wondered about those chores he alluded to the other night, at he'd said made sense. Anyone would have made Zancón for a t wasn't only his dress and tattoos; the man owned an attitude that d gangster.

the other hand, Emilio Prada cleaned up very well. He was the re of an attractive young man when he wasn't trolling for gay e was probably a lot he could do for the Saints.

vo men remained inside the apartment for thirty minutes or emerging with boxes and suitcases. Emilio was clearing out. ver the attack at my home or merely to escape my clutches? le of both. He'd sure turned rabbit when the firebomb hit

borhood was old enough to have alleys behind the yself out a back gate and made it to my Impala before turned north on Coors. They were probably headed for

was only a couple of blocks ahead of me, but s farther down the street. Was the gangster guarding erely going his own way? With one car between pala, we eased to a stop at a traffic light. Emilio turned east onto I-40.

hevy trailed the Fairlane onto the expressway dropped abruptly into the broad Rio Grande nd on the far side of the river, Albuquerque's pressive from this viewpoint. The massive ated the eastern horizon. A speck in the o. Zancón goosed his car as soon as he nd we closed enough on the Mustang to t lane and enter the maze of blue-striped interchange. I wasn't close enough to or the overpass leading north. Zancón st past the interchange.

"I don't want a file opened, Gene. Not until Del decides complaint. Okay?"

"Sure. But the patrol officers will report the firebo~ other shit leaks out, that's just too bad."

"Fair enough." I gave him the details.

When I finished, he eyed me doubtfully. "You s a file opened on the blackmail attempt?"

"That's Del's call, not mine."

"That was true until they threatened you ' way. Still, it looks like you could use some h

"No question about that."

"You used the K-Y Lab for the no† "They're as good as anybody, so that '

"But I sure would like to know 2223 on Juan Tabo. And where th'

"As long as we can open what I can do. After all, it's a '

"Appreciate the effor† over here, you know."

"Hey, what are fr'

"Yeah. Appreci'

He shrugged

As soon as ' I locked the ho'

Twenty still in fror he answ to get ' hour st

li~ settleu unoccupieu here there was i. could approach or i~

very pict
trade. The~

The t
more before
From fright o
Probably a lit†
my window.
This neigh
houses, so I let n
the other two cars
the freeway.

Zancón's For
Emilio's Mustang wa
the hustler's back or i
the Fairlane and my In
had made it through and
Minutes later my C
ramp where the highway
Valley. Sitting on low grou
skyline was singularly unin
bulk of Sandia Peak domi
distance was probably Emi
merged with freeway traffic, a
watch Emilio switch to the rig†
exits and flyways of the Big I
determine if he took the exit south
gave me no clue as he continued e

b~
Za
fro
lan†
him
but w
hood.
scream~
On

If Emilio was running for Mexico, that was not necessarily a bad thing. He was pretty well bled dry of information and would be out of harm's way. Besides, he was dead right; the blackmailer was probably someone I'd already interviewed. Or somebody close enough to be alarmed by my questions. That meant the puzzle was now mine to figure out. Even though I had no idea of what was really going on, that thought was strangely uplifting. As I had learned long ago, there were always two stories unfolding: the apparent one and the one lying undetected below the surface. The surface plot was slowly coming into focus; the other one remained murky.

I pulled out my cell and called Gene. He agreed to put out a "report location only" bulletin on Emilio's Mustang.

Chapter 9

I SAT in the office Monday morning trying to go over notes from the investigation, but Paul's image kept intruding. Finally I gave up on working and simply sat back in my chair to consider what was happening to me. Why was I becoming so wrapped up in this extraordinary young man? Maybe that was why. Extraordinarily handsome. Extraordinarily athletic. Sexy. Interesting. Just sitting and talking to him engaged all my senses. He hadn't led a very complicated or unusual existence for a South Valley kid, yet because it was *his* existence, it became complicated and unusual to me. I shook my head and sighed. This was getting way past the physical, and because of it, the physical was immeasurably better.

He'd left last Thursday night, actually Friday morning, without making any arrangements for later. Maybe I could sneak out for some pool therapy. I'd been a little less than consistent about it lately, as he had been quick to remind me.

A phone call from Richard Harding was a welcome interruption. His electronics guru had found no evidence of hacking into his computer files, although he cautioned there was no way to be absolutely certain. Wasted words because I already knew that, plus I wasn't sure if I could believe him or not.

I hung up wondering what had been accomplished. Probably nothing. Evidence of a break-in would prove something; absence of such evidence was meaningless.

Del phoned, interrupting that thought. "Addleston knows," he blurted. "I can tell from the way he acts."

"Well, that's no surprise. Sturgis's promise not to mention it to his brother was halfhearted at best. The last time we talked, you were going to warn the partners."

"I haven't gotten around to it yet. This thing has me rattled to the point where I'm not thinking straight."

"Where's that steely-eyed, iron-nerved lawyer I used to know?"

"He's still in here somewhere—I think. Vince, will you go see Sturgis and tell me if I'm being paranoid. I need to know for sure if he spilled the beans to his brother, but I'm not ready to confront Addleston yet. The office politics are too complicated."

"Okay, but there's something about this situation that doesn't make sense, not for a simple blackmail scheme. What are you involved in that warrants a threat against me? A rivalry for a law partnership wouldn't take things that far, nor would a labor union battle over an organizing attempt. I'm having trouble stretching this thing to the level of a death threat."

"Somebody's just trying to scare you off, that's all."

"That might be true, but doesn't a threat on my life raise the stakes in a court of law? And I told you about the attempt to torch my place. That is definitely an escalation. Hell, it's an overtly criminal act."

"That's true."

"Del, here's the point where I have to get personal—really personal. Who are you seeing right at the moment?"

"Seeing? Well, nobody at the present."

"Any recent breakup?"

"Not since Emilio."

"Anyone who's jealous enough to go off his rocker?"

"Absolutely no one. I've been so busy lately, I'm practically living the life of a monk. Well, there was that lawyer in Dallas a few days ago, but that was entirely casual. And the blackmail attempt predated him. No, there's no one I'm intimately involved with, now or in the recent past, who would try anything like this. Nobody except Emilio."

"How about anyone who might resent your lifestyle?"

"You mean like someone who hates gays? I'm sure I'm surrounded by them. We all are. But there have been no incidents lately."

"You're a pretty good lawyer. You win more than your share of cases. Have there been any recently that might have sent a losing defendant off on a tangent?"

He cited a few of his more adversarial cases, and I wrote them down so Charlie and I could check on the parties involved. I hung up after assuring him I'd go see Sturgis.

DECIDING A face-to-face meeting would be more productive than a phone call, I headed for UNM. There was a parking spot on the street, so I jaywalked across Central to the C&J building. The professor was in his office shuffling papers at his desk. His face turned cautious when I rapped on his door.

"I thought I might be hearing from you again."

That comment confirmed Del's worst fears. "You let me down, Steve."

His expression turned sheepish. "Yes, I'm afraid I did. James and I had lunch the other day, and he confided he was up for a partnership. When I heard his potential rival in the matter was Mr. Dahlman, I'm afraid I let the cat out of the bag. I do, however, feel justified in my indiscretion since partners in a prestigious law firm should be of good reputation."

"I'm shocked to hear you say that, Professor."

He looked genuinely surprised. "Why?"

"Isn't it a bit hypocritical to consider a gay attorney as somehow less qualified than a straight one?"

Momentary confusion crossed his face. "Yes, of course it is. But that's not the way I looked at the situation. I merely assumed that if Mr. Dahlman was under the threat of blackmail, something unpleasant might come of it, such as bad publicity."

"We're all vulnerable to pressure from others to some extent. It merely seems strange that one member of the gay community sees nothing wrong with torpedoing another—simply for being gay."

Sturgis flushed with anger. "You're welcome to take that attitude if you wish. Life is more than one's sexual orientation, you know."

"You're preaching to the choir, Steve. I'm as gay as you are."

His look and body language told me he hadn't suspected. "You've learned to hide it well."

"That may be, although I suspect it's simply me being me."

My mission accomplished, there was no point in trying to dump a bigger load of guilt on him, so we exchanged strained good-byes. I gave Del the bad news on my cell from the car.

Charlie was waiting for me when I got back to the office. He'd satisfied himself that the Blah-firm receptionist was clean. Belinda had worked for the partnership for ten years, and her husband, Yul Gerard, was an engineer for the local power company. However, Charlie's poking into the Royal Crest had turned up a maintenance supervisor with a record.

"His name's Luther Hickey. Went down for knifing a guy."

"What's his story?"

"Hickey was a crew chief for an oil-drilling company down in Hobbs with a rep as a good worker but a hard drinker. At a company Christmas party a few years ago, he got into it with another worker. Claimed the guy was making indecent remarks to his wife. During a dustup, he stabbed the guy. Wasn't fatal, but he went down for a nickel at the state pen on the south side of Santa Fe anyway.

"Hickey was paroled after three and a half years, but he ran straight into the problem most ex-cons have. No one would hire him. He finally landed a job with Royal Crest Management. He's called a supervisor, but all that really means is he does the maintenance on his shift. He's not making much money, and his wife and family left him. He's a bitter guy, BJ."

"Did he have any sort of relationship with Del?" I asked.

"You mean Del's lifestyle? No, I don't think he's Del's type. Stocky, hairy, and rough. He'd probably haul out his knife if he got propositioned that way."

"You think he's a homophobe?"

"That wouldn't surprise me. He seems like a hard case all the way around."

"Anything to tie him to Emilio?"

"No, but Hickey was on the premises a lot, so he probably knew who came and went all the time. He might have met Emilio. He could have drawn his own conclusions even if he didn't meet him face-to-face."

Charlie hadn't talked directly to Hickey, but had gotten all of his information from coworkers, neighbors, and by checking his record. When I asked for a description of the man, he handed over a copy of Hickey's mug shot and a company group photo of the local staff. "Like I said, stocky, hairy, and rough looking. His ears look like his papa used to haul him around by them when he was a kid."

I studied the photos, confirmed what Charlie had said, and thanked him for a job well done.

HICKEY WASN'T on Emilio's list, either by name or by description, but Charlie spent the next two weeks digging into his background and associates while I ran down two men I'd added to the list recently. One of them had looked promising, but neither led me anywhere.

One afternoon in mid-July found me sitting in the waiting room of the James, Jamieson & Smith law office on San Pedro. A very nervous

Estelle Bustamante kept glancing up from the receptionist's desk. She'd almost jumped out of her pretty skin when I walked through the door and asked for an appointment with James or Jamieson—or even Smith. Sotto voce, I assured her this was not an attempt to sabotage her job or sink her reputation. From the way those big brown eyes kept flicking in my direction, she did not totally buy my declaration.

Eventually the most colorless man I have ever seen outside of a true albino strode down the hall. Although he stood at least six three, he couldn't have weighed more than 140–50 at the most. His hair was like dry winter grass, his irises the color of oyster shells. All that kept him from being completely bland was a pronounced bluish tinge beneath his eyes and around his cuticles.

The body might have looked anemic, but the rich bass booming out of his thin chest was healthy enough to reach every part of the building. "I'm Roger James. What can I do for you, Mr. Vinson? I should let you know that I've heard of you. Sherry DeVine is a friend of mine, and she told me how much you helped with her problem."

"Not much of a recommendation, I'm afraid. I normally don't do domestic work, but I knew Sherry back when she was Sherry Robinson. Jerry even longer. How do you know them?"

"Her, not him. My wife and I belong to a bridge club. We became casually acquainted with Sherry there. At any rate, how may I help you?"

"Mr. James, I am a licensed confidential investigator with a reasonably well-balanced clientele, except I'm lacking clients directly or indirectly tied to organized labor. As that is an area that interests me, I'd like to correct the deficiency."

His eyes turned a bit grayer. This guy knew a fairy tale when he heard one. He cleared his throat. "I will certainly let my partners know of your interest. However, as you can imagine, we already work with a couple of your competitors. Both, I might add, come out of the labor movement."

"Duly noted. I must also be candid and let you know I've worked with a lawyer in the Stone, Hedges, Martinez law firm once or twice."

"I see. That, of course, might present a conflict of interest. They represent Premier Tank & Plating, with whom we are engaged in a dispute."

"An organizing attempt, as I recall."

"Yes. The union believes management has used unlawful practices to discourage an honest vote of its workers in the matter."

"I suppose that would put me outside the pale, so to speak. I'm curious. Is the union game as rough as it was in the old days?"

"If you mean do plant managers hire scabs to knock heads when legitimate workers protest, not so much anymore. Neither side shoots at the other, at least not normally."

"That's progress, I suppose. How about intimidation? You know, threats, blackmail, that sort of thing."

"That depends on your definition and probably your viewpoint. I'm sure there's been a little 'who was that woman I saw you out with the other night' sort of thing. But threats of physical violence? Outright blackmail? No, I don't think so." He paused and gave me a cool look. "Mr. Vinson, are you here as a representative of the Stone firm?"

He had me unless I weaseled.

I weaseled. "The Blahs have not hired me to investigate the matter or gather information on their behalf."

"The Blahs?"

I chuckled. "That's what the guys down at the police station call the Stone firm. You know, Stone, Hedges, Martinez, Blah, Blah, Blah."

He laughed aloud. "That's rich. The Blahs. It fits them to a T. I've got to pass that one along."

"So long as it's not for attribution. Well, you have my card. If something comes up where there is no conflict of interest or divided loyalties, I would appreciate your consideration."

I left after accomplishing nothing more than forming a healthy respect for at least one of the partners in the law firm and confirming what I already knew from newspaper accounts—they were, in fact, counsel to the union in the Premier battle. Of course, I'd also put myself on their radar screen, but so what? If they were involved in the blackmail attempt, I was already there.

Chapter 10

I ARRIVED home late that afternoon, still antsy since the firebombing. My contractor still hadn't gotten out to clean up the mess on my porch. The day had been taken up by other cases we were working, so little progress had been made on Del's problem. As I headed for the den, I was drawn to my front window by the sound of an idling motor in time to see Gene crawl out of a departmental Ford. Some cop habits die hard; he'd parked in front of the neighbor's house. I opened the door as he walked up to the porch.

"Am I interrupting anything?"

"Not a thing. I just got home myself. Come on in. Coffee? Cola? If you're off duty, I can fix you a stiff drink?" I led him down the hallway.

"You trying to get me busted for DWI?"

"Okay, a not-so-stiff drink."

He grunted and slipped out of his suit jacket, tossing it over the back of a chair. "I'm off duty."

"Still bourbon and branch water?"

"No ice." He plodded along behind as I went to the bar in one corner of the den to fix his drink. He rested his elbows on the counter and looked around. "I always liked this place, but I have to admit I'm a little surprised you kept it."

"Why?" I glanced up from pouring jiggers into two heavy tumblers. "Tonic or bottled water? I'm having bottled."

"That's okay with me. This is a settled neighborhood. I imagine most of your neighbors are retired folks."

"They are."

"I thought, with all your money, you'd want to be living where it's happening. You know, with the hip crowd."

"Where do you live, Gene?"

"You know where I live. You've been there enough."

"In a nice, settled North Valley neighborhood with its share of old fogies, right?"

"Okay, I get your point. I like living where I do because it's peaceful, and the Lord knows I need peaceful after a day at the police department." He reached for the glass and paused with it halfway to his lips. "If you can call a house with five kids peaceful."

"At least it's a different sort of brawl from what you run into at the station house. And I like this place for the same reason. I can relax."

"I've always wondered if the neighbors knew your folks hit it big? I mean, they kept on living the same way they always had. Same car. Same house. Same furniture. Same everything."

"So far as I know, no one was aware my dad invested some money in a little start-up business that paid off for him."

"A little start-up business that moved to Seattle and became Microsoft. Refresh my memory, how many millions did you say he walked away with?"

"Twelve, but don't spread that around."

"Twelve million bucks. You know, that would almost support a wife and five kids."

We both laughed.

"What brings you to the Vinson household? Since you never visit socially, I assume this is business."

He took one of the two recliners facing a long leather couch and had a sip of his bourbon before answering. "Ex officio business. Like you asked, I put out a bulletin on that fancy blue Mustang the hustler drives."

He left the rest of the thought hanging in the air, forcing me to ask. "Get a hit?"

"A couple. One in Santa Fe and another in Taos."

"When?"

"Santa Fe this morning, Taos this afternoon."

"Hmm. Emilio either knows someone in Taos he can hole up with, or he's headed to Colorado. Did he pick up the mail from box 2223?"

Gene shook his head. "Nope. Per standing instructions Del's manila envelope was remailed to the main post office on Broadway. But *somebody* picked it up from box 1525 there." We worked on our drinks in comfortable silence until Gene held out his glass for a refill. "Does the name John Wilson mean anything to you?"

"Not a thing. Is that the guy renting the box?" I got up and went back to the bar.

"Both of the boxes in question. At least that's the name on the cards."

"Don't you have to present ID to rent a post-office box?"

"That's the drill. But how many ways do you know to get a false ID? Anyway, it wasn't picture ID, so there's no photo scanned into the system, but I talked with the clerk who handled the rental."

"And?" I handed him his refill.

"And she remembered the guy. Vividly."

"Made an impression, did he?"

"Bombshell. Said the appearance didn't exactly go with the name Wilson, but he was slender with dark hair and brown eyes. Oh yeah... and handsome as an Irish devil."

"Son of a bitch! Emilio Prada. I let that little prick pull the wool over my eyes."

"He's not the only good-looking guy around, and the girl wasn't swooning over a queer."

"Doesn't mean a thing. You'd never know it if he didn't want you to. The kid can be as macho as the next guy. Did you pick up an address?"

"A number in the 9900 block of North Fourth. Don't bother. I already checked. It's phony."

"Thanks. You've pointed me in a new direction."

"We aim to serve. Too bad you didn't get the plates on that truck when your porch got torched. When you gonna get all that sooty mess cleaned up?"

"Got somebody coming next week. Have you found the truck yet?"

"The Open Space guys found a smoldering hunk of molten metal that could have been your vehicle. A '98 Chevy pickup stolen on the Westside."

"Red?"

"Yep, although it was sorta hard to tell. The crime-scene guys couldn't pick up anything useful. Whoever set it on fire must have doused it with a whole lot of gasoline—inside and out."

I frowned. "Someone stole a pickup to attack me and then torched it. That raises the stakes a little."

"Could be, but vehicles get stolen every day. That said, watch your tail. Somebody's serious." He played with his glass but waved away my offer of another drink.

"Did the canvass of the neighborhood turn up anything?"

"Nobody saw a thing, except the old lady across the street."

"Mrs. Wardlow."

"Yeah, that's her. She told the cop the red pickup slowed down in front of your house for a second and then peeled out. She saw the flames and dialed 911."

"Could she identify anyone?"

"Nope. But she said there were two of them."

We nursed our own thoughts for a minute, and then I went personal. "How are Glenda and the kids?"

"As well as can be expected. Not looking forward to dragging the whole tribe around the state fair this year. We're getting older, which means we're slowing down while the kids are speeding up."

"Take heart. They'll hit their prime about the time you and Glenda reach your dotage. Then they can change *your* diapers."

"Now there's a pleasant thought. Is there anyone for you at the moment?"

I hesitated before shaking my head. Paul wasn't really "anyone" in the sense Gene meant, although he was getting close. "Not right now."

"That's sad. If I was in your shoes, I'd let Dahlman crawl out of his own shit and probably pray he didn't make it. The guy let you down, BJ. Big time."

"That's water under the bridge. Right now his money's as good as the next client's."

When we'd run out the string on the case and the latest news about family and shared friends, Gene got up to leave. He paused at the front door. "Any more threats or incidents?"

"Nothing."

Our attention was pulled to the street as an old Plymouth coupe eased to the curb in front of the house. Gene gave me a quick look.

I hoped my sudden joy wasn't evident. "Relax. It's a friend."

"Okay. If you're sure you know who's friend and who's foe."

Paul reached the front stoop before Gene had a chance to get away. The two regarded one another warily. The smile on Paul's lips died as the one on Gene's grew.

"Sorry." Paul started to reverse course. "Didn't know you had company."

"Just leaving." Gene stepped forward and held out his hand. "Gene Enriquez, BJ's old partner before he got himself shot all to hell and gone."

"Oh." The simple expression likely told Gene all he needed to know. "I'm Paul Barton. A friend of Vince's... uh, BJ's."

"Come on in," I said to my confused friend. "Be with you in a minute."

I walked Gene to his car and watched as he paused to glance back at the house. "Slender, dark-haired, brown eyes, and handsome as an Irish devil. I've heard that description recently, haven't I?"

"It wasn't Paul," I said firmly.

"If you say so." Gene crawled into his vehicle and repeated himself, "If you say so."

I returned to the house to find my guest standing uncertainly in the foyer. "Sorry if I messed anything up. It's just that I hadn't seen you at the pool lately. You need to keep up that therapy, you know."

"I know, and I will. I promise. No, you didn't interrupt a thing. I told you before—you're free to come over anytime. Gene's a good friend from the old days."

As we walked down the hall toward the den, he allowed his shoulder to brush mine a couple of times. "Does he know? About you, I mean?"

"They all know. I never made a secret of being gay. Never flaunted it in anyone's face, but I never tried to hide it either."

"Didn't they resent it? I mean, you hear stories about cops hanging their gay comrades out to dry."

"Never ran into that sort of thing. Oh, there were those who shunned me because of who I was, but not many. A couple had harsh words, but they were few and far between. Nothing I couldn't handle."

"How about your partner? Did he have trouble with it?"

"He was ragged on some, but a wife and five kids gave him plenty of cover. Most of the guys probably felt he had proved his manhood." I shrugged. "People who didn't know us might have figured we had something going."

Paul halted in his tracks and looked at me. "Why do they think we screw anyone in pants? Anywhere. Anytime. Like that's all we ever think about."

They were serious questions, but I didn't have any ready answers. Without another word we went into the den, where I fixed him a drink. I'd had my limit with Gene.

Paul toyed with his rum and Coke as we stood at the bar. "I was afraid to come over tonight."

"Why?"

"You haven't been at the pool lately, and I thought maybe you'd gone to the YMCA or somewhere. Because of me."

I smiled. "Do I detect some insecurity here? No, I've just been putting in long hours on a case. I'm not trying to avoid you. To the contrary, I've been plotting to find extra time to spend with you."

"That would be great. What's the case tying you up in knots?"

"Somebody's trying to blackmail a local lawyer."

"That sounds exciting."

"Nothing exciting about it. It's just work."

"What does a PI do in a case like that?"

"Plods all over town asking questions."

"What kind of questions?"

"Sometimes some very personal ones. Awkward ones."

"Don't people resent that?"

"Some do. Some don't give a damn."

"And it's the ones who resent them that get another look, huh?"

"That's a natural reaction, but it isn't always accurate. Some people just don't like others snooping into their lives. And the guilty are often the coolest under fire."

"Speaking of fire, why is your front porch burned to a crisp?"

"You noticed that, huh?"

"Hard not to."

"Yeah, I think I got too close to someone in this case, and they're warning me off. Got a contractor coming out next week to clean up the mess."

His eyes bored into mine. "Are you in any danger?"

I laughed it off. "No more than usual."

"I hope not. I wouldn't want another hole in you. One is... you know, intriguing. But two? That would be scary."

I touched his hand resting on the bar. "Don't worry. I'll be all right."

THERE WAS something urgent, something frantic about Paul's lovemaking that night. It was both exciting and off-putting. As we lay, coming off an adrenaline high, I watched him by the ambient glow of the nightlight from the adjoining bathroom. The inevitable comparisons rose unbidden to my mind.

Del's beauty required gestures and a voice to endow it with masculinity. Emilio's good looks were in-your-face flamboyant and overtly sexual. Paul's were quiet and solid and altogether more erotic. His comeliness would mature and serve him well for a lifetime.

"What?" he demanded. "You're staring."

"I'm overdosing on eye candy. Damn, you're sexy, Paul." I touched an eyelid, intrigued by the silky caress of long sable lashes.

He barked a laugh. "Yeah, right."

In that moment I realized he did not understand how attractive he was. The fact only added to his charm.

He turned into me, resting his left leg atop my thigh. "I wasn't kidding, Vince. I was *really* afraid you were avoiding me when you didn't come to the club."

I tousled his hair. "No way. But I probably should."

He drew back. "Why?"

"Because someday I'm liable to lose control and plant a kiss, shocking all the old fuddy-duddies in the club."

He laughed. "They're not all fuddy-duddies. We have some younger members. Guys your age, and even a few mine."

"You mean all the kids and grandkids of the original club members? Fuddy-duddies in waiting and fuddy-duddies in the making. Do any of them know what a man their lifeguard is?"

His laugh turned into a boyish giggle. "Just this one beat-up detective who has a hang-up about a scar on his leg." He promptly disappeared beneath the covers to plant a gentle kiss on said blemish. When he came up to hover over me, I saw the mirth give way to dismay. "I… I've got something to tell you."

I touched his smooth cheek involuntarily but held my tongue.

"I'm transferring to the Medill School of Journalism at Northwestern University next semester."

My heart turned cold. "But Northwestern's in Illinois!"

"Yeah, Evanston. I don't want to go, Vince, but… well, I do too. It's one of the best journalism schools in the nation. It's a real opportunity. But I hate to leave Albuquerque—you."

Fighting conflicting emotions, I pulled him to me and hugged him fiercely. "I'm happy for you. What brought on the change?"

"I got a scholarship. One of my professors at the U is a graduate of Medill, and he went to bat for me. It's a full scholarship. All I have right now is the New Mexico lottery scholarship."

"Paul, I can help with your schooling. It would be a privilege." Mistake! His muscles tensed, confirming my blunder. "Only because of my interest in your future, not for any other reason."

He relaxed and rose to his elbows, examining me closely. A reflected shaft of light caught in his eyes, making the pupils glow uncannily. "I know. And thank you, but this is something I've earned for myself. And it will take a load off my mom."

He had confided in quiet moments that his widowed mother was still working two jobs to keep her household together. Living at the dorm this semester was an extravagance he'd decided he needed in order to fully experience college life, but to offset the added cost, he worked a few hours each week in the school cafeteria in addition to his job at the country club.

I surrendered to the inevitable as gracefully as possible.

"I'm going to cover the cost of your move and get you set up in Evanston. No argument. It's a farewell gift to a very special friend."

He was still and silent for a bit, and then the awkward moment passed as he moved into my arms.

Chapter 11

EARLY THE next morning, I polished off the bagel, cream cheese, and lox that Paul had prepared and watched him push his plate back from the edge of the table. He glanced up and smiled when he caught my eye.

"I've been wondering how you dealt with being gay in the Marine Corps? That's supposed to be the ultimate man machine."

I laughed. "It's like anything else. It's got a little bit of everything in it. But to answer your question, mostly I did without. There was one guy, another lieutenant, who helped me come to grips with a few things."

"Like what?"

Fifteen minutes later I realized Paul had been conducting an interview. He got me started talking about what interested him, and prompted me with a "who, what, when, and why" whenever I flagged. That was the first time I realized a journalist did much the same thing I do every day of the week. And Paul was very good at it.

After he left I dawdled at the dinette with a second cup of coffee while my restless mind seesawed between Paul's departure and Del's stubborn problem. Worse, I couldn't avoid thinking about the *possible* connection between them. There are times my brain seems hardwired toward the suspicious. The connections my devious head made were both inevitable and odious, but they wouldn't go away.

James Addleston, Steve Sturgis, Paul Barton, Emilio Prada, and Del Dahlman. One way or the other, they all tied together as the two lawyers battled it out over a coveted partnership position potentially worth millions. Of course, it could all be happenstance, but one thing preyed on my mind more than anything else. This new scholarship of Paul's to one of the most prestigious journalism schools in the country came in the *last semester of his undergraduate career*. Was Sturgis the Medill alumnus sponsoring Paul at Northwestern? The professor was a client of Emilio's. Did Paul and Emilio know each other? It was possible, of course. Both of them frequented the C&W Palace on East Central, and two such extremely attractive guys might well have gotten together, especially with a mutual friend to introduce them. Someone like Sturgis, for instance.

I set my cup down so hard the coffee dregs sloshed onto the table. Ignoring the mess, I mentally recoiled from my thought processes. Paul fit the description of the man who rented the post-office boxes as readily as Emilio did.

With dragging footsteps, I went to my bedroom and shuffled through snapshots of Paul I'd taken recently. Selecting one, I glanced at it fondly. Dressed in black jeans and a red form-fitting pullover shirt, he stood in front of the fireplace in the den with a broad smile on his face. His black hair was slightly long and unruly, like a kid's. I reluctantly slipped the photo into my pocket along with the one of Emilio and Estelle.

As Paul had remarked, my pool therapy had been hit-or-miss lately, so after cleaning up, I took a quick trip downtown, hoping to clear the calendar before heading for the North Valley Country Club. Hazel came in early, confounding my effort to slip in and out of the office, but I brushed aside her attempts to order my day and hurried out, promising to call later.

I laughed all the way down the stairs. Why did I keep her around if I spent so much time avoiding her? Good question, easily answered. Because I loved the old gal, that's why. When Mom was alive, she'd been like a spinster aunt. A nosy, interfering old biddy whose wisdom and experience and unquestioned devotion was well worth the effort.

PAUL WAS in the shallow end of the pool, giving a swimming lesson to a matron of a certain age who was almost certainly the wife of one of the fuddy-duddies in waiting. He gave me a sly wink while supporting the lady's bare abdomen as he instructed her in the art of aquatic kicking. She went under when he took away his hands. She surfaced, laughing and sputtering and clinging to Paul's sleek form. She probably took the dive in order to feel him up.

Dismayed by my reaction, I hit the water and went about my regimen with uncharacteristic fervor. I was exhausted by the end of my prescribed laps. I noticed the two of them watching as I crawled out of the water and collapsed onto a lounge chair. I dried my hair with a towel and wiped the water from my face; sun and evaporation took care of the rest.

I closed my eyes and was drifting off when a soft baritone startled me. "Hello, Mr. V."

I snapped to a sitting position.

"Whoa," Paul said. "Didn't mean to shake you up."

Mr. V—that was what Emilio called me. Did it mean anything? Paul and I had agreed he would address me more formally in a public setting, and that sounded both respectful and familiar.

Or had he picked it up from Emilio?

"Hi, Paul. Guess I was dozing."

"Not surprising. You really went at it hard this morning. In the pool, I mean. Well, the other too."

"Yeah, I got it done, but I had a little trouble with it."

"Amazed you had the energy to take it on." He dropped his voice. "I know I wouldn't have."

"I've got to stop letting this case take up so much time. It's a troublesome son of a bitch." I mentally kicked myself for deliberately baiting the individual who was rapidly becoming the most significant person in my benighted life.

But he ignored—or missed—my invitation to ask about the case and flashed another smile. "You'll crack it. I've got confidence in you."

"Thanks."

Were the words sincere, or was I being flummoxed by yet another pretty face? I generally had confidence in my judgment of others, but it looked as if I'd been wrong about Emilio—not to mention Del. *That* had been a big miscalculation. Now I questioned my reading of Paul. A worm of self-loathing wiggled in my belly.

"Can I get you anything?"

When I declined he returned to his duties as lifeguard.

After showering off the chlorine and dressing, I reclaimed my car and headed straight for UNM.

I wasn't so lucky this time. Professor Sturgis was teaching a class. Nonetheless I waited, brooding over my dark thoughts so much that when he finally appeared, I belligerently demanded an audience.

As we settled down in his office, his puzzled look let me know he'd caught my mood.

"Steve, I'm disappointed you did not honor my request to hold this investigation confidential."

"Sorry, but I thought I'd explained that already."

"You did, but I've uncovered some information recently that disturbs me, and I think you're more deeply involved than you let on."

Astonishment blanked his features. "How is that?"

"I think you're part of this blackmail attempt."

"What?" Sturgis didn't appear angry, merely surprised.

"I need those photos and the negatives. The time for screwing around is over."

"I wish I could help, but I don't have them."

"Does your brother?"

"If he does, he certainly didn't get them from me. I've told you before, BJ, I merely saw the pictures. I have never possessed them."

"I heard what you said. But if this thing blows open, it could cost you your reputation. Your job, even."

"That's ridiculous. I'm tenured, and short of criminal activity, nobody's going to fire me. And I assure you I have indulged in no criminal activity." I opened my mouth, but he forestalled me with a wave of his hand. "As far as my sexual orientation, if that's what you're alluding to, it's an open secret within the department."

"But how would the department view sleeping with one of your students? Would that be enough to jeopardize your tenure?"

My heart sank as his eyelids flickered and his lips tightened. "I have done nothing improper, certainly nothing to merit the interest of my department head."

"Even if you had a relationship involving a student under your authority? It would raise a number of ethical, if not legal questions. Pressuring a student for sexual favors in exchange for grades, for example."

"Absolute rubbish. I can justify every grade awarded to any of my students."

"How about a scholarship?"

Irritation gave way to anger. "How dare you make such insinuations? I am a professional, Mr. Vinson, and I do not take advantage of my students for personal reasons. Now please leave. And phone my secretary if you want to see me again."

I crawled into the Impala feeling as if I were soiling the seat covers and headed downtown, parking in my own spot at the lot on Copper. Then I walked to APD to complete the second part of my odious mission.

To stroll downtown Albuquerque was to yo-yo through time. A block due east of me sat the Hyatt Regency and the Plaza Tower, representing the new. My office building, a sandstone structure recently painted an atrocious white, represented Albuquerque's past. At Fifth and Central Avenue NW, the famous KiMo Theatre with its incredibly intricate Indian

Art Deco curlicues and flourishes provided a similar contrast to the new multi-screen movie complex four blocks away.

The Albuquerque police headquarters building was a freestanding edifice across Marquette Avenue from City Hall. I'd not yet decided whether it was a matter of security or the joy of inconveniencing the public that motivated law enforcement authorities to require citizens to walk around to the north-facing entrance on Roma.

The APD entryway was small with a glass-enclosed alcove to the left for filing and receiving records. A row of bolted-down plastic chairs and an awkwardly placed table for filling out forms were probably uncomfortable by design. The double doors at the back of the foyer gave access to the building proper, but a security station blocked the way. After studying my ID and bullshitting a minute, the attending officer verified Gene was in the building and sent me on my way. Threading the corridors to his office was like old home week. That picked up my morale a bit, but handing him the two photos sent it plunging again.

"You got me to thinking, partner. Maybe you ought to show these photographs to the mail clerk and see if she can identify either man. Who knows, maybe I'm wrong."

Gene gave me a look—one that said "Who do you think you're fooling?" and "I understand your pain" all at the same time. He tapped the snapshot of Paul smiling into the camera. "You sure about this?"

"Yeah." My voice held a sigh. "I'm confident it wasn't him, but we might as well remove all doubt."

"Makes sense. I'll try to get by the PO before the end of the day. I'll call when I know something."

"Thanks, I'll owe you one."

"More," he shot back. "One *more*."

HAZEL MIGHT be overbearing at times, but she knew me well enough to get out of my way when I entered the office. She allowed me half an hour to glance through the messages on my desk and return a couple of calls before knocking on my door. I knew it was time to clean up my attitude when she actually waited to be invited inside.

In truth Hazel was good for me. Before long she had me immersed in the details of a couple of other investigations and the daily routine of the office. I climbed back on my roller coaster when I tried Paul's cell number without success.

Shortly after lunch Gloria McInnes called to tell me she'd compared the prints from Luther Hickey's APD card to those on the extortion envelopes. They did not match, but that didn't necessarily mean anything; there had been two men in the red truck involved in the Molotov attack against my house.

It was time to check out this ex-con maintenance supervisor for myself. Before leaving the office, I studied his sheet and examined the two photos Charlie had turned up. Then I hooked a small tape recorder to my belt and headed for the car.

The Royal Crest was a white five-story concrete building designed before architects began draping everything with glass. It had a well-settled, snobbish, self-satisfied look about it, as befitted one of Albuquerque's classier apartment addresses.

I eased the Impala into a visitor's spot and walked around to the underground parking garage entrance. It wouldn't take much to get past the steel mesh barrier that slowly rose and fell to accommodate tenants' vehicles as they came and went. Then I approached the front entrance across a ribbon of pebbled concrete snaking in gentle curves between twin expanses of close-cropped green grass. No flowers. I rang the buzzer marked Manager at the front entrance and negotiated my entry by means of a talking black box.

Eventually the door buzzed, allowing me access to a large entryway with a bank of mailboxes to my right. This opened onto an even larger reception area furnished with heavy but comfortable-looking divans and chairs upholstered in faux white damask with lots of pink and green blossoms embroidered into the fabric. Every flat expanse of shelf and table in the room held a vase of flowers. I suspected many were silk. There were also plenty of mirrors in gilt frames scattered around the walls.

The assistant manager met me in the reception area, checked my credentials, and then, without expressing the slightest degree of curiosity, directed me to the basement where the maintenance supervisor's office— make that cubbyhole—was located. Luther Hickey was not in said cubbyhole, but I spotted him coming down the hall with a wrench in his hand. He slowed as he approached.

"Help you?" Tapping the business end of the wrench in the palm of his right hand took some of the cordiality out of his words.

Hickey stood an inch or two over my six feet, but he was twice as wide as I was. His mug shot had reflected a fit man. A drilling rig probably kept the fat off him, but he'd gone flabby during or after his stay in Santa Fe. That and his unkempt beard and hair, both prematurely gray, revealed a man who groveled in his own misery. I suspected one of his few pleasures in life was feeling sorry for himself.

I flipped on the recorder before he reached me. "Luther Hickey?"

"Yeah. That's me."

"Mr. Hickey, my name is B. J. Vinson. I'm a confidential investigator. I need to ask you a few questions."

"About what?" The tone indicated I wasn't going to get far with him.

"About one of your tenants."

"Ain't allowed to talk about none of the tenants. Can't even tell nobody if one of their dogs takes a shit on the carpet. Just have to clean it up without saying a word."

"This is more serious than crapping on the rug. And if you won't talk to me, I'll phone your probation officer and have him ask the questions."

"Fuck the probation officer. You reach for a phone and you'll be sorry."

"I believe that was a threat."

"Naw. Just saying I won't give you the time of day, you do that."

"That's not the way I heard it, especially with that wrench in your hand."

He looked down at the heavy tool in his left hand. "Yeah, and I know how to use it too."

"That *was* a threat, Hickey. Enough to send you back to Santa Fe."

"I was just saying I been working on some equipment with this wrench and know how to use it. You think I meant something else, it's your word against mine."

"No contest. All I have to do is press a complaint, and you're gone."

He pursed his lips like he was about to whistle and gave me a long stare. When I didn't break, his stance eased. "Okay, ask, and I'll decide how much to talk."

"You know Mr. Del Dahlman?"

"The fruit in 5100? Yeah, I know him. We're big buddies."

"How's that?"

"He stops up his crapper and he calls me. Every time. Always calls me."

"That happen often?"

"More'n it oughta. If you ask me, he tosses his used rubbers in the stool."

"I take it you don't think much of Mr. Dahlman."

"Probably think about him the way he thinks about me."

"How often are you in his apartment?"

"Like I say, ever time he stops up his stool."

"Is he always present when you go inside?"

"Hey, wait a minute. I ain't no thief. I didn't take nothing outa his place."

"No one accused you of it, Mr. Hickey. I'm merely trying to understand how this works."

"Yeah, sometimes he's already gone when I respond to his call. But I don't touch nothing but what I'm supposed to."

"Do you leave a note telling him what you've done if he isn't there?"

"Nope. Just do my job and leave. If it didn't get done right, he calls again. But I always do it right the first time."

"Have you ever given anybody else access to his apartment?"

"Huh?"

"Have you ever let someone into his place?"

"Naw. Get fired for that."

"How about admitting someone to the lobby to leave a message for him?"

"That's the front office's job, not mine."

"That didn't answer the question."

His eyes narrowed. "No. I never let nobody in that didn't belong here."

"Then how did that envelope get stuffed into his mailbox?"

"What envelope? I don't know nothing about no envelope. Hey man, I stick to my part of the building. The mechanical room's down here. I don't go up to the lobby unless the manager calls me up for something. This is bullshit, and I'm through answering your fucking questions."

I considered taking up his challenge by calling the probation officer but decided that would accomplish little. Instead I'd have Charlie call in one of his retired buddies to do some surveillance on the man.

"All right, Mr. Hickey. You write down my name, address, and telephone number so you can contact me in case you remember something, and I'll go away and leave you alone."

"There ain't nothing to remember. What's this about anyway?"

"It's about extortion. A crime that can get a man a lot of years in this state. Especially if it's his second fall."

Blood rushed to his face; his cheeks turned a rosy red. The long greasy-looking beard twitched. His lips tightened. "You son of a bitch, I ain't trying to hold nobody up."

"Knock off the attitude, Hickey. You're an ex-con on probation for damned near killing a man. Show me some cooperation or I *will* call your probation officer."

"All right, give me your fucking card but don't expect no calls."

"I'm out of cards. Write down the information."

"Who'd you say you was? Let me see some ID." After I held my PI license in front of his eyes, he brushed by me on the way to his broom closet of an office. Once inside he rooted around for pen and pad, finally managing to come up with a scrap of paper and a pencil. He wrote down the information I fed him and then looked up from the desk.

"There now. Satisfied?"

I snatched the piece of paper from the desk and turned around to leave. "I changed my mind. You probably wouldn't call, anyway."

"Already told you I wouldn't."

Once back in the Impala, I took a look at the scribbling. It was poor penmanship, but I couldn't tell if it matched the writing on either of the envelopes. Charlie could take it to the K-Y Lab tomorrow. Maybe Gloria or one of her coworkers could analyze it for me.

I knocked off in the middle of the afternoon, and since I'd skipped lunch, I picked up a pan pizza on my way home. But the recollection of my meeting with Steve Sturgis that morning came back to kill my appetite. Viscerally I connected the pizza with my misery and ended up throwing most of it in the garbage. Unable to sit still, I gave the house an unneeded dusting.

Around ten the phone rang. I knew who it was even before glancing at the caller ID. Although I forced a cheerful tone, my heart was filled with dread.

Paul answered my greeting with a tirade. "What do you think you're doing? You went to see my professor? Are you jealous or just crazy?"

"Calm down, Paul."

"Calm down? You accused one of my teachers of sleeping with me. Are you trying to torpedo my scholarship? I never figured you for that kind of guy, Vince."

"You've got it all wrong. I went to see Professor Sturgis on a case matter. It wasn't personal. I never mentioned your name once."

"No, you just mentioned screwing a student and a scholarship all in the same breath. You might as well have spelled out my name. And for your information, I've never gone to bed with Sturgis."

"Then why did he think I was talking about you?"

"Because he hasn't gotten a scholarship for anyone else, that's why. But that's beside the point. It *was* me you were talking about. You know it, and so do I."

"All right, I let a professional situation get a little personal. But my visit to Sturgis was justified, something I had to do."

"Do you think the professor and I are trying to blackmail somebody with dirty pictures?"

"How do you know what case I was talking about?" The words were out of my mouth before I could swallow them.

"Because Sturgis told me, that's why! Well, for your information, I don't have any pictures of that lawyer, dirty or otherwise. Never seen them and don't want to. And if I did, I wouldn't stoop to trying to squeeze money out of the man. I work for my living!"

"Paul, please understand. It's something I had to do. I owed my client that much."

"But you didn't owe me a thing." His voice was strident. "And I came within an ace of turning down a sweet scholarship just to stay here with you. Man, what a mistake that would have been."

"Look, let's sit down and straighten all this out."

"No way. Those days are over, Mr. Vinson. I don't ever want to see you again. I'll quit my job at the country club so you can use the pool without embarrassing yourself."

"That's not necessary. I'll use the Y until you head off to Northwestern."

"Wouldn't want to inconvenience you." With that acid comment, he broke the connection.

I sat with the dead phone in my hand for a long minute while my world turned sour. Undigested pizza sat heavily in my stomach. My old bullet wound ached. I'd lost something rare and precious, all because of my ham-handed approach to the job.

Damn Del Dahlman and the train he rode in on!

Chapter 12

AFTER A miserable night, I got up on the wrong side of grouchy, feeling empty yet unable to face breakfast. I hungered for one of the Denver omelets Paul made so well. I wanted to watch him wake up. Talk to him. Laugh with him. Let him ask a thousand who-what-why questions about my life. I wanted *him*.

Moving as if underwater, I mindlessly went about the routine of cleaning up. I needed to get some things done, but as I wasn't fit for human contact, I steered clear of the office and started retracing my steps.

While picking up a single-use camera at the nearest drug store, I went surly with the clerk and was immediately contrite. My problems were not hers; doubtless she had enough of her own. I crawled back into the car and snapped twenty-four random shots on the way to the South Valley.

Rory Tarleton's homestead was considerably tidier than on my first visit. No one answered my knock, and there was no sign of him in the darkroom at the rear of the place. I was just slipping back into the Impala when the roar of an engine caught my attention. Rory rolled down the road on a US military Indian motorcycle, complete with sidecar, and parked in the drive beside the old Toyota up on blocks. The antique motor stroked smoothly, a testament to his mechanical skills.

"You again," he groused. "What you want this time?"

"What the fuck's your problem?" Groping for an attitude change, I sighed and glanced around. "Looks like I did you a favor. The place looks 1,000 percent better. Now if you get rid of that junker, the joint will look decent."

"No way. That Toyota'll run like a top when I get through with it. I'll double my money."

"Like you will with the bike? It's new, isn't it?" It wasn't new, of course. It was probably a leftover from WWII.

He puffed up and smiled. "Yeah, just picked it up a few days ago. Didn't take much work to get it purring. Whadda you want, anyway?"

I held out my camera. "The same deal you made Emilio. By the way, have you heard from him?"

He shook his head. "Not since them pictures. Same deal? Okay, for fifty bucks I develop, print, and forget them. I'll let you know when they're ready."

"Nope. I'm gonna watch you work. Just like Emilio did."

He shrugged, jiggling his beer belly. "Whatever. But I get paid up front."

"No problem." I peeled off some bills Del would eventually replace.

The next hour was devoted to staying out of Tarleton's way in the cramped little shack behind the house. Even by the muted glare of the hazy red light he'd snapped on, I could see he wasn't duplicating the negatives—if such a thing was even possible.

Tarleton was giving me funny glances by the time he draped the last print over an old-fashioned heat drum. He flipped on a sixty-watt bulb as the first photos peeled off the dryer. Grabbing the first three, he shuffled through them before facing me with a bayonet in his hand.

"What the fuck's going on, Vinson?"

"What do you mean?"

"Them pictures ain't nothing. You coulda gone anywheres and got them done for ten bucks tops! How come you brought them here?"

"Wanted to watch you work."

"You still looking for them dirties Emilio had?"

I nodded. "Trying to trace them from development to the blackmailer."

He relaxed and buried the tip of the long bayonet in the wall beside his table. That was his stress reliever—the planking was pretty well splintered.

"You lied to me. About one thing, anyway."

He wrapped his fist around the hilt of the bayonet. "About what?"

"About the way Emilio paid for your skills. You got an administrative separation from the Corps, didn't you? And here you had me fooled by that kiddy porn with little girls."

Anger suffused his heavy features, but he relaxed almost immediately. "Wasn't fooling nobody. Sex is sex. 'Sides, Emilio kinda looks like a girl if you squint your eyes. And he paid me the fifty too, just like I said." A foxy smile crawled across his lips. "So by rights, you still owe me."

"In your dreams, Tarleton."

He smirked. "That's okay. Be kinda hard to take you for a girl. Besides, you're too old for me."

"You like twinks, huh?"

He shrugged. "Well, you satisfied I didn't steal none of your pics?"

"Yeah, but that doesn't mean you didn't swipe some of Emilio's. He might not have been watching as closely as I was."

"Like hell! He was right there with his nose stuck in ever step of the way. Now get the hell offa my place. And I hear any talk about my discharge, I'll come looking for you. You hear?"

"I hope they let you take retirement."

Rory looked confused at my switch in attitude, but he answered anyway. "Yeah. Barely."

As I walked down his short, dusty driveway, he came out onto the front porch. "Hey, Vinson, anybody ever tell you, you got a cute butt?" His raucous laugh brought up phlegm. He hawked and spat in the yard.

As soon as I got to Five Points, I pulled into a parking lot and dialed Paul's cell. It went to voice mail. Then I searched my notes for Estelle's work number. She answered on the second ring, smoothly singing the name of the James, Jamieson & Smith firm, but went silent when I identified myself. Reluctantly she agreed to meet me during her lunch period in the Smith's parking lot at Lomas and San Pedro.

I killed the rest of the morning by meticulously going through Emilio's list. I had located most of the men he knew by name, but it was slow going trying to find anonymous men by description alone.

A little after noon, I drove to the supermarket and waited for Estelle. She looked worried when she got out of the Taurus a few minutes later.

"I'm not looking to hassle you. Just need to go over a few things again. By the way, how's your little boy?"

That brought a half smile. "Just fine. Growing more every day. I can't stay long. I only have half an hour for lunch."

"We won't be long. Have you heard from Emilio since we talked?"

She shook her head. "No. I have heard nothing."

"He took off somewhere, and I need to talk to him again. His car was spotted in Santa Fe and Taos. Do you know if he has friends in either of those places?"

"No, no one. Oh, yes, he had a… uh, what do you call them? A trick? Yes, he had a trick in Santa Fe he told me about. A big shot. A banker he saw sometimes. I'm sorry, I don't know his name."

"That's okay. At least you gave me a place to begin."

Estelle thought for a moment. "Have you tried his cell phone?"

"He has a cell?"

"Yes, at least he did when he was with me."

"You told me you didn't know how to get in touch with him."

"I forgot about the phone. And I don't even know if he still has it."

My brow furrowed. I distinctly recalled asking Del in the initial interview for Emilio's number. Estelle apparently saw my confusion.

"No one knew about it; not even Mr. Dahlman."

"Do you remember the number?"

"No, but I have it at home."

"Can you get it for me?"

"May I borrow your cell?"

I handed it over and watched as she dialed. After a moment she greeted her grandmother. I spoke enough Spanish to understand she asked the old woman to look in her jewelry box for a small address book. Within two minutes the little prick's phone number was in my hands.

After I thanked Estelle, she hesitated before getting into her car. "Mr. Vinson, I appreciate the way you spoke to Mr. James without involving me. I hope he was able to help you."

"He eased my mind a little. And you're welcome. But there is one thing I'm curious about. Did Emilio know any of the people working in the JJS office?"

"No, I am certain he did not."

"Could he have met one of them? As a pickup?"

"I don't think so. He knew where I worked, and if he had done that, he would have bragged about it. No, I'm sure he never met any of them."

"Thank you."

I waited until she left the parking lot before flipping open my cell and dialing Emilio's number. It rang until it went to voice mail. The voice asking me to leave a message sounded like Emilio's, but I declined the invitation.

What kind of investigator was I, anyway? True, my client had thrown me off track about a phone, but there *had* been a clue. The second time I went looking for Emilio at the C&W Palace, I'd observed Puerco Arrullar making a call. Since Emilio was supposed to be servicing a client at the time, it was likely he'd been contacted by cell phone.

It was possible the succession of "lost" cell phones Del had told me about had been one of the chores Emilio performed for Puerco's gang.

Or perhaps selling what he got for free was Emilio's way of making an extra buck or two.

When I got back, Hazel pushed me to take care of some mundane office tasks—signing this, okaying that, until I finally snapped at her. Looking wounded, she withdrew and closed my door a little too firmly, the opening shot in her long-suffering mother routine. Moments later her frosty voice informed me Detective Enriquez was on the line.

"I checked with that postal worker at the main office," Gene said. "She identified one of the pictures."

"Which one?"

"Prada."

"The hustler hustled me."

"I thought you'd be pleased, given the other one is your mint of the month."

"Now, Gene—"

"I'm sorry, but I gotta pull your chain once in a while. That's all the payback I ever get."

"Yeah, right. Do me a favor, will you?"

"Another one?"

"Yeah. Will you return the pictures to me? I need Prada's for the file, and I'd hate for Paul's to get into your system for no good reason."

"He's already in it. Don't tell me you didn't check for a sheet?"

"Of course not!" Then I screwed up my standard of ethics by asking why he was on record.

"Nothing serious. Drunk and disorderly at an off-campus beer party. Got into a fight with another guy, barely missed being charged with assault."

"Oh, crap. Is it still pending?"

"Naw. He got fingerprinted, mugged, and slammed into a cell overnight. The judge let him go with a warning."

"When was that?"

"A year back. Nothing before or since."

"Thanks. I owe you."

"Man, do you ever. But there's more. One of the guys in the Gang Unit tells me Barton flirted around with one of the gangs back in high school. There's no evidence he actually joined, but there was some sort of blood connection, I gather."

"Which gang?" I asked with my heart in my throat.

"Probably the Santos Morenos. That was their turf, even back then. I can check it out if you want."

"No, thanks. Let me do it."

I hung up and processed what I had learned. The system snares a lot of young men for one thing or the other, and Paul's charges hadn't been serious. A wake-up call was probably what he needed at the time.

The other thing bothered me, but maybe it shouldn't. Every kid in Albuquerque was exposed to a gang like the Saints sooner or later. And in Paul's part of the South Valley, half the people were related by blood or marriage. The fact Gene's contact was vague about the details was both good and bad: bad because whatever brought Paul to his attention was enough for him to remember it years later; good because it meant Paul hadn't been seriously involved with the Saints or any other gang.

Finding some comfort in that thought, I turned to how Emilio had snookered me. I dialed his number and tried to determine if the voice mail recording was Emilio's voice. Probably, but I still wasn't sure. Of course, that didn't necessarily mean anything. I don't put my voice on the cell I carry; I use the prerecorded message. At least the service had not been interrupted, but given his history with other phones, it was anyone's guess who would eventually answer the ring.

And then I remembered something else. The day I'd hauled him home to grill him, we'd been heading for the front door when he stopped in his tracks. At the time I thought that was because of the firebomb attack. But he'd halted a fraction of a second before I heard the truck motor outside the house. He stopped when I said we'd catch the blackmailer through the mailboxes he'd rented if questioning johns didn't do the trick.

Son of a bitch! He knew who stole the negatives from him. He'd figured it out that very instant, and it was enough to send him running.

Unable to sit still that night, I went to the C&W Palace, unsure of what was I hoping to find. Emilio was in Santa Fe or Taos or points north, so it was unlikely I'd find him at the Saints' table. Maybe I expected to experience a revelation by merely staring at Puerco's fat shoulders. Or was it Paul I hoped to see? Whatever it was, I didn't find it. I spent half the time dialing Emilio's phone and listening to it shunt me off to a talking computer. I finally went home and turned in.

Awakening from a restless sleep in the middle of the night, I grabbed the phone and punched in Emilio's number. After a moment his baritone answered. Taken by surprise, I almost launched into a tirade, but good sense prevailed.

"Emilio, this is B. J. Vinson. We need to talk."

I was speaking into the ether. The line was dead. That, of course, finished off my night. I tried calling a couple more times, even leaving brief, nonthreatening messages. He did not return my calls.

It was difficult to get my motor running the next morning. I contacted Charlie by phone and asked him if he'd learned anything new about Royal Crest. He hadn't, but his questioning of the staff had begun to raise the anxiety level of the manager, so I told him to lay off the questions and put somebody to watching Hickey. Then I moped around the house doing Internet background searches on a couple of the johns I'd recently identified from Emilio's list.

PULLING AN end run around Miss Snoot-in-the-Air, I called the Blah firm at five minutes after noon the next day and slid right through to Del before he escaped to what was probably a power lunch at the Petroleum Club with Someone Important.

He agreed to meet me that afternoon for drinks at his downtown country club. I understood his choice of locale as soon as I saw him at the bar, dressed in golf slacks. I waved away his offer of a drink.

"Why didn't you tell me Emilio had a cell phone?" The attack wasn't fair because Estelle had said Del didn't know about it, but it established the pecking order for the meeting.

He looked confused. "I did. I told you I'd bought him three or four of the damned things. He just couldn't—"

"Well, he has one now. And it's active."

"You talked to him?"

"For about one second at two o'clock this morning. As soon as he found out it was me, he hung up."

Del looked thoughtful. "That probably means he's still around, doesn't it?"

"Not necessarily. Some of these throwaway phones piggyback off major provider networks. They're nationwide."

"How about Mexico? Will they work down there?"

"Don't see why not, but the last sighting was north, not south. His car was seen in Santa Fe and in Taos."

"He's headed for Colorado?"

"Why did you say that? Does that ring any bells?"

"No, but if he's running, Taos is on the way to Colorado."

"Maybe. Del, have you heard anything else from the blackmailer?"

"Not a peep. That's unusual, isn't it? He should have reacted to my note by now."

"Might not have had the opportunity. I haven't told you yet, but Emilio was the one who rented the post-office boxes."

"Emilio? When did you find that out?"

"Gene Enriquez just told me. But don't jump to conclusions. That doesn't necessarily mean this is Emilio's deal."

"The hell you say! He was the one with the pictures in the first place, and if he rented the blackmail boxes, that's proof enough for me. The fact he's running and nobody is putting pressure on me is just icing on the cake."

"That's true on the face of it, but I've learned he started doing chores for people. Sometimes it was probably for money, and sometimes it was to get in good with someone. It's *possible* he rented the boxes for someone without knowing their purpose. That's why I've been trying to get in touch with the bastard. Even if he didn't know why they were rented, he knows who told him to rent them. And that's who we want to get to."

"I still say that's bullshit."

"Maybe, but this thing is beginning to look a little more complicated than it first appeared. If Emilio were trying some extortion on his own, he'd be more up-front about it. I'm going to keep an open mind until I catch up with him."

"You mentioned Gene Enriquez. You involved the police?"

"Yes and no. Once my house was firebombed—"

"Your *house* was firebombed?"

"Yeah, a couple of Sundays ago. Not much damage, but a neighbor called 911. Gene heard the dispatcher's call go out over the air and showed up. I had to tell him something, so I went off the record and filled him in. He's been helping out where he can. Like finding out who rented the mailboxes."

"And you're sure that was Emilio?"

"The postal clerk identified him from the picture you gave me."

I allowed Del to vent a little before I asked about the status of the Premier-union tussle.

"Some nastiness, but it's not excessive. Harding tried to have some picketers arrested—against my advice, I might add. Not much more will happen until the employees vote on organizing the company."

"When is that scheduled?"

"January."

"Emilio must have been pretty comfortable with his setup with you. Why do you think he deliberately sabotaged the arrangement?"

"I'm not sure he's capable of a long-term relationship, no matter how good it is. But in the end, it was a struggle for control. He'd started asserting himself, making demands. If you really want to know what I think, I believe the little shit wanted to prove he could get away with what I couldn't—bringing in someone else to share a very private and personal liaison. He's a cocky bastard."

"Well, let's see if we can scare up the cocky bastard." I took out my phone.

No one answered Emilio's cell, so I left another message. Del grabbed the instrument and added fifteen seconds of vitriol. Despite the words I sensed an unuttered yearning in his voice.

I caught his eye when he handed the phone back to me. "Anything new with your competition? Addleston?"

"No, we're both being as civil as possible. There's no clue from the partners who's going to be selected. Hell, it might not be either one of us."

"The Blahs are a staid old firm. Aren't you a little young to be considered for a full partnership?"

"Why do you keep calling us the Blahs?"

"Never mind. Just answer the question."

"Nobody else brings in the dollars I do. Right now I've got a hand in a merger that will bring the firm over $500,000. And that's just one deal."

"Any problems with it?" When he shook his head, I said, "Look, Del, I need to know everything you're working on, especially any criminal cases. At least run over the cases with me, and we'll argue about naming the clients later."

No wonder he was so hard to reach. For the next fifteen minutes, Del cited a litany of cases involving tax planning, setting up new businesses, reorganizing old ones, partnership disputes, minority stockholder complaints, and a host of other boring cases. But none of them were before the criminal bar. Nor was there anything that was likely to generate an attempt to compromise an opposing attorney.

"It doesn't add up," I said. "There's nothing here to make anyone desperate enough to resort to blackmail. Charlie and I took a discreet look at those contentious cases you gave me. We couldn't find anything there either. Are you sure there's nothing else? How about that big merger you mentioned? Anyone stand to lose money on that?"

"Not that I can tell. Control of a major local business will pass to an even bigger regional company, but the local owners will end up with a pot full of money."

"Is it a friendly takeover?" I asked.

"They were invited in over the objections of a faction of the board."

"Bad blood?"

"Nothing serious," Del said.

"You represent the regional company?"

"I'm local counsel for them, yes."

"When is it supposed to come off?"

"Right after the new year—for tax purposes."

Then I took him through his relationship with Royal Crest's management company. It was landlord-tenant. Nothing more. No disputes or complaints.

"I use the place to sleep, and that's about all," he said.

"And to host your guests."

"Well, that too."

I scratched an itchy place on my chin. "Do they know you're gay?"

"Probably, but I don't know for sure."

Del maintained he had no contact with Hickey, the maintenance supervisor, except when he had a mechanical or electrical problem that needed taking care of. He confirmed that Hickey had been in his apartment for such repair work, sometimes when Del wasn't around.

"You think he rifled my place while I was gone?"

"I wouldn't put it past him, would you?"

He shook his head. "No, I wouldn't."

"How about when Emilio was living there?"

"Surely you don't think Emilio would have gotten together with that big, hulking brute?"

I rolled my eyes. "Emilio would get it on with a moose, if the moose paid him. But I was thinking Hickey could have been in the apartment while you and Emilio were both away. He could have found the pictures and the negatives."

Del looked doubtful. "I don't think so. Emilio kept the pictures in his backpack, and he hauled that around with him all the time. I don't ever recall him leaving it behind in the apartment."

"Could he have left it in the Mustang in the parking garage?"

"He didn't park in the garage. He parked in the lot. I suppose he could have left it overnight, but it would have been unusual."

"Did you have copies of the pictures?" I asked.

"No, I didn't."

"Why not? Emilio enjoyed hauling them out and looking at them from time to time. Didn't you?"

"I probably would have gotten around to asking for a set sooner or later. But then we started having our problems."

Getting slightly irked at having to drag every detail out of him, I asked who took the pictures.

"Emilio. He set up a tripod and tripped the camera with a timer." Del sat with his head down for a moment. "So, you think Hickey's the one, huh?"

"He's a possibility. I've only talked to him once, and he wasn't very cooperative. But he has a record."

I declined Del's invitation to dinner, and as I started to leave, he thought of something else.

"You asked about criminal cases. The closest thing I have is acting as attorney for a woman who's a witness in a criminal matter. The court simply appointed me to look out for her interests since she was peripherally involved."

"What's the case?"

"A double homicide of two drug dealers up in Santa Fe last year, a husband-and-wife team. Gilbert and Helen Zellner. I say Santa Fe, but it actually happened somewhere between Santa Fe and Española."

"How does your client fit in?" I asked.

"She was the girlfriend of one of the guys accused of doing the shooting. She claims she wasn't involved in the murders. It could be she's being cooperative to save her own skin, but I don't know that. Frankly it's not my job either. I'm merely charged by the court to see that she's legally protected during this process."

"Who is she?"

"It's public record, I guess. Miranda Skelton. She's an Española girl. Ran around with a local biker gang called the Iron Crosses. Hell's Angels wannabes. Even so, they're badasses. Her boyfriend, Melvin Whiznant, is the Cross leader. He and his partner in crime, Jaime Rodrigo—called Adder on the street—are both in jail awaiting trial for the murders."

"Christ, Del, why didn't you mention this before?"

He shrugged. "Slipped my mind. In the first place, it's a minor housekeeping chore for the court. It doesn't amount to a hill of beans. In the second, it has nothing to do with Emilio. Nothing whatsoever."

"When's the trial?"

"After the first of the year."

I shook my head. "I wish you'd told me about it before. Do you realize everything's coming to a head at the first of the year? The Premier-union fight, the partnership announcement, the merger, the murder trial. Everything."

"Guess that's right."

"If it were me, I wouldn't be sleeping too well."

"It's not like anyone's trying to get rid of me. They're just trying to compromise me."

"Well, they want *something* from you, and it isn't $5,000."

Chapter 13

I CALLED Paul from home that night. This time when I got his voice mail, I left a message, an abject apology, and a request for him to please phone me that bordered on begging. My chest cavity felt hollow; the air around me seemed too thin to sustain life. I hung up, hoping against hope he'd been listening and would rush to accept my invitation to at least remain friends.

Of course it didn't happen.

Exhausted, I turned in early and overslept the next morning. I rushed through my shower and shave and threw on clean clothes. On the way downtown, I phoned Charlie Weeks and asked if he'd been able to put anyone on Hickey's tail yet. He had, but there was little to report. Hickey apparently lived in a duplex near Bell and San Pedro SE in what is commonly called Albuquerque's "War Zone." He'd gone home after work, and his tan 1996 Mercury Mystique sat at the curb all night. Around ten two unidentified men showed up with a case of beer, and the door hadn't opened again for the rest of the night. After Hickey reported in for work this morning, Charlie's man—yet another ex-cop named Alan Mendoza—had gone to a nearby police station to see if he could find a mug shot to identify the two visitors. Then he intended to go home for some shut-eye.

After I heard Charlie out, I asked him to nose around the Zellner murders while I looked into the merger deal Del had mentioned. Del had declined to identify either his client or the target company, but a couple of acquaintances in the investment business, including the one who handled the bulk of my trust, ought to know something since the local company was supposedly a big one. Actually it wasn't a strain; my man knew exactly whom I was talking about.

"High Desert Investments," he said without hesitation.

"Billingham's company?"

"The same."

Like many before him, Horace Billingham Sr., the family's patriarch, came to Albuquerque in his early twenties to die. Back in those days,

Central Avenue was known as TB Road because of the old Memorial Hospital and the Presbyterian Sanitarium. But New Mexico's clear, thin air did more for Billingham's failing lungs than all the doctors in the world. He survived and prospered. Within five years he had established a highly successful mortgage business. As the company grew, he installed family members in key positions. A year ago he had relinquished the presidency to his elder son, Joseph, although he remained Chairman of the Board. Horace Jr., a contemporary of mine, was now a senior vice president. The old man's daughter, Louise Billingham Fields was something—secretary, probably—and her husband, Frank Fields, a stuffed shirt if there ever was one, held down the Treasurer's slot. A split within that board would provoke a fierce family fight, and every one of them knew how to roll around in the dirt.

Rumor held that the proposed merger with Vestmark Mortgage Company, a large Texas firm, was in trouble. Joseph had sandbagged old man Billingham, but the word in the financial community was the patriarch had recovered and come out fighting. Horace Jr.—or Whorey as he was known back in our school days—had swung over to the old man's side, most likely hoping to end up as Crown Prince of Billinghamshire.

Normally a merger fight wouldn't involve attempted blackmail and threats of mayhem, but the Billinghams weren't your normal entrepreneurs. They were a mean nest of vipers and merited careful examination.

I put in a phone call to the Billingham I knew best—Horace Jr, an old school buddy—but was told he was out of town. Better than a week passed without a callback. I used that time to track down two more of Emilio's johns and satisfy myself they were not connected to Del's case. I also spent the time worrying about the strange silence from the extortionists. Either this wasn't as serious a matter as I'd thought, despite a death threat, or they were lying low because of my investigation.

Eventually I was ushered into Horace Jr.'s presence. He rose from behind an immense oak desk, dressed in typical banker's attire, although more like a New York mortgage banker than an Albuquerque one. The blue-gray three-piece suit was Italian cut; the red power tie neatly dimpled. A prominent beak that definitely was not a British nose dominated his saturnine face. Some astute Billingham ancestor likely changed the family name back in the mists of time.

I'd never set foot in the Billingham Building before, so I surveyed the office curiously. The walnut wainscoting and the dark fuzzy wallpaper I associated with old-fashioned parlors weren't Whorey's style. This room reflected the tastes of Horace Sr., who glared down from an immense portrait mounted on the wall behind the big desk.

Whorey noticed me taking in the room and growled in what was intended as an amiable manner. "Not bad, huh? Good to see you, BJ. Sorry to be so long getting back to you, but I was out of town. It's been awhile. Looking good, boy."

"So are you, Whorey."

"Those were the days, huh? Always liked to be called that. It was spot-on as a nickname. Never lacked for the stuff. Except," added the man who had waved his daddy's money around like a sexual lightning rod, "I never had to pay nothing for it."

"You miss them? Those days, I mean?"

"Yeah. I do. Those were good times, huh? Damned near won the state championship our senior year, didn't we?"

I laughed aloud. "And cried like babies when we lost by an extra point."

"We did, didn't we? Whole damned football team broke down like kids. Hell, we *were* kids."

"More than we would ever admit."

"Right." The man's face closed up and a glint of suspicion surfaced in his eyes. "What can I do for you? I'm sure you didn't come here to relive our high school days."

"Word on the street is the merger's dead, and you're the guy who put a halt to it."

Whorey beamed and adjusted his perfectly aligned tie. "So that's the word on the street, is it? Well, it's not dead yet, but I expect it will be soon. I kinda got the upper hand on the deal."

"How did you manage that? With your picture gallery?"

His jaw dropped. "How'd you know?"

"Just a guess. But then, I know how sly you can be. When greed gets in the way, reason doesn't always work. When reason doesn't work, a man sometimes has to take the extra step. And greed's what's at the bottom of the merger, right?"

"Damned straight. And that's all it is. Can you imagine turning over Albuquerque's leading business to some Texas conglomerate? It's criminal."

"Why are you against the buyout? You'd net a pile of money if it goes through. And I'm sure Vestmark would recognize your value to the company."

Billingham ruined his image as a buttoned-down businessman by slouching in his high-backed executive's chair and absently juggling a lead crystal paperweight with a sizeable gold nugget embedded in it. "I'm already sitting on Fort Knox, so why trade being a big bug on the lily pad for being a little one in the pond?"

"Makes sense."

Whorey gave me a level look. A confession of sorts would follow. Horace Billingham Jr. had always been eager to share secrets. "I considered coming to you for help, but I figured you were too straight and narrow for the job." He laughed aloud. "Well, not *straight*, maybe, but I didn't figure personal surveillance was your thing."

"You guessed right. I wouldn't have enjoyed sitting on Joseph's tail 24-7."

"Figured. So I brought in somebody from Phoenix. A good man with long-distance lenses. Joe's always screwed around on his wife. She knows and ignores it." Then he virtually mirrored Del's description of his predicament. "But pictures are something else. Hard to ignore them. And the old man would have gone apeshit if he saw them."

"Do I know her?"

He smirked. "You do, but I can't say more than that. You understand."

"Yeah, I do. Confidentiality's my bread and butter." I relaxed in my chair, initially unaware my muscles had tightened when he began to confess. "I thought for a minute you had the goods on somebody in Vestmark."

"Don't need to. Squeezing Joe's balls is enough. He'll waffle for a while, but then he'll fall in with the old man and me." Whorey paused and gave a sly grin. "Tell me, did you get what you came for?"

I laughed as I stood. "You're too sharp for me. Yep, got what I came for."

"You gonna tell me which minority stockholder you represent?"

"Wouldn't dream of it. You don't want to know, anyway."

"Naw. You're right. Don't wanna know."

"One more thing. Why go to Phoenix for a PI when there are plenty of them right here? It's bound to have cost a lot more money."

"There's times when cost isn't everything, you know. I needed Joe cold, and he's got as good contacts in this town as I do. So I went for someone he couldn't compromise."

"Good thinking."

I felt a little greasy as I exited the Billingham Building.

WHEN I returned to the office, Charlie Weeks filled me in on what he'd learned about the Zellner murders. Gilbert Zellner and Helen Martinez Zellner had been found shot to death in their Mercedes between Santa Fe and Española this past February. The husband-and-wife team was well known to northern New Mexico lawmen. Both served time for drug dealing, but that didn't prevent them from manufacturing crystal meth at their ten-acre hideaway in the rolling hills north of Santa Fe. Most homegrown labs were able to produce something like a weekend supply of meth, but the Zellner operation was considerably larger than that. It fell short of the big Mexican warehouse operations but was big enough to attract attention. The Iron Cross Club handled some of the Zellners' product.

When the couple showed up dead, authorities assumed rival drug makers from Mexico or southern Colorado had been the culprits, until a young woman named Miranda Skelton confided to a girlfriend she had witnessed the murders. Miranda was a strange creature; her biker chick's brashness was overlaid with a coed's naïveté. Apparently she was up for anything—except cold-blooded murder. Once whispers of the girl's confession to her friend reached official ears, she was hauled into Santa Fe, where she exposed the entire tragic event.

According to Miranda, her boyfriend, Melvin Whiznant, known by the sobriquet of Head Cross, and his lieutenant, Adder, had killed the two drug dealers in a dispute. The Iron Crosses wanted total control over distribution of the meth and ended up with nothing except more trouble than they could handle. To make matters worse, if Whiznant was convicted of these killings, it would be his third major felony. Even if he managed to escape the death penalty, he wouldn't be coming home again.

Understanding that Miranda was the key to the case, the police tucked her away in a nice safe cell, as a material witness until the trial. When defense counsel insisted on deposing the state's witness, the court had called on the Blahs for someone to look out for her interests. Del ended up as her guardian by the luck of the draw or because it was his turn in the barrel—depending upon the way you viewed the assignment.

Here was a promising new lead, and Del's lame excuse for not mentioning it before bordered on the dumb—hell, on the brain-dead. I phoned to fill him in on the Billingham interview but ran head-on into his version of Hazel. Finally I settled for leaving him a pithy message informing him his merger was probably off and that we had to have a serious talk about Miranda Skelton.

Disgusted with my client, I stalked out into the bullpen and announced I was taking a few days off.

Hazel took my announcement well. In fact, she brightened perceptibly. "About time. Where are you going?"

"Going? I'm not going anywhere. I'll just kick back and try not to think about business for a long weekend."

"A weekend?" She grimaced. "That's not taking time off, BJ. The Santa Fe Fiesta starts soon. Why don't you go?"

"If it's a fair I want, the state fair's about to get underway right here in Albuquerque."

Now fully in her take-control mode, she started making plans. "No, you need to get out of town. Monday is Labor Day, and they're burning Zozobra up in Fort Marcy Park next Thursday night to kick off the festivities. Take the whole week and enjoy yourself."

Every year since God was a baby, our neighbors to the north have held a Fiesta. As the opening act, they fire up a giant marionette called Zozobra, or Old Man Gloom, to burn up everyone's troubles. I hadn't attended the ritual since my high school years, and the idea held some attraction.

Hazel was good at reading me and sensed weakness. "It's the perfect thing to make you forget all this Dahlman mess. Take a long drive through the northern mountains; the trees are already turning up there. Go play golf in Los Alamos. You always liked their course. Then you can come back to Santa Fe for Zozobra on Thursday."

With no better idea, I acquiesced, although I refused to do the motor-tour bit. Instead I agreed only to drive up to Santa Fe on Thursday for an overnight stay. Hazel grunted at the partial rejection of her plans, but before the afternoon was over, she barged into my office and laid a ticket on the desk.

"What's this?"

"Admission ticket to Fort Marcy Park."

"They charge admission now?"

"Of course." Her jowls jiggled in agitation. "How do you think they raise all that money for charity?"

"They raise money for charity?"

"A bunch. You're booked at the La Fonda, but only for Thursday night, and we're lucky to find that. I had to call on a friend." She predictably paused for me to ask for details. Yeah, right. I wouldn't touch that one with a stick.

"Everything's booked solid from Albuquerque to Raton. Has been for weeks," she said.

I still refused to bite. "Thanks."

"Humph," she groused. Then she paused and added, "It's a single."

"That's fine by me."

"And it's in the name of David Herring."

"Who the hell is David Herring?"

"The fellow who made the reservation."

"How am I supposed to pass myself off as—"

"You're a former Marine, an ex-cop, and a high-powered PI. If you can't find a way, you're in the wrong business."

Taking her advice, I didn't worry about it. Besides, she'd fix it long before I arrived at the La Fonda.

I WENT to the North Valley club Saturday, ostensibly for physical therapy in the pool, but actually on the off chance Paul would agree to go with me to the Zozobra burning. Alas, another lifeguard presided over the swimming pool. Had Paul followed through on his threat to quit his job? I made some inquiries and determined he was still on the club's payroll.

Late Sunday morning I took a leisurely shower, dressed, and went to church, something I do off and on. I'm a believer in a higher power, although it is not firmly defined in my own mind. I was raised in the church and attended regularly until my late teen years, when I began to suspect who I was. Then disenchantment set in—big time. How could a loving God simply write me off because I wasn't like other people? After all, He'd made me that way; there was no doubt of that. I was not the product of a broken home. It was not the lack of a strong father figure or the presence of a smothering mother that made me gay. No, my sexual orientation was hardwired.

After reaching that conclusion, I rebelled and stopped going to church. If it didn't want me—the way I was, not the way it demanded I be—then to hell with it. So I lived for years with something lacking in my life. It was in the Marines, of all places, where things were reconciled to my satisfaction. A fellow junior officer with a brand-new degree in ancient languages opened my eyes. He showed me how those damning passages in Leviticus and Deuteronomy and Kings and elsewhere had been perverted to reflect local prejudices by the substitution of a Greek verb here and an Aramaic noun there and applying what had been intended as a proscription against temple behavior to the general demeanor. Maybe this didn't explain things for the rest of the world, but it gave me enough to once again accept the embrace of organized worship.

On the way to the nearest Blake's drive-in after church, I turned on my cell and checked my voice mail. I was hoping my elusive client had tried to contact me, but it was the smoky, sexy voice of Emilio Prada in my ear instead.

"Hiya, Mr. V. Know you been trying to reach me. I.... well, I guess it's time we talked. Gimme a call, and maybe I'll drive down and meet you pretty soon. Let me know if that's okay. Uh, I guess you figured out this is Emilio. See ya."

I listened to the message twice more, trying to pin down something in the kid's voice. Finally I identified it. It was worry, if not downright fear. No one answered my return call, but I left a message on his voice mail saying I'd be in Santa Fe Thursday afternoon and was booked at the La Fonda that night. "Driving down" most likely meant he was north of us, possibly in Taos, so it would be easier to make his move if I went part of the way to him.

There was no return call. Nor did Emilio answer my subsequent attempts to reach his number.

I HAD planned to keep Labor Day labor-free, but it didn't work out that way. I was rereading James Lee Burke's Edgar Award–winning *Black Cherry Blues*, featuring his Dave Robicheaux character, when I was interrupted by a phone call from Charlie.

"It's Alan Mendoza, BJ; he's in the hospital. Well, he's in the UNM emergency ward. They'll probably let him go when they get through treating him."

"What happened? Will he be all right?"

Charlie told me Alan was sitting on Luther Hickey again last night when those same two guys showed up. This time they made him. Hickey walloped on him some, but Alan claimed he would be all right. He'd have a shiner for a few days, but nothing was broken. His wife, Alice, was there with him… as was Charlie.

"I'll be right down," I said.

I pulled into the parking structure at the west end of the Richardson Pavilion at UNM Hospital twenty minutes later. Charlie was waiting for me in the overcrowded waiting area of the emergency room, but he'd greased the wheels and soon had us back where a doctor was just finishing up with Alan Mendoza.

"I don't want you getting in any more fights for the next two weeks," the pretty black woman said. "I won't take it kindly if you undo all of my work."

Alan, a broad, swarthy man about Charlie's age who could have been her grandfather, gave her a big gap-toothed grin. "Might get in one tomorrow if I knew you'd be my doctor."

"You do that, and I'll show you what pain really is!"

She patted his cheek, beamed at us, and told him he was ready to check out at the front desk. A second later we heard her cheerfully greet another patient hidden by a curtain next door.

"What happened, Alan?" I asked.

"Those two guys Hickey had a beer party with a couple of nights ago showed up. They gave me the evil eye when they went in, but once the door closed behind them, I figured everything was copasetic. Early this morning—it was still dark—the door opened and Hickey and one of the others came out of the apartment. I was wondering where the other one was when he bashed in the window right at my head. The guy musta crawled out of a window at the back and snuck around behind me. He got me by the neck so I couldn't start the car. After that, they wrestled me out into the street and started beating on me."

Alan had been lucky. A car had turned down the street and his assailants took off in Hickey's Mercury. The driver of the car stopped and called for an ambulance.

"Thank God. Did you get his name?" I asked.

"Nope. He hung around until the meat wagon showed up, and then he took off."

"Why the hell would Hickey do something like that? He's bound to know that'll send him straight back to Santa Fe. Were any words exchanged? Did you argue with them? Threaten them?"

"Nope." Alan groaned as he moved to emphasize his point. "It was just a bashed-out window and then wham-bam-thank-you-ma'am."

"Hickey's lid's not screwed on tight," Charlie said. "I called the station, and the boys are looking for him and his pals, but they're in the wind. He knows you put Alan on him. Tell him, Alan."

"His two buddies held me while Hickey delivered the beating. Two or three times, he said to 'tell that nosy PI this is what's coming to him if he keeps fucking around.'"

"Tell him what else he said," Charlie prompted.

"Said 'that pansy in 5100' was going to get the same treatment."

I looked at Charlie. "Did you tell the police about the threat?"

He nodded. "Yeah, but I'll let you warn Dahlman."

Alan added, "I was able to ID one of the guys with Hickey. His name's Jackson Starbucks." Alan tried to laugh, but it turned into a pained grunt. His hand automatically went to cradle his bruised ribs. "Honest to God, that's his name. Found a sheet on him. He was at Santa Fe the same time as Hickey. Went up for attempted murder during a domestic dispute."

"Nice bunch of people. We'll take care of all of your medical expenses, okay? Send the medical bills and the tab for your broken window to Hazel. Charlie will see that you get home all right."

"My wife's down at the pharmacy filling the doctor's prescriptions. Don't worry about me. Just find that fucking madman."

Del didn't answer his home or cell phones, but I got through to him at the office. Apparently he didn't observe Labor Day either. Thankfully there was a way of bypassing the switchboard for after-hours incoming calls.

"You okay?" I asked.

"Yeah, why wouldn't I be?"

I told him about the beating Alan had taken and the threats made against the two of us.

"So Hickey's the one behind the blackmail scheme?"

"That's possible. Or he could just be a homophobe that I sent spinning out of control when I interviewed him. But this Zellner murder thing can't be dismissed. I haven't finished looking into that at this point."

"So what do we do now?"

"The police are looking for Hickey and his friends. As soon as they run him down, Gene and I will question him. The other day I tricked him into writing down my name and address and got the handwriting sample to Gloria down at K-Y. Maybe she can tie him to the blackmail envelope and the threat to me. But until they catch him, you should watch your back."

"I think I'll stay at the hotel next door tonight."

"Probably a good idea."

I considered doing the same thing… but what if Paul had a change of heart and tried to contact me? No, I'd go home and lock the doors behind me.

A LITTLE later, as I got out of the Impala in my driveway and was halfway to the back door, Luther Hickey suddenly blocked my way. There was a sneer on his shaggy face as he tapped a metal baseball bat into the palm of his right hand—just as he had toyed with the wrench when I'd interviewed him in the basement of the Royal Crest.

Chapter 14

MY FIRST thought, a totally irrational one, was that I was going to have to delist my home telephone number. My second was closer to being on the mark—my Smith & Wesson M&P Shield, 9 mm semiautomatic was locked in the trunk of the Impala. Unloaded!

A millisecond later, the skin on my back puckered and the scar on my thigh burned as I focused on the man brandishing a baseball bat.

"What are you doing here, Hickey? This is private property. You're trespassing."

He laughed, revealing yellowed teeth in the middle of his matted beard. "Trespassing? That all you can come up with? You think trespassing's what I got on my mind?" He took a step forward. I retreated two. "If I'm going back to the pen, it's gonna be for something big."

"What are you talking about?"

"About you wrecking my life, that's what." We did the two-step again. I was now at the edge of the driveway.

"You're crazy. All I did was ask you some questions."

"All you did was come to where I work and ask your questions, getting my boss all goosey. Then you had somebody come and talk to him about the ex-con in the basement and the queer on the fifth floor. Then you put some Mexican creep outside my place to watch everything I do. You know what all that adds up to?"

I held my tongue. He'd either talk himself up for something or out of something. The ball was in his court.

"Me getting fired, that's what. It's a lousy fucking job, but it's the only one I could find. If I'm going down again, I'm going down for something that'll earn me some respect up there in Santa Fe."

"Hickey, don't be a damned fool. You can handle what's coming your way right now. But if you go any further, you'll spend the rest of your life behind bars."

"Fuck it. At least I'll have a roof over my head and three squares a day."

He set his stance. I knew what was coming next. So be it. I hadn't been in a real dustup recently. Maybe this was what I needed.

"Yoo-hoo! Mr. Vinson? BJ?"

The thin, frail voice startled both of us. I glanced over my right shoulder and saw Mrs. Wardlow, my across-the-street neighbor, standing at the end of my driveway. Her helmet of blue-white hair glowed like an angel's halo.

"I saw a big hairy man go into your backyard. I'm afraid I called the police. I hope that's all right."

The word *police* released both of us. Hickey telegraphed his swing, and the bat took out a chunk of brick from the corner of the garage. If I hadn't jerked out of the way, it would have taken off my head. I barreled into him before he had a chance to recover. His body odor almost did me in as I drove my shoulder into his chest. I bounced off him. He grunted and reeled backward but didn't go over. He still held the bat loosely in his left hand. I kicked him in the soft underside of the wrist. His hand flexed, and the bat flew up and tumbled over my head, crashing down onto the hood of the Impala. I heard it clank onto the concrete driveway.

Even absent the weapon, Hickey was capable of doing major harm. His eyes went to slits as he gathered himself and started to move. I threw myself to the ground and rolled into him, catching him in the shins and dumping him on top of me. The force of the blow drove the air from my lungs, rendering me helpless for a precious few seconds, but Hickey got to his feet. All I could manage was to twist over to see if he was coming to finish me off.

He wasn't. He'd gone over hard. Hickey was hurt, but he wasn't finished. I struggled to my feet. He bled copiously from a cut on his forehead where he'd bounced off the brick walkway. Blood from his nose soaked his heavy beard. His eyes wandered around wildly before managing to fix on me. His rage restored him in a hurry.

He paused as car doors banged and my neighbor's frantic, quavering voice urged someone into the backyard. Hickey apparently realized the cops had arrived and decided to finish what he'd come for. That was okay. I wanted some satisfaction as well. He lowered his head and lumbered forward. But he was unsteady, and I sidestepped and delivered a hard jab to his ribs. He let out a gasp but whirled faster than I expected. Hickey was a brawler, but I was a fighter. I kept my distance and let him do the hard work.

On his next lunge forward, he clipped my left shoulder. I used the momentum that created to spin into his left side, delivering him a brutal blow to the ear. I could almost see the bells that set off inside his head. I followed up with a left to his nose, but I'd lost some of the power in that arm, so it didn't hurt him much. I backed off and watched as he gathered himself for another go at me.

When he moved I timed his rush and flexed my right foot into his left knee. He lurched sideways right into my roundhouse. He did a one-eighty and blundered into my birdbath, breaking the concrete stand. Hickey sprawled on the ground, making no effort to get to his feet.

By then two uniformed patrolmen had arrived, batons in hand.

Holding both arms over my head, I stood stock-still. I wasn't about to provoke them while they figured out the situation. "I'm B. J. Vinson," I yelled. "This is my home. I'm former APD, so I know the drill."

"Just hold it like you are, man, till we get this all straightened out."

Mrs. Wardlow was right behind them. "Well, of course, this is Mr. Vinson. He's been my neighbor for years. This other bozo is the troublemaker." She picked up Hickey's bat and grasped it like a seasoned Isotopes batter. "He attacked Mr. Vinson with this."

After things settled out, I thanked the cops, kissed Mrs. Wardlow's powdered cheek, and watched them haul Hickey off. Then, after statements were given and everyone had left—and my heart rate settled down—I dialed Del's cell phone and told him he could go home.

I LOOKED at the man seated opposite Gene and me in the police interview room—a bear of a man with a white bandage across his forehead and a swollen, crooked nose. Luther Hickey looked almost like a teddy bear compared to how he looked yesterday afternoon in my backyard. Fury no longer burned from those dark eyes. Now he was simply resigned to what would come next. The three of us were alone in the room; Hickey had waived his right to an attorney.

He shifted his glance from Gene to me. "What's he doing here?"

"We have a few questions for you."

"Kinda questions?"

"Like why you tried to blackmail Mr. Dahlman in 5100?"

"I what? Fuck, I didn't do no such thing. Blackmail him how? The whole apartment house knows he's queer as a two-headed toad. And besides, who gives a shit? Now, if he had a dog and it crapped in the hallway, they'd all be up in arms. But he can bring in his faggot friends and do fuck-all in his apartment, and nobody gives a damn."

It was the opening round in an hour's grilling of the ex-con. Gene came at him every way he knew how, and then I took over. He denied having any pictures, or ever *seeing* any pictures, of Del and Emilio. In the middle of it, the detectives Gene had sent to search Hickey's car, apartment, and cubbyhole at the Royal Crest reported they'd come up dry. Gloria pretty much finished things off when she phoned my cell to say Hickey's handwriting didn't match the extortion envelopes. Finally we gave up and had him returned to the cellblock.

"Sorry, BJ, we can't tie him to the blackmail scheme, but at least he'll be out of circulation." Gene scratched his left ear. "I understand the DA's going to press deadly assault charges, so you'll probably have to testify."

I watched the guards march Hickey down the hall. "No, he waived counsel. And when you charge him with assault on Alan Mendoza and me, he'll confess. He wants to go back to Santa Fe."

"That's sad. You gotta be down really low when the pen looks better than what you have on the outside. But there are people like that. We'll see he gets his wish."

I waited until I was back at the office to phone Del. He heard me out.

"Do you think he is involved?"

"In all honesty I don't think so. But we'll keep looking to see if he ties into anyone else we're looking at."

Del indulged in some cussing. At length he sighed. "I was sure you were going to tell me this nightmare was all over."

"No such luck."

Chapter 15

My LAST Zozobra, back when I was a sixteen-year-old high school sophomore full of piss and vinegar, had come in the midst of a vicious and unresolved battle to determine who I was. Susie Garcia's perky breasts and Billy Balkins's—Ballsy to his intimates—lanky physique both stimulated my raging adolescent libido. At that moment in time, the internal confusion over which of the two was more important to me eclipsed the excitement of Zozobra's demise. My recollection of the event was reduced to the loud groans and moans of the flaming marionette, most likely because they mimicked my own smothered gasps of frustration.

For years legions of locals and guests from all over the world have scribbled their cares and woes on scraps of paper to go up in flames with Old Man Gloom in the desperate hope that the year's hardships would die with the frightful ogre. I was more than ready to be freed from my plague of problems—both professional and personal.

I arrived in the capital city early Thursday afternoon and checked into the La Fonda Hotel. I took time to have a late lunch of hot pepper steak in the restaurant and to have them pack me a corned beef on rye to take with me. If I recalled correctly, it would be a long time before I had an opportunity to eat again. In a nearby shop, I bought a canvas tote bag, a small blanket, and a supply of snacks and bottled water.

I intended to hoof it straight up Washington Street to Fort Marcy Park to beat the mob, which was expected to number over twenty thousand this year. Instead I was lured into the town square. The burning of Zozobra traditionally opened the Santa Fe Fiesta, and an art-and-food street show was already going strong on the plaza kitty-cornered across from the hotel. Rows of colorful tents reminded me of woodblock prints I'd seen of medieval European fairs.

The plaza generally attracted pretty good crowds on any given day, but there were literally throngs of people tromping the grass as they moved from one booth to the other. I had no interest in buying anything; nonetheless, I shuffled along with everyone else to look at an astounding array of goods: paintings, Native American pottery and jewelry, Mexican tinwork, and Spanish retablos. Some of it was pretty good stuff, and I ended up spending a few dollars on a silver ring with a thunderbird motif and a couple of strands of heishi with a few turquoise nuggets scattered throughout. Hazel would like the necklace. The ring? Well it would probably fit Paul's finger… if he ever bothered to speak to me again.

I added the purchases to my tote bag and turned away from the booth in time to spy two young men ahead of me. I had only a fleeting glimpse through the crowd before they turned left at the end of the row of booths. Had that been Paul? It sort of looked like him… in a way. I would probably have dismissed the idea if the other man with him hadn't resembled Emilio. That possible combo was too much to simply ignore. Damn, why hadn't I glanced up a moment earlier? With my curiosity meter in the red zone, I pushed through the holiday browsers, earning a dirty look or two along the way.

When I reached the end of the line of booths, I paused to scan San Francisco Street, but the two men I'd spotted were nowhere in sight. A bunch of people rushed here and there or strolled along like they had nothing to do. I went down the next line of booths, shoving my way through the throng and making a nuisance of myself. More glares.

I spent an hour vainly searching, although I did spot two young men who could *possibly* have been the couple I'd seen. Neither Paul nor Emilio was anywhere on the plaza or across the street where more Native American vendors sat in the overhang of the old Governor's Palace, selling wares spread on brightly colored blankets. I searched every side street in the vicinity before finally giving up and heading to Fort Marcy Park.

There had been some changes in the eighteen years since I'd last attended a burning. The most obvious one was the security. I was early enough that the crowds hadn't really started gathering, but it still took me a while to get through the security check. They searched me as thoroughly as the air transit people had done the last time I flew commercially. Teams of uniformed officers circulated inside the gate, usually a Bernalillo County sheriff's deputy paired with a Santa Fe police officer. As Bernalillo County was Albuquerque, not Santa Fe, they were probably Gang Unit deputies.

As soon as I passed into the Fort Marcy Ball Park proper, I came face-to-face with other radical changes. Although Kiwanis teams worked year round building the giant puppet we were going to burn tonight, the final construction—or more properly, the final erection—took place on the field. In the old days we came early, along with a host of children, to watch this final step in old Zozobra's creation. Not now. He already stood on a huge stage fenced off from the public area. I used to walk down to the big marionette and stuff pieces of paper containing my written woes and cares into the monster's legs to be destroyed when he went up in smoke. Uh-uh, not now. To collect the scraps of paper, the *Santa Fe New Mexican* staffed a booth with people. They even provided the pencils and paper. At the proper time, they would haul the box of woes to Zozobra for incineration. The new arrangement took some of the magic out of it.

I was early enough to find a good spot to throw my blanket down and establish my claim. This year the big effigy's robes were white with black and crimson belt, buttons, and bow tie. His oversized head was topped with bright yellow streamers representing hair. Huge, round red eyes glared from ebony sockets. Heavy crimson lips outlined in black framed a sneering mouth.

"Does it really work?"

The voice at my side startled me. A man about my age stood staring at the towering monster. He was my height and weight, with a smooth milk chocolate complexion.

"The last time I did this I was sixteen, and it sure as hell didn't take care of those problems."

He grinned. "Only time did that, I'll bet."

Enjoying the byplay, I raised my voice over the gathering crowd. "Crystallized them, maybe, but didn't snuff them out." I noticed he had no blanket… or supplies of any other kind, for that matter. I scooted over and patted my blanket. "Join me?"

He sat down. "Thanks. My name's Darrel." His grip was firm.

"I'm BJ. Are you a foreigner or a Santa Fean?" The question was pure chitchat. The odds of a thirtysomething-year-old black man being a native of Santa Fe were modest at best.

"An immigrant from Mississippi. You?"

"Born and bred in Albuquerque. To these people, that not only makes me a foreigner, but the Antichrist, as well."

Darrel turned out to be an architect recently lured to the City Different by a local firm, so this was his first Zozobra. As we sat on the blanket, we shared the bottles of water and power snacks I'd brought along. He was pleasant company, and I was able to satisfy some of his curiosity about the history of the place he now called home.

Speaking loudly to be heard over the crowd, I told Darrel how the Santa Fe Fiesta was a celebration started back in 1712 by the Marquis de Peñuelo, the governor of New Spain, to mark the reconquest of the city by Don Diego de Vargas following the Pueblo Revolt.

"They say that makes it the oldest civic celebration in North America."

He put his lips to my ear. "You seem to know a lot about it."

I turned my head and leaned in close. "I've been nuts about local history ever since I learned to read. My… uh, best friend and I used to take weekend trips all over the state. We found some interesting things. This is one of the more dramatic."

"I've read about de Vargas and the Po'Pay revolt. Was that the start of burning up all your troubles in a big rag doll?"

He snatched his hand off the grass as someone came close to tromping on it. I glanced around. Our immediate area was getting pretty packed. Some were sitting, as we were, but others stood and unconsciously pressed forward, testing the boundaries established by the blanket we sat on. Many in the crowd were dressed in colorful costumes, adding to the pagan atmosphere of the night. A lot of them were on cell phones, frantically trying to find family or friends in the swarming sea of humanity.

At that moment the canned music died, replaced by a live band that was no less noisy. I leaned toward Darrel and shouted an answer to his question. "No, that came along later. In 1924 a Santa Fe artist named Will Shuster borrowed an idea from Mexican folklore and created a puppet he burned in his backyard to entertain friends. He named it Zozobra. That's anxiety or gloom in Spanish. So he started a tradition of burning up people's problems. Eventually he moved the burning to the city plaza, but when it got too big, they moved the whole shebang here to Fort Marcy Park."

The people in front of us were seated as well, so we still had a view of Zozobra. He was constructed of wood, cloth, papier-mâché, and chicken wire, and stuffed with shredded paper, supposedly old police reports, paid mortgages, anything that caused angst.

Darrel eyed the monster and shouted. "That sucker must be fifty or sixty feet tall."

"Sometime back Shuster signed over all the rights to Zozobra to the Kiwanis club, and they made a moneymaking project out of him. For charity, of course. They tell me the club expects to raise fifty or sixty thousand dollars for charities with this burning. Over the years they've collected over a half million to sponsor scholarships, youth projects, pay handicapped youth camp fees, and things like that."

"That's good stuff," Darrel yelled. "Got to see if I can get hooked up with an outfit like that."

"They'd be happy to have you."

Something thumped me in the back of the head. I turned to see a woman holding a big purse. She and her companion were standing on my blanket. She muttered an apology. I glanced at my watch—7:00 p.m. Still an hour and a half before the real show began, and we were already losing space to the pressing mob.

"I see he's animated," Darrel said.

The puppet's limbs were twitching. His head moved back and forth as if he were surveying the crowd. Occasional amplified moans and groans overpowered the noise of the mob.

"Yeah, he sets up quite a racket when he's burning."

"So he goes out with a bang."

"A groan and a moan and a screech and a bang." I wasn't certain how much of this he was hearing. "You'll see for yourself before long."

The crowd grew larger, noisier, and more restive as evening arrived. Booze was banned in the park, but flasks abounded, and they sure as hell didn't contain sassafras tea. Another band had taken the stage, and if anything it was more enthusiastic and louder than the first. Every thump of the bass reverberated inside my chest. It was just like being at an outdoor rock concert. Pretty soon we'd have to give in to the press of people and stand up, but first I shared my corned beef sandwich and some water with Darrel.

After that we stood, and I tried to retrieve my blanket. There were too many people standing on it, so I abandoned it to its fate. Eventually the decibel level grew to a pitch where conversation became impossible.

We stood and craned our necks to do some more people watching. Just as I figured my back was going to give out, a blare of trumpets heralded the approach of the traditional procession from St. Francis Cathedral. The Conquistadores Band approached the base of Zozobra's stage from a gate that spared them from having to squeeze through the mob. Immediately "The Star-Spangled Banner" blared through the speakers, and the crowd sang—no, shouted—along.

Then the tempo switched from triumphant to funereal. Black-robed and hooded Kiwanis members led the parade bearing the effigy of the Mother Mary in the persona of La Conquistadora. Gloomies, eight- and nine-year-old children who dance as ghosts around Zozobra, preceded the Fire Spirit Dancer, Queen of Gloom, Gloom Princesses, handlers, dignitaries, and a seemingly endless host of others.

As darkness fell a synthesizer blared when white-sheeted Gloomies began cavorting before Zozobra. The Fire Spirit Dancer, clad in a flowing red costume, drove away the mischievous children in an acrobatic dance originally created by a New York ballet dancer. A drum crew added to the din of the frenetic synthesizer. A band added brass and reed instruments as the dance reached its tempestuous climax. Then the master of ceremonies stepped forward and whipped the assembled crowd into a chant of "Burn him! Burn him!"

As the demand for his death grew, Zozobra flailed and roared in protest. I could almost believe he was some grotesque human personification facing a burning at the stake. It was eerie.

At last, Santa Fe's black-suited mayor took the stage to solemnly pronounce the death sentence to the screaming crowd. Instantly weird green lights lit the periphery of the doomed monster. As the official stepped away, the crowd broke into the chant again. Cries of anticipation reached a crescendo, grown men shouted, women screamed, and children yelled. And *everyone* pressed forward for a closer look. For a moment, I wondered if I'd be able to draw another breath. The panic passed, although the pressure continued to mount. The noise was indescribable.

Then the Torch Handler gave in to the demands of the frenzied crowd by touching a brand to the skirts of the giant. Old Man Gloom's grunts and groans became squeals of agony. His arms flailed helplessly as a white-hot blaze raced up his loins. Thousands of throats let out a deafening roar when the first fusies, little containers of black powder concealed in the marionette, fired off. The band struck up the Mexican revolutionary tune "La Cucaracha."

The animated creature continued to flail as parts of him began to come apart. Gloom was now totally consumed by flames. His lower jaw fell away, blasted apart by fireworks concealed in his head. The roaring fire reached for the sky. It was a miracle half of Santa Fe wasn't incinerated by now. Of course, Zozobra's auto-da-fé came at the end of New Mexico's monsoon season when the countryside was wetter than usual—at least in theory.

A deafening roar came from the crowd as the personification of anxiety came apart. A flaming arm fell to the ground in a burst of sparks. The massive fire seemed to exert a magnetic force, drawing spectators at the rear to press even harder against those in front. The conflagration turned the chilly night warm as Old Sourpuss disintegrated before our eyes.

I stole a glance at Darrel. His eyes were glued to the dying monster. He trembled from unconcealed excitement.

The raging inferno collapsed in upon itself and became a mere bonfire. Immediately the most spectacular fireworks show I'd ever seen began. Rockets flared, shells burst. Vivid, vibrant colors filled the entire sky.

When it finally ended, I experienced an anticlimactic feeling, reinforced by the long, laborious, and sometimes contentious process of exiting the park. Egress was limited to a few routes, and for half an hour, the mob pressed toward the exits, carrying Darrel and me along with it. I spent most of my time trying to keep from tromping on the heels of the guy in front of me. Still it was a more or less orderly crowd. I heard a great deal of laughter as though the demise of Gloom had in fact freed the minds of the spectators.

Where were all those people going? Some were headed to the Armory for the *Gran Baile*, a fancy dance. Many would go to bars to sate their thirst while reliving the event; more than a few would retire to homes and hotel rooms to play out the savage sexual excitement of the evening.

"Man, that was something!" Darrel said as if in a daze. I suspected he was speaking to himself rather than to me. "Never seen anything like it. Of course, coming from Mississippi, I don't cotton to hoods and bonfires too much."

"Different time, different place, different message."

I concentrated on shuffling one foot after the other as soon as a space opened up in front of me. As we neared the exit, I had a momentary glimpse of Del and a couple of other Blah-firm attorneys on the bridge that fed the crowd over the ditch and out onto the street. I hadn't spotted them again by the time Darrel and I shook hands and parted, he for home, and I for the La Fonda.

Chapter 16

WELL RESTED and congratulating myself for skipping the wild parties that undoubtedly followed last night's burning of Zozobra, I turned my thoughts back to Del's problem. Still puzzling over the situation, I went outside for a few brisk turns around the city's historic plaza. The booths cluttering the square were closed at this early hour.

Since Emilio hadn't put in an appearance or gotten in touch with me yet, I figured my best bet would be to try getting a line on the banker Estelle had mentioned. Maybe Detective Arthur Hartshorn, an old friend from my cop days, might be able to help identify him. Artie kept his nose to the wind, which meant he knew a little about the gay scene in town. And if he didn't, he had associates who did.

But the banker would have to wait until after I'd had some breakfast. The La Fonda restaurant had a good reputation, and that was saying something in a town filled with more first-class restaurants per capita than any place between St. Louis and San Francisco. As I reentered the lobby, a couple brushed past me.

"Imagine! A murder. And we were there last night."

A murder? I viscerally connected "last night" with the Zozobra affair but immediately shut down that train of thought. I had come north to shed at least some of my worries, not to assume someone else's. But for the clumsy way I'd handled things, Paul would be there with me, wearing the silver ring I'd bought yesterday afternoon. Was that symbolic or not? Anyway, we would have forgotten everything except what excitement we could spark between us.

The restaurant's staff agreed to serve one of the La Fonda's famous *enchiladas con queso* even though it was not yet time for the luncheon menu. The place was almost empty, but the staff scurried around getting ready for the noonday crowd. As I ate I enjoyed looking at the high-ceilinged Pueblo Revival interior that recalled New Mexico's territorial past.

Pleasantly sated, I pulled out my phone and tried Emilio's number again. It was probably a waste of time, but who knew? Abruptly the line opened on the other end. There was silence except for some traffic noise.

"Hello, Emilio?"

A strange yet oddly familiar voice demanded to know who I was.

I went defensive. "Who are *you*?"

"Who're you calling?"

Tired of playing Who's on First, I snapped, "I must have dialed a wrong number."

"Are you trying to call a fellow named Emilio Prada?"

A dark cloud of unease settled around me. "Yes, that's right."

"This is Detective Arthur Hartshorn of the Santa Fe Police Department. Who is this?"

"Artie? This is B. J. Vinson. What's going on?"

"BJ, where are you?"

"At the La Fonda."

"You better get over here right away. Fort Marcy Park. Near the entrance to the ballpark."

The line went dead as I got to my feet. Filled with dread, I dropped money on the table and hurried out the door. The trek to the park seemed longer than last night's, and it was uphill all the way. Deep in my soul, I knew the murder the couple in the La Fonda lobby had been talking about had reached out and snared me.

Just before I reached the entrance to Fort Marcy, I saw a group of people behind the fence in a stand of trees not far from a pile of ash and charred rubble—all that remained of Zozobra. A figure moved away from the rest and met me halfway across the field. Santa Fe Detective Arthur Hartshorn.

"BJ." His brown hair had gotten a little less brown and a lot thinner since I'd seen him last, but he carried his sixty years well. Except for the gray eyes—they'd always looked ten years older than the rest of him. Artie was about four inches shorter than I was, but we both weighed in at around 170.

"Hello, Artie. Please tell me this is not what I think it is."

"Afraid so. Your friend's down there behind that tree. Dead as Old Man Gloom. Were you here in the park last night?"

I nodded. "Right over yonder as close to the front of the crowd as I could get."

He motioned to the form on the ground in the distance. "Did you see this kid here?"

"Nope."

"I gotta ask this, BJ, you know that. Was this Emilio Prada one of your, uh...?"

"Nope. Never made it with the little bugger."

"Then how come you called him this morning?"

"I've been trying to get in touch with him for a couple of days. He ties into an investigation I'm conducting for a client. Can I see him?"

"If you know him by sight, you can make the ID. Then we gotta go down to the station and get a statement. Okay?"

"Sure. No problem."

He moved off toward a small group of police hovering around a body. One man, whose shape reminded me of a koala, seemed to be in charge. Artie introduced him as an OMI—Office of the Medical Inspector—doc named Mueller. I saw no evidence of the crime-scene unit, so they must have already come and gone.

"Are you a friend of our victim here?" Mueller asked in accented English.

"No. I knew him, but we were not friends. He was a person of interest in an investigation I'm conducting."

"BJ's a PI," Artie explained. "Used to be an Albuquerque cop."

"Ah." The word came out just short of the German *ach*. "Then you can identify him for us."

In my experience most bodies are ghastly before an undertaker gets to them; Emilio was the exception. He was as handsome in death as he had been in life. His brow was clear, his features relaxed. A slight waxen pallor was all that told you he was not asleep. That and the caked blood on his expensive windbreaker. A lot of it had puddled beneath him.

"That's Emilio Prada," I said. "What happened?"

"Looks like a stabbing, but the autopsy will tell us for sure," Mueller said.

Doctors from the OMI, not coroners, performed all the autopsies in the state of New Mexico. "You'll be taking him to UNM Hospital in Albuquerque?"

"Yes, yes. But it will be a day or two before any autopsy is completed."

"Will you be the one performing it?"

"Possibly."

"May I have access to the results?"

"You must speak to Detective Hartshorn about that." He turned to his assistants. "Okay, let's load 'im up and move 'im out." The play on the old *Rawhide* phrase uttered in guttural German-accented English sounded off-key under the circumstances.

"Any idea how long he's been dead?" I asked Artie.

Mueller answered my question as he watched his assistants place Emilio on a gurney. "Torso's in rigor, but not the whole body. So anywhere from twelve to eighteen hours."

"Twelve hours would put it at around ten thirty last night. Hell, there were thousands of people here then."

Artie grimaced. "Yeah, looks like he bought it right in the middle of the big shindig. Of course, down here in the tree line behind the puppet, he wasn't so visible."

I shook my head. "How did this happen? There was security up the kazoo around here last night."

"Yeah, booze is banned too, but I'll bet you saw plenty of it."

"Some. But a knife?"

"Who knows? Might not be a knife. Hard to tell the difference between a gunshot and a stab wound sometimes. Maybe somebody went through the security checkpoint, and then someone else handed him a shiv or a piece through the fence."

I eyed the area. "Can you fix a point of entry or exit?"

"Are you kidding? With that many people tromping around?"

"When did you find him?"

"Around four this morning."

"Somebody shoulda spotted him," I said.

"Somebody probably did—several somebodies, in fact. They all likely figured he was passed out drunk."

"With all that blood?"

"Nobody got that close. Shied away on purpose, I'd guess. Until one of the patrols spotted him. They protected the area as much as they could until crime scene and OMI got here. Let's go back to the station house for a little talk."

The drive to the police station wasn't far, but a short drive on the City Different's narrow old-world streets is often a quicker walk. One doesn't get in a hurry in Santa Fe. Artie had chosen to walk to the crime scene, so we chatted about the old days until we were seated in his office. Then he turned to business.

"What's your connection to this guy?" His eyebrow arched, silently asking the question already answered back at the park.

"Like I said, he was involved in a case I'm working."

"What's the case? You want to fill me in?"

"It's sorta sensitive. Can you give me some time?"

"Murder's sorta sensitive too. Come on, BJ, you know the drill."

"Okay, but let me call my client first. Give him a heads-up."

"Like to accommodate you, you know, for old time's sake. But let's have our talk first. By the way," he added in a falsely offhand manner, "the kid had your name and number on him… in addition to one other. You know of any connection between him and an Albuquerque lawyer by the name of Del Dahlman?"

I bowed to the inevitable. This was going to get headlines, but there was nothing I could do about that. Since Artie already had Del's name, it would be best to make a clean breast of it. Artie listened to the whole tale without interrupting.

"You were standing not more than a hundred yards from where the guy died, maybe even *when* he died. Were you with anybody?"

"Local architect named Darrel. We met at the park. It was his first burning, and I tried to explain the thing as best I understood it."

"Darrel, huh? Darrel who?"

"Don't know. We never got around to last names."

"What'd you do after the burning?"

"Went to my room at the La Fonda and turned in. I was waiting for Emilio, actually. I'd left a message on his cell phone saying I was registered at the La Fonda. But he didn't show up or phone, so I had a good peaceful night."

Artie stretched his back muscles. "Given what you told me about his relationship with Dahlman, it looks like this could be a gay catfight. Or maybe the kid propositioned the wrong guy and it's a hate crime."

"Possibly, but I think it's connected to my case."

"He have any relatives who need notifying?"

"Probably, but they're all down in Mexico. The kid came from somewhere around Durango."

"Better notify the Mexican authorities, I guess." Artie sighed. "This is another one the county's going to have to bury, I suppose."

"Not if you find his automobile. That'll pay for a pretty fancy funeral. It's an '04 Mustang convertible. Electric blue with gold trim."

"You don't happen to know the plate number, do you?"

"New Mexico vanity plate BIGBOI."

"He didn't look so big stretched out on the grass like that."

I grimaced. "Death seems to shrink us all. Look, you heard what Mueller said. Will you share the autopsy results?" I paused and addressed the obvious. "After I'm ruled out as a suspect, that is."

"Once that's done, I don't see a problem."

Artie leaned back in his chair and started with the questions again—some pretty penetrating questions. Aware I was a potential suspect, I answered very carefully. Artie showed me a photo of a big knife the officers found not far from where Emilio died. At this point they were assuming it was the murder weapon. The blade was about halfway between a Marine Corps bayonet and a bowie knife. The kid's blood encrusting the tip made the thing appear even nastier.

He also had photos of the piece of paper they'd found in Emilio's pocket with my name and phone number written in a crude cursive script, not block letters like the ransom notes. Since Del's data was scribbled just above mine in the same laborious manner, I surmised it was Emilio's handwriting. The paper was torn from a cheap, lined writing tablet.

"So, you didn't see this kid last night?" Artie started around the bend again.

"No, but it wasn't from lack of trying. He finally phoned back a few days ago and said we'd better meet. Maybe he was beginning to feel threatened for some reason. When he didn't respond to any more of my calls, I left a message saying I'd be at the Zozobra burning and was staying at the La Fonda."

"So he coulda been trying to find you at the park." Artie scratched his head. "Hard to see a pissant blackmail attempt leading to murder. Still looks like a gay bashing to me."

"I'm convinced it's not a gay killing, Artie. But I have to admit the other doesn't make a whole lot of sense either. Everybody knows Del's gay. It's the TV and newspaper publicity he's worried about. Photos that sensational would likely cause a stir."

"Hell, nobody could publish them if they're as raunchy as you say."

"It would be easy enough to upload them on the Internet. Then the media would sit up and take notice."

"I guess," Artie allowed. After a pause he asked the question I'd dreaded. "You know where your client was last night?"

"You'll have to ask him. I'll see that he phones you, okay?"

"Yeah, you do that."

An hour later, Artie had my statement on paper. Finding no fault with the document, I signed it, and after agreeing to a search of my luggage and car, I was allowed to leave. An associate of Artie's walked me to the La Fonda and went upstairs so he could check out my room and overnight bag. When he finished there, I went to the front desk to turn in my key and settle my bill while he headed for the garage. I warned him there were weapons in the vehicle and showed him my carry license before handing over my keys. By the time I got to the garage, he'd finished the search. He returned my keys and left for the station.

As soon as he left, I dialed the Stone law firm. I cut off Del's secretary before she got three words into her usual stonewalling routine. "Listen to me very carefully. If I don't speak to Del Dahlman within the next five minutes, I guarantee you'll be out of a job."

Del exploded into my earpiece thirty seconds later. "Vince, what do you mean threatening my secretary? I'm in the middle of—"

"Del, shut the fuck up and listen! Emilio Prada's dead. He was stabbed to death last night in Santa Fe at Fort Marcy Park—at the Zozobra burning. You were there. I saw you."

"What? Emilio's dead?" He had an odd catch in his voice. Apparently there was no cure for Prada fever. Well, I understood that; I was still perversely fond of the prick on the other end of this phone call.

"I spent the morning with a Santa Fe police detective who found our names and telephone numbers on Emilio's body, so I decided to make a clean breast of everything rather than risk alienating the lead investigator with a claim of client privilege. You need to start putting your house in order. The world's about to come down on you like a ton of bricks."

Del spouted some four-lettered legalese before returning to the problem. "I *was* at the burning last night, but I was with five or six other lawyers every minute of the time. And I can prove it. No way I could have killed Emilio."

"No, but you could have hired it done to keep him from publishing those pictures."

"Hired it done? Who would I have hired?"

"Me, for instance."

He took another expression directly from the lawyer's handbook. "Oh, fuck! It *will* look like that to some people, won't it?"

"Yep, to those with nasty minds. The detective handling the case in Santa Fe is Artie Hartshorn. I suggest you contact him and volunteer a statement. Phone him first and offer to come up for a face-to-face interview. I'll go up with you if you want."

"Thanks." His voice took on a note of sadness. "So he's really dead, huh? He was a despicable little shit, but—"

"Yeah, I know. But right now you need to concentrate on Del Dahlman. For example, do you still have those pictures I returned to you?"

"I destroyed them right away."

"Be sure you tell Hartshorn that. Look, I'm headed back to Albuquerque now. I'll talk to you this evening. Call me at home. And tell that ice cube guarding your door that when I call, you're to be notified immediately. Things are going to heat up, and a ten-minute delay getting to you might prove costly."

"Okay, I'll fix the problem."

We were silent for a moment, doubtless sharing thoughts of Emilio. He'd been brash and opportunistic and had cost me a precious personal relationship.

"He didn't deserve to be murdered," Del said before hanging up.

"No. He didn't," I said to a dead telephone line.

I CAME out of Santa Fe on I-25 and headed toward Albuquerque on automatic pilot.

Was Emilio killed to prevent a meeting? That made no sense. No one knew I would be at the burning except Hazel. I drew a sharp breath. Nobody but Hazel and *Emilio*. Maybe he confided in someone he shouldn't have. Why hadn't he come to the La Fonda instead of looking for me at Fort Marcy Park in a crowd of thousands? Did he feel safer in the middle of a mob? If that was the case, why didn't he call so we could have talked our way toward one another? Had there been someone with him he hadn't yet managed to elude?

I shook my head. So many questions, so few answers. He probably died less than a hundred yards from me when one phone call that never came might have saved his life.

Del's presence in Fort Marcy Park last night was a dose of bad luck, but there was no use worrying about it now. I hoped to hell he had stuck close to those other lawyers the way he claimed. That reminded me of the fleeting glimpse of someone who looked like Paul in the crowd with another man. Could it have been Emilio? Could Paul have—?

I shook my head. Not Paul. He was too decent.

As the Impala crested a rise and began the swift drop toward the bottom of the long hill south of Santa Fe known as La Bajada—literally The Hill in colloquial Southwestern Spanish—an automobile suddenly loomed in my rearview mirror. It took a long second to realize it was an electric blue Mustang ragtop. Before I could react, the Ford swung to the left and drew abreast of me. I couldn't identify the driver through the raised tinted windows during the few seconds before it muscled past and swerved right, trying to force me off the road.

The steep grade beyond the shoulder would have rolled my Impala, but the other driver had tried to catch my front panel with the rear of his vehicle instead of smacking solidly into my side. I stood on the brakes. The Mustang's rear bumper ripped off with a bang, spraying steel and chrome and plastic all over the highway. The Impala went into a skid. As I fought to bring the Chevy under control without going over the side, the Mustang fishtailed wildly. Emilio's wet dream would have tumbled over the embankment but for slamming into a road sign hard enough to send it back onto the asphalt.

I ground to a halt with the Ford's mangled rear bumper wedged firmly beneath my vehicle's chassis. After wasting a moment to calm my nerves and get my breathing under control, I checked all around to see if other bad guys were coming for me before grabbing the cell phone and punching in 911. As it rang, the Mustang moved slowly down the highway. Either it was badly damaged or the driver was considering coming back to finish the job. I reached beneath the seat and grabbed my backup weapon, a Colt Junior, .25-caliber semiautomatic. With a wary eye on the retreating vehicle, I quickly related the details of the attack to the emergency operator and asked her to notify Detective Hartshorn. By the time I hung up, the Mustang had disappeared over the far hill.

A green Porsche breezed around me without slowing, jump-starting my faltering heart. A Lincoln with Colorado license plates was more considerate. The middle-aged driver tucked in behind me, got out of the car, and offered help. Concealing the small pistol in my right hand, I told him the authorities were already on the way. After the tourist left me his name, address, and cell phone number in case he was needed as a witness, the Lincoln pulled back onto the freeway, heading south.

I got out and took emergency flares and bright red warning triangles from my trunk to place them on the road behind my disabled vehicle.

Then I tried to reach Gene, figuring he might be able to apprehend the Mustang from the south, since there were not many ways off the interstate between here and Albuquerque. It took ten minutes to locate him, but after I explained what had happened, he went to work setting up a roadblock. Artie was doing the same thing from the other side, I imagined.

A black State Police cruiser, lights flashing, pulled up behind my car, which was blocking the right lane. A tow truck wasn't far behind. The trooper was a young guy I didn't know, but after I casually tossed out the name of the District 1 commander—the rookie's home base in Santa Fe—his attitude eased. He took down the information and allowed me to read his report and correct a couple of minor points before motioning the wrecker to haul my Impala up on its flatbed. The old car was a no-frills vehicle, but it had served me well for the last couple of years. Probably time for a new one. Now I wouldn't have to repair the dent Hickey's baseball bat had made in the hood.

The state trooper gave me a ride back to Santa Fe, where we huddled with Artie Hartshorn. As we were wrapping it up, the state cop, whose name was Pachenco, received a call. Emilio's Mustang had been spotted heading east on a dirt road running across the Santo Domingo Pueblo. It was unclear if the tribal police were in pursuit.

"Somebody was keeping an eye on you, BJ," Artie said. "You notice a shadow?"

"No, but I wasn't looking for one. My guess is somebody was hanging around the park this morning to see how things went. They trailed us to the station and then followed me to the La Fonda."

"Why would they want to take you out?"

"Because I'm investigating Del's blackmail demand. That's the only connection there was between Emilio Prada and me."

Artie thought for a moment. "Well, the bozo in the Mustang cost you a car, but he did you a big favor."

"How's that?"

"He moved you to the bottom of the suspect list in the Prada killing." The Santa Fe detective frowned as if he had suffered a sudden pain. "And this probably blows the hate crime theory out of the water too."

I RENTED a Ford Focus and once again headed for Albuquerque, a little jumpy any time a vehicle overtook me on I-25. I barely noticed the rolling hills and the wildflowers and sage I usually found so comforting. The distant Jemez Range to the west looked secretive, repelling instead of attracting me. As my rental topped a hill north of the Santo Domingo exit, an ominous column of black smoke to the east drew me off the freeway and along a rough dirt road toward the mountains. In less than a mile, a reservation cop crawled out of his parked patrol car and waved me down. The dark, husky man looked me over suspiciously.

"Gotta turn back. Can't go no further." His tone was clipped and no-nonsense.

I glanced at the column of smoke rising from behind the sand dune over the man's shoulder. "What's the problem, officer?"

"This is Pueblo land. You gotta get back on the highway. Can't cross over here."

Aware that non-Native traffic regularly used this road to connect with the highway running between the old mining town of Madrid and Santa Fe, I nodded toward the greasy smoke. "Because of that?"

"That's right."

"Let me hazard a guess. It's a 2004 blue Mustang with gold trim. Plate reads 'BIGBOI.'"

The tribal lawman stepped back. His hand did not quite reach for his weapon, but it twitched. "How do you know that? You responsible for this? Get outa the car." He got it all out in a single breath.

Moving slowly, I complied. He backed off a good six feet as I closed the car door behind me. "I know because the bastard who was driving it tried to run me off the road on La Bajada. You can confirm that with State Police Officer Pachenco, badge number 2901. Pachenco hauled me back to Santa Fe so I could rent this car and go home to Albuquerque. I guessed what had happened as soon as I saw the smoke."

"What do you mean?" He squinted at me suspiciously.

"His car was almost disabled by the crash. I called 911 and then talked to Detective Artie Hartshorn of the Santa Fe Police Department, who's investigating last night's murder of the owner of that car."

"Murder?" He lost his squint and went round-eyed.

"A stabbing. Probably by the bozo who tried to kill me."

"What's your connection to the man who was stabbed?"

"I'm a licensed private investigator."

After I gave him the short version of recent events, he contacted his superiors at the Santo Domingo Pueblo station. I used the opportunity to call Gene, who grasped the situation quickly and asked to speak to the officer. Eventually the cop, whose breast tag read Watchi, handed my phone back to me and relaxed a little. I asked if there was any chance I could take a look at what was left of the Mustang.

He shrugged. "Why not? I doused it with my fire extinguisher, but it didn't do much good. Whoever set the fire soaked it pretty good with gasoline. Who in the hell carries around that much spare gas?"

"These guys did because they planned to burn the Mustang all along. It was stolen and possibly evidence in the murder. They probably filled up a couple of jerry cans in Santa Fe."

We topped the sand dune, and what the officer had said was true. The once-beautiful car was now a blackened wreck. The interior was either burned to a crisp or melted into mush. The only things still afire were three of its four tires.

"Well, we're not going to get anything from that. You find any tracks?"

"Yeah." Officer Watchi moved past me out onto the desert hardpan to point out a single set of footprints. "The perp went a quarter mile up to the top of that hill before heading back to the road."

"Went to high ground to call for help, I'll bet."

"Yeah. Then he struck out for the road about a quarter mile east of the burning vehicle. From there I'd say he met up with a car."

"Anything else?"

"The vehicle pulled a U and drove back to the spot where the Mustang was hid behind the hill. Looks like two individuals got out of the car."

"A car, not a motorcycle?"

"Uh-huh. Why'd you ask that?"

"The guy who got killed might have been mixed up with a motorcycle gang. Did the car that picked up the driver of the Mustang come in from the west? From I-25?"

"Yep."

"The Porsche!" I told him about the green Porsche that had roared past me after the Mustang disappeared over the hill. "Dollars to donuts that was a confederate watching his tail."

He grabbed his shoulder radio as I clawed for my cell phone. Artie and his partner showed up thirty minutes later. Another state trooper arrived right behind them. The FBI would probably show up next. They had jurisdiction over major crimes on reservations, and the torching of a murder victim's car on Pueblo land likely qualified.

Chapter 17

LATER THAT afternoon my rental car breezed past Sandia Pueblo and approached the recently rebuilt Tramway intersection.

Enough was enough. I took the exit ramp west and headed home, punching in the speed-dial number for my office as I navigated the curve. Although Hazel had already heard the news, she spent five minutes satisfying herself my carcass was intact. Like I said, a mom at heart. Then she turned professional and rattled off the day's events and waited, probably with pen poised, for me to provide instructions. Few were needed because she'd already taken care of most of the details.

As I pulled into my driveway, I saw something affixed to my front doorframe. Reaching for the little Colt now tucked into my belt, I crawled out of the car and looked around cautiously. Nothing stirred except a curtain on the front window across the street. Mrs. Wardlow might be old, but not much escaped her notice. She was a one-woman neighborhood watch committee.

The envelope on the doorjamb beside the screen was held in place by a small knife. A slight bulge alerted me to something other than paper inside the packet. Backing away without touching anything, I placed a call to Gene. An hour elapsed before his disreputable brown sedan pulled up in front of the house. He looked tired as he plodded up the sidewalk.

"Roadblock didn't catch anything," he said. "Neither did Santa Fe's. That Porsche is probably halfway to Mexico by now, or else it's chopped up in some back-alley shop and already inventoried for parts. They'll make more money on it that way." He pointed to the front door with his chin. "Another present?"

"Yeah, and it looks like there's something in the envelope besides a note."

His brow furrowed. "Do we need the bomb squad?"

"No, it's too small for a bomb. But I didn't want to touch anything until you got here." I indicated the neat white brick house across the street. "Chances are Mrs. Wardlow saw who put it there. Or the vehicle they were driving. She notices everything that goes down on this street. We need to have a word with her."

"Well, if you don't think it's a bomb, let's see what we've got." Gene skirted me and climbed the steps to study things without touching the knife. "The other message was shoved through the mail slot, wasn't it? So the blade's deliberate. A message within a message, so to speak."

"That's what I figure. They killed Emilio with a knife, albeit a considerably bigger one."

"That it is. Artie faxed me a photograph of what they think is the murder weapon. Big sucker."

"But not too big to be concealed in clothing. I figure it's homemade. Somebody ground a piece of steel into a blade and made a hilt for it."

"Lotta trouble. Why not just buy an anonymous blade somewhere?"

"Harder to trace. Or maybe somebody's just into making knives. It wasn't a bad job. Showed some skill."

"Well, this one looks store-bought. It's a miniature hunting knife. Buy them anywhere. Not much chance of running it down." He peered closely at the envelope. "You're right, there's something inside. Let's get some crime-scene techs out here."

"Why? There's not going to be anything on it. No prints, no DNA, no nothing. These guys are too careful."

"These guys? What makes you think there's more'n one of them?"

"Because there were two in the truck that firebombed my house. And because somebody picked up the bastard who tried to run me off the road."

"Yeah, there's that. Okay, there's more than one of them."

"And besides, I've learned a few things since I talked to you last."

As we waited for his team to arrive, I shared my latest theory about the motorcycle club double murder.

"Artie told me about that. The witness's name is Miranda Skelton, right? If I understand it, all Del's doing is protecting her rights. Making sure she doesn't get screwed over by the system."

"That's what they say, but the Santa Fe DA already has her in protective custody so nobody can get to her."

Gene snorted. "If you believe that, you wasted eight years on the force. Best way to get to a prisoner is through another prisoner, you know that."

"Yeah. But Del's connection is too obvious to ignore. *Somebody's* trying to blackmail him. And for peanuts."

"True. Have you checked with Del to see if he got a message too?"

"No. Guess I'd better do that."

I delivered a warning to my unhappy client, who said nothing had been delivered to the office; he didn't know about the apartment. He agreed to call me if he found anything. Del wanted details on what had gone down up in Santa Fe, but I put him off. Gene's people arrived as I hung up, and after a thorough search of the grounds and the house, Gene and I walked across the street to question my neighbor while they worked on the knife and envelope.

No one of my acquaintance more aptly fits the description of a "prim and proper old lady" than Gertrude Wardlow. Seventy-odd years had given her masses of soft, carefully powdered wrinkles, but her bright blue eyes were as beautiful today as they undoubtedly had been when Herb Wardlow first started courting her. I had never seen a single white hair out of place, even in a stiff wind.

She didn't wait for our questions.

"I saw it all." She spoke calmly in a carefully modulated voice, a frail hand at the lace collar of an old-fashioned housedress.

"Did you call it in, ma'am?" Gene asked.

"I had the phone in my hand when BJ showed up. So I let him do it. I'll give you my statement now. This dark green Porsche pulled up, and a man got out of the passenger's side and put that thing on your door while the driver waited with the engine running. He just plunked it right on the frame and ran back to the car. The wheels made an awful racket when the driver took off down the street. A terrible waste of gas and good rubber, if you ask me."

She had little more to add. The man who got out of the car was young. How young? Well, young. And he was slightly built. Dark? Fair? Dark, she thought, but her eyesight wasn't all that good these days.

I took out my card and put in in her hand. "Ma'am, I don't think anything else is likely to happen, but I want you to have my cell phone number in case you need to reach me."

"Thank you, BJ. That's very thoughtful of you. I'll put it away where it will be handy."

"Don't hesitate to call me or the police if you see anything—and I mean anything—that doesn't look right."

As we trudged back across the street, Gene said, "Well, we know the Porsche was the pickup car and it came down to Albuquerque."

"Yeah, straight to my front door."

"Cheeky bastards, aren't they?"

The technicians were photographing a note spread out on my kitchen table. Unlike the last one, it had been hastily scribbled, not made from words and letters cut from magazines or newspapers. There hadn't been time for that.

"Maybe they made a mistake with this one," Gene observed. "You know, being in a hurry and all."

"Maybe. But if there are fingerprints, I'll eat my hat."

"Do you own one?"

"Yeah, a Stetson, but it's too expensive to grill. We'll make it my golf cap if I'm wrong." I bent over the table without touching anything. "What's that?"

One of the technicians stirred a small pile of metal until it took the shape of a gold cross on a thin chain.

"A Latin cross," Gene said.

"It's Emilio's. I've seen it around his neck."

"Well, that ties this attempt on you into the kid's murder."

"I'd say the fact they were driving the murdered man's car pretty well established that. Let's see what the note says."

Printed in block letters with a lead pencil, the note was short and to the point.

You shoulda listened. Now what happened to the kid is on your back. You don't want the same, stop poking around. You cost the lawyer a bunch of money. Send $250,000 in small bills to the box number. No more stalling. We don't have the money by the end of the week, you're next. Or the queer lawyer is.

"Well," Gene noted, "it's not peanuts anymore. The stakes just went up."

"In more ways than one."

"No fingerprints," one of the techs said. "We'll have to take things to the lab to look for anything else."

Gene agreed, and after the two men packed up and left for downtown, we got Artie Hartshorn on the wire in Santa Fe.

"Dicky Dominguez ain't gonna be happy," Artie said after he heard us out. His voice sounded weary over my speakerphone.

"Dicky Dominguez?"

"Owner of the Porsche. If it's in Albuquerque, it's in little pieces by now."

"Who is he?" Gene asked.

"Local big shot. Richard Dominguez, executive vice president of the Cibola National Bank, a luncheon buddy of the governor and a golfing partner of the archbishop."

"How come he's not president of the bank?" Gene's voice held a touch of sarcasm.

"Because his papa hasn't retired yet."

"Artie," I said, "Emilio Prada had a contact in Santa Fe supposed to be a banker. Could this be the guy?"

"By contact, you mean…?"

"Yeah, a client. It was supposedly a recurring thing."

The line went silent for a moment. "Yeah. Could be, I guess. Dominguez is a pretty macho bastard, but you gotta wonder about a grown guy answering to Dicky. Maybe I oughta go ask his two former wives and the current Mrs. Dicky."

"So it's possible?"

"Yeah. Dicky likes to lord it over people, and I could see him dominating a pretty queer as easily as a pretty woman. Uh… sorry, BJ."

"That's okay. I'm not pretty. You think Dominguez will talk to me?"

"Dominguez will talk the arm off anybody. Whether he'll listen while *you* talk is anybody's guess."

"I'm more interested in this motorcycle club," Gene said. "We can't ignore the fact Dahlman represents the woman who's a potential witness against two gang members in a double homicide case."

"It's not them," Artie responded flatly.

"How do you know?"

"The Iron Cross is a small club. Half a dozen members and a couple of girlfriends. The two leaders of the gang are the ones accused of the Zellner murders, and they're in custody. When Prada was killed, three others were locked up for public fighting on the plaza."

"That leaves one member at large," Gene said.

"Yeah. Up in Colorado. He was spotted in Trinidad and told friends there he was headed to Denver. Denver cops just located him for us. It wasn't him that did Prada. He was on the road to Colorado by the time the hustler died."

"The girlfriends?" Gene again.

"There's only two of them—besides the Skelton girl, that is—and one was in jail for mixing up in the fight. The other one's under the watchful eye of her grandmother, who's as tough as any jail warden I know. Anyhow, they're all too young and inexperienced."

"Artie, you know the young ones—" I began.

"Yeah, yeah. Nothing's more dangerous than an American teenager. But trust me, it wasn't these guys."

"What was the fight on the plaza about?" Gene asked.

"Rival gang. These penny-ante cycle toughs handled the meth distribution from Española north to the Colorado border for the dealers they killed, but they were trying to muscle in on the drug trade in Santa Fe. That territory's already taken, so they ran into trouble."

"Who handles the territory?"

"Some of your locals. Those bastards calling themselves the Santos Morenos."

Gene and I exchanged looks.

"The Saints own Santa Fe?" I asked. "And they were up there Thursday night?"

"They were the other side of the dustup on the plaza that morning. Some of them were in our lockup. We're a nonpartisan police force. We arrest anyone who disturbs our peace."

Chapter 18

I TOOK the wheel of Del's Volvo so he could study my statement to the SFPD. Driving him to Santa Fe for his interview with Artie Hartshorn reminded me of the old days when we took weekend and holiday trips as often as we could. Those had been great times. He was carefree and inquisitive and a fantastic traveling companion back then, almost as fascinated by the local lore as I was. We checked out nearly every state and national monument in New Mexico, making up names and personalities for the people we imagined once lived and worked and played there. Del, in his idealism, imbued them all with noble qualities. My Marine and police experiences led me to color them in darker tones.

To keep from racing headlong down nostalgia lane, I reminded myself this was a different Del. He had lost that charming naïveté and his unbounded enthusiasm for discovering what lay just around the corner. Absorbed by the profession he had chosen, Del tackled his workdays seemingly unworried by blackmailers and threats of mayhem. Sadly he was also less curious about adventures yet to come.

Some people consider the hour's drive north to Santa Fe boring, but it never struck me that way. The countryside was crammed with history if a person took the time to look. Denver is not the only mile-high city in the Southwest. Albuquerque sprawls at the foot of the Sandia and Manzano Mountains at pretty much that altitude, and the road to Santa Fe climbs another fifteen hundred feet along its sixty-odd-mile stretch.

Del sighed heavily and dropped the papers he was holding into his lap. "After all that's happened, I can't believe these guys still expect me to pay their blackmail demand. Only now they want 250 grand. They must be crazy."

"They probably believe they're in a stronger position now that they've demonstrated a willingness to kill for what they want."

"Jesus, Vince, could those pictures of Emilio and me really have cost the guy his life?"

His rhetorical question did not require an answer. In the silence that followed, the hum of the motor seemed loud. Outside, dark sage and rabbitbrush lined the shoulders of the road with autumn flowers adding dashes of color: scarlet Indian paintbrush, pink and orange trumpet phlox, whitish Rocky Mountain pussytoes, blue and violet gilia—and, of course, the ubiquitous sunflower. If it were a little later in the year, I would be dodging windblown tumbleweeds scurrying across the highway.

Del's voice interrupted the comfortable, bucolic mood I'd slipped into. "Emilio wasn't all bad, you know."

"I know. Basically he was a good little street thug simply exploiting his looks to make a living."

"Like thousands of others around the world. We're lucky. We never had to scratch for our existence like that. Not that it was a bed of roses for me. My folks worked hard just to make a living, but we never went hungry or wondered where we'd lay our heads at night." Del sighed again. "I'm not going to pay the extortion demand. Damn the consequences."

"No, you're not, but you're going through the motions. You know, send an envelope stuffed with paper. If they're using the same post-office box, then they don't know we're onto their little mail-forwarding scheme. We'll catch them when they show up to collect the money."

"Do you still believe this is connected to the Zellner murders?"

"Someway, somehow. It's the only thing that makes sense. Luther Hickey seemed to be a likely suspect, but neither Charlie nor I have been able to tie him to the ransom demand."

"He pled out to assaulting you?"

"Yeah. I think going back to the pen was a relief for him."

"Weird."

"That describes him all right. By the way, do you know a Santa Fe banker named Dominguez?"

"Yeah. He's the principal stockholder in the Cibola National Bank. Herman Dominguez."

"That must be the father. How about the son? You know him?"

"Dicky? I've served on some committees with him. Charitable stuff, mostly."

"What's your take on him?"

"Complicated man. Confident, but mostly because his father owns the bank he works for and has more money than even Dicky can spend in one lifetime. Uncertain of himself in some situations, probably for the same reason—his old man. He knows he'll never be the banker Herman is, but he's a good public relations man. When the father goes, we'll see what kind of businessman he really is."

"He might have been a client of Emilio's. Did he ever make a move on you?"

"No, but it wouldn't surprise me if he tried. Dicky's a sexual predator. He has a reputation for chasing the ladies, but it wouldn't be hard to see him going the other way so long as he got his ego scratched. It's not a stretch to say he's into domination. And under the right circumstances, Emilio was willing to play that game." There was a catch in Del's voice. "He used to fantasize about getting you in bed with us. He was certain you were man enough to handle us both."

Not about to touch that one, I indulged in a sigh of my own. "Thanks for the rundown on Dominguez."

"You're not suggesting Dicky would be mixed up in this, are you? He sure doesn't need the money, and he'd be a fool to risk everything he has in a game like that."

"This has never been about the blackmail money, at least not until somebody murdered Emilio. Now the killers may need money to get out of town. This whole scheme was designed to gain some leverage over you. Somebody thought that if they demanded a paltry $5,000, it would be less trouble for you to pay than to put up a fight. They just couldn't figure how to get past the suspicion they'd come back for more."

"So why do they need leverage?"

"Possibly because someone wants to get to your client, Miranda Skelton."

"Hell, all I'm doing is making sure she doesn't get screwed over."

"Then somebody wants her screwed over."

Del thought for a moment. "So you no longer believe it's connected to Harding's fight with the union or with the Billingham takeover?"

"No, I don't. But we have to keep an open mind."

We fell silent again as the Volvo breezed past the San Felipe Pueblo lands and approached the Santo Domingo exits. Near the interstate, a tribal-owned service station sat on high ground boasting cheaper gas by virtue of the elimination of state fuel taxes. In the distance off to the west, the blue-hazed, pine-shrouded Jemez Mountains beckoned. Directly ahead, the towering Sangre de Cristos already sported a modest snowfield.

We completed the long climb up La Bajada, topped the rise, and saw Santa Fe sprawled before us. As usual the first thing that caught my eye was the old state penitentiary sitting ominously on the south side of the city. The place was closed now, but it was supposedly still haunted by the tortured souls of thirty-three inmates slaughtered in the unbelievably savage riot of 1980.

I'd seen pictures of some of the decapitations and torture while I was at APD, and I wished I hadn't. The brother of one of my friends was up there in Cellblock 4 where they housed the snitches and sex offenders and the vulnerable. That's where most of the murders and mutilations took place. I can still remember the family's terror until they knew he was safe.

Half a mile farther down the road, my sphincter puckered. "Tighten your seat belt. There's a car coming up behind us. Fast."

"You think it's them?"

"Dunno. But after last time, I'd rather be prepared than surprised."

"How do they know we're on the road? You think my phone's tapped?"

"Probably not, but have you noticed anyone following you lately?"

"N-no." His stammer let me know the thought had never occurred to him.

"Hang on, here they come."

The black silhouette on my tail veered suddenly to the left, and a big SUV blew by, leaving the Volvo shuddering in its vortex. I caught the distinctive license plate.

Del swiveled to scan the road behind us. "Where the hell is his State Police escort?"

New Mexico's governor-in-a-hurry disappeared down the road ahead of us.

"Probably back there somewhere trying to catch up."

The man was notorious for rushing from one function to another. Several citizens had complained publicly about his penchant for air-lane speeds on roadways. He'd promised to slow down—and probably had—but that still left mere mortals eating his dust.

ARTIE HARTSHORN didn't much like the idea of me sitting in on the interview, but finally agreed. He led Del through his association with Emilio Prada from beginning to end, and Del didn't flinch, answering each question head-on. After Artie had approached things from about three different angles, the detective sat back in his chair and relaxed.

"That's it. I appreciate your cooperation, Mr. Dahlman. I'll have to check out a couple of facts, but I believe you're in the clear."

"Thank you, Detective. May I ask a couple of questions now?"

"Answer what I can, but you understand it's an ongoing investigation."

"Clearly. Vince… uh, BJ is convinced this whole blackmail scheme is connected to the Zellner murders in some manner. Do you share that conviction?"

"I try to keep an open mind, Mr. Dahlman. At this point, I'm not married to any theory. But I can't honestly see how they're involved."

"I'm intrigued by the relationship of the Santos Morenos to the Zellners," I said. "The last couple of times I saw Emilio, he was with some of the Saints."

"Well, there you go," Artie said. "The Saints were archrivals of the Iron Cross bunch, and if Prada was a Saint, the Crosses might have taken him out."

"He wasn't a gang member, but he was on the fringe. Besides, you're talking out of the other side of your mouth. You claim the Crosses were out of business."

Artie flushed. "Okay, maybe the Saints caught him with the Crosses and took him out. You know, because of the rivalry. The Saints control the drug business from Albuquerque to Santa Fe, and the Iron Crosses were trying to slice out a piece of it. It wasn't in the Saints' interest to want the Zellners dead and out of business."

"What if they wanted to take over the manufacturing end of the trade?" I asked.

"Why? Making the stuff is physically dangerous, and it's the high-risk end of the business. Both of the Zellners had already taken a couple of falls. No, it doesn't make sense."

"How strong is the case against Whiznant and Rodrigo?" Del asked.

"Pretty decent, I'd say."

"You have the weapons?" I asked. Artie frowned, so I pressed him. "Any forensic evidence at all?"

"Some," the detective admitted slowly. "Enough so the district attorney figures he has a case."

Del shook his head. "He needs my client's testimony to make it stick."

"Puts the lid on the jar, I guess."

"So an attempt to intimidate me—her lawyer—could be the motive for the blackmail."

"Intimidate you into what? You can't make her disappear, make her lie. Nothing like that."

"No, but I could scare the hell out of her. Screw her down so tight she might not sound credible on the stand. I can probably terrify the woman so much she'd refuse to even take the stand."

"That merits a hard look at an Iron Cross-Santos connection," I argued.

"Shit, BJ, when the Prada kid was killed and somebody tried to run you off the road, the Iron Crosses were outa commission. When you got the last demand for payment, they were all behind bars or up in Colorado. I'm telling you it wasn't them."

"Well, who does that leave?"

"Nobody connected to the Crosses."

"Unless there's someone you don't know about," I suggested. "Like somebody who finances the whole deal. Underwrites the cost of manufacturing the meth and its distribution."

"You talking about a banker?" Artie's eyebrows climbed toward his receding hairline. "Damn, a *real* banker. You're talking about Dicky Dominguez."

"I don't know who it might be, but since you brought up his name, don't you think it's suspicious his car was involved in the attempt on me?"

"I checked, and he was in a loan committee meeting when that happened. His car got boosted off the street right in front of the bank."

I sat up straighter. "Off the street? You know any other bank executive who hunts up a parking spot on a street crowded with tourists?"

"Aw, you're grasping at straws. Dicky has an assigned spot in the bank's lot, but he was running late for his meeting and found a space on the street right in front of the bank. He told his secretary to move the car before the parking meter ran out. When she went to do it later, the Porsche was gone."

"I think he had a connection to Emilio Prada. Can't prove it. It's merely a suspicion. Emilio was connected to the Santos Morenos. If Dominguez was banking the Zellners or the Iron Crosses, that links them all together."

"You're reaching again," Artie objected. "I know you, and you know Mr. Dahlman. That links us together. Does that mean we're all confederates in a crime? What you're suggesting is that Dicky deliberately put himself on our radar screen by providing a car—an easily identifiable car—for those thugs to run you off the road. Ridiculous."

"It does seem a little over the top. But this thing was put together on a moment's notice, after someone saw me in a huddle with you. They needed a powerful car as backup for the Mustang, and Dominguez had one. He sounds arrogant enough to believe he could get away with it."

"Where were you parked that day?" Artie asked.

"In the La Fonda's garage."

"And the La Fonda's right across the square from the Cibola National," he noted. "You're right, BJ, it was a spur-of-the-moment plan. They spotted you, needed a second car, and there was that green Porsche staring them right in the face. So they took it. About sixty seconds is all they'd need. If you ever find that car in one piece, you'll see it was hot-wired."

Artie hand-brushed his thinning hair. "Look, BJ, this is dicey. Dicky carries a lot of clout in this town, not to mention the influence his father has. I gotta give this some thought."

I asked Del for his opinion.

"Dicky Dominguez needs drug money like he needs a hole in the head. But the danger of the thing might just turn him on."

"If Dominguez provided a connection for Emilio to the Iron Crosses, maybe the kid was trying to play both sides," I said. "The Santos might not have liked him helping the Crosses squirm out from under murder charges."

"You know for certain Prada was involved in the blackmail attempt?" Artie asked. With a sideways glance at Del, he added, "Aside from being one half of the couple starring in the photoshoot, that is?"

Del didn't even flinch as I answered the question. "The postal clerk identified Emilio as the man who rented the contact box. The latest blackmail demand instructed Del to mail the money to that same box number."

"So they haven't tumbled to the fact you're watching it. That doesn't sound very professional to me. Are we dealing with amateurs here?"

"Possibly. They've been pretty cagey so far, but this might be the break we need."

EVERY DOWNTOWN building in the City Different pretended to be an authentic colonial edifice reluctantly outfitted with electricity and modern plumbing. The Cibola National Bank was no exception. I pushed through the heavy double doors of the two-storied stucco building and walked into a lobby as determinedly Old World as the La Fonda Hotel's.

A white marbled floor with flowing brown streaks. Straight-backed couches and casual chairs carved in the old Spanish style and padded in rich gold and orange with an occasional green thrown in relieved the cold, business atmosphere of the place. The tellers' cages had the look of the thirties banks that John Dillinger used to rob, although the machines behind them were modern computers. Square, faux Doric columns embedded in the walls at regular intervals lent it a rich and powerful aura.

A pert, thoroughly modern receptionist with strawberry tresses seemed to be guarding the offices at the back of the building, so that was where I headed. She smiled brightly and chirped an offer of assistance.

"Mr. Dominguez, please. Uh, Mr. Richard Dominguez."

We sparred a few minutes over my identity and business, but eventually she ushered me into an office that would have done a territorial governor proud.

Roughly thirty by thirty feet square, the room was crammed with solid, heavy, age-darkened furniture upholstered in gold and scarlet and designed to impress, and it accomplished its goal admirably. A massive desk that looked to be pecan wood to me, carved with ornate curlicues, practically rendered Dominguez a dwarf. That desk and a matching sideboard the size of a small truck, both beautifully handcrafted, were probably the only true antiques in the whole place.

It was only when Dominguez rose from his chair that he revealed his true proportions. It wasn't his six-one height; it was his mass. The thick torso reminded me of Puerco's neck and shoulders, but whereas the gangster's were porcine, Dominguez's were bull-like. He was not fat; he appeared trim for a man of his girth. The flesh on the backs of his hands was golden and sprinkled with black hair, but his face was swarthy, made even more so by dark pouches beneath big, expressive eyes studying me with an intense curiosity.

"Mr. Vinson."

He toyed with my name as if it were familiar to him. This, I was immediately convinced, was Emilio's john in Santa Fe. The man was a hunter. Emilio would have looked like attractive prey to him. It would be difficult to figure out who took advantage of whom in that arrangement.

I clasped the outstretched hand in a silent match of strength and resolve. Then he gestured me to a seat with the huge desk conveniently between us.

"Dicky"—I deliberately used the diminutive—"I was sorry to hear your Porsche was stolen recently. It was equally distressing to find the car was involved in an attempt to run me off of La Bajada."

"That's where I heard your name. I'm glad you weren't injured in the accident. But I assure you I was right here—"

"Yes, I understand you were in a loan meeting at the time. But that's not why I stopped by to see you. I could bullshit for a few minutes and try to convince you I need some Santa Fe banking services, but that would merely waste time, and neither of us can afford that. So let me just come out with it."

I had his attention and was ready with my bluff. "I have some photographs I believe you would like to retrieve in exchange for some I need to recover."

The banker's immense brown eyes—which almost, but not quite, saved his face from being coarse—changed in a subtle way. Those eyes and their bruised lids had no doubt gained Dicky Dominguez admission to a number of bedrooms over the years.

"I don't take your meaning, Mr. Vinson."

"I mean Emilio Prada, Dicky. And please don't insult my intelligence by giving me the 'I don't know anyone by that name' routine."

"I *have* seen that name recently. That was the man killed in Fort Marcy Park, wasn't it?"

"Yes. And he was your sometime lover."

He bristled. "I assure you I don't know what you mean. If there's nothing else, as you say, I'm a busy man." The words were stern, but the outrage was missing.

"You're right, he was the man murdered at Zozobra's burning. Well, since you have no interest in the photographs I hold, perhaps they should be turned over to the police for their investigation into his death. Who was the officer in charge? Artie Hartshorn, wasn't it?"

His eyes did their flickering trick again. "I don't know how I can help you, Mr. Vinson." He shot his cuffs, flashing the heavy gold watch on his wrist in a practiced move. Doubtless it was a genuine Rolex. "But why would private photographs be of interest to the police?"

"It's the nature of the photos. They might open a new line of inquiry into the murder."

"Uh... you say you're attempting to recover a set of photographs, as well? Then I assume those snapshots might establish an equally convincing motive." Dominguez examined me closely for a reaction. He received none. "I also assume you represent an attorney in Albuquerque."

The fact I was not responding to him must have rattled Dicky at bit. "Gossip has been floating around," he said. "You know how this town is—one big rumor mill. I assure you there are no such photos of me."

"Very well. Then I guess that's the way we'll leave it."

"So long as we are clear on one point. Any photographs remain private. Is it agreed?"

Did he know he had just undermined his forceful declaration of a moment ago? "Not at all. You are free to do as you see fit. As am I."

Dominguez sucked wind. He'd realized his blunder. "Come on now, be reasonable."

"Are you saying you have photos to trade?"

"No, I am not. I'm merely curious about the ones you claim to be holding."

I considered my options and made a decision. "Mr. Dominguez, I think we've reached an understanding. You play your cards close to the vest, and so will I." I stood to take my leave. "I see no profit in revealing any embarrassing pictures—for either of us."

I felt the pressure of his gaze all the way down the long marble corridor and out the great double doors. Although there was nothing overtly menacing in Dicky Dominguez's demeanor, I was relieved to be out in the open air.

What had I accomplished? He had admitted nothing overtly, other than he was aware of the photos of Del. But that knowledge convinced me Dominguez and Emilio had shared a history. The significance of their relationship remained unclear. Even so, I felt compelled to swing by the police station and share the interview with Artie Hartshorn.

Then, because I'd sent Del to Albuquerque in the Volvo, all I had to do was find a ride home. After renting yet another automobile, I eventually arrived back in my office to find an urgent message to call my client. I chose to go see him instead.

Chapter 19

A SVELTE young woman of about thirty led me through a rabbit's warren of hallways at Stone, Hedges, Martinez to one of the grandest conference rooms in the Southwest. Trimmed in basic mahogany with a massive teak table and leather chairs—Moroccan, I assumed—the room was already sumptuous, but gold-encrusted ashtrays, cut crystal decanters heavy with lead, and excellent original oil paintings on the walls raised it to another level. No Western art for the Stone firm—except for one Georgia O'Keeffe, which oddly enough fit in rather well with the five European impressionists adorning the walls. The six-foot portrait of Gerald Randolph Stone, the dour founder of the firm, painted in blacks and browns and mottled flesh tones was the only jarring note.

The fact my green-eyed escort was the formidable roadblock I'd run into every time I called Del escaped me until he introduced us. Collette Brittain was worlds away from my unflattering mental image. She packed more into a five-four frame than many women far more statuesque. I liked her heart-shaped face framed by honey-brown hair worn in a short bob.

Del, who was preparing the room for a meeting, brushed aside Ms. Brittain's offer of refreshment and got right down to business. He was steamed. "I think you're wrong. The extortion attempt doesn't have anything to do with Miranda Skelton and the Zellner murders."

"Enlighten me." I glanced out of the large windows toward the Sandias. It was an illusion, but we seemed to be on a level with the TV towers on the peak. It was a spectacular view.

"When I got back from Santa Fe this morning, I had a visitor. Horace Billingham Jr. waited forty minutes in the receptionist's area for me. Have you ever known Billingham to wait forty minutes on anyone? Not even five minutes."

I shook my head. "What did he want?"

"First a little background. After you clued me that the Vestmark takeover of High Desert was going to fail, my clients decided to play hardball. Joseph Billingham had legally executed certain documents as president of High Desert Investment Bankers, which encouraged Vestmark to incur expenses in the logical, reasonable expectation the acquisition would take place. They were none too happy when word came down it wasn't going to happen."

"So? Acquisitions are subject to stockholder approval, aren't they?"

"Yes, but who are the stockholders? The Billinghams hold 80 percent of the common stock. I've been very careful with this thing, Vince." Del rose and paced the room.

The plush blue pile of the carpet rendered his footsteps silent, but his vigorous passing ruffled one of the packets meticulously laid in double rows down the long conference table. The flutter aroused my curiosity about the subject of such a power meeting.

Del continued. "I made sure Joseph Billingham had the authority to proceed with negotiations. Joe even showed me proxies representing a majority of the shares. So when you told me of your conversation with Horace Jr., I alerted the acquisition team from Vestmark. Even with this warning, they were shocked when Joe turned down their offer. Couldn't believe they'd been had like that."

Del sat down opposite me. His bulky gold cuff links left marks on one of the fancy blue Stone, Hedges folders holding the upcoming agenda. "On their instructions I sent notification of intent to sue for breach of contract, not only to recover costs but also for damages. Apparently the two Horaces aren't taking it well. Junior wouldn't come to see me without specific instructions from the old man."

"Okay, that's the background. Now what did Whorey say?"

"Made a threat. A bald-faced threat." Del turned red. "Claimed everyone in the countryside would know the kind of man I was." He lifted his hand to forestall my interruption. "When I asked what that meant, he weaseled."

"Nuts, Del. He'd probably been weaseling from the time he set foot in the office. You can't read anything into that comment."

"That wasn't all. He said 'a certain pansy lawyer' needed to be taken down a notch or two, and the Billinghams were just the ones to do it."

"Those were the old man's words. Whorey might be a throwback to the Neanderthals, but even he knows the political and social climates have changed with respect to homosexuality."

"You're right, it was Horace Sr.'s message delivered by Horace Jr. But think about it. The man admitted he was using photographs to pressure his brother. Sex pictures, if I understand the thing right. Doesn't it stand to reason he'd use the same thing on me?"

"Sure it does… if he had any. But I can't tie him or any other Billingham to Emilio, and I looked. I take my job seriously. Besides, even old man Billingham would draw the line at murder."

"There are a few things in his background that might make you think twice about that. He's ruined more than one former partner. Trampled them underfoot on his way to the top. Maybe he hired the Santos Morenos and things got out of hand."

I grimaced. "Well, at least you buy into my theory it's the Saints doing the dirty work."

"Makes sense. Horace Jr. has plenty of contacts in the valley. They tell me he used to spend half his time down there chasing women. Maybe he didn't intend for the killing to take place, but the Saints do things their way, not his."

"There are a couple of holes in that theory. Hire the Saints to do what? The timing's not right."

But maybe that wasn't true. Whorey was shrewd enough to look for dirt on his opponents as insurance in case hijacking his brother's vote didn't work. Perhaps Whorey had gone to his friends from the old days for help. We used to joke he would make a better gangster than business executive.

"Even if you're right about the Saints going too far, old man Billingham's smart enough to know when things are starting to go south. He'd draw in his horns, let the acquisition go through, and count his money."

"The old man, maybe, but I'm not so sure about Junior. He's not the brightest bulb in the family chandelier. At least go see him and tell me what you think."

WHOREY READILY agreed to a meeting even though it was after normal business hours. He came downstairs to admit me to the Billingham Building.

"Thought I might be hearing from you," he said on the elevator up to his floor. "You represent Dahlman, don't you? That's why you were nosing around the other day."

"Yes, but not for the reason you think. I have no interest in whether or not Vestmark acquires High Desert."

"Maybe not, but your boss does. He's Vestmark's lead counsel."

"That's true. And it's also true I reported our conversation to my client last time."

He opened the door and allowed me to precede him into his office. The painting of his father put me in mind of Stone dominating the Blah's conference room. Had both of those old pirates used the same artist?

"Appreciate you being so up-front, but you always were an up-front guy. I have to tell you, I admire you, BJ."

"And why is that?"

"You might be homo, or gay, I guess they call you fellows now, but you never flaunted it in anybody's face. Pretty good record for a gay: football, Marines—and an MP officer to boot—Albuquerque Police Department. That's about as macho as things get around here. Well, except maybe—"

I headed him off at the pass. "Except for leaving a string of satisfied women in my trail."

Whorey laughed aloud. "Yeah, that. I won't even ask about a string of satisfied guys."

"Good. Then we can get down to business. Del Dahlman doesn't take threats very well."

His thick eyebrows climbed. "Who threatened him?"

"'A certain pansy lawyer needs to be taken down a notch, and the Billinghams are just the ones to do it'? Sounds like a threat to me."

"Naw." He played with a yellow-gold signet ring on the little finger of his right hand. "That's more in the line of a promise."

"Come on, everybody knows Del's gay. He's never made a secret of it."

"Knowing it and seeing it is two different things."

"Are you threatening to blackmail my client with photographs?"

He snorted. "Of course not. We're just talking here. Look, I'm no dummy, BJ. I know about all I can do is crimp his style a little."

"The threat implies more. Like, for instance, you have something to show the world. Since it was photographs that did your brother in, I assume that's the basis of your promise."

Whorey made a face, the result of trying to grimace and grin simultaneously. "Been rumors floating around about some pictures of Del. Figured that's what you were sniffing out when you came to see me the first time." He paused and sighed. "That's what I asked for, you know. I told that Phoenix PI to get me some compromising photographs of Del. He got some, but they don't amount to diddlysquat. A couple of shots of Del in a gay bar. Big deal. Besides, this was all the old man's idea. He thinks fairies still slink around in public restrooms afraid to show their faces to decent folks."

"I'd like to see your investigator's report, at least the portion on Del."

He pinched his lips together and wrinkled his forehead—Whorey's attempt at deep thought. "Don't see why not. Not much there."

He rummaged around in his oversized desk and came up with a few files. He sorted through them and tossed the one labeled with Del's name over to me.

The letterhead read *Hartz Investigations* with an address on Van Buren in Phoenix. Hartz appeared to have come up with nothing except some photos of Del at one of the city's gay bars with his hand on a companion's arm. The guy was obviously not a minor, and the touch wasn't lascivious. Neither it, nor the one of Del dancing with the same man, rose to the level of good extortion material.

"Tell me, Whorey, do you still see your compadres in the valley?" I handed the file back across the desk.

"Not in five years." Then, Whorey being Whorey, he confessed. "You know, when you try to screw one of their sisters, those guys turn sorta clannish. For a couple of years, it was worth my hide to venture down there. Not so bad anymore, but nobody's too pleased when I drop south of Barelas Road."

I used that opportunity to do some reminiscing about the old school days, lingering long beyond his capacity to keep secrets. It was dark outside when I got up to go.

"Now you answer a question for me," he said as we walked to the building's locked double doors. "What's this really about? You were after something the first time you came in here, and you're still looking for it. I was on the mark, wasn't I? It's those pictures of Del, right?" Billingham halted in his tracks. "Son of a bitch! It *is* pictures of Dahlman. How bad are they? They might be worth a little money to some folks."

Intuition told me the Billinghams, rats though they were, were not at the bottom of this extortion attempt. "Don't know what you're talking about. Thanks for the info, Whorey."

Chapter 20

THE NEXT morning, I gazed forlornly at a framed photograph of Paul on my desk at home as I phoned a former APD officer who was now on the Phoenix police force. He had run across Hartz a couple of times, and although the record showed no complaints filed against the PI, he agreed to ask around the department for me.

That done, I dressed and drove to a Chevrolet dealership on Lomas Boulevard NE. I'm a creature of habit. My first car had been a Chevy Impala, as had my last. Unless the new models had a serious defect, my next one would be as well. With the insurance company check for my wrecked car in my pocket, I parked the rental Ford and went inside. Fred, the friend who had sold me the last two cars, was no longer with the agency, so I dealt with a stranger. That might be a good thing. Fred and I had known each other's tricks so well there wasn't much to our negotiations. So instead of being disappointed, I considered dealing with a new salesman an opportunity.

I walked straight to a silver Impala with gray trim. A man, who had introduced himself as George Uttley, trailed along in my wake. "I want this one."

He took another look at the business card I'd handed him when we introduced ourselves. "No you don't. Come with me."

I followed him to the back lot where he stopped before a white, four-door clone of my wrecked Impala—except, of course, the new 2007s had undergone a major redesign.

"I see you're a PI, so this is the baby you need. This Impala SS is powered by a new 303 horsepower, 5.3 liter V-8 engine, but it's got what we call Active Fuel Management technology. That regulates between an eight-cylinder and a four-cylinder operation for improved fuel economy. She's got the power when you need it and has pretty efficient gas consumption when you don't."

Uttley might prove a worthy opponent after all. He'd zeroed in on my needs with one look at my card. Point for him.

"The '07s have a tire-pressure monitor, a new 7.0 Generation OnStar system offering Turn-by-Turn navigation, sixteen-inch, five-spoke cast aluminum wheels, XM Satellite Radio, and leather-trimmed seats as standard equipment."

I needed to take him down a notch or two. "I don't need a sales pitch. I'm going to buy a car. An Impala, in fact. Driven them for years, and I'm comfortable with them. It all boils down to the deal, Mr. Uttley."

"Is there a trade-in?"

"Only in the form of an insurance check. Some joker totaled my car."

"Are you financing with us, or do you bring your own?"

"My options are open."

"So you want us to place the financing for you?"

"Possibly." I glanced at the sticker, took in the optional equipment—this one was loaded—and started the dance. "I'd guess this was a custom order that fell through."

Aha! He had a tell. A wrinkle appeared between his eyebrows as he suppressed a frown.

"Whatever the reason, it's available. And it won't stay around for long. Not a beauty like this."

I took in the total at the bottom of the invoice and named a figure.

"But that's below our costs," he objected.

"It's got some luxuries I don't need. I'm willing to pay for them, but only at a discount. As far as the invoice price, you'll more than recoup what I'm offering with your year-end bonus package from the manufacturer. Take it or leave it."

"I'll have to consult with my manager."

"Why don't we both talk to him?"

We talked our way through the sales manager and into the presence of the finance guru, who wasn't too happy when I handed over the endorsed insurance payment and hauled out my checkbook. He had been looking forward to making up some of what I'd managed to shave off the deal by adding a point to the interest rate, which would come back to the dealership. Wasn't going to happen.

After they promised delivery later in the day, I drove to Advanced Car Rentals and turned in my Ford. They gave me a ride back to my office, but instead of going inside, I headed straight up Fifth to APD headquarters. On the corner of Marquette, I gave a mental nod to the larger-than-life sculpture of a Pueblo couple with their child in a cradleboard.

A couple of gang squad members agreed to look for a connection between the Santos Morenos and the Phoenix PI, Hartz. They also gave me the goods on Whorey without having to consult the records. One of the sergeants in the squad confirmed Whorey's tale about getting crossways with his old cronies in the valley by putting the moves on a girl—who turned out to be Zancón's sister—but gave the tale a different ending. The exchange of some Billingham money apparently put Whorey back in the good graces of his former friends.

My confidence in the Zellner connection slightly shaken, I went upstairs in search of Gene Enriquez. Since instructions for delivery of the extortion money had not been altered, we decided it was time to mail the "payoff."

In case someone had a sample of his handwriting, we called on Del to hand-address an envelope stuffed with paper cut to the size of US currency. We also insisted he personally drop the envelope at a mailbox near his office. There was no evidence of surveillance, but why take chances?

The package would arrive at the Ship-n-Mail on Juan Tabo tomorrow morning. I set up casual surveillance at that location even though we knew the package would simply be remailed to the main post office.

There would be another delay until the envelope showed up back at the North Broadway PO, probably sometime on Monday. Then, of course, we had to wait for someone to pick up the envelope. Gene wasn't satisfied with my arrangements and made certain both boxes would be under close scrutiny 24-7.

Agreeing on our next move sparked a minor dispute. Artie Hartshorn, principally concerned with solving a murder on his home turf, wanted the recipient, whoever it turned out to be, immediately arrested and interrogated. Assuming he would be a gofer and not a principal, Gene and I favored putting a tail on the individual. That ran the risk he might open the envelope and discover the scam. To discourage this, we'd sealed the envelope with liberal amounts of packing tape, the kind that's damned near impossible to open without a blowtorch.

SATURDAY AFTERNOON, while Charlie Weeks loafed around keeping an eye on the Ship-n-Mail, I set up a stakeout of my own.

Paul lived in a Pueblo-Spanish, territorial-style dorm named after one of the Spanish conquistadores. Earth-brown and thick-walled, it housed the body but did little for the soul, or so he had often complained. The only public parking, near the sports field, wasn't an ideal spot for surveillance, but it was the closest I could get. Dragging out my binoculars, I settled down to wait as patiently as if he were a client's target. An hour into my watch, he emerged with another young man and headed for the student parking lot. Unwilling to confront him in front of a friend, I dithered over the ethics of following him. I was an investigator, not a stalker.

Nonetheless, that's exactly what I'd become. I was oddly relieved when the pair stopped by a neighboring dorm and ushered two young ladies into Paul's dilapidated old Plymouth before exiting the UNM campus—with me in tow. They headed east up Central Avenue.

So Paul's interest in a woman was okay with me, while an obvious attachment to another male would have been difficult to handle. He'd told me more than once that he only dated women when he wanted to go dancing. And he loved to dance.

Then I recalled double-dating with a buddy in my college days as an excuse to share in my friend's pursuit of sexual excitement, however peripherally. Another unwelcome thought followed. Had it been Paul at Fort Marcy Park with someone who looked like Emilio the night of the stabbing?

I shook my head to dislodge such ideas and eased up on the gas. Even though I wasn't worried about Paul recognizing my new Impala, there was no need to ride the Plymouth's tail. The four were decked out in denim, so they were headed for the C&W Palace.

A couple of miles up the road, I turned into the big parking lot. Paul's old jalopy was easy to spot among the shiny late-model pickups, SUVs, and sedans. Although there was a vacant space next to the Plymouth at the rear of the lot, I chose to park half a block away. The air smelled of ozone as I exited my rental and strode toward the entrance to the big barn. We'd likely get a shower tonight, but it probably wouldn't amount to much. The monsoon season had passed, and it was far too early for spring showers. We'd have snow before those showed up.

I paid the cover charge, grabbed a scotch neat, and took a table for two near the dance floor to get an idea of what was happening. Although it was early, the place was already half-full. A rattle of drums heralded a new musical number, and the guitars swung into the beat of Patsy Cline's old classic "Crazy." Despite my penchant for classical music, that is one country lament I'd always liked. Nobody can do it like Patsy, although these guys made a better-than-average effort. For a few moments, the music distracted me. The sight of Paul slow-dancing with one of the coeds brought me back. If she were merely a diversion, he was a hell of a lot better at acting than I had ever been.

Watching Paul on the dance floor would have been more enjoyable if not for the leaden feeling in my gut. He had been enthusiastically and unequivocally mine, at least until he left for Medill, but I'd let Del Dahlman screw that up for me too. No, that wasn't fair. My results-driven sense of the job got in the way of our relationship. It had nothing to do with Del. The client could just as well have been Sherry DeVine or anybody else. The responsibility was mine. Mine alone.

The realization did nothing to ease my mind. I kicked back the chair, got up, and stalked to the far side of the cavernous joint where the Santos occupied their usual table. I was looking for a good fight—a knock-down, drag-out, bruising slugfest, something I hadn't indulged in since my Corps days, except for the brief one I'd had with Hickey. But was I crazy enough to provoke a fight with this bunch?

A delayed sense of reality caused me to back away. Too late. Puerco glanced up and met my gaze. His eyes glowered even as his lips curled into a thin smile.

"Lookee who's here. Milio ain't here, man. Hell, he ain't nowhere. Case you ain't heard, he got his ass killed."

"Yeah, I heard." The acknowledgment sounded civil to my ears. Hopefully it did to his, as well. "Have they caught whoever did it?"

"You tell me. You the ex-cop with friends in the pig shop. What they tell you about it?"

"Just that he got stabbed up in Santa Fe."

"S'what I heard. Too bad. He wasn't a bad dude—for a queer."

"You know, I wondered about that."

"About what?"

"Why you let him hang around. You know, him being queer and all."

"Ain't you heard? It's against the law to discriminate. Long's they behave around me, anybody's welcome." He gave a short laugh. "Even ex-cops."

Zancón spoke up from across the table. "Even *queer* ex-cops."

Puerco's head whipped around. "No call for talk like that."

The chastened hood actually hung his head, staring at the table for a long moment before snatching up his glass and taking a long swig.

Puerco turned genial. "Sit down and have a beer. On me."

"Had two scotches already, and that's my limit."

"You 'n' Milio get things settled before somebody took him out?"

The question was innocent enough, but there was an edge to Puerco's voice. I shook my head. "No. Didn't manage to straighten it out."

Jackie Costas, the Haitian thug, horned in. "What was it, a date?"

"Business," I answered shortly.

"Hell, with Milio, a date *was* business."

"Maybe, but it wasn't my kind of business."

"What was your business?" Puerco asked. "Maybe we can help."

"Don't think so. It was something that happened a long time ago. But thanks for offering."

With a casual wave, I turned to walk away—and ran squarely into Paul Barton, who was carrying two cocktail glasses full to the brim with a pale liquid. He recoiled, almost spilling the drinks. I wanted desperately to acknowledge him, but was unwilling to single him out for the Saints. So I muttered an apology and stepped around him.

Outside in the parking lot, I realized I was leaving without accomplishing my mission of having a private word with Paul. To apologize. To grovel, if it would do any good. I wondered if he'd been headed to Puerco's table. No, he was carrying the wrong kind of drinks for that collection of misfits. He'd been going back to his college friends.

LATER THAT night, as I threw off the covers and sat on the side of the mattress, my resolve failed. I picked up my cell and dialed. The phone rang for a long time before a distant voice answered.

"Hi, Paul." The lump in my throat made me feel like some lovesick teenager. "It's Vince. Just wanted to apologize for not speaking to you earlier, but there were some bad dudes at my back, and I didn't want to single you out to them." Silence. "Anyway, felt I owed you an apology. Another one."

"It's okay. I see those hoods there all the time. Known some of them all my life. Surprised you were talking to them."

"Case I'm on." I regretted the words the moment they came out of my mouth. "It makes me do things I don't want to do sometimes."

"Yeah. I noticed."

I grabbed something out of the air—anything to keep him on the line. "You made an early night of it. It's not even midnight."

"Is there anything else?" The voice was as cold now as when we last spoke.

"Just that I'd give anything to undo what I did. I'm sorry I bothered you, Paul. Good night."

I wasn't certain which of us hung up the quickest.

Chapter 21

THE TELEPHONE woke me early the next morning. I fumbled for the receiver, coming wide-awake at the sound of the voice in my ear.

"Vince, it's me, Paul. Sorry to call so early, but I'm due out on the tennis court in a few minutes. That's why I was back at the dorm so early when you called last night. Anyway, I wanted to get this out of the way."

"It's okay." I sat up in bed and ran a hand through my hair. "Get what out of the way?"

"I guess it's my turn to apologize. I'm sorry about the way I've treated you, but I was hurt and had trouble letting it go. I know you were just doing your job. You don't know that much about me, so I can see you have to be careful and cover all the bases. In fact, I ought to tell you something. I'm—"

"Stop right there, Paul. I know everything I need to know about you. I knew in my heart you couldn't be involved in the case I was working on, but I let Sturgis get under my skin and said some things I shouldn't have. That doesn't normally happen, but then someone I care for deeply isn't usually mixed up in my business either." I shut up, hoping I hadn't said too much.

"I understand."

"No, you don't. But you're going to prove my point by forgiving me, aren't you?"

"What point?"

"That I know all I need to know about you. You're a decent man and a fine human being. That's what counts."

A subdued laugh came across the line. "Most of the world considers me a pervert and a pedophile in the making."

"Most of the world are insensitive clods without a clue. But I'm right, aren't I?"

"About the world?"

"About you."

Silence. "Yeah, I guess I can let it go. Sturgis was an ass about it for a while, but he's more or less back to normal, and I still have the scholarship. No harm done, right?"

"Just to some egos. I am sorry, Paul. Sorry for hurting you, and... and sorry for depriving us of what we had."

"There was something there, wasn't there?"

My throat tightened at his use of the past tense. "Yeah. Was, and is. At least on my part."

He didn't respond immediately. Finally I heard a breath expelled. "Mine too. You're an exciting man, BJ."

BJ, not Vince. Despite the conciliatory words, he was holding back. "Can I buy you breakfast?" I asked.

"I don't think so. I'm not sure we should get together again. That wasn't why I called. I just wanted to clear the air."

"I understand." But I didn't. I didn't understand at all. "When you're ready, I'm here. Go whip some ass on the tennis court."

ON MONDAY the office seemed a bleak place before Hazel arrived. The ransom envelope stuffed with trimmed newspaper had been mailed on schedule but could not possibly be picked up before late morning, at least according to Gene. Nonetheless, I was revved up and ready to go. Being here at the office was better than moping around the house, endlessly mulling over my conversation with Paul. That was the theory at any rate. But my mind refused to focus on the printed words in the case folder of a teenaged girl missing from her St. Louis home and rumored to be in Albuquerque. A Marine buddy had referred her parents to me. It was another one Charlie would have to work.

Hazel showed up, and after a few minutes in the outer office, she invaded my space to deliver a cup of fresh-brewed coffee and a transcribed phone report on Ira Hartz. According to my Phoenix PD contact, the PI was legit.

By eleven my patience had run out. I called Gene. He had heard nothing but agreed to contact his man at the post office. Another frustrating hour elapsed before I heard back from him.

"Got a problem."

A great opening line. "What is it?"

"The envelope never made it to the Broadway post office."

"What?" I bolted out of the chair. "How can that be? I thought we had all the bases covered."

"Dunno. To be precise, I don't know that it didn't reach the PO. All I know for sure is it wasn't delivered to the proper box."

"Could they have screwed up and shoved it in the wrong place?"

"Kyle Hewitt claims nothing at all has been delivered." Hewitt was the inspector the local postmaster appointed to work with the police on the case. "I'm headed up there right now. I'll call when we know something."

"I'll come with you."

"Sorry. Official folks only."

"This could be bad. If that envelope was delivered, the blackmailers know they've been scammed."

"And there are already death threats on the table. So stick close to the office and home until you hear from me."

Gene didn't wait for me to protest; he simply hung up the phone, forestalling my outburst. The first thing to do was alert Del to a possible disaster. He'd done his job well with Collette Brittain; my call breezed straight through to his office. He didn't take the news any better than I had.

After a little cussing, he started rationalizing. "Maybe they just misplaced it. I understand that happens a lot. You know, temporarily lost. They'll find it and put it in the right box."

"Maybe, Del. But we have to be prepared for a major snafu. If that envelope got delivered, they know we're onto their game. They've killed once. Why would they hesitate to kill again?"

"But I'm no good to them dead."

"Think about that. If they want to frighten the Skelton woman, you being dead would do just fine."

"The court would simply appoint someone else. No, if—and I say if—this involves the Zellner murders, somebody wants to compromise my witness. Killing me won't accomplish that. And if you're wrong and it's the Billinghams, they have nothing to gain by killing me. By the way, did you see Horace Jr.?"

I filled him in on my conversation with Whorey. "If the Billinghams are behind this, they've lost control of the thing. It wasn't a Billingham who put a knife between Emilio's ribs."

"How about that Phoenix PI? Is he capable of it?"

"He checks out clean. Been in business ever since he retired from the Maricopa County Sheriff's Office about five years ago. We can probably strike him off the list. But whoever did the actual dirty work now has a problem. He's got to clean things up. And since they've threatened me and actually tried to kill me once, it stands to reason I'm to serve as your horrible example."

"Why would they think killing you would intimidate me?"

"Well, in the first place, I'm working for you. That would make my murder a direct threat to you. And because of Emilio, we have to assume they know our history."

"If that's the case, they know there's nothing between us now."

"Think like a thug, Del. All queers are miserable weaklings who panic at the first sign of danger."

"So one or the other of us might die because of a stereotype, huh?"

"Wouldn't be the first time."

"Vince, maybe a long vacation would be a good idea."

"Forget it. The resolution to our problem lies in solving this thing, not in running away from it."

"If you really believe somebody's trying to force me to give them a leg up in the Zellner murders, there is only a limited window. Once Miranda takes the stand, they've lost the game."

"If they can't frighten you by getting to me, that leaves you hanging in the wind. They'll wait until the eve of the trial and then kill your ass. That would certainly bring the proceedings to a halt—at least temporarily. And if they can't intimidate you physically, they'll carry out the threat to go public with the photographs before going to the trouble of killing you."

Del uttered some of his four-letter legal terms.

Gene phoned on the heels of my conversation with Del. He sounded frustrated. "I don't know what went wrong, BJ. They've gone through whatever process they have to look for lost mail and didn't locate the envelope. I don't know how the fuckers did it, but we've been flummoxed. I've had a man up here since early morning, and he's kept an eagle eye on box 1525. Claims nobody approached it."

"Cameras?"

"Yeah, and they bear him out."

"Could the envelope have reached the box late Saturday and been picked up on Sunday?"

"Shift supervisor says no."

"So that means somebody at the PO intercepted it."

"Shift supervisor says no," Gene repeated. "But that must be what happened. The problem is, that's a federal offense, so the postal authorities and possibly the FBI will be the ones to investigate it. We'll be out in the cold. They'll let us look over their shoulder, but that's about all."

"Gene, are you free to meet me right now?"

"Yeah, sure. Where?"

"The Ship-n-Mail Store at 3301 Juan Tabo. And bring your big shiny badge."

"Thirty minutes."

It took me one of the thirty to root through my notes and find the name of the kid who clerked at the Ship-n-Mail—William Mackson. Then I hit the road.

WHEN WE entered the store, the face behind the counter was unfamiliar. But the dumpy girl in pigtails was just as pimply and precisely as helpful as her predecessor. She answered questions about Mackson with an eloquent shrug.

"Don't know him."

"How long have you been working here, Miss?" Gene asked.

"All day." She read our faces and added. "But I worked at another Ship store, so I know the routine."

"We need to speak to the manager."

"That's me." She began to sound worried.

My partner grimaced. "Then I need the manager's manager."

"Oh, you mean the owners. They're not here right now."

Gene's hand on the counter twitched. "I can see that. I need them. *Now*. Do you understand me?"

"Y-yes, sir." The teen's eyes resembled Ping-Pong balls. "They're at the store down by the university."

By the time Larry Abbott, one half of the husband-wife team who owned three local Ship-n-Mails including this one, arrived, Gene had Kyle Hewitt, the postal inspector, standing at his side.

Abbott, a small man with a penetrating gaze, was in a belligerent mood. "What's this all about?"

Hewitt blinked at him. "We need some information on a former employee named William Mackson."

"You could have asked me that on the telephone. You didn't need to haul me all the way up here."

"Yeah," Gene said, "and we can still have this conversation down at the station house."

"I don't think you understand the gravity of the situation," Hewitt said. "An important piece of mail has gone missing. Disappeared right out of your store."

"Now tell us about Mackson. Why was he let go?" Gene asked.

Abbott cleaned up his attitude. "He wasn't. Uh, I mean he wasn't fired. He put me on notice a couple of weeks ago that he was quitting."

"So he wasn't working here Saturday?"

"Well, yes, he was. But he called me after closing Saturday and said he couldn't come back. Left me in the lurch for the Monday shift."

"He say why he quit?" I asked.

Abbott looked as if he was trying to remember who I was. "He said he wanted to go out for the debate team or the chess team. One of those teams at his school."

"You have any problem with him? As an employee, I mean?" Gene asked.

"No, not really. He did his work but wasn't too good with customers. He'll never be a salesman."

Apparently that was a mark of failure to Abbott.

Gene, Hewitt, and I left the store to huddle in the parking lot to discuss the possibility the envelope had disappeared out of the back door of the store.

"Could be," Hewitt admitted. He stood a couple of inches shorter than I do and weighed thirty or so pounds more. "And it might have been a postal clerk who took it."

"So we don't know any more than before," Gene said. "Anything develop down at the main office?"

Hewitt shook his head.

"Look"—I thumped my fist into my palm—"we need to talk to the Mackson kid. I made such a deal out of trying to find out the name of the box holder, he's bound to remember every piece of mail addressed to it."

Gene glanced at the list of past and present employees the Ship-n-Mail owner had provided. "Mackson goes to Eldorado High. I don't want to drag him outa class, so let's give him time to get home."

"We need to see what he knows right now," I said. "We can't afford to wait. We've got to run that envelope down before it's delivered."

"Face it, BJ. It's already in the hands of the blackmailers."

Despite that gloomy assessment, Gene called the Eldorado principal and asked to have Mackson detained after class. Since his nondescript sedan fairly screamed "police undercover vehicle," we probably looked like a swat team trying to travel incognito as we pulled into the sprawling parking lot, but we didn't even rate a glance. These kids were so blasé, nothing short of drawing blued steel would impress them.

"Cripes, look at these cars," Gene groused. He waved a hand at row upon row of gleaming vehicles as we strode toward the administration building. "How can high school students afford Caddys and Jags and Lexuses?"

"Mommy and daddy," I answered.

He smacked his lips in disgust. "Yeah. Like somebody else I know."

Properly chastened, I shut up. I couldn't help it if my folks left me a bundle. Besides, I drove a Chevy.

The Eldorado campus was a sprawling affair of modern buildings with lots of brown brick and gray concrete, with a fierce-looking eagle, their mascot, prominently displayed. Billy Mackson sat in a vacant classroom off the principal's office, looking just as frail as the last time I'd seen him and a great deal more frightened. As we walked in the door, he leveled an accusing glare. The kid clearly blamed me for mixing him up in this business.

The school principal sat in on our session, but since Mackson was eighteen, there was no need to call in his parents. I kicked off the questioning.

"You remember me, William?"

"Yeah." After a quick glance at the principal, he straightened in his chair and changed his answer. "Yes, sir. You're that private investigator who tried to trick me into telling you who rented a box at the Ship-n-Mail where I worked." He smirked at the payback.

"That's right. You remember the box number?"

He frowned, but came up with the answer. "Uh… 2223."

"Right. Remember what you told me?"

"Yeah, that I couldn't tell—"

"We're way past that, Billy. You told me there were instructions to remail the envelope to box 1525 at the main post office."

"Did not. Well, I told you it was supposed to be rerouted, but I didn't give you the new box number or say where it was located."

"That's right, you didn't. But now that we know you recall things so clearly, Mr. Hewitt has some questions for you. He's a postal inspector."

"Uh… okay. I mean, sure."

"Was there a delivery to that box on Saturday?"

The kid shrugged. "I guess."

"You're sure or you guess?" Hewitt's voice grew sharper, his bulk more menacing.

"Yes, sir. A big, thick envelope."

"What did you do with it?"

Mackson's hand went to an angry red blemish on his cheek, but he caught himself and dropped his arm to the table. "Checked the instructions on the box, wrote the reroute information on the envelope, and put it in the bin for the truck to pick up and take it back to the post office."

"Did you see it picked up?"

"Saw the bin picked up, but I didn't see the envelope again after I put it there."

"Who was the carrier who made the run at the store?"

"The regular guy. You know, the one who usually brings us our mail. Matt's the only name I know him by."

The more questions Hewitt asked, the stiffer Mackson's spine became. That was normal; the kid was beginning to understand something serious was going on.

We left the rattled teenager to the tender mercies of his principal and reconvened outside. The kid's recollection of the mailman jibed with what Hewitt already knew; the Ship-n-Mail was on Matt Sylvania's route.

"If it were up to me," I said, "I'd check to see if Mackson is a biker. Same for Sylvania."

"You still trying to tie this into the Iron Cross murder thing?" Gene asked.

"Makes as much sense as anything else."

"What are you guys taking about?" Hewitt asked.

"BJ thinks this has something to do with a double murder up between Española and Santa Fe. Some motorcycle badasses called the Iron Crosses are accused of killing two meth dealers."

Hewitt turned to me. "How's that connected to the blackmail attempt and the theft of this piece of mail?"

"I don't think the blackmail demand is about the money. Someone wants to force my client to do something, and the only thing he's working on that even remotely ties in to criminal activity is this murder case."

I suffered a twinge of guilt about not sharing my investigation of the High Desert acquisition fight and Billingham's clumsy attempt to pressure Del, but there was no way that related to this thing.

"Okay," Hewitt said, "I'll ask around and see if anyone knows if Sylvania is a biker. But he's not the only one who could have snatched that envelope. If it got into the system at the main PO, any number of people could have nipped it."

"Then you've got a lot of ground to cover," Gene said. "Right now, BJ and I have to go warn his client the envelope might have been delivered. If it was, our attempt to run a scam on these guys has been exposed and we don't know how they'll react. The Prada killing is tied up in this thing, so Dahlman needs to be prepared for the worst."

We returned to the Ship-n-Mail to recover my car and to drop off Hewitt so he could get started on his end. Then Gene and I headed downtown in tandem.

Halfway there my cell phone rang.

Chapter 22

"DEL? Is that you? Speak up, I can't hear you."

"Yeah, it's me. Where are you?" He sounded shaky, distant.

"Gene and I are headed to your office. Be there in five minutes. Where are you? There's a bad echo."

"In the parking garage under my building," Del said. "Ditch Enriquez and meet me somewhere other than your office or mine."

"What's happened?"

"Tell you when I see you, and it's not good. I don't want the police involved."

"Too late. Gene's car is right behind me. If it's as bad as you say, he's a level head. Something we can probably use."

Del dithered for a few seconds before conceding. "Okay. I'm on the move now. I'm being watched, but I'm on the Bluetooth so nobody can tell I'm talking to anyone."

"Okay. Park near the federal courthouse and enter through the south entrance. Walk straight through and out the north side. Gene will be there. Pick out the most nondescript brown four-door Ford you see. That'll be him."

"I can't walk out on the street. I—"

"Do it." I broke the connection and dialed Gene's cell.

A second later he disappeared around a corner. I drove straight to the parking structure across the street from the UNM Medical Center on Lomas and Campus, trailing a line of cars through six interior levels dark enough to require headlights. When I arrived at the top tier, I parked sloppily, making sure to take up two spaces. I moved so that Gene could pull in beside me as soon as his car nosed into sight fifteen minutes later.

I climbed in beside Gene. "Okay, fill me in."

"They contacted me," Del said from the backseat.

He gasped as a shadow fell across the window beside him. I glanced up as a young man threaded his way between the Ford and my Impala. He clasped the hand of a little girl and was speaking to her animatedly. The top level of the structure was open to the elements, and I'd counted on the sun's glare to prevent anyone from noticing us. Apparently it had worked with the young father… or perhaps he was merely wrapped up in his daughter.

"Contacted you?" Gene exclaimed. "Hell, BJ, they assaulted him in the parking garage. He's bleeding all over my backseat right now."

I twisted around to look at Del. "Do you need a doctor?"

He straightened his spine and shook his head. "I had come out of the elevator and started for my car when somebody came up behind me and put a knife to my throat. Told me they were through playing around. They knew I'd put paper in the envelope instead of money. Gene told me the envelope was delivered. How did that happen?"

"We think somebody filched it. What happened next?"

"The guy told me to tell Miranda Skelton not to testify. She could say she didn't remember or she'd been lying before, anything except tell the truth about what really happened."

"So it *is* the drug murders."

"Tell him what happened next," Gene said.

"I started to reason with the jerk, but he wasn't in the mood. He took the knife away from my throat and slashed an *X* across my back." Del lifted the coat he held in his lap. It had a gaping hole in the back. "Sliced up the jacket of a thousand-dollar suit."

No wonder Del had been hesitant about walking around on a public street. "If he just shredded the jacket, why are you bleeding?"

As if reminded of his discomfort, he eased forward in the seat. "The blade scratched me a little. I'll be all right."

"So quit bellyaching about a damned jacket. There's a lot more at stake here than some expensive cloth." Del gave me a surprised look but didn't say anything. "Did you get a look at your assailant?"

"No. He told me that ripping up my suit was to show they were serious. Said I'd already got Emilio killed, and they'd kill me too if I didn't cooperate. I tried to tell him that wouldn't accomplish anything because the court would appoint someone else. He laughed and said my funeral would at least buy some time."

"You didn't get a look at him when he left you standing with your jacket in shreds?"

"Not a glimpse. Before he left, he told me to look down at my chest. There was a red dot centered right over my heart."

"A laser aiming device," Gene said. "These guys have some sophisticated weaponry."

"More likely a plain old laser pointing device like you use in conference rooms."

Del ignored me. "Christ, Vince, that was the scariest part of it. Somebody had a gun aimed at me. He told me not to move until the dot went away. Man, I froze there imagining some doped-up gangster giving in to an impulse to squeeze the trigger. It was almost five minutes before that red dot disappeared. By then the guy with the knife was long gone."

"Yeah, but not the gunman," Gene said.

"Maybe not, but I wasn't about to go looking for a criminal with a gun. I got in my car and pretended to be recovering from shock. Hell, I *was* recovering from shock. But I managed to punch in your cell number before driving off."

"Let's get a crew over there to see what they can find." Gene reached for his car's radio mike.

"No!" Dell yelped. "He said no police. Warned me if the police got involved, people would die, starting with my client."

"If it's so easy to reach your client, why not just kill her and be done with it?" Gene asked. He raised a hand to forestall my objection. "I know, I know. People who are locked up in the pokey get compromised all the time, but they rarely get killed. After all, there would be a finite number of suspects, and there are too many snitches in the jailhouse to risk that. No, if anyone's gonna be hit, it's you or BJ."

"That's comforting." Del rolled his eyes.

"So that means you have to involve the police," Gene continued. "Otherwise you're sitting ducks."

"I can take care of myself. And so can Vince." As if surprised by his own bald statement, Del looked at me. "I guess you have a say in this too."

"The police are better equipped to deal with these things than we are. They have the manpower to give you protection and the informants to gather intelligence. I contracted with you to root out some information, not to protect you from harm. That job belongs to Gene and his people, but whatever you decide is okay by me."

The detective shook his head and snorted in disgust. "I expect macho crap like this from bull-headed cops, but not from two intelligent...." His voice faded away.

"Say it," Del pressed him.

"Okay, I will. Two intelligent queers like you. Who're you trying to prove your manhood to anyway?"

Del flushed. "Pictures of Emilio screwing me to the contrary, I'm as much a man as you are."

"Don't get your bowels in an uproar. Gene's trying to make a sensible point."

Del clenched his fists and ground his teeth. Then he sagged back, no doubt smearing more blood on the seat covers. "I know. I'm sorry I dragged you into this mess, but it's done now and I don't know how to undo it."

I lifted my fist, thumb up. "At least this puts to rest the Billingham nonsense. Does everyone concur we can drop that investigation?"

Both men nodded.

"Del, your thousand-dollar suit jacket probably delayed things a little. Nothing's happening on the Iron Cross case until January, right? As far as they know, you're terrified and willing to cooperate. Sometimes stereotyping comes in handy."

"Wrong," Del said. "There's a meeting tomorrow with the Santa Fe district attorney. He's extending immunity in exchange for Miranda's testimony and releasing her, pending trial."

"Isn't it too late for that? Her grand jury testimony is already on the record."

"Miranda was originally a target, so she refused to testify. She took the Fifth. After he got his indictments of Whiznant and Rodrigo, the district attorney dropped the charges against her. Then she blabbed to the wrong person and found herself back in hot water. The DA declared her a material witness and put her in solitary."

"If they didn't need her testimony to indict, why do they need her at trial?" I asked.

"The Rules of Evidence don't apply in a grand jury. They do in a criminal trial. That makes the burden of proof a hell of a lot tougher. If she testifies and comes across as believable, she makes the state's case stronger."

"Let's face facts, fellows," Gene said. "You have no option but to report today's events to the court. The last thing you want is Miranda Skelton running around free where she's an easy target."

"You're right, of course," Del conceded. "But I want to be as low-key about this as possible."

"Okay, I'll have somebody scout out the garage to see if they can find anything to help identify the thugs who braced you today. They'll be discreet. And they probably won't find a damned thing."

We spent a few minutes discussing damage control, but the only thing we could come up with was to cancel tomorrow's meeting with the DA.

"Last time I heard," Gene said, "the court's obligated to keep defense counsel up-to-date on events in a trial. So I'm not sure how confidential you're going to be able to keep this."

"His Honor may consider special circumstances apply here since the defendants are trying to intimidate the state's primary witness." Del's voice held a wisp of hope.

"You can prove that, can you? Didn't think so," Gene said. "So you're betting your ass on the common sense of a judge. Glad it's yours and not mine."

"At any rate we want the defense to know the meeting with the DA is cancelled," I said. "Del, you'll just have to be creative about the reason why."

As I got back into my car and watched Gene pull away to take Del back to the federal courthouse, I paused to rethink our conversation. Miranda Skelton was reasonably safe so long as she remained in solitary confinement. Del had gone along with scrapping tomorrow's meeting for two reasons: she was more vulnerable while free, and the blackmailers might consider the cancellation as caving in to their demands. It was worth a try.

That, of course, made me the number one target. Why? Because I was the fellow muddying the water in their little pond. If that kind of pressure didn't bring Del to heel, he'd be second on their hit list. As he correctly pointed out, his death would merely delay the trial.

Del's encounter with the hood in the garage worried me enough to phone Charlie Weeks. He grasped the situation quickly and agreed to keep an eye on Hazel. That done, I bearded the lioness in her den, albeit from the relative safety of a cell phone. As anticipated, Hazel voiced a few strong opinions on the subject; the first of which was that Del Dahlman had done it to me again. When I told her Charlie was on his way to the office to babysit, the telephone almost blistered my ear. I hung up right in the middle of her diatribe. When the time came to pay for that little stunt, I'd claim it was a dropped call.

It seemed wiser to work from my home for the moment, so I started the car and rolled down the exit. Resisting the temptation to swing by the country club for a glimpse of Paul, I left the university area and drove straight to Post Oak Drive. As I turned onto my block, I passed two men tinkering with a motorcycle at the side of the road. Odd enough to catch my attention, but not alarming.

Stowing my vehicle in the garage seemed prudent under the circumstances. I locked the Impala and closed the double doors, making certain they were secure. All right—so it was like wearing a belt *and* suspenders, but sometimes that's not only appropriate but also judicious.

A cautious stroll around the place to scope out the backyard for skulkers and the shrubbery for miscreants revealed nothing amiss except a couple of bald spots in the greenery. Some of the lawn sprinklers needed adjusting. Was the same thing happening to the grass around front? I latched the gate firmly behind me before making my way down the driveway to check on the turf. The rose bushes running along the edge of the house needed pruning. And weeding. There was always something.

I smiled as the curtain at the picture window across the street twitched. Resisting the urge to wave to my inquisitive neighbor, I mounted the steps to my front porch, where I paused. The hair on the back of my neck rose at the sound of an approaching motor.

I whirled as a motorcycle roared to a stop in the middle of the street. The driver and the man in the saddle behind him both raised their arms. I dropped to the floor and rolled toward the porch's solid stone balustrade. The roar of a heavy-gauge handgun all but drowned out the dull purr of the deadlier automatic weapon. Bullets smacked into the stone at my head. Chips from the wooden railing along the top rained down on me.

In the sudden silence that followed the gunfire, I heard excited chatter. The gunmen should have roared away, but they hesitated. My mouth went dry. The old wound in my leg throbbed. They were coming to finish the job. I fumbled the small Colt semiautomatic from my jacket pocket. It was no match for the gunmen's firepower, but it might be enough to keep them from coming any closer. Just as I bounced up from behind the banister, a thin, quavering voice demanding to know what was going on sent me into shock. Gertrude Wardlow, bless her meddlesome soul, had the same effect on the gunmen and me: the world seemed to freeze.

Two hoods in black leather with opaque helmets masking their features paused in the act of reloading. The man on the back carried what looked to be an Uzi. The driver had just popped a fresh magazine in a bigass handgun. Beyond them, and in my direct line of fire, stood my white-haired neighbor. So much for trying to draw blood from the bad guys.

Deliberately aiming to the left, I chewed up the trunk of a weeping willow my mom had planted when I was a toddler. The pops my tiny pistol made were laughable. But they got the bozos' attention. I bellowed for my neighbor to run for cover and dropped to the floor again. A fusillade shredded the remainder of the wooden railing over my head.

The throaty growl of a heavy motor echoed up and down the street. The bike's wheels screeched. The stench of burning rubber blended with the odor of cordite, a hideous olio. I was halfway to my feet when another round of gunfire drove me flat again. But instead of the thud of bullets against brick or flying woodchips, there was a scream and the sound of breaking glass from across the street.

Chapter 23

I SCRAMBLED to my feet and vaulted the ruined railing. My neighbor's frail form lay facedown and motionless on the lawn across the street. Her print housedress bunched at one side, revealing a pale thigh circled by an old-fashioned garter. I sprinted across the street. "Mrs. Wardlow! Mrs. Wardlow!"

"BJ?" Her voice was hushed. "Is that you?"

"Yes, ma'am."

"Oh, thank goodness." She rolled over onto her back and tugged at the skirt to restore her modesty. She sat up, taking the time to primp her short, permed hair before speaking. "I was afraid you were injured."

I gave her a quick once-over. There was no sign of blood as I helped her to her feet. "Thank God you're not hit. Are you all right… uh… otherwise? You know, your heart and all."

She brushed her elbows and once again fussed with her hair; despite everything it still looked as if she'd just left the beauty salon. "Gracious, I must look a sight. My heart? It's just fine, thank you. Why wouldn't it be?"

"It's not every day you're in the middle of a gunfight."

"That's true. It's been almost thirty years."

I took an involuntary step backward. "You were involved in a shootout thirty years ago?"

"Let me see. Yes, the last one was just about thirty years ago. My Herb and I were both in the Drug Enforcement Agency. We transferred to the DEA when it was formed in 1973. This is not the first time I've been shot at."

"I'll be damned. But has anyone ever blown out your windows before?" I nodded over her shoulder to the gaping hole that had been her squeaky-clean front window. Jagged shards of glass hung like crystalline stalactites from the mangled sill. Glittering splinters littered the front porch of the once-neat, white-painted brick house.

Mrs. Wardlow put a blue-veined hand to her mouth. "Oh, dear! I should have gotten my service revolver instead of hitting the deck like a rookie."

I couldn't help it. I burst out laughing. "It's a good thing for those guys you didn't. Don't worry, Mrs. Wardlow. I'll see everything's replaced." It certainly wasn't the violence that was rattling her, more likely the potential cost of repairs.

"It's… it's not that. It's just that Herb is on the mantelpiece. I hope he's all right."

That was a stumper until it dawned on me she meant his ashes were there. "If he isn't okay, we'll get him a nice new urn. No argument, now. I'll pay for everything."

"That's very kind of you. Your business must be doing very well."

Surreal. The neighborhood had just been shot up, and here we stood politely discussing mundane matters.

"Insurance." I gave a wink to put an end to the matter.

The neighbors had gathered in clusters to gabble and gawk. Gene had been right; I lived in a geriatric community. This was probably the most exciting thing to happen here since a hot air balloon landed in the middle of the street two years ago during the International Balloon Fiesta.

A couple of braver souls started toward us, but someone among the group had been more practical that either Mrs. Wardlow or me. The first police cruiser arrived with siren blasting, sending them scuttling back to their yards. A familiar brown Ford showed up hard on the heels of the patrol car.

Gene strolled across the street. "Guess we figured wrong."

"Dead wrong. Somebody's very nervous about something."

"I'd say so. Looks to me like all that secrecy hocus-pocus didn't work. You were followed, my friend."

"Don't think so. When I turned onto the street, there was a bike parked at the side of the road. A couple of guys were working on it. Or pretending to."

"So your house was staked out." Gene turned to my neighbor. "You all right, ma'am?"

"I'm just fine, thank you."

"Well, what can you two tell me?"

I took the lead. "Two men on a big motorcycle were about all I saw. I was busy ducking, but I think it was a Harley. The shooters wore black leather and helmets with tinted faceplates. I couldn't describe either one of them. The rider on the back had an Uzi; the driver, a very large semiautomatic. They were dead serious about it, Gene. They would have come up on the porch to finish the job if I hadn't pulled out my popgun. That, and Mrs. Wardlow yelling at them from across the street, that is."

"Bad move, ma'am. I can tell you from experience he's not worth getting shot up over."

"Don't give me that, young man. I know you two were partners when he was a lawman. I think you would have risked your fanny for him."

"Maybe so, but I'm—"

"She's ex-DEA, Gene. Don't give her any lectures."

He looked at her with new respect. "Then maybe you saw a little more than he did, since you weren't hiding your eyes."

"Not much, I'm afraid. I don't see all that well anymore. That motorcycle, or one just like it, had gone up and down the street a couple of times over the past hour and a half. Casing BJ's house, as we now know. I considered calling the police, but decided they weren't doing any harm beyond making a lot of racket. My mistake.

"The cycle was black. No trim or designs that I saw. New Mexico license plate, but I couldn't make out any numbers. BJ's right; it was a Hog with beer cans and oversized boots. It was a kicker, I think, but it didn't look classic, so it must have been a seventies or eighties model."

We both blinked as she described a Harley-Davidson FL with can-shaped covers on the front forks and oversized tires. *Kicker* meant the machine didn't have an electric starter. Mrs. W hadn't finished.

"Both of the men were short and stocky. No more than five six or seven, but that's about all I saw. Oh, and the back warmer had an automatic weapon. BJ is probably right about that too. It was an Uzi. The men's clothing looked old. Leather, but old. Their brain buckets, however, were new. The heavy plastic ones that completely cover the head, including the face."

We exchanged glances, tipped our nonexistent hats, and abandoned the field to a superior force. That old lady, dim eyesight notwithstanding, had caught details I missed while ducking for cover. Of course, during her DEA years, bikers and drugs went hand in hand. I had no doubt the plucky widow could have thrown a leg over the saddle and booted that bad boy the length of Route 66—at least once.

A CANVASS of the neighbors added little to Mrs. Wardlow's observations. A citywide alert failed to intercept a motorcycle with driver and passenger. Assuming the second man bailed somewhere along the way, the cops stopped virtually every cycle they came across without finding the correct one. Gene searched police records for some sign of a vehicle like the one my neighbor described, but my ex-partner came up blank.

I called in a favor or two and had Mrs. Wardlow's picture window glazed before the afternoon was over. The contractor, already scheduled to repair the fire damage on my porch tomorrow, agreed to restore her interior, as well. Herb had, indeed, been scattered all over the carpet. I was horrified, but my amazing neighbor merely observed her husband probably enjoyed the first light of day he'd glimpsed in fifteen years. She was contemplating vacuuming him up and depositing him in a mason jar so they could share the morning sunlight, but I prevailed upon her to go with me to pick out a suitable urn.

My house had come out relatively unscathed. The stone balustrade was pitted from absorbing most of the force of the bullets, but the railing and some woodwork near the door would need replacing. Amazingly only a single bullet hole starred my front window. The contractor could take care of that damage, as well.

The police forensics people loaded their equipment and departed after measuring and picking up brass and photographing rubber burns on the pavement. I refused the plainclothes watchdog Gene pressed on me and earned a stern rebuke from my ex-partner before he left. The only concession I made was to strap my S&W 9 mm handgun in plain sight on my belt.

An hour later an old Plymouth ground to a halt in front of the house, drawing me outside and sending window curtains flicking all up and down the street. My nervous neighbors likely anticipated more excitement. A cop would probably be here within minutes.

I watched from the porch as Paul climbed out of the car and stood gaping at my ruined railing. After a moment his gaze shifted to me.

"You all right?"

"Yeah. Fine."

"Everyone's talking about it at the country club. I was about to leave for class when I heard the buzz. I had to come over. I hope it's all right."

"It's not only all right, it's great. Come on in."

He glanced at his watch. "For a minute. I've gotta get to the U."

I ushered him inside, and we stood in the foyer while I described what had happened. The concern written across his face sent my heart soaring. A moment later he proved he cared by moving into my arms.

"Damn, Vince, I was scared to death. Wild rumors claimed dead people were scattered all over the neighborhood. Somebody saw a bloody body on the lawn. I was afraid something bad had happened."

I was about to clarify the *body* situation when a car screeched to a halt outside. I pushed Paul back against the wall and pulled my weapon as I looked out one of the two small windows cut high into the front door. A blue-and-white was parked behind Paul's car. One policeman was on the radio checking the license plate; the other one got out of the cruiser and warily approached the Plymouth.

I relaxed and holstered my pistol. "False alarm. It's some minders Gene put on my tail. I'll let them know everything's okay. Come outside with me so they can see you."

Paul followed me down the steps while the two cops, both now standing on the sidewalk, nervously fingered leather holsters.

"It's okay, fellows. I'm B. J. Vinson and this is Paul Barton, a friend of mine who heard what happened and came to make sure I was all right."

The suspicion faded but did not disappear. The older, heavier officer circled around us in a practiced maneuver, making certain there was no at gun at my back. I automatically scanned their nameplates: Kennedy and Olguin. They worked smoothly, moving so they covered us from either side. I stepped away so they could see no invisible thread tied me to my visitor.

"Nice to meet you, Mr. Barton. Uh, Mr. Vinson, Detective Enriquez wanted me to check the house again to see if we missed any projectiles in the front room. Is it okay if I go inside?"

I motioned to the door. "Be my guest. Paul and I will wait right here."

Still wary, Officer Kennedy entered the house. I knew he wanted to make certain no one else was hiding inside. His hand was on his holster as he passed through the door. Olguin remained with us. By the time his partner returned, the thin rookie hadn't spoken a word.

"Okay, sir," Kennedy announced from the steps, "we'll be leaving now. You need any help, give us a call."

"Will do, and thanks. By the way, mention my guest's name to Detective Enriquez. He'll recognize it."

As we watched them leave, Paul muttered. "They were checking me out, weren't they? Like a perp or something?"

I nodded. "A nervous neighbor probably saw a strange car at my curb and panicked."

Paul laughed. "If they think that pile of bolts is a gangbanger's car, they don't know much about gangbangers."

Enjoying his mirth, I chuckled. "That's for sure."

"This is on that big case, isn't it?" Paul leveled his gaze at me. His lips twitched. "Let's go inside, Vince. I want to make love."

I smiled. "What about your class?"

"Screw the class."

Chapter 24

I WAS living a Dickens novel—"it was the best of times, it was the worst of times." Paul's embrace was exactly what the doctor ordered, but his proximity was distracting at a moment when I needed to remain focused. The extortionists had escalated things exponentially, and I had to be at the top of my game.

Paul stayed overnight, and for those twelve hours, I thought only of him and how he made me feel. As he dressed the next morning in my bedroom after his shower, I ignored the ringing telephone, preferring to watch his graceful reverse striptease. The voice booming over my answering machine finally snagged my attention.

"This is your San Diego compadre. You 'n' me need to meet, Sonny. I'll call back." As I scrambled to reach the phone, Tarleton hung up without leaving a number. The caller ID registered Unidentified.

Paul looked at me quizzically, but I shrugged off the call as a confidential informant. Just then the doorbell chimed. Still besotted with Paul, I answered it without taking precautions. Fortunately, Gene stood on the other side of the door.

"Christ, BJ, you didn't even check the peephole. This is being careful?"

"How do you know I didn't?"

"Well, did you?"

I sighed. "No."

Gene eyed my guest but made no comments, other than to bring me up-to-date on the lack of progress and cuss me roundly for opening the door without knowing who was on the other side. Then he left, taking the steps down to the sidewalk in a stiff-legged gait that signaled he was pissed.

A few minutes later, I watched Paul's beat-up Plymouth pull away from the curb. Had he understood how important he was to me? Had he come because I needed him or because he needed me? Did it matter?

His car rounded the corner, putting an end to the wonderful interlude. Bracing myself, I prepared to face down my secretary in her—make that *my*—office. It was difficult to remember who paid the bills when dealing with Hazel Harris. No matter how much I dawdled, the ride took only fifteen minutes. When I entered the portals of B. J. Vinson, Confidential Investigations, she was waiting for me.

Hazel stood in the doorway, as solid as a brick outhouse, blocking my way. She settled her glasses on the bridge of her nose and scanned me up and down. Once satisfied all of my various parts were still in place and functioning, she started in on me.

"You oughta tell that… that *lawyer* to take his case and go stuff it. I told you no good would come of this."

"Yes, Mother."

"Don't take that tone with me, Burleigh J. Vinson. Use the sense the Good Lord gave you and send him packing."

"Yes, Mother."

Hazel puffed up but held on to her temper. "Well, you have other clients too, you know. There is a whole stack of messages on your desk."

With that she flopped down at her desk and grabbed some papers, aggressively stuffing them into a file folder. Something suspiciously like a sniffle came from her.

"Look, you were right, and I was wrong. But the genie's out of the bottle now, and the bad guys aren't going to listen when I don't want to play anymore."

She swung around to her computer, and I didn't quite know what to make of the maneuver. It could be a rebuff or a way to hide her red eyes from me, or maybe she simply had work to do.

Laying a hand on her plump shoulder, I considered the two most prominent women in my life at the moment. One was a doughty old warrior, the other a suffocating motherly type. Troupers both. "I'll be careful until this is over. I promise. It's you I'm worried about. Where's Charlie?"

"I sent him after a can of coffee. We're out."

"I told him to stick close. Don't send him off on errands."

She did sniffle then, but her fingers continued to dance across the keyboard. "He has stuck close. The old fool wanted to stay at my place last night."

"Good. I hope you let him."

"Of course I didn't! Well, I did, but he slept on the screened-in porch. There was a locked door between us all night long."

Smiling at the mental image, I went into my office to deal with that host of telephone messages she'd mentioned. Most were expressions of curiosity or concern from friends and acquaintances over the shootout. A couple were from reporters—I threw those in the wastebasket. Yesterday's shooting had been the lead story on all the local late-night newscasts.

One of the telephone slips contained an unfamiliar number. "Hazel, what's this 343 prefix? It doesn't have a name on it."

My guardian angel appeared in the doorway. "He wouldn't leave his name. Called a couple of times but only gave me his phone number late yesterday afternoon. Said to tell you he wanted to talk to you Marine to Marine."

Tarleton. The old gunny had tried to reach me at the office before looking up my home number in the phone book. I was going to have to reconsider that listing. "Okay, I know who it is."

As soon as her keyboard began clicking again, I punched in his number. The phone rang a long time. Eventually, Tarleton answered.

"Gunny, it's B. J. Vinson.

"About time. Probably oughtn't talk to you now. Not after you being on the news."

"Didn't know you were shy. Besides, you called for a reason. What was it?"

"You still looking for them pictures that pretty queer had?"

"Still looking. What can you tell me?"

I heard a rasp as he apparently scratched his chin. "What's it worth?"

"Depends on what it is."

"What if I know who took the negatives offa him?"

"That might be worth something to the police. It's a murder case now."

"No! No cops. Cops and me don't get along." He dropped his voice. "I fixed up that Toyota and sold it. Made a decent profit too. Got my motorcycle tuned up and ready to go. Thought I might like to try Utah or Wyoming, or someplace I ain't never been to. That's what retirement's for, they say. Traveling."

"So, what's stopping you?"

"Need a bit more cash to get outa town in style."

"How much more?"

"I was thinking something like five thousand."

The exact amount the blackmailer first demanded. Coincidence? "I doubt it's worth that, but my client might go for a thousand. You have the negatives?"

"Shit, no. You ain't listening, Lieutenant. I said I might know who has them."

"So tell me, and I'll see you get the money."

"You might be an ex-gyrene, but you was an officer. You was a noncom, I might be tempted to trust you. But you wasn't, so I don't. Look, I'll meet you wherever you say. But it's gotta be quick."

"You knew who had them all along, didn't you?"

"Hell, I ain't a fucking liar. I didn't have no idea. But the other day somebody showed up and wanted some prints made off the same negatives I developed for Emilio."

"Did you make the prints?"

"Yeah. And right after that, I got a bad case of wanderlust."

"If you feel threatened, let me send a detective I know. He's good at watching a fellow's back."

"No way, man. No cops. I see the law, I don't show my face. You wanna meet or not?"

"I want to meet. How about the Frontier Restaurant. You know it?"

"Yeah. It's a little public for me, but okay. Bring the money. I ain't meeting to swap war stories. When?"

"Half an hour."

Tarleton grunted agreement and slammed down the phone. My hand rested on the receiver as I debated calling Gene. But Tarleton had agreed to a public meeting, so it wasn't likely he was planning my assassination. After grabbing some cash from my floor safe and making sure Charlie Weeks had returned to cover Hazel, I went to my car.

All the way up East Central I mentally kicked myself. Rory Tarleton was the only guy I knew mixed up in this biker thing who *was* a biker. Emilio had conned me from the beginning. Maybe Tarleton had too. Was he leveling about making prints for somebody, or was he involved somehow and planning on cutting his losses? Then it hit me. The only thing stolen from Emilio was the roll of negatives. The blackmailer was preparing to take his next step and needed prints for that. Maybe Tarleton was telling the truth.

The Frontier, a white brick building with a yellow roof ripped right off a country barn, was not only a café but also an institution. Located directly across Central Avenue from the University of New Mexico's main campus, it had fed generations of students on relatively inexpensive yet excellent fare.

After waiting thirty minutes and sampling some of that excellent fare, I was merely impatient. Tarleton would likely stake out the place to make certain no cops showed up, but after an hour and a half, I was worried and started out for the South Valley. Halfway there I tracked Gene down on my cell, and he agreed to meet me at Tarleton's place.

When I arrived minutes later, the Indian, its sidecar packed with Rory's belongings, sat in the space formerly occupied by the Toyota on blocks. Tarleton was serious about getting out of town.

Something was wrong. In his present frame of mind, he'd have checked out a car pulling into his driveway. No point in waiting for Gene or the car he'd undoubtedly send as backup. I warily approached the front door of the small house. There was no answer to my knock. Tarleton could be out back in his darkroom finishing up some final work, but I didn't think so.

The plain plywood front door stared back at me blankly. The knob turned at my touch. I drew my weapon and entered quickly, stepping to the side of the open doorway to avoid silhouetting myself. The room was empty. The place stank of stale cigarette smoke and a hint of something sharper, like a men's locker room. Marijuana. The sun streaming through the open doorway lit a cloud of swirling dust motes.

The old house seemed to sigh around me. I went through the place room by room. Empty closets. Abandoned litter in the bedroom. Filthy bathroom stripped of personal possessions. But it looked more like Tarleton tearing through his house collecting his belongings than intruders ripping up the place in search of something.

By the time the back door loomed ahead of me, I wished Gene were here. Rusty hinges set up a loud protest as I pulled the door open enough to give me a limited view of the big backyard. Nothing threatening. The screen screeched as I eased through it. My back prickled; I felt exposed.

A raucous crow complaining somewhere nearby fell silent. A breeze stirred two tall elms near the back fence. Dry leaves rustled with a clamor that could have covered the advance of a squad of infantry. A sudden whoosh of wind lifted litter from the bare earth. I spotted movement and whirled with my gun thrust in front of me.

The crow examined me with bright, interested eyes from a clothesline post.

I carefully swept the entire yard while the sun retreated behind a heavy cloud cover. The light dimmed ominously. I sagged against the adobe wall of the house as my mind reeled backward in time.

I hadn't spotted the man that day my APD career ended because my attention had been diverted then too. He'd almost gotten the drop on me. I saw again the vivid orange-yellow flash from his gun barrel. The deafening explosions of two gunshots echoed in my head, as real as they had been two years ago. I flinched, reliving the hammer blow of the bullet to my thigh. My mind's eye misted with blood—my blood.

I grunted and clutched my scar. My resolve weakened and I wiped sweat from my brow; I fought the need to back away, to wait for the cops. A shiver swept down my back, but waiting wasn't an option. I pushed off the building and limped forward, reeling like a drunk. It took a long thirty seconds to reach Tarleton's darkroom.

The door stood ajar. I shuffled forward and thrust my head through the opening like a striking snake, jerking back instantly. No movement inside. Darting from bright sunlight into the shadowy gloom of the building temporarily blinded me. Almost panicked by my inability to see, I froze against the interior wall as a heavy stench clogged my nostrils. Slowly my eyes adjusted to the semidarkness. The place was in shambles, total devastation. Photographic equipment littered the floor, smashed bottles of reeking chemicals burned my sinuses, and the worktable sagged on its side, three of its four legs splintered. Tarleton's bayonet lay on the floor in the middle of the shack.

My gaze moved from the blade to the hand grasping the hilt, then traveled up the inert arm. Tarleton lay crumpled in the corner. I knelt at his side. No pulse. The body was warm and blood was everywhere. Fresh blood. My knee was soaked in it. I recoiled and got to my feet. This killing was less than half an hour old. As I stood gawking at violent death, I noticed the tip of the gunny's bayonet. It was coated with gore.

"You put up a fight, Sarge. Semper fi." I reeled out the door.

The backyard was still deserted, but there was a trail of blood leading from the darkroom to the back fence. I hoped the fucker died.

Sudden noises from the side of the house startled me. I whirled in a shooter's stance. I was preparing to move my finger into the trigger guard when a uniform emerged around the corner. Instantly, I pumped my gun hand into the air. The astonished cop, a middle-aged veteran gone careless, yelped "Police!" and clawed for his weapon. A second officer yelled the same warning and added "Drop your weapon!.

I complied immediately. A cop's bullet is no less lethal than a criminal's. My S&W hit the grass with a thud. "I'm a PI. Former cop."

"On your belly. Hands on your head."

I knew better than to object. Aiming a weapon at an officer of the law is a fast way to die. It would take very little to escalate this thing. Turning slightly in order to fall nowhere near my pistol, I went prone, my hands clasped at the back of my neck. In seconds my arms were twisted behind me. Steel bracelets bit into my wrists.

"There's a dead man in the shack," I said. "Murdered."

"You kill him?"

"Not me. I came to meet him."

"Then how come you got blood all over you? Your pants are soaked in the stuff."

"I checked to see if he was still alive."

The veteran's partner, a young man probably just out of the academy with pumped arms and tapered torso, tore my wallet out of my pocket. "Shit, this guy's the private eye Enriquez told us to watch for. Vinson."

"That's me." I spat out a mouthful of grass.

"Why didn't you say so?" The senior officer grabbed me by the arms and yanked me to my feet.

"Things were a little tense. Thought it better to simply obey orders."

The cop I'd almost shot moved in front of me and compared my flesh-and-blood features to the photo on the driver's license in his hand. His nameplate read "Findlay," which virtually described him: black Irish going to pot. He squinted as he read. He probably had glasses stowed away somewhere on his equipment belt but was too vain to use them.

"Yep, it's him. Guess you are an ex-cop, Vinson. Most guys woulda started protesting and ended up getting their butts shot off."

"You're right. For eight years before I got shot. It wasn't an experience I care to repeat."

"What about this murder? Is it Tarleton?" Findlay motioned with his head for his partner to check out the shack, but he made no move to free my wrists from the handcuffs.

"Yeah, it's Tarleton. How do you know him?"

It was obvious he considered freezing me out but changed his mind. "Had a few complaints from the neighbors. He was a little too fond of the booze. Chased a couple of citizens with a bayonet when they came over to complain."

"Yep, he's dead," the second cop confirmed as he rejoined us.

I nodded. "Point of exit's over there. There's a trail of blood from the darkroom to the back fence. They probably came in the same way. Yeah, *they*. It would have taken more than one to deal with Tarleton. He might have been rum-soaked, but he still knew his business."

"You want me to call it in?" the junior officer asked.

"Naw. Enriquez will be here any minute. He can handle it any way he wants."

As if calling the devil up out of hell, Gene arrived, trailed by his current riding buddy, a sandy-haired six-footer named Carson.

"What's going on? How come you have my ex-partner trussed up?"

"Your partner?" both street cops asked at once.

"Unless you've got a good reason not to, let him loose and tell me what's happened."

They saw to the shackles; I did the filling-in part.

Gene kept me there until the crime-scene unit arrived. After I showed them where I'd walked and everything I'd touched, Gene and I retired to the front porch to discuss the situation. After we'd wrung every detail dry, I shook my head.

"So far as the extortionists knew, Del was cooperating. He cancelled the meeting with the DA, and that should have satisfied them for the moment. But they came after me and took Tarleton down. Why?"

"Because you're a pain in the ass and you're getting too close. Tarleton's a clean-up job. Who knew he was meeting you?"

I shook my head. "No one I know of. Of course, he could have told someone, but I doubt it. He was too seasoned a Marine to go around flapping his lips." I reconsidered that statement. "He was selling me information for a thousand dollars. He claimed he knew who stole the negatives from Emilio. Maybe he thought his silence was worth more to someone else."

Gene shook his head. "Dumb move. Did he say who the thief was?"

"No, he wanted his money first."

"Okay, let's go over everything again."

After he led me through my story one more time, Gene relieved me of my handgun to test for recent firing—even though at this point

Tarleton's murder looked like a stabbing rather than a shooting. Then he released me before returning to the backyard to rejoin his team.

I pulled away and drove down the dusty street, uncomfortably aware I had not been completely truthful with my old friend and partner. There *was* someone who knew about my call from gunny. At least, he'd stood at my side and heard Tarleton say we had to meet.

Had Paul returned to my life out of concern for me... or for something else?

Chapter 25

I RATIONALIZED my suspicions away by the time the Impala reached downtown. If Paul had been involved in this mess, he wouldn't have pulled away over my confrontation with Professor Sturgis. He'd have remained close to keep tabs on me regardless of anything and everything. True, he asked questions, but about a whole host of things, not just Del's case. That was natural; he was training to be an investigative journalist. If he had insinuated himself into my life in order to spy, he sure was doing it in a roundabout manner. But maybe he was just there to gauge the temperature.

I had trust issues ever since Del betrayed me. I hoped for the best but expected the worst and was seldom disappointed. So maybe my willingness to believe, or at least suspect, Paul's betrayal was born of that mindset—a matter of connecting dots that were in reality only spots dancing before my eyes.

As I prepared to turn into the parking lot on Copper, I spied a TV news van. The Tarleton murder, no doubt. How had they tied me to it so fast? Not wanting to face television journalists while wearing blood-soaked trousers, I headed straight home. Something else was bothering me, and this was the perfect opportunity to pursue it—right after changing clothes.

William Mackson had quit his job at the Ship-n-Mail. Maybe his excuse about joining the chess club was perfectly valid. But then again, maybe it wasn't. Kyle Hewitt would rattle the cage at the post office, but I wasn't certain he would be as aggressive with the privately owned mail drop's staff.

The Eldorado principal, although none too happy to see me again, told me what time Mackson's last class of the day ended. He also grudgingly checked to see if the kid had a club meeting of any kind afterward. That one was easy. Billy Boy didn't belong to any clubs—no school-sanctioned after-hours activities of any sort.

Lounging around a high school campus these days wasn't easy for an adult, but I found the security cop on duty and chatted him up. We had a couple of mutual friends at APD, and he'd heard about my shooting. That gave us something to chew on while I kept my eye on the door to the chemistry lab where Mackson was finishing his scholastic day.

When the bell finally rang, an astonishing range of young men and women spilled out of various buildings. Astonishing because some of them didn't even seem to have reached puberty while others were already young men and women, at least physically. This was the age when Mother Nature played weird tricks on unsuspecting youngsters.

I pointed out William Mackson as he passed, but the cop didn't know anything about the kid. I thanked him for his time and company and excused myself, claiming a need to get out of the parking lot before the traffic rush began. The cop laughed aloud. Too late.

The clamor of chattering adolescents and the roar of hyped-up engines made a dizzying mélange of color and noise. Clouds of dust, overly rich carburetor fumes, and an occasional diesel exhaust added to the general confusion. A sizeable portion of the country's oil imports could have been eliminated had these kids formed an orderly exit line, but some serious machismo was on display in this vast parking lot. Lead feet fed accelerators too much gas, wheels rolled mere inches, heavy brake action brought vehicles to a standstill only millimeters from crushing fenders. It was a massive game of chicken. Everyone tried to rev a motor louder than their neighbor's, even if the neighbor drove a muscle car with quad pipes. The internal combustion engine, like the Colt revolver of old, was a great equalizer. Some of the geeks turned into raging bulls within the isolation of their vehicles.

I suddenly felt old. Back in the dark ages, I used to go on eager display like that too.

Ahead of me, Mackson walked straight toward a line of motorcycles. To my surprise he stopped beside a late-model green Kawasaki Vulcan power cruiser. I shouldn't have been so surprised. His brand-spanking-new leather coat looked to be fake to me, but it was meant to mimic a biker's jacket. Mackson's Kawasaki was not brand-new, but Mackson was brand-new to the Kawasaki. He fished around in saddlebags studded with chrome doodads we used to call fiddly bits and came up with a fish pot for a helmet—in other words, a cheapie. He threw a leg over the beast and staggered as he took the weight between his knees. The kid was definitely not an experienced rider. Even so, he was out of the lot before I could get my car in line to play double dare with a bunch of drivers with more testosterone than brains. I expected the curses, but the guy who yelled *Pops* at me was a little over the top.

By the time my Impala hit the street, Mackson was nowhere in sight. Gambling he'd go home, I headed for the address written down in my pocket notebook.

The Mackson family's residence was located in a low-income housing project dropped right in the middle of an affluent Northeast Heights neighborhood. Billy had parked his shiny new wheels in the driveway of a house that looked exactly like the one to the left and the one to the right except for the personalized clutter attending each. The kid emerged from the house, now dressed in fake leather pants as well as the new jacket.

There is a perfectly logical explanation for why bikers prefer leather duds, other than wanting to look like outlaws. Leather not only protects against the wind and cold better than most materials, it's also tougher, saving a guy a couple of yards of skin in case of a wipeout. Given the awkward way Mackson fought the machine as he backed down the steep incline of his driveway, I prayed the plastic jacket would hold up like real cowhide.

Billy appeared oblivious to my tail as he drove straight to Jill's, a fast-food teen hangout on Eubank near Los Altos Park. I ordered a milkshake from curbside service and watched him through a big plate glass window as he sat inside eating what I suspected was a juicy burger and soggy fries. That explained his acne but not his skinny build.

Mackson ate alone, an island around which his schoolmates moved as though he were nothing more than an obstacle in their path. I could see his head move each time the door opened, although I don't think he was expecting company, merely desperately craving it.

He ate as slowly as he could, but eventually Billy went back to his bike, attempting a little swagger. He failed miserably. As the kid pulled on his jacket and swung a leg over the machine, he stumbled and nearly fell. Glancing around to see if anyone had noticed, his eyes landed squarely on me. If anything was needed to convince me William Mackson had a guilty conscience, the shock twisting his features at that moment did it. He pulled on his helmet and hit the bike's electric starter, but he wasn't totally in control as he zoomed toward the exit. The Kawasaki ended up halfway in the street before he managed to come to a full stop. A car approaching from his left gave a sharp blast on the horn and swerved around him.

That was more than Billy could handle. The machine got away from him. He sideswiped the divider and did a somersault over the handlebars. He wasn't going fast enough to do much damage, but the fall had to hurt. I halted behind his overturned bike and put on my flashers to keep traffic from running up my tailpipe. By the time I got out of the car, Billy had picked himself up and was limping toward his bike. The panic on his sallow features stirred some pity in me. The kid was a loner using a big piece of machinery he couldn't handle in a pathetic attempt to fit in. Mackson probably didn't even like motorcycles.

"Let me help you."

He flinched from my touch as if it were poisonous. "I-I'm okay." He came down on his ankle wrong and grunted.

"No, you're not. You twisted your ankle and banged up your knee." I pointed to a rip in his new britches spotted with blood. "You get in the car. I'll wheel your bike back to the restaurant. You can pick it up later."

"No, I can ride it home."

"We do it my way, or I'll call a cop and report an accident. What happened, anyway?"

He tried to smile but failed. "Not used to my bike yet. I'll be all right."

"Have it your way." I pulled out my cell phone.

"What are you doing?" His voice bypassed panic and went straight to frantic.

"I'm calling the cops to report an accident. Of course, if we stand here arguing much longer, I won't need to. Someone will do it for us."

His eyes went wild, scanning the street in both directions. "O-okay." He hopped over to the bike and inspected it for damage as I lifted it upright.

"Seems okay." I mounted the machine and hit the starter. The motor caught and the beast rumbled beneath me. "Get in the car. I'll park the bike and alert the manager so he won't report an abandoned bike."

Actually I tipped the guy twenty bucks to keep an eye on it until Mackson could pick it up later.

No cops had arrived by the time I waded back through the traffic stacking up behind my Impala, so we pulled away without trouble. Billy tried not to let it show, but he gave a barely suppressed sigh of relief. A peculiar odor flooded the cabin. It took me a moment to realize it was fear leaking out through William Mackson's sweat glands. I hit the button to lower the windows. The kid's wet upper lip and dripping forehead decided my line of attack for me.

"Okay, Billy, I'll make you a deal. I won't report you to Detective Enriquez or Inspector Hewitt if you tell me all about it."

"About what?" The kid's question came out as a whine. One more little push would probably do the trick, so I pulled out my cell again. "Don't do that." Mackson reached out as if he was going to snatch the phone from my hand. Then he drew back. "You promise? You promise you won't tell?"

"I promise, providing you tell me everything, including names. But I can't keep them from finding out as a result of their own investigation. You need to be prepared for that eventuality."

"Oh shit," he moaned. His side of the car grew more pungent. The fake leather jacket wasn't helping his perspiration problem.

"Who approached you?"

His shoulders slumped. "Guy from school. He knew I worked at the Ship-n-Mail."

"And?"

"And he told me he wanted me to do something for him."

"When was this?"

"The day after you came nosing around."

With a lot of prompting, Billy Mackson's story emerged. A kid named Milt Zorn had struck up a conversation with him. Starved for companionship, Billy had responded eagerly. After only a couple of hours of bumming around together, Milt moved on his target. All he wanted Billy to do was to watch a certain box in the store and give any mail addressed to it to his new friend. It was okay because John Wilson, the box holder, was Milt's stepdad. He was supposed to pick up some important mail while Wilson was out of town, but his stepdad forgot to leave the key with him, so Milt needed Billy's help.

Billy had put up a weak struggle until his new friend said his stepdad had this neat motorcycle for sale cheap to the right buyer. How cheap? How much did Billy have? He'd managed to save three hundred dollars from his job. That would do the trick. So Zorn got a thick envelope full of worthless paper plus Billy's three hundred dollars, and Billy got a valuable motorcycle plus a probable criminal record. I felt sorry for the kid.

"Billy, you realize you're in a spot, don't you? And I'm not talking about breaking federal laws by stealing mail."

"What do you mean?"

"Your story doesn't hold up. You already told me there were instructions to forward mail from the box, so you knew the request from this Zorn guy wasn't kosher. Now, you're mixed up in an attempt to blackmail a prominent lawyer to influence a witness's testimony in a double-murder case."

"What? I-I didn't know. I just—"

"You just stole the payoff envelope and messed up the police's opportunity to identify the blackmailer."

"Oh *man*! But I didn't steal it. I just gave it to the owner's son... or stepson."

"How do you think that's going to turn out? Look, you're the low man on the totem pole, and you're probably telling the truth when you say you didn't know what was involved. Nonetheless you participated, and you're going to have to face up to it."

"Oh Lord." Billy moaned.

"Now you've given me the next guy in the scheme. And when I confront him, they're going to know there was only one way I got to him—through you. Just this morning the man who developed the photographs used in the extortion attempt was murdered because he tried to get in touch with me. And he was a Marine gunnery sergeant."

This unwelcome bit of news reduced Mackson to meaningless mumbling.

"I think you need protection. Let me take you to the detective you met the other day."

Chapter 26

IN CASE something new emerged, I was allowed to sit in on William Mackson's interrogation by Gene and Kyle Hewitt with the strict proviso to "keep my mouth shut." Nothing I didn't already know surfaced, and when it was over, Gene sent a couple of uniforms to bring in Milton P. Zorn, aged eighteen.

As soon as Mackson was taken to a cell, Gene and I headed for the Metropolitan Forensics Science Center on Second Street NW. There was nothing new on Tarleton's murder. OMI hadn't yet performed an autopsy on him, but we hoped the lab could tell us something.

They couldn't; it was too soon for any positive results. And because it was coming up on 5:00 p.m., there weren't likely to be any today. The sergeant heading the team sent to pick up Zorn called Gene on his cell to say they couldn't find him. The kid appeared to have vanished.

With nothing more to be accomplished there or at APD, I returned to my office. The TV news van had vacated the parking lot at Fifth and Copper and gone elsewhere in search of sensational stories. No reporters ambushed me as I climbed two flights of stairs. I searched the lobby from the third-floor balcony and saw no newshounds on the lookout for me. The danger, however, lurked elsewhere.

As I walked through the door, Hazel confronted me with a look of utter disdain. *"That's* what you call being careful?"

It must have been a rhetorical question because she pulled on her coat, grabbed her handbag, and marched out the door.

"Lock up when you leave." Her tone was dismissive but short of rude.

Charlie Weeks was half a step behind her. The former cop must have tapped his contacts at headquarters for information on the Tarleton killing, otherwise Hazel would not have left without wringing every last detail from me.

Never comfortable carrying more than a hundred dollars on my person, I returned the Tarleton payoff money to the safe and plopped down at my desk, exhausted. Must be getting old. Couldn't be anything as mundane as stress.

The telephone sat on my desk, making psychological demands on me. It was time to report to my client, although he seemed more or less superfluous in the matter now. Things moved right along regardless of what he did. With a sigh I picked up the receiver.

A call to his cell phone went straight to voice mail. The Stone firm's switchboard was closed, but after hours there was a way to get past the system to reach individuals. I meticulously followed the instructions of a computerized voice and eventually reached him.

"I heard," the flesh-and-blood Del said after I penetrated all the electronic roadblocks. "How did Tarleton fit into the picture?"

A perfect opening for delivering bad news, so that's what I did. Del was silent as I told him of the latest events, including the fact Tarleton had made prints for the extortionists from the negatives stolen from Emilio.

"Thanks for telling it like it is," he said. "I've already made the partners aware of what's going on. I also phoned the Santa Fe district attorney and briefed him on our problem. I should have done it a long time ago. Now the extortionists no longer have any leverage over me. They probably already know Miranda is going to testify, and there's nothing they can do to stop it."

"Things have moved beyond that now. Tarleton's killing was part of a cover-up. They didn't want him to identify the individual he made the prints for. There's no other reason for his murder. They're cleaning up behind themselves, and that kid, Mackson, would have been next if I hadn't got to him first."

"He's in custody?"

"As we speak. Gene will screw him down tight. They'll have trouble getting to him, but that leaves the next link in the chain still at large, another high school kid named Milt Zorn. The cops didn't manage to pick him up today."

"Is he a gangbanger?"

"No. At least he hasn't been identified with a gang yet."

"Vince, you were right about the reason for this blackmail attempt, but are you any closer to figuring out who's behind it? I've talked to Detective Hartshorn up in Santa Fe, and he still insists the Iron Cross members couldn't have killed Emilio."

"The best bet is the Santos Morenos. I can't prove it, but since we know the direction the wind's blowing, maybe APD and SFPD will come up with something. They have a lot more resources than we do."

"What about the blood on Tarleton's bayonet?" Del asked. "That should give the police DNA."

"Yeah, but DNA's useless unless you have something to compare it with. Besides, DNA testing typically takes weeks."

I heard him snort. "DNA tests take around sixty hours."

"Yeah, but the labs are overwhelmed."

"How about a private lab, like the one you used to check the blackmail envelopes?"

"That's a thought," I said. "Are you willing to cover the cost of a test by a private lab?"

"In a heartbeat. You know, whoever's behind this is more afraid of you than they are of the law. That's why they came after you. You have to be careful."

"That goes for you, too, Del. Remember, if everything else fails, killing you will at least delay the trial."

"I know, and I'm packing these days. Enriquez helped me expedite a permit to carry. Besides, I'm not quite as vulnerable as you are. My apartment building has security and a guard on duty in the parking lot at night."

"Don't get overconfident." Del had no experience surviving on the streets, and that's what this amounted to. "Don't forget your slashed jacket and the red dot on your chest in the parking garage."

After hanging up I consulted my notes and completed a detailed report—the timeliness of which could be important if any of this ever came to trial. Day had long since turned into night by the time I snapped off the office lights and prepared to leave. My paranoia rising, I stood in the darkened window and craned my neck, trying to see my car in the parking lot at the west end of the building. Everything looked quiet, but there was enough darkness out there to shroud an army bent on mischief. Mischief? Murder was light-years beyond mischief.

I called up the elevator, lamenting the fact that my peashooter was locked in the car. As soon as the automatic doors opened, I pushed the down button for the lobby and raced to the stairs, hustling to the first floor, where I eased out of the stairwell. The ninety seconds it took to reach and unlock my car left my neck pimpled with gooseflesh. After locking myself inside, I groped around under the seat for the .25. The feel of the little Colt in my hand gave me more security than it merited. I drove out of the parking lot and headed for Central Avenue.

A few years ago, the downtown area would have been deserted at this time of night, but urban renewal had been successful in bringing citizens to the clubs and cafés and movie screens strung up and down Central and along the two blocks of Fourth Street that had been converted into a pedestrian mall. Now uniformed cops on bicycles mingled with cars and strollers.

Just minutes earlier I'd been ready to fold my tent and steal away to cover my head in a warm bed, but the moment I fired up the Impala, I got a second wind from somewhere. Anxiety? Adrenaline? Whatever it was, I decided to take advantage of this unexpected energy. I headed up the hill to the C&W Palace, ostensibly to check on Puerco and his bunch.

Who was I kidding? I was hoping to run into Paul. But if I wanted to see him, why not simply phone him? I didn't have an answer.

As soon as I took the first sip of my drink, all that newfound energy evaporated and dumped me at a small vacant table near the dance floor. On reflection it wasn't a bad place to be. Paul came to the C&W for one reason: to dance. As up-front as he was about his sexuality, he was never quite at ease on a dance floor in a local gay bar. Me even less so. What was that all about? We were both comfortable with who we were, so why get hung up on the small details? Anyway, that was why he always came to the C&W with a coed.

Midway through my third drink, I realized I was violating my self-imposed rule of no more than two alcoholic drinks at a time—and Long Island Iced Tea wasn't the drink for that. Made with vodka, gin, tequila, rum, and triple sec, with a proportionally small amount of sour mix and cola, the drink had a high alcohol concentration. I plopped the tall glass on the table and pushed it away. A DWI charge would be disastrous.

As I listened to the same music by the same bands, played for the same patrons as during my previous visits, I wondered if they ever tried new numbers. That wasn't fair. They probably did, but to my tin ear, all C&W music sounded alike.

I had lived my entire life in this city and knew a fair number of people, so it was disconcerting to realize there was not a single familiar face in the C&W that evening. Well, that was not strictly true. Occasional gaps in the crowd revealed glimpses of Puerco and his gang holding down their usual table. They were a single-minded group. None of them ever got as far as the dance floor. They preferred to sit and drink, raising occasional bursts of raucous laughter. There were plenty of noisy people elsewhere in the vast building, but their laughter conveyed a sense of good cheer while the Santos's held an underlying air of menace.

I lurched to my feet and threaded my way across the dance floor, making straight for the group. Why? A whim. More likely an alcohol-induced sense of bravado—or suicide. Since surviving attempts on my life and almost interrupting the murder of Rory Tarleton, I was feeling pretty damned invincible.

Puerco spotted me first. Not much escaped those small, piggish eyes. The man had probably spent a lifetime guarding his back from someone: the law, rival gangs, challenges from his own people. That was how he'd survived this long.

He watched my approach solemnly before breaking into a phony smile. "Well, if it ain't the washed-up cop turned private investigator. Hello there, *Mr.* Vinson." The slight inflection on *mister* implied the courtesy title wasn't entirely courteous.

"Puerco." I swallowed the urge to address him as Mr. Pig. "This seems to be your home away from home."

"Might say that. They treat us good here at the C&W."

"Zancón." I saluted the gang's second-in-command as my eye roamed the table. The usual contingent was present, except for the Haitian thug, Jackie. "I see you're all here tonight—mostly. Have fun." There was a sudden tightening around Puerco's eyes just before I turned to walk away. Why the hell had I added that *mostly*? Nervous shivers ran down my back, flushing away that brief feeling of invulnerability.

I had made it through the crowd of dancers when I heard my name called. I turned. Paul approached with a big smile lighting his face. To my eyes he was a young man greeting his lover; to my mind he was the potential enemy. Angry with myself I thrust away the treacherous thought and met him, grasping his outstretched hand.

"Hoping I'd see you," I said. "You here with anyone?"

He grimaced. "Yeah, with a girl and another couple. But I can make it an early evening if you want." He sobered suddenly. "I heard what happened in the South Valley today. You all right?"

"Physically, I'm okay. But being a witness to bloody murder is hard on the nerves."

"I'll bet. Look, can we find a place to talk for a minute?"

"Sure. I left a drink on a table over there if someone hasn't appropriated it yet."

No one had, so we both sat down. The tiny table put us into intimate proximity. Paul studied my half-empty glass and picked at a bar napkin before meeting my eyes.

"Vince, I know it's not my place to invite myself, but… well, I want to move in with you. At least for a little while."

My heart went on a rollercoaster ride as I listened to him.

"It's not that I need a place to stay, but I thought maybe you could use the company. I know this is a rough time for you. Besides, I could sorta watch your back." He grinned. "Of course, I do that whenever I have the chance, but you know what I mean."

"I understand. You want to babysit me." I paused to choose my next words carefully, but the alcohol in my system wasn't making it easy. "I'm a big boy. Been watching out for myself for a long time."

His smile died. "I'm sorry. I was just—"

Halfway panicked by his reaction, I touched his arm. "Paul, there's nothing I'd like more than having you with me. But with everything that's been happening lately, I can't allow it. I can't expose you to danger you're not equipped to handle. It comes with my job, and I'm trained to deal with it. But I don't want you living in fear of your life because of me."

He seemed to buck up. "Okay, I guess I understand that. But I'm coming over tonight, and I'm not leaving until tomorrow morning, danger or no danger. If that's all right with you." He straightened his spine. "Hell, even if it's not. I'll camp out on your front porch and cause all the neighbors to talk if you don't let me in."

My resolve crumbled. "Don't plan on getting much sleep."

"Hah!" he said with a laugh. "I'll wear you out, and then I'll sleep like a baby."

"You go back to your friends. I'm going home now to rest up."

"You better. You're gonna need it."

I watched him walk away and wondered what I'd done. Had I invited the enemy to my home or placed the man I loved in danger because of my own selfishness? It was almost certainly one or the other.

As Paul disappeared into the crowd, my gut clenched. Puerco Arrullar stood nearby, eyeing me closely. As soon as he realized I'd noticed him, he flashed a gang sign and moved off in the direction of the men's room. I felt as if a snake had invaded my private space.

Chapter 27

AS ANXIOUS as a teenager before a first date, I tried to keep busy while waiting for Paul. A part of me—the brain part—hoped he wouldn't show. The rest of me could hardly contain itself.

After slipping my small pistol into a drawer of the bedside table, I went into my home office and created a phony Del Dahlman file, filling it with a few pages of hastily written pages of official-sounding gibberish. After adding the pocket-sized tablet I used to scribble notes to myself, I laid a two-inch length of thin white thread on top of the materials. Finally I placed a letter opener across the file folder. If anyone—Paul—looked inside, he'd place the knife back as carefully as possible, but he might not notice the thin filament inside. Then I took a quick shower and shaved.

When Paul rang my doorbell shortly before midnight, I left the foyer lights off and turned on the porch light. His freshly scrubbed appearance indicated he'd made a few preparations of his own.

"I'm here and I'm primed and I'm ready to keep my promise," he announced as he strode inside. He turned and gave me a grin. "About wearing you out."

Within the hour he had delivered on his promise; I was sated and could hardly keep my eyes open. Nonetheless, when he finally snapped off the table lamp and settled down beside me, I came wide-awake. Good Lord, was I afraid of him? The gun in the drawer at my shoulder made me ashamed. No one as delightful and loving as this man could possibly betray a trust. I suppressed a sigh. Of course he could. Recorded history was full of such treachery.

Mortified by my thoughts, I pulled him to me. He nestled into my arms and murmured, "Good night." In the grip of powerful, conflicting emotions, I held him close, pressing my face against the soft, damp hair at the back of his head. Embarrassed by my suspicions and chastened by my reactions, I whispered a desperate mantra of love until I finally nodded off.

It was an uneasy rest. Normally when I drink too much, the alcohol puts me out. Not tonight. Every time Paul moved, I woke, tense and alert—and halfway sick to my stomach. I swore off Long Island Iced Teas at least twice. Eventually morning arrived and I opened my eyes to find Paul staring at me from the other side of the bed.

He stretched lazily. "Morning. I gotta get moving. Early class."

"Morning," I responded as he bounded out of bed. "I'll fix you something to eat. What would you like?"

"Just some toast and chocolate milk if you have any. Gotta watch the waistline, you know." He patted his flat swimmer's belly.

"Don't worry about it. It's being watched—closely." I admired anew the magnificent grace of youth as he strode into the bathroom to shower.

I was relieved when he made no attempt to plan the evening during our quick breakfast. Well, the brain part of me was.

Later I watched his car drive out of sight before going into my home office. The file lay apparently undisturbed with the letter opener askew on top. Opening the folder carefully, I found the almost invisible thread in its proper place. Weak with relief I clung to the back of my desk chair until strength returned to my legs. Even my seminausea from last night's third drink eased a bit.

ACCORDING TO Gene, Milt Zorn's family lived in an upscale neighborhood a few blocks south of Eldorado High. The kid's father was alive and kicking and an integral part of the family. So much for the story that John Wilson was the kid's stepfather. When I showed up on his doorstep, Zorn Senior glanced at my license and slammed the door in my face. I wasted the whole day and half the night parked down the street, hoping for a glimpse of Milt.

There were no alleys in this part of town. Houses shared a common concrete block wall along the rear of their respective yards. It was possible Milt had made his way across the neighbor's property and hopped the wall, but it was more likely he had skipped. Unless, of course, he'd been snatched. But given his father's reaction, that was unlikely. The kid had probably taken off the day we questioned Mackson at school.

Throughout the day, Hazel had been on the phone, pestering me with requests. We had a new worker's comp surveillance case, which I told her to give to Charlie. One of my regular clients, a large life insurance company, wanted us to look into a death claim they suspected was suicide.

That one could wait since they'd be in no hurry to pay the claim anyway. She also needed my signature on a few things, not the least of which was her paycheck. I'd suggested placing her on the main account—she already had her own petty cash account—or getting a signature stamp for her, but she declined. According to Hazel, she handled everything else in the office but didn't want to be responsible for the money too. On her last two calls, she'd mentioned Charlie's paycheck, which caused me to smile. Something was definitely developing there.

As the day wore on, I recovered from last night's drinking, but that merely made me hungry. I ate the sack lunch I hadn't wanted when I made it, and emptied the car of every candy bar, cracker, and crumb I'd left in it. Then I tried to concentrate on Del's problem, but the memory of last night kept intruding. Paul was an odd mixture of youth and maturity. At times he was aggressively virile, totally dominating me. In the next moment, he could be achingly gentle, anxiously begging to know if that—whatever *that* was at the moment—was okay.

The thought he might not be what he seemed—at least in our relationship—kept intruding. I'd lost him once, thanks to my ham-handed handling of Steve Sturgis, and I recalled the despair of believing he was gone from my life forever. Now he was back, and I wasn't sure I was prepared to face another estrangement. That shook me. Had I sunk so low I was willing to compromise a case to satisfy a personal need? Had my ethical standards flown out the window at the appearance of a handsome young man with an easy, charming manner—and great sexual prowess?

Giving in to a growing sense of unease over sitting motionless on a darkened street for hours at a time, I terminated my vigil just before midnight and headed home. Halfway there I changed my mind and turned south. I'd rather take care of things now than try to beat Hazel to the office later this morning.

Headlamps in my rearview mirror kicked up my pulse rate. A tail? As I caught Lomas Boulevard and turned west, the other car turned off on a side street. Why was I so damned jumpy? Maybe a better question was why had I opted to go driving downtown in the middle of the night?

The parking lot at the corner of Sixth and Copper NW was quiet, disturbed only by the faint sounds of revelers a block east on the mall. Mine was the only car in the lot when I switched off the lights and killed the engine. Still anxious I sat for a moment in the darkness, studying my surroundings uneasily.

Perhaps this wasn't such a good idea after all. I hesitated, weighing my options. Thirty minutes now would save me a couple of hours later. I hadn't been followed—that car had gone its own way long before I reached the office. APD headquarters was only a couple of blocks away with cops coming and going at all hours. Maybe I was working myself into a lather for nothing. I was here, so I might as well get it done.

Making sure my .25 was tucked in my belt, I got out of the car, unlocked the door to the building, and entered through the west lobby without encountering a guard or anyone else. Management had part-time security, meaning that on certain unspecified nights, an after-hours guard was on duty. At other times we made do with a roving security patrol. Once inside my footsteps rang on the tile floor, the hollow sound rising five stories before echoing back, an eerie phenomenon that occurred only at night when the building was more or less deserted.

A sudden clang from somewhere above sent my heart rate soaring until I realized one of the cleaning crew had dropped a broom or a mop.

I opted to walk up the two flights of stairs, and when I emerged from the stairwell my hand automatically went to the little pistol at my belt. The balcony running around the perimeter of the entire third floor was empty. I glanced over the banister. There was no one in the lobby far below.

Tomorrow I'd buy some stronger firepower. Gene still hadn't returned my 9 mm pistol, and there was little possibility of getting it back anytime soon since the labs were backed up—a euphemism for seriously underfunded.

As the door to my office suite clicked behind me, I gave an involuntary sigh of relief. I'd been more worried than I'd realized. Hazel had been busy piling my desk high with things requiring my attention. I reviewed the reports she'd drafted and looked over a couple of new assignments that had come in today. After making a few changes to the documents and signing the checks she was so anxious about, I flicked off my desk light and swiveled to face the wall of windows behind me.

I liked this view. The abject darkness, broken by pools of light receding into mere pinpoints gave the illusion of serenity. Under that calm cloak, I could almost believe the good citizens of Albuquerque were safely tucked in bed, sleeping soundly and dreaming of peace and goodwill.

I called home and picked up the messages from my answering machine. Most were duplicates of messages left at the office. Del wanted to know if there was anything new. Gene said they'd traced Milt Zorn to a Southwest Airlines flight to southern California. Stealing mail from the postal service is a federal offense, so Kyle Hewitt's people were handling things at that end.

Then Paul's baritone came over the wire wanting to make sure everything was all right. He planned on hitting his own bed early in deference to the calisthenics in mine the previous night. Paul had my cell phone number in case of emergency but never used it. Influenced by television gumshoe programs, he claimed to be afraid the phone might ring at an inopportune moment, placing me in danger.

The last message really caught my attention. Mrs. Gertrude Wardlow, my plucky neighbor across the road, had noticed a suspicious car passing up and down the street two or three times earlier in the evening. She suggested I use extreme caution in returning home. Wondering why she hadn't alerted me by cell, I checked and found I'd switched to vibrate after I got tired of Hazel's calls while hunkering down in the car. Mrs. W had left a message and then doubled down by calling my home phone. What a wonderful old gal.

If this mess kept up much longer, my staid and stolid neighbors would ask me to move. On second thought, most of them hadn't had this much excitement in ages. Safe, or presumed safe, behind their windows and drapes, the old geezers probably scanned the street every night to check on "that private investigator fellow" down the street before going to bed.

Resisting the temptation to sack out on my office couch, I got up, stretched, and started to leave. An indistinct noise from the landing—a footfall, a shoulder brushing against the wall, *something*—stayed my hand on the doorknob. The door was a solid plank of heavy oak, but a panel of frosted glass to the left darkened momentarily as a shadow passed across it. After five minutes of inaction, I cautiously cracked the door. A quick look up and down the landing revealed nothing alarming. If anyone was on this floor, he wasn't visible, but a side hall leading to the restrooms lay between the elevators and me. Was someone waiting in ambush there? I stepped out onto the landing, locked the door, tugged the peashooter from my belt, and turning away from the elevators, made for the stairwell.

I did not hear my assailant's sneakers on the carpet behind me until it was too late to face him, so I dropped to all fours. He tripped over my legs and fell, landing with his body sprawled halfway across mine. Before he had time to recover, I gained my feet and sagged against the metal banister at the outer edge of the landing. Clinging to my back, he came up with me, flailing with a knife. When the blade nicked my right arm, I panicked, twisting away from the blade and straightening to throw him off my back.

Time switched to slow motion. The man clawed at my shirt for a moment. Then his center of gravity shifted. He slid over the railing. I clutched at his legs but couldn't hold on—he fell with a terrified scream. I leaned over the railing and watched him flip on his back during the forty-foot drop to the hard, polished tiles below. He landed with a terrible suddenness and a sickening thud. A dark corona haloed his head. The blood and the clatter of his knife across the baked clay squares kick-started my brain and released my frozen muscles.

Twisting around, on guard for other assailants, I spotted the weapon I'd lost during the attack, so I scrabbled across the floor and snatched up the Colt. Pressed against the wall, I frantically swept the landing in both directions.

Voices! From above.

I aimed two landings above me—too far for accurate shooting—but maybe the killers didn't know that.

But there were no killers, only a frightened cleaning crew jabbering in excitement and cringing as I pointed my weapon at them. The prudent thing would have been to retreat to the safety of my office and call the police. Instead I fished my cell out of its holder and dialed 911.

By the time the cops arrived, I had wits enough to go downstairs and let them in. The sergeant in charge was Walker Robins, an old police academy classmate. He took one look at me, grimaced, and placed a call for Gene. Then he grabbed my shoulder and turned me around.

"Hell, Vinson, you're bleeding. Somebody call an ambulance."

"I'm okay. It's just a scratch."

"Well, your scratch is filling up your shoes. Get the docs here pronto," he ordered one of his uniforms.

Robins turned to view the body sprawled on the lobby floor, running a fleshy hand through what had been a bright carrottop. Now it was thinning and fading to a rusty brown. "You know him?"

"No. But he came up from behind and attacked me as I left the office."

"Wonder how he got in?"

"It wouldn't be hard to hide in a broom closet or someplace like that until the building was locked up for the night."

"You'd think some of the cleaning crew would have stumbled over him, wouldn't you? Cardenas, you 'n' Hooker go round them up and see what they know. All right, BJ, you wanna tell me what happened?" He checked the small slice on my right arm as I talked.

I'd finished relating the events of the evening about the time Gene arrived and then had to do it all over again. The officers had trouble finding a knife until I recalled the sound of metal skittering over tiles and directed them to the other side of the open atrium. The blade had come to rest beneath a big green leaf drooping from a terracotta pot.

Eventually an ambulance arrived. A couple of EMTs bandaged me up but lost interest when I rejected their suggestion of stitches. They cautioned me to get a tetanus shot and went on their way.

Gene insisted on being Gene, that is, a careful and thorough policeman. We walked the scene step by step, he confidently, me on increasingly feeble knees. After I'd gone through the whole thing three more times, he plopped me down on a chair in the lobby. The crime-scene team arrived on the heels of the OMI people and chased everyone away.

After Gene wrapped things up, he insisted on a patrol car delivering me home. I balked but agreed to allow a cruiser to follow me. Exhausted but afraid sleep wouldn't come, I tried dictating a report to bring Del's file up to date, but made a mess of it. Tired of reliving these last tragic hours, I tumbled into bed without even undressing and promptly zonked out—only to hear the nauseating sound of a bursting pumpkin again and again in my restless dreams.

Chapter 28

THERE WAS no avoiding the news media this time. A shootout on a quiet North Valley street and a murder in the South Valley piqued their interest, but a gruesome death in a downtown office building was more than they could stand. I was forced to run gauntlets of reporters at home and at the office.

Hazel handled them better than I did. Her snarled "no comment" had a finality to it that even the most intrepid understood.

My responses must have been more tenuous because one novice news puppy kept peppering me with the stupidest questions imaginable—how did it feel to send a man tumbling to his death?

How did she think it felt? That query was as bad as wanting to know if it hurt getting shot. You bet—like a son of a bitch.

It was almost noon the next day—make that later the same day—before we gathered for a consultation in my office. Gene Enriquez of the APD, Kyle Hewitt of the US Postal Service, and a deceptively mild-mannered little man named Henry Young from the district attorney's office joined Del and me. On the speakerphone, Artie Hartshorn represented the Santa Fe Police Department. No one believed I had committed a crime in the early hours of this morning, and that was reinforced by the fact we were meeting in my office, not at APD. But we needed to make sense of the whole tangled affair, including last night's attack.

Gene got things going. "The bozo who tried to knife you was a character named Alonzo Johnson. He sometimes went by the moniker of Lonzo Villarreal. Johnson was his daddy's name, Villarreal his mother's. Ring any bells?"

"Nope. He have a record?"

"Long one. Mostly minor stuff. Some drug dealing, an assault or two, but they were bar fights, not assassinations."

"Get anything from the cleaning crew?" I asked.

"Not much. A couple of the women got nervous when they were cleaning the rest rooms on your floor but swear they didn't see anyone."

"I don't understand it, Gene. Nobody knew I was coming back to the office last night, although I had the feeling I was followed downtown. It was strong enough to spook me and put me on my guard."

"We found a cell phone on the guy set to vibrate," Gene said. "My guess is he hid out and was prepared to wait until you showed, whenever that might be. Even overnight if need be. You probably *were* followed until they were certain you were headed to the office. Then they broke off and alerted Villarreal."

"And if I didn't show, he was going to wait all night?"

"Probably. That's how determined these people are. That ought to tell you something."

"Was the man a gang member?" the assistant district attorney asked.

"Associated with some gangs, but there's no clear evidence he was a member of one. He always denied it. He was more of a freelancer, I guess you'd say."

"Who'd he pal around with?"

Gene named members of two or three local gangs, but none of them were connected with the Saints.

"Any contact with the Iron Crosses?" Artie's disembodied voice asked.

"Not on the record."

"Was he a biker?"

"We don't know that much about him, but we'll find out for you," Gene said.

"Mr. Dahlman, what's your take on all this?" Artie again.

"Well, Detective, I'd say your double-murder trial will proceed as scheduled. With all that's happened, even the extortionists must realize they can no longer compromise me. Things are far too public now. My law partners are aware of the blackmail attempt. You gentlemen know what's involved, and we all understand the motivation for the threats."

"Agreed," Artie answered. "We know everything except the who."

"I have a few ideas about that," I said. "If you look hard enough, you're going to find a connection between this Johnson—or Villarreal—and the Brown Saints." I ignored Artie's exasperated grunt. "And when

Inspector Hewitt runs Milt Zorn to ground, he's going to find a connection there, as well."

Artie couldn't contain himself. "That's crazy, BJ. The Crosses and the Saints were at one another's throats, have been for years. There's been so much blood spilled between those two groups, there's no way one is doing a favor for the other."

Gene agreed. "That's my intel too. In fact Puerco Arrullar and this fellow Whiznant have butted heads before. Puerco's got a nasty scar on his belly, and Whiznant's got one in his shoulder. They exchanged those four years ago right here in Albuquerque. Both of them served a little time for that."

"Come up with a better answer," I said. "Emilio Prada was more or less running with the Santos Morenos. He was getting protection from them in exchange for some favors—like renting those mailboxes, for example. Their association was a new development, and frankly, a bizarre one. Arrullar's crew would have nothing to do with a queer hustler unless they needed him." I paused. "Emilio was probably telling me the truth when he said he didn't know who stole the negatives for the blackmail pictures. But when I started questioning him, he put two and two together."

"So this Prada fellow figured it out and wanted in on the action, is that it?" Young, the ADA, asked.

"That makes sense. When I started showing up to ask Emilio questions, it was the Saints who helped him pack up and get out of town." I thought for a minute. "Gene, why don't you check out a fellow who runs with them by the name of Jacques Costas."

"The Haitian? Why?"

"I was at the C&W Palace the other night. The Saints keep a table there, and the usual group was drinking and having a grand old time. But Jackie was missing. That was the day after Tarleton was killed."

"You're thinking it's Haitian blood on the victim's bayonet?"

"It's worth checking out."

"When you find him, I think we have enough to get a warrant for his DNA," Young said.

"*If* we find him." Gene came back at him. "There was a lot of blood on that bayonet. Whoever got stuck, got stuck good." He nodded at me. "What's your take on Tarleton's murder?"

"More or less what you spelled out the other day. He was a danger to them because he could finger whoever ordered those prints. Maybe he tried to cut himself in for a piece of the action, or was afraid the Saints would start slamming doors behind them."

"You think Tarleton killed Emilio?" Del asked.

"Possible, although I don't think so. But he knew too much for somebody's comfort, so they went after him."

"Sorta strange they made that move right after he called you," Gene said.

Was something gnawing at my old partner? "The fact they were able to take him out up close and personal is another argument favoring Puerco and his crew. It took some serious muscle to kill that old Marine."

"Now that you guys have got this thing all solved, you gotta explain it to me," Artie said dryly. "The Iron Crosses and the Santos Morenos would rather kill one another than cooperate. Hell, BJ, nothing would serve the Saints better than for Whiznant and his buddy Rodrigo to go up for life. That tears the head off the Crosses and leaves the drug trade in the north to the Saints. Why would they go to such extremes to quash a witness who'll send away the guys trying to cut in on their operation? Explain that to me."

Shit! What if I was wrong about this? These guys were competent professionals, and they had the same set of facts I did. I rubbed my tired eyes. Well, for one thing, they hadn't done the footwork, hadn't stared down Puerco and his bunch as I had.

I cleared my throat and tried to counter Artie's reasoning. "Blood's thicker than water—"

"No shared blood between them except what they spilled," Artie said.

"And what's thicker than blood?"

"Money," Gene and Del chorused.

"Right. The Crosses are paying for the Saints' help," I said.

Artie continued to object. "There are no Crosses left. The club fell apart when we arrested the two leaders. All Arrullar and his group had to do was walk in and pick up the pieces. No need to commit murder to reap the benefits. Hell's bells, now they've even got the Feds down on them. It's an unreasonable risk."

"To us, maybe," Del said. "I'm not sure how a thug would see it."

"Puerco's an arrogant shit," Gene mused. "Maybe he figures he can get away with anything he puts his mind to."

"Well, he figured wrong," Kyle said. "He's got three law enforcement jurisdictions going for his throat if your supposition is right."

"It is. When we finally get to the bottom of this, you're going to find Puerco and his Santos Morenos."

ADA Young turned to Del. "Well, you're wrong about one thing, Counselor. The Santa Fe murder trial is very vulnerable right now. Given the extremes these people are willing to go to, if they can't intimidate you, they might figure on eliminating you."

"That would merely delay the trial."

"And possibly terrify the witness into silence. And, of course, they might eliminate her, as well."

"That would work to the detriment of the defense. It's the old question of who benefits?"

"Yes, that works sometimes," Young agreed. "But if we're trying to pin these murders on the defendants' bitterest rivals, I'm not certain the doctrine of who benefits would suffice. Especially in a capital murder trial. One thing is clear, gentlemen—you must all be very careful until this thing is over."

That seemed to put the cap on the meeting, but Gene hung back as the others left. "I notice you didn't mention your boyfriend."

"Paul? Why would I?"

"Maybe because you weren't up-front with me. When I checked on you the morning Tarleton was killed, Paul Barton was at your place. The patrol I assigned to keep an eye on your house after the shootout says his old jalopy was in front of your house all night long. Then I found out Tarleton phoned you at home to ask for a meeting. Is that right?" I reluctantly acknowledged it was. "Did Barton hear the conversation?"

"There was no conversation. I didn't make it to the phone in time, so it went to the answering machine. All Paul heard was a voice saying we had to talk. Tarleton didn't identify himself beyond saying he was my old San Diego buddy, or words to that effect."

"Enough so someone in the know could figure out who it was."

"Yeah, I guess. You've got more, haven't you?"

Gene nodded. "Paul's mother's name is Luisa Maria Arrullar de Barton. She's Puerco's father's sister. His aunt."

"Shit," I said with a sinking heart. That was why Puerco gave me the eye the other night at the C&W. He saw me talking to his cousin. But as I recalled the incident, my morale picked up a bit. If Paul had been a co-conspirator, Puerco would have passed us without calling attention to himself.

"Does his mother have a record?" I asked.

"Not even a parking ticket. She was married to Paul Barton Sr. for years until he died when the kid was about ten. The old man was a carpenter. Made a decent living for his family, but after he died of TB, Mrs. Barton fell on hard times."

"She works two jobs to keep the family going," I said.

"True. Plus she got some help from Puerco's father until he died. Maybe Puerco called in a marker."

"You're wrong, Gene. The kid's clean. I've laid traps for him, and he didn't tumble once. This other thing has to be coincidental."

"Then why didn't he tell you about the family relationship and clear the air?"

"There was no reason to. The Santos name never came up in our conversations." I hesitated, recalling the night I told Paul the Saints were involved in a big case. "Well, that's not strictly true. He knew they were involved in something I was working on. But hell, Gene, you don't go around volunteering your cousin's a hood unless there's a reason."

The detective gave me a long, searching look. "If you say so."

"Besides, he tried to tell me something about his background once, and I cut him off. I think he intended to tell me about his blood ties then, but I said he didn't need to prove his trustworthiness to me."

"Hope that wasn't a mistake." Then my friend—my ex-partner— pulled a heavy-caliber Ruger semiautomatic from beneath his suit jacket and handed it over. "Watch your back."

Gene had no sooner departed than Hazel buzzed to say Paul was on the phone. The sinking feeling in my stomach said a lot about how firmly I believed what I'd just told Gene.

"Sorry to bother you, Vince." Paul's voice was full of concern, but was it genuine? "I had to know you're okay."

"I'm fine, Paul. The other fellow's not so good, but I'm all right."

"I thought maybe you'd call and let me know you were okay."

"I was going to as soon as I found a minute. The whole thing didn't happen until after midnight, and I've been tied up with the authorities."

"You're not in any trouble, are you?"

"No. The police have the knife he cut—was trying to cut me with. How did you find out?" The oblique reference to my wound set the scratch to burning.

"Are you kidding? It's all over the news, and I read about it in the *Journal* when I stopped at the Student Union for a salad. When is this going to be over?"

"Soon, I hope."

"Will you be careful? Please."

I swallowed around a lump in my throat. *He cared!* "As careful as I can."

"Is it okay if I come by tonight?"

"Not a good idea. I won't be home tonight. I have a new lead to run down."

"Oh, okay. Maybe I'll drop by tomorrow after I finish at the library. Around sundown."

I couldn't muster the courage to deny him. "Fine, but I'm not sure what tomorrow will bring."

"No big deal. If you're not home, I'll head on back to the U."

As soon as Hazel saw I was off the phone, she asked if I wanted a corned beef on rye for lunch. The thought of food made me nauseous. To foil her attempt at mothering me, I told her I had a late lunch meeting. She raised her eyebrows but let it go.

While Gene and Kyle and Del were out doing their thing, as was Artie up in Santa Fe, I needed to come up with a way to convince them my theory about the Santos Morenos was correct. Gene was a good cop, but he wasn't on board yet—although Paul's tenuous connection to Puerco nudged him in my direction. All right, it wasn't tenuous; it was blood.

I sank back in my chair and went semicomatose. My mind refused to function as the host of feelings bottled up inside me sought avenues of escape. As they surfaced one by one, they inevitably led to only one person: Paul. My response to him was so fucking overwhelming it was off the charts, even beyond what I'd felt for Del. It was obvious I'd fallen for him. Hard. The kind of hard that raised goose bumps at the thought of him, sent tremors of excitement throughout me at the mention of his name, and muddled my brain at the sight of his lean frame walking toward me.

The timing couldn't be worse. My entanglement with him was throwing me off my game and putting me at undue risk. And if I was in danger, he might be as well.

A shiver wracked me; he was screwing up my ability to think straight. Was my obsession with Paul Barton getting in the way of resolving this case?

Chapter 29

I DROVE home from the office to clean up and change into my western duds. It was time to make my move. If Jackie Costas was dead or dying from Tarleton's bayonet, the Saints had a problem. When the Haitian's body surfaced, his DNA would connect him to the former Marine. After that their delicate truce with the valley street cops would be upset. Homicide Division would be all over the gang.

I drove through the C&W Palace parking lot to make sure Paul's Plymouth wasn't there before entering the noisy barn. I wandered the perimeter of the nightclub to check out the situation.

Even before I reached the Saints' table, Puerco was aware of me. One of his gangbangers had sidled up and whispered in his ear. A lookout posted in the lot, no doubt.

"You're starting to feel like a boil on the butt," Puerco said when I walked up. "You know what I do when I get one-a them nasties? I lance the fucker, drain the pus, and pretty soon it ain't a problem anymore."

"Here's a thought, Puerco. Keep your butt clean, and you probably won't have any boils."

A couple of the Santos came up out of their chairs. Puerco flushed a deep brown, but it was too much to hope he would burst a blood vessel and solve both of our problems. He settled back and scanned the table, sending a secret signal to calm his restless boys.

Zancón, his right-hand man, remained cool throughout the exchange. He was the dangerous one.

I headed straight for what I hoped was Puerco's tender spot. "Where's Jackie tonight?"

The dangerous gleam in the hood's eyes said it all. What had they done with the body?

"Last I heard he was headed back to Port Prince, or whatever place he come from. Decided he didn't like the States. Probably the poor quality of the cops."

"According to the police, he didn't get on an airplane headed for Haiti or anywhere else. Same for Amtrak."

Puerco gave a swinish snort. "Naw. He left like he come. Over the nearest border. Or that's what they tell me. How come the cops looking for him anyway?"

"Homicide's on his trail for some reason. If those guys are after him, it's serious. But they'll find him. You can probably do yourself some good if you contact Detective Eugene Enriquez and point him in the right direction. I can give you his number if you want."

"Why'd I do that? Screw 'em. They can find Costas without my help."

"You're right, they can. I was merely trying to be helpful. By the way, you remember me looking for Emilio a while back?" The gangster merely stared. "Well, that situation's defused now. Seems somebody was trying to blackmail this attorney with some racy pictures. Won't work now. He told his law firm about the photos. For some reason he also reported the extortion attempt to the local DA and to the one up in Santa Fe. In fact, he told everyone who'd listen. So that takes the heat off him."

"Why do I care?" Puerco growled.

"No reason. Well, you guys have a good evening."

I SLEPT very little that night.

The picture window in my darkened living room gave me a decent view of Post Oak Drive in front of the house. Lying on the couch to alternately catnap and watch the street for suspicious activity to the music of *Tosca* and *Otello* made for a long night. Ironic how murder and mayhem in two magnificent operas seemed romantic while the real thing was altogether different. Stray thoughts of Paul kept stirring the witch's brew of my emotional cauldron.

Nothing moved outside except the cop car cruising the house every few hours. Puerco was apparently smarter than I was. He was letting me stew in my own juices. Either that or he had no more idea of how to bring this thing to a climax than I did.

As soon as it was light outside, I nodded off and slept for three straight hours.

My ringing telephone woke me—Hazel checking up on me. After I assured her I would come in before long, she bluntly told me Del's case was taking up too much of my time and energy. That point was hard to argue.

She morphed from mother to office manager, reminding me I'd accepted a stolen identity case from a local lumber magnate. His daughter, a sophomore at UNM, was the victim, and he hadn't been satisfied with the progress APD detectives had made on the case. Now he was beginning to feel the same way about our efforts. Charlie, she reminded me, was occupied with the worker's comp and insurance death claims he was handling.

Sounding more confident than I felt, I told Hazel this would soon be over and cajoled her into running down the leads she'd already found on the Internet. In truth she was perfectly capable of handling the whole ID-theft thing.

That out of the way, she demanded decisions on a list of things that more or less rendered my appearance in the office meaningless. So I cleaned up and settled down in my home office to bring my notes on Del's case up-to-date. Unlike on television, no obscure clue suddenly popped into the clear light of day to propel me into action.

Frustrated, I leaned back in my father's leather swivel chair and glanced around the office. This room had been his—and still was. I had changed very little except for replacing his old desktop computer with a faster, more powerful machine and adding a scanner and copier. Otherwise the room was as he left it. The dark walnut paneling, the ivory ceiling, the cowboy and Native American artwork, the small MacNeil bronze serving as an expensive paperweight, even the old-fashioned Schaeffer fountain pen and mechanical pencil desk set had been his. It was almost as if he were looking over my shoulder and speaking to me in his gentle voice.

Be thorough, son. Thorough and careful, and nobody can fault you.

Don't take so many risks. That was Mom. *Last night was pure foolishness.*

And it had been. Deliberately goading a feral boar while he was feeding and counting on him to spin out of control was downright stupid.

Or was it? How did I know he hadn't? He could have set the city afire while I brooded inside my own home. I grabbed the phone and started dialing.

It took five minutes to get Del. He reported nothing unusual in his day so far. It took longer to run down Gene Enriquez, whose voice matched mine for weariness and frustration. He took out some of that frustration on me when he learned of my face-off with Puerco at the C&W last night.

"Jackie's dead, Gene. That nonsense about going back to Haiti was the clincher. If the guy was still ambulatory, Puerco would have spouted some bullshit—like the Haitian was off on a job assaulting some poor citizen or stealing a grandmother's pension check or something. But he put the final touch to the thing. Said Jackie was gone for good."

"You may be right about him being dead, but a body has a nasty habit of showing up no matter where it's hid. Someday a coyote will dig up his corpse out on the mesa and scare the bejesus out of some poor hiker."

"Yeah, but by then it'll be too late. We need to locate Costas faster than that."

"Last trace we can find of him was with his live-in girlfriend before Tarleton bought it. The woman's Haitian, too, and she claims he's gone home. But she didn't make it sound permanent like Puerco did."

"Anything new on Zorn?" I asked.

"Kyle's people have him in custody in San Diego. Kid was trying to join the Navy to see the world. Now he's seeing the local jailhouse. So far he hasn't given up anything or anybody."

"He's our best bet to tie the Saints into all of this."

"A scared high school kid is a mighty poor bet."

"What else do we have?"

"Nothing. The Metro lab didn't do any better at raising forensic evidence on the extortion envelopes and notes than K-Y. The logic of our theory about all this mess will escape any impartial jury pool I know of. Young Mr. Zorn is it."

"You get anything else out of Mackson?"

"Not a thing, and he'd have blabbed if he knew something. In fact, our problem now is to keep him from making up things he thinks will make us happy."

"Poor kid."

"He's old enough to know better. Now he's learning the Feds' spanking is going to hurt more than his mama's." He paused and worked around to what interested him. "What about your friend? Anything new there?"

"Haven't seen him. He called to make sure I was okay after the attack at the office, but I discouraged him from coming over." I neglected to add I expected Paul that evening.

"Good. Keep him at arm's length."

"Gene, let's assume for the moment you're right about him. Maybe we can use him if he's the fox in the henhouse. Feed him some information and see if he leaks it to Puerco. When the Santos act on it, we'll know you're right."

"And what gem do you intend to impart?"

"Working on it."

I SPENT the rest of the morning trying to concoct a story to provoke Puerco into acting rashly. All I could come up with was the fiction that neighbors had seen a seriously injured or dead man carried down the alley behind Tarleton's house the day he was killed. The police had a description of at least one vehicle involved, but weren't releasing any information at the moment. They'd made some progress in tracing the movement of the mysterious car and expected to have something concrete soon.

Would that string of monumental lies be enough to rev Puerco's motor? It was pretty thin.

Now it was a matter of waiting for Paul to come over to feed him the poisoned apple. Lord, how would I pull it off? We didn't normally discuss my cases, so how would I even bring it up without tipping my hand? I'd figure it out somehow. More to the point, was I capable of loving him one moment and setting him up for a fall in the next? My present train of thought sent me on the hunt for an Alka-Seltzer to settle my roiling belly.

When reason won't work, resort to rationalization, I always say. If the information failed to get to Puerco, wouldn't that prove Paul was no spy? My theory collapsed under its own weight. If Puerco simply did nothing, we'd never know whether Paul had passed the information to him because it's impossible to prove a negative.

After lunch I decided another nap would make me sharper for my ordeal that evening. It was downright tragic that I considered a tryst with Paul an ordeal.

I'd just fallen off the sleep cliff when the ringing telephone dragged me back to consciousness. I must have sounded terrible because Gene became instantly alarmed. I shook my head to clear away the cobwebs and then assured him everything was okay.

"Zorn volunteered to come back to the state. The marshals are flying him out. He'll be in my office about three. Want to sit in?"

"Sure, if it's okay with the Feds."

"They won't be a problem, but Daddy Zorn's getting a lawyer for Junior. If he insists, we'll have to throw you out. But what the hell, if we don't try, we won't know, right?"

"I'll be there."

I hung up, feeling a surge of excitement. Maybe I wouldn't have to put Paul to the test after all.

Before heading downtown to police headquarters, I detoured by Mrs. Wardlow's house.

She cracked the door cautiously but threw it wide open when she saw me. "BJ, how nice. Won't you come in?"

"No, thank you, ma'am. I'm due downtown in about thirty minutes, but I want to warn you to be careful. Things are beginning to move on the case that's caused so much trouble."

She beamed. "Why, thank you. That's very thoughtful of you."

THE CHARTERED jet was late arriving at the Albuquerque Sunport, so Gene, Kyle Hewitt, and I brought one another up-to-date as we waited in a police department interview room.

The postal inspector was none too happy I'd braced Puerco at the C&W last night. "What the hell were you thinking, man? That's a good way to wake up one morning and find your head's missing. Those guys aren't just dangerous, they're deadly."

"As soon as I found out about it, I alerted the Gang Unit," Gene said. "They have a pretty good handle on the Santos Morenos and say it's caused no dustup they can see."

"The squad have any thoughts about my theory the gang's involved in the Iron Cross case?" I asked.

"They expressed some surprise and a whole lot of doubt. There have been a lot of back-and-forth trips to Santa Fe and points north, but you'd expect that if the Saints are expanding their territory to fill the vacuum after the Crosses fell apart. Incidentally the Gang Unit's looking for Costas. They have a complaint he sliced up his woman's old boyfriend recently. If they find him, they know he's on our list too."

There was a knock on the door. A middle-aged man with a shock of suspiciously perfect yellow hair entered. Everyone else in the room had already gone to light woolens, but Reggie Smith seemed quite comfortable in thin silk the color of milk with a dash of coffee thrown in. The noted defense attorney might be flashy, but no one ever accused him of being fashionable.

He shook hands all around. When he came to me, his eyes widened, but it was obvious he wasn't really surprised. "BJ, why are you here?"

"By invitation."

"BJ is the one who followed the trail to your client."

"Ah, I see. But I still don't understand why it's appropriate for him to sit in on this interview."

Gene hopped on that one quickly. "Is there going to be an interview?"

"Certainly. That's why we're all here, isn't it? By the way, I'd like to thank the postal service for saving my client the cost of a ticket back home."

"Way I heard it, he was trying for a ticket elsewhere," Gene said.

"Yes, well, he had some romantic notion of joining the Navy and sailing around the world."

"Maybe he can work it into his schedule in a few years."

"Let's not rush to judgment, Detective Enriquez. We'll see what develops."

"What about BJ here?" Gene shot a thumb in my direction.

"He's welcome to stay as far as I'm concerned. At least for the moment. I thought my client would have been here by now."

"Plane was delayed getting out of San Diego."

"I see. Well—"

We will forever be ignorant of the bit of wisdom Reggie Smith was about to impart because right then two US Marshals arrived with Milt Zorn, turned him over to Kyle Hewitt, and headed out to look for a good café.

ADA Henry Young entered the interview room hard on their heels. It looked as though things were about to get underway.

Chapter 30

ZORN WAS a slightly heavier and tougher version of Billy Mackson, although by now a good deal of the toughness had leached away. Big gray eyes sat in deep sockets on either side of a high-ridged nose that made me question the kid's peripheral vision. His thick, mousy hair gave him a fuzzy look. To someone like Mackson, the guy probably seemed cool, if that's a word the kids still use. To me he just looked like a scared kid in hot water over his head.

Milt kept his eyes averted, staring at the floor, the table, anywhere to avoid human contact, but he darted quick looks from beneath heavy brows now and then. He obviously wasn't prepared for the display of power arrayed against him.

His lawyer stepped up to start earning his pay. "Son, I'm Reggie Smith. Your father hired me to act as your attorney in this matter. Do you understand?"

Milt gave a quick nod and concentrated on a scratch in the department's steel table. We had yet to hear his voice.

"Good. Now before we begin the formal interview, I need to ask if you're all right? Have you been mistreated? Do you need anything to drink or eat?" The questions earned a shake of the head. "Very well." Smith addressed the rest of us. "Gentlemen, I need a few minutes with my client before we proceed."

"Just one minute, Counselor," Young, the assistant prosecutor, said. "I'm certain Mr. Zorn has already been informed that the federal authorities will be pursuing mail-theft charges against him. Technically he remains in their custody at this time, but I think it appropriate to let him know the State is investigating other criminal matters. Depending upon what we learn from him today, we may or may not be leveling our own charges.

"Now we will excuse ourselves while you consult with your client," he went on. "Mr. Zorn's father and mother are waiting outside. As he is eighteen years of age, we do not consider it necessary for them to sit in on our session."

We trooped out of the room, passing the Zorns, father and mother, as they went into the interview room to meet with Reggie and their son. The senior Zorn was a big bluff man with thick glasses and an even more pronounced nose than his son's. He wore a stubborn air, and I had the feeling he didn't realize the seriousness of his son's problem. Mrs. Zorn, on the other hand, looked whipped. She sat leaning forward over her purse, refusing to meet anyone's eyes.

We passed the Zorns again as we returned to the interview room. A heated, half-hour argument must have taken place in there before Reggie was ready to proceed. To my eye nothing had changed, except that Milt's mother now seemed almost despondent.

Because our interest at the moment was the younger Zorn's involvement with Del's blackmail case, Gene handled the interview, which was being recorded. He identified each of the eight individuals crowded into the room. The place already seemed stuffy, and we hadn't gotten past the formalities yet.

Once the interview began, it dragged on interminably while Reggie constantly referred to the copious notes he'd made while consulting with Milt and his parents.

Mild-mannered Henry Young had had enough. "Mr. Zorn, we have evidence that you bribed William Mackson, a clerk at the Ship-n-Mail on Juan Tabo, to steal mail from a certain box and turn it over to you. What I want now is the name of the person who asked you to make those arrangements and your motivation for agreeing to the request. You should understand, Mr. Smith, that I will bring criminal charges against your client, including conspiracy to commit capital murder, if he fails to cooperate."

The kid visibly wilted before the prosecutor's onslaught, but Reggie Smith smiled as if he had found a worthy opponent.

After a lot of back-and-forth, and some posturing on both sides, Reggie worked out the deal he wanted for his client. Young agreed not to prosecute Milt if he gave us what we wanted; however, the ADA carefully explained that the federal authorities were free to proceed with the mail-theft counts. Even so, this got the Zorns' son and heir out from under the threat of capital murder charges. In my opinion, the state would have had a hard time making them stick anyway.

Twilight was falling before things really started moving. Once Young and Smith stated the parameters of the deal for the record, Gene took over the questioning.

"On or about September 20, did you approach William Mackson, a clerk at the Ship-n-Mail store on Juan Tabo NE, and ask him to give you any and all mail addressed to box 2223?"

The kid sat with slumped shoulders and answered in a husky baritone. "Yeah. Uh, yes, sir."

"Even though you were not the box holder?"

"Yes, sir."

"Did Mr. Mackson agree to do as you asked?"

"Yes."

"Why?"

Now that the spotlight was on Billy Boy's shortcomings, the kid's spirits rose a bit. "He's a dork. A puppy dog. Always trying to get tight with us, so I knew he'd go along."

"Us? Who is *us*, Mr. Zorn?" Gene asked.

Under Gene's determined questioning, Zorn admitted he took advantage of Mackson's desire to be accepted by the regular guys at school by hanging around with him a bit before asking him to filch the mail. To cinch the deal, he'd added the bribe of an expensive motorcycle for a mere $300.00. When he balked at revealing where the bike came from, Gene came at him from another direction.

"Why did you want the mail from that particular Ship-n-Mail box?"

Milt stirred in his seat, scuffed his shoes on the floor, and clenched his fists. "Somebody asked me to get it for him."

"Who asked you to intercept the mail?"

The kid was beginning to understand the possible consequences of his actions—consequences levied by people outside this room. He had trouble getting the words out and glanced at his attorney.

"Go ahead, Milt. Answer the question," Smith prompted. "You're protected under the agreement."

"Right… protected," he mumbled, deftly understating his fear. "It was a guy named Zancón."

"Are you speaking of José Zapata, the man whose street name is Zancón?" Gene asked.

"I guess. I just know him as Zancón."

"Describe him," Gene snapped.

Milt stumbled around grasping for words, proving to me, at any rate, that he wasn't very observant. In the end, however, he gave a more or less adequate description of the hood.

"Is he the man who gave you the motorcycle?" When Zorn stared mutely into space, Gene hardened his voice. "Answer the question."

"Yeah, Zancón gave it to me. You know, for Mackson."

"How do you know Zancón?"

The kid slid a long look at his attorney. "From around."

"You have to be more specific."

"Do I have to? I know him. Isn't that enough?"

"We need to understand your relationship to this Zancón fellow."

"He was my dealer."

"Your drug dealer?"

The answer was barely audible. "Yeah."

"What?"

"Yeah, he sold me drugs."

Gene eyed the kid for a long moment. "Did you buy drugs for the purpose of selling them on the Eldorado campus?"

"Don't answer that," Smith said. "That is outside the scope of our agreement, Detective. Bring it back, or the interview's over."

"All right," Gene agreed amiably. "Mr. Zorn, do you know of any gang affiliations this Zancón has?"

"He's something in the Santos Morenos. One of the bigwigs."

"And how do you know this?"

"I saw him with the big boss once when…. Well, I saw them together once."

"Together like friends?"

"Together like business."

My cell phone went off at that moment. After silencing the ring, I left the interview room to take the call. I did not recognize the number but I did know the high, nervous voice.

"Mr. Vinson? BJ, is that you?"

"Yes, ma'am." I answered Gertrude Wardlow's tremulous query.

"Oh, I'm so glad I reached you. Something happened a moment ago, and it's got me worried."

I clenched the phone tighter. "What happened?"

"You know that young man who comes to visit and sometimes stays overnight?"

I felt my cheeks redden. "Yes, ma'am. You must mean Paul. Paul Barton."

"Is that his name? He's such a handsome youngster."

"Yes, ma'am. But what about him?"

"Well, I saw him park his car like he always does and watched him go to your door and ring the bell. When no one answered, he started back to his car. And then this big white van roared up and two men got out. They got into a fight, BJ. Right out there on the street. And I'm afraid your friend was injured. One of the men hit him with something, and then they put him in the van and drove away."

My heart virtually stopped and then raced at an alarming rate. "They kidnapped Paul? Did you call the police?"

"Yes, I reported it right away, and then I called you. You said it was all right to—"

"Absolutely all right, Mrs. Wardlow. Did you get the license of the van?"

"No. My eyesight, you know." She sounded apologetic. "But it was an older model Econoline. I'm pretty sure of that. White."

"Thank you, ma'am. Stay inside your house with the doors locked until the police get there or I arrive. Will you do that?"

"Oh, yes. I'll do that."

I hung up and stormed back into the room. It took some doing, but eventually I pried Gene out of the interview long enough to give him the news.

Chapter 31

"IT'S A trick. A trap," Gene insisted after he returned from asking Young to take over the interview. "They know I'm onto Barton. They're just trying to give him some cover. And they'll probably take your ass out while they're doing it."

I swallowed my anger. "*How* do they know you're onto Paul?"

He shrugged. "I don't know. You told him, for all I know."

"I didn't. And what if you're wrong about him?"

"If I'm wrong, how'd they know he was gonna be at your place?"

"They probably didn't. They were looking for me and took him when I wasn't there. Puerco saw us together at the C&W the other night. If you're wrong, Gene, an innocent citizen's been kidnapped and probably hurt. And either way, it ties into this case."

"Okay, so let's get out to your place and see what's up."

My Impala rode Gene's bumper on a mad dash to the North Valley, until I realized the foolishness of driving so recklessly. I eased off to put some distance between the vehicles and raised Charlie Weeks on my cell phone. He agreed to stay close to Hazel.

Three blue-and-whites were already on the scene when we arrived. Night was falling and the cruisers' flashing light bars turned the residential street into a dizzying strobe. Some of the cops, spotlighted by powerful flashlights, clustered around Mrs. Wardlow standing on the lawn across the street, while others were taking digital photos of everything in sight. Mrs. Wardlow was gesturing this way and that like the agent in charge she once had been. Neighbors huddled in pools of light on their porches or peeked from behind drapes. The adrenaline on Post Oak Drive NW was running high.

"BJ!" My neighbor broke away from the policemen who dwarfed her slight figure. "I'm so glad you're here. I'm afraid your friend is in serious trouble."

After that dramatic introduction, the widow, clasping a wool sweater around her shoulders against the night chill, clearly relished retelling her tale. One day I was going to sit down and hear her story. Regrettably she was able to add little to what she'd told me on the telephone. A police sergeant picked up the tale when she finished.

"We got an alert out on the van immediately. Intercepted three answering the description within ten minutes, but they weren't the right ones. I figure they switched vehicles within the first mile or so."

"There's blood on the ground, did you check any of the vans for blood?" Gene asked.

"There's blood?" I rushed across the street.

An officer intercepted me. "You can't come any closer. The technicians are on their way."

I was close enough. The streetlight revealed a small rusty stain on the asphalt beside Paul's Plymouth. They'd caught him as he was getting into his car.

"Hey, Detective," a uniform called from his patrol unit. "They found a white van parked on a street four blocks over. Ran the plates, and it was reported stolen this afternoon."

"That's it," Gene said. "Maybe they screwed up and left prints this time." He called to the officer who was monitoring the unit's radio. "Tell them to boot the crime-scene guys in the ass. I want them over there right away. And have somebody canvass the neighborhood to see if anyone saw the switch. We need a description of the transfer vehicle."

The next hour was as frustrating as any I've ever endured. I stood at my picture window and watched the forensics team arrive in vans and a mobile crime lab. They cleared the site and took photographs of their own. Then they set up a laser scanner to measure distances and placed alphanumeric coded markers that identified blood, hair, or anything else they might find. The fact so few had been put down was frightening. They weren't finding very much. The criminalists and the technicians went about their tasks in such a deliberate, careful manner that my blood pressure about tore off the top of my head.

Gene and the department were doing everything humanly possible to find Paul, but to me it was taking an agonizingly long time. At one point my ex-partner thought we'd caught a break when they located a witness who was able to describe the second vehicle.

I was in the passenger's seat of Gene's Ford, ready to go interview the source before he'd taken two steps. "Come on, let's go!"

He leaned into the driver's side window. "Hold your horses. The guy's being interviewed. They'll get whatever info he has."

"We need to be there, Gene."

"Calm down. We'll—"

"This is *Paul*, Gene. They've got Paul."

"And we'll get him back. But not by running all over the countryside every time someone reports in. You're a better cop than that."

I leaned back in the seat and sighed. He was right. I'd been a pretty cool customer when I was on the force. But now…?

Then a call came over his radio that dashed my hopes. The car was found abandoned in a West Central Avenue parking lot. The perps had made another switch.

Trying to figure out the purpose of the snatch was driving me crazy. If it was payback, then Paul might already be dead. I prayed it was something else.

Then Gene did the worst thing he could have done… from my standpoint, at least.

"BJ, let's be rational about this thing. You're not helping things by tromping on my toes and getting in the way. What these guys really want is to flush you out. So I want you to go in the house and stay there until I get a better handle on this."

"If you think—"

"That's an order, BJ. Of course, I could always haul you down to the station and have someone interview you for the next couple of hours. Your choice."

The front door no sooner closed behind me than my skin itched. The inactivity was going to suffocate me. I headed for the bar and poured a bourbon neat. Normally the worst thing in the world to do, but I needed something to steady me.

Then my cell phone rang. The caller's number was blocked.

"You missing something?" the voice on the other end asked. "Like maybe your new boyfriend?" A harsh laugh rattled the receiver. "You got a thing for pretty boys, ain't you? This one's as sweet-looking as Milio."

The caller's voice had hovered between the familiar and the strange, but the way he enunciated Prada's name brought it into focus. I reached for the portable recording machine on my desk, attached its rubber suction terminal to the cell phone, and switched on the device.

"Hello, Puerco. I always thought you were a fellow in control of things. Guess I was wrong."

Making no effort to deny the identification, Puerco slipped into his own persona. "Wrong how? I got total control, in case you ain't noticed. You the ones chasing your tails."

"Let's see. You've managed to bring the Albuquerque Police Department, the US Postal Service, and probably the FBI down on your back. That doesn't sound like control to me. Sounds like you went off into outer space."

"I'll show you who's in space, man!" Puerco shrieked. "I'll send you pretty boy's right hand."

"You do that and he's worthless to you." I broke into a cold sweat. The thug was crazy enough to do it. "What do you want?"

"What do I want? I want what you owe me, you white... fairy... motherfucker."

"I owe you?"

"Fucking A! You cost me a million bucks, man. That's what you owe me."

Suddenly all the pieces fell into place. "Is that what the Iron Crosses promised you for getting their people out from under a double-murder charge? They were conning you, man. They don't have that kind of money."

The silence on the other end of the line told me I'd hit the nail on the head. I halfway expected him to ignore my comment, but he didn't.

"No, but the two they iced did. The Head Cross, you know, that guy Whiznant, found their stash."

"The drug trade in the north is worth more than $1,000,000. Why not just let the Crosses stew in their own juices and take over?"

"We will anyway. At least, we'll split the territory with the guys moving down from Colorado. But a fresh million finances a lot of meth. Look, Vinson, I ain't no fool. I know the kid's not worth a million to you, but I figure he's worth something. Maybe a couple hundred grand. Then there's that old busybody across the street. Probably worth something to keep her healthy. That fat secretary of yours is gold-plated too. I hear she's like a mama to you. The queer lawyer you and Milio used to share's gotta have some value. And you—you're worth the whole nut all by yourself. And I know you're good for it. Milio told us how that lawyer was always bragging you was rolling in dough."

"Why'd you kill Emilio, Puerco? He was harmless."

"Who said I killed him?"

"Look, we're talking on cell phones. There's no way I can trace your call. So tell me why you killed Prada."

"That one's on you, man. You kept pushing him, and he was weak. That's the thing about queers. They're weak bastards. Ever notice that? Oh yeah, you're one of them, ain't you? Well, nothing personal. So here's the deal. I want a million bucks in small bills. Nothing marked. My guys are good with money. They can spot marked bills, no trouble at all. And I want it tonight."

"Tonight? You're crazy. You know better than that, Puerco. Where am I going to get a million tonight? Everything's closed."

"Your problem, not mine."

"Look, I can come up with the money, but it's going to take some time."

"You ain't got time. Leastways, your lover boy ain't."

I momentarily lost my cool, but maybe that wasn't a bad thing. Puerco needed to know I wasn't going to fold up and give in to unreasonable demands. "If you want your money, he comes back in one piece and breathing on his own. And let's get one thing straight right now, you fucking asshole. If he doesn't come back whole, then your ass is gone. It's over. I'm not a cop anymore, Puerco. I can do things they can't."

"You through? You think you can scare me? You're nothing but a over-the-hill, fairy punk. I ain't scared of queers."

"Then I will kill your ass without thinking twice about it, Puerco. It'll be like making bacon out of a slaughtered hog. Then Zancón can sit in your chair and be the big man."

There was silence on the other end of the call. Had I pushed too hard? I turned reasonable. "Okay, if we're through playing macho tag, let's get down to business. Tonight's impossible. Probably take me most of tomorrow to arrange a loan from the bank or to liquidate something to come up with that kind of money. You've got to live with that reality, or else we're spinning our wheels."

"All right. You got until tomorrow. But you try anything, and the kid pays."

"Your own cousin? You'd cut up your own flesh and blood?"

"You know about that, huh? Look, I didn't get to be top dog by favoring blood. Paul coulda joined up, but he thought he was too good. You get my meaning?"

"I get it, okay. You won't hesitate to kill him. So how do we do this?"

"You'll make the delivery tomorrow night—in person. I'll call you on this same number with instructions. And keep the cops outa this."

"No way. They're swarming the streets right now. Your thugs snatched Paul right out in daylight. Hit him on the head. The whole neighborhood saw it."

A dry laugh. "For all the good it did them."

"I want to know he's all right, Puerco. How badly is he hurt?"

"Bump on the head. He's fine for right now."

"I want to talk to him."

"Yeah, right."

The line went dead.

Chapter 32

AFTER LISTENING to the recording of Puerco's call twice, Gene sighed and dry-washed his face with a broad hand.

We stood beside the desk in my home office. He looked exhausted. Conversely, Paul's abduction had energized me.

"Do you believe me about Paul now?"

Gene shrugged. "Doesn't matter if I do or don't. We can't take a chance on his life. But you know he could be playing along with them to get his share of the money."

I leaned forward and got in his face. "He's not. Don't forget that's his blood in the street."

"What's a little blood for a share of $1,000,000?"

"Dammit, Gene! Now you're just being stubborn."

"Ain't love grand? If he's not one of them, how'd Puerco get your cell number?"

"It's stored in Paul's phone. Or he could have gotten it from Emilio. I told you I left a couple of messages on his phone."

"So what are you going to do? Can you come up with that kind of money in twenty-four hours? Maybe Dahlman can."

"I don't need his help." My chair squeaked as I sat down to start making plans. "I'll go to the bank tomorrow morning. I've got enough stocks and bonds to cover the loan."

"Even with collateral, a loan that big will take some time."

"I'll have to shake the tree pretty hard, but I should be able to get the money by Puerco's deadline. The problem's going to be getting enough cash together. My bank might not have enough on hand. They'll have to collect enough from the other banks."

"You don't want to try stuffing a bag with newspaper?" Gene asked.

"They're not going to fall for that again."

"You're lucky Puerco's a twentieth-century crook. Otherwise he'd have told you to wire it to a Swiss bank account."

I shook my head. "He knows I wouldn't do it. He's got to hand over Paul in exchange for the money."

"At least his game makes sense now. Providing, of course, he wasn't lying about a $1,000,000 payoff from the Iron Crosses."

"I don't think he was. The Zellners had been dealing meth for a long time, and there's a lot of money to be made in the stuff. So the murder victims are financing their killer's escape from justice. If Whiznant and Rodrigo can slide out from under the murder charges, they'll fade into the woodwork, leaving the Saints with the million *and* the territory. If things had gone right, Puerco would be sitting pretty."

"But they didn't, and you know what that means," he said.

"Yeah. His goals have changed. Now he needs the money to set up someplace new. Someplace where he'll be safe from extradition."

"And he'll clean up after himself before he goes."

"If you're saying he's planning on killing me, don't waste your breath. He'll kill Paul too."

Gene splayed his hands. "If you know that, why not be rational and let the police handle the payoff?"

"Who are you, and what did you do with my ex-partner?"

"Yeah, well, I had to try, didn't I?"

"But I'll need your help."

"That's why I'm here. Just don't get my ass shot off, okay?"

I paused for a moment before speaking again. "How do you think Puerco will set this up?"

"He'll have you meet them out in the middle of nowhere and shoot you as soon as he verifies the money's real."

"That's what I figure too. And where's the biggest middle of nowhere around here?"

"The West Mesa. That's where most of the bodies turn up. Hell, that's probably where Jackie Costas is buried."

I gave him a thumbs-up. "Right on the first try."

"BJ, I can't provide much cover out there at night. There are too many ways in and out, and the roads are rough enough to require headlights. Lights, even parking lights, can be seen for miles. Of course, there are plenty of other places to rendezvous. The Sandia foothills, for example, or the Cibola National Forest, Tijeras Canyon, the South Valley—just to name a few."

"Yeah, but I think it'll be the West Mesa."

"Okay, I'll contact the Open Space boys first thing tomorrow and have them brief us on likely meeting spots. They patrol the mesa regularly—at least the Volcano Park and Boca Negra Park areas."

"Good idea. We need to warn them not to screw up the deal."

"Think I'll get hold of the rangers in Cibola and alert them too." Gene made a notation in his pocket notebook. "I'll put a chopper on standby."

I nodded, although I suspected a noisy helicopter would prove a death knell for Paul. "Let's cover all the bases we can. We'll make tentative plans even though we can't firm up anything until we know the actual location. More than likely, Puerco will hold off contacting me until after dark tomorrow night."

"And speaking of Puerco and the phone, hand over that tape. It's evidence. I want to be able to convict the bozo when he shoots you full of holes."

After Gene left I tried to get my head on straight. I needed to be out in front of this thing. If I was right about where the exchange would take place, the high mesa on the west side of Albuquerque presented a number of obstacles and one possible advantage. I mulled the situation over for half an hour before booting up my desktop and searching the Internet. Data relating to daytime wind currents, wind speeds, and thermal columns was abundant, but the same was not true of night conditions.

I printed out all the useful information to study later. Then I went out to root around in my garage. My old paraglider was right where I'd left it a few years ago. I spent a few minutes checking it out to make sure everything was in working order.

I SLEPT on the idea of dropping in on Puerco from the sky, and in the cold light of day the plan, while admittedly harebrained, seemed as good as any and better than most.

My banker took my early phone call and consented to see me in an hour. While my company account didn't merit that kind of attention from a bank, my trust fund did. Gene agreed to meet me at the bank. Somebody was bound to be keeping an eye on me, so a confab in a neutral corner seemed prudent. I instructed him to take the side door, the one leading to the building's elevators, as that would be less obvious to any watcher.

Stan Goodman, a senior vice president of the Central Avenue National Bank and an old friend of my father's, preferred to conduct business at his desk out on the carpeted, open area on the west side of the bank's ground floor. The Central Avenue was housed in one of Albuquerque's original 1920s "skyscrapers." Crowned with medallions, swags, and pilasters, it looked like a bank building was supposed to look.

The interior reinforced the impression with ornately patterned forty-foot ceilings, marble flooring, brass railings, and an entire wall of twenty-four-foot arched windows. In case anyone from off the street missed the point, a massive steel vault door in plain sight behind the teller cages confirmed this was a bank.

Goodman was a little surprised when I insisted on moving into his private office. He was astonished when a detective from the Albuquerque Police Department joined us, but downright flabbergasted at the request for an immediate loan of $1,000,000.

"Good Lord, BJ!" His thin gray moustache twitched; the first sign of distress I'd ever observed in the normally unflappable banker. "You're good for it, of course. There's plenty of collateral available, but a loan of that size has to be approved by the loan committee. It will take a few days."

"Stan, I don't have a few days."

The banker blinked a couple of times as he heard me out and then excused himself to go upstairs to consult with his superiors. I took the opportunity to run my rescue idea by Gene.

"Are you fucking crazy? You want to paraglide to the ransom site and take them by surprise?"

"Crazy with worry, maybe, but I'm not a lunatic."

He snorted. "Then how did you come up with a lunatic solution?"

"Desperation, Gene. Desperation."

"You don't even know Puerco's going to want to meet on the mesa. It might be in a warehouse somewhere, or in the Sandias, or who knows where?"

"I realize I'm banking heavily on the site, but think about it for a minute. The idea works equally well for the foothills, for the Sandia Indian Reservation, for the South Valley hayfields, for a number of places. Maybe even as far as the Rio Puerco country. But we both know he's going to wait until the last minute to give me the time and place of the meet, so it's got to take place within no more than an hour's travel time from my house. That limits his options, and the fifteen miles from my driveway to the top of the mesa meets that time frame—even traveling at the speed limit."

"So does the South Valley. So does the foothills area," Gene said.

"True, but the mesa makes more sense for other reasons. There are only a couple of main roads in and out of the Cibola National Forest, especially on the eastern side of the Sandias. It would be too easy to block their escape."

"Let me get this straight. You plan on launching a paraglider from the summit of Sandia Peak in the dead of night—night jumping's an illegal act, by the way—soar across the entire Rio Grande Valley, and surprise a bunch of armed killers, thereby rescuing your lover boy?"

"That's about it."

"I see. In this dream of yours, is an army of law enforcement officers floating down alongside you to provide support?"

"No, an army of law enforcement officers is going to approach the area from different directions and wait for my signal before rushing Puerco and his gang. And no SWAT unit, Gene. They'd take over the whole operation."

Gene shook his head. "And we oughta let them. When did you last strap on that glider?"

"Before my gunshot wound."

"Aw, crap! How do you know you can even fly the damned thing anymore?"

"It's like riding a bicycle. Once you master it, the skill's yours forever."

"Pardon me if I don't buy that wagonload of pumpkins. And let's get one thing straight. SWAT's going to be right in the middle of this. We need them."

"Okay, but you keep control of the situation."

"Do my damnedest. But what if it's not the mesa? Say it's a warehouse, for instance?"

"Then I'm screwed, unless I can manage to land on the roof."

The banker's secretary tapped on the door and asked us to join Stan in the president's office upstairs. Wilfred Wiseman, Central Avenue's chief executive, was older than sin, reminded me of pictures of Machiavelli, and was the nicest guy in the state of New Mexico. He wasted no time.

"Stan's going to prepare the paperwork. You go over to the brokerage house and arrange for them to bring us about two million dollars in stocks and bonds. We'll have your money by early afternoon. Sorry to ask for so much collateral, but we're doing an end run around the loan committee, and I want to be able to justify our actions."

"I appreciate the cooperation, Mr. Wiseman. I need small, unmarked bills. Will that be possible?"

"I believe we can put together a million in hundred-dollar denominations, with some cooperation from the other banks."

"That should be satisfactory. I'd like the currency in four or five sturdy canvas bags like the armored car services use."

"Not a problem. And I sincerely hope you secure your friend's safe release."

CHARLIE WEEKS and Del Dahlman joined Gene and me in the bank's boardroom. Charlie was a trouper and made no objections, but Del was as firm as my ex-partner in telling me exactly how nutty my plan was.

"Has it ever been done before?" he asked as he ended his dissertation.

I shrugged. "Damned if I know. But I'll tell you one thing, Del Dahlman. A few years ago, if you'd been the one kidnapped, I'd have jumped off the frigging mountain for you."

That shut him up, but Charlie immediately raised an issue I'd been trying to ignore.

"Hazel's gonna be a problem."

"Which is why she isn't at this meeting. We'll present her with a *done deal*. At least the planning stage will be. I'll just have to go deaf for the rest of the day. You have any problem with the role I've laid out for you?"

Charlie shook his head. "Sounds simple enough to me. I just pretend to be you and drive right up to the hoods with the money."

"You realize there's some danger, don't you?"

"For all of us, but I can handle what comes my way. We don't look much alike, but I guess I can fool them in a closed car. At least for a while."

"Del, will you do what I ask?"

"These guys are looking at you, not me. I'll go about my business, but keep me informed, okay?"

"Let me explain something. Puerco Arrullar has made a threat against you, Hazel, and my neighbor, Mrs. Wardlow. I want all three of you in my house until this is all over. Gene will have a street full of police officers in the vicinity and two in the house with you. If things go wrong, that thug's liable to come after you."

"Look, I sit around on my butt all day as it is, but being cooped up with Hazel for half the night? That's cruel and unusual punishment. Give me something less dangerous—like jumping off Sandia Peak with you."

Gene tried again. "He made a threat against you too. The smart thing is for you to hole up in that house with the rest of them and let us handle the Brown Saints."

"It won't work. In the first place, he's going to expect me to be on the scene. If I'm not, he'll kill Paul."

"That doesn't hold water. You're sending Charlie as your stand-in. If things go the way you plan, Puerco won't even see you until the last minute. Let's follow your plan, but let a trained police officer with paragliding skills take your place on the mountain."

"Nobody respects the dedication and ability of the Albuquerque Police Department more than I do, but I *am* trained, remember? I've got to do this, Gene. Paul Barton is in this mess because of me, and I've got to get him out of it. Now how about the equipment and cooperation I need?"

"What if I say no?"

"Then I'll do it alone."

"I could slap your ass in jail overnight, and that's probably what I oughta do. But I'll play my part—under protest. I hope you realize if you get shot up, I'll get raked over the coals. Probably end up back on night patrol for the rest of my career."

"I know, and I apologize for that, but have a little faith, will you?"

THE REMAINDER of the day was spent playing hurry up and wait. I spent part of it rechecking the condition of the paraglider in the garage. Then I fretted until the bank delivered the money. The hardest part of that deal was getting them to do it in a public manner, wheeling an armored car ostentatiously down my block and unloading four canvas bags of cash in front of the house. That caused a flutter of curtains up and down the street, but I was counting on another kind of watcher somewhere in the vicinity. I wanted Puerco to know the money was available.

Police cars came and went throughout the day as shifts changed, and one of them, carrying the communications and night vision equipment I required, backed into my driveway. The cruiser remained there so the paraglider could be stuffed into the trunk after dark. At five thirty, Charlie Weeks arrived with Hazel. She'd almost finished delivering her tirade by the time Del showed up around six. Mrs. Wardlow joined us right after that.

My cell phone didn't ring until almost nine o'clock, by which time I had hunkered down in the backseat of that same police cruiser now parked in a Smith's supermarket lot at the far eastern edge of the city. I quickly activated the recording device and answered, trying for a fine mixture of anxiety, which was easy, and confidence, a little harder task.

Puerco didn't fool around. "West Mesa. You got till ten o'clock to get to the top of the mesa. After that the kid starts losing fingers and toes."

"No need for that." I gave Tom Clark, my police driver, a thumbs-up. He immediately climbed out of the vehicle to raise Gene on a handheld radio. It was a go, and my partner needed to get his people moving while I kept Puerco engaged in conversation.

"I'm satisfied with the deal so long as you agree this takes care of the problem. No more demands. No more threats."

"I get my money, that's the end of it."

"Good. I have to warn you the other people you mentioned are all here at my house, and there are cops all over the neighborhood."

"Cops know what's going on?"

"Of course they do. I told you yesterday my neighbor called them. They knew about the kidnapping before I did. There was no way to prevent their involvement, so I used it to my advantage. Yours too."

"How's that?"

"The more of them tied up here on Post Oak Drive, the fewer you have to worry about. Now what are my instructions?"

"Put the money in Barton's old Plymouth. Backseat, not the trunk—"

"I don't have the keys to Paul's car."

"Check the floorboard." He gave an ugly laugh. "But you'll have to punch out a window. My boys didn't want no neighborhood thief to boost your ride. Drive to Coors using Paseo del Norte. Take Unser past the Petroglyph Park and up the escarpment. Drive to the road that takes you to the park. You know, the one where they fly model airplanes all the time."

"La Boca Negra?"

"I guess, but turn north away from the park. Drive two miles and stop in the middle of the road. Somebody'll direct you from there."

"I've never been in Paul's car. I don't know if the odometer works."

"Then guess at it. You'll see a flashlight when it's time to stop. And come alone. When you see that flashlight, get out of the Plymouth and open the trunk and all the doors. Better not be nobody hiding in that car. All I wanta see is you and my money. You got it?"

"Got it. And Paul?"

"When I count the money, you get your honey."

"Is he all right?"

"Still nursing a headache, but he's okay. Whether he stays that way is up to you."

"One thing, Puerco. I'll have a police escort to the top of the escarpment. That's the only way the detective in charge will agree to the deal. He doesn't want me hijacked on the way to meet you. Don't let the police convoy spook your men."

"I said no cops!" Puerco shouted.

"Not my call. If I refuse, he'll confiscate the money and the deal goes down the drain. He's as serious about this as you and me."

"Their doors stay shut and they turn around as soon as you're up on the mesa. Somebody'll watch them out of sight, so you better be sure they don't try to pull no tricks."

"Anything else?"

"That's it, motherfucker. Be there by ten."

SGT. CLARK, my driver, switched on the lights and siren and roared out of the parking lot. We hit I-40 East and breezed through Tijeras Canyon in record time, but it was going to be close. Even with the edge we'd gained by waiting for the kidnapper's call virtually in the mouth of the pass through the Sandia and Manzano Mountains, it was still nearly an hour to the peak's summit. Sgt. Clark was determined to shave ten minutes off that time—or kill us in the effort.

He hit the exit at the cement plant, blew by the busy bar on the right, and ran the red light controlling traffic coming off westbound I-40. He ate up the long stretch past the fire station, the Italian restaurant, and a couple of service stations, but when we turned west onto the summit road, our pace slowed considerably.

Typical of mountain tracks, the road took a tortuous route up the east side of the mountain. The cruiser's headlights cut a faint tunnel through the absolute darkness. We were further slowed by the danger of wildlife crossing the road. As a teenager I had once confronted a black bear and her cub shuffling across the asphalt. More than once I'd nearly run up the tailpipe of tourists halted in the middle of the road to ogle mule-deer feeding on the shoulder.

Faint traces of snow clung to the south-facing road banks, although none had fallen in the valley to the west of this massive hunk of rock. The lights atop the television towers came into view as we neared the summit of Sandia Peak. Clark turned into the parking lot below the gift shop and spoke for the first time since we'd left Albuquerque's city limits.

"The rangers are gonna steer clear of this area for a couple of hours. It's illegal to launch after nightfall, you know. I'm gonna hang around and help until you're airborne, but I'm gonna do it with my eyes closed, if you get what I mean."

"Right. Thanks. I shouldn't have much problem launching alone, but I appreciate the company—just in case."

He pulled as close to the observation deck as possible, and we walked the rest of the way. I lugged the big bag containing the paraglider; Clark trailed along behind with the remainder of my gear.

"Thought you'd use a power unit," the sergeant observed. "Doing this with air currents alone makes it kinda dicey. It's gotta be forty or fifty klicks, even as the crow flies. Not much chance of finding a cloud street."

He was referring to those extended columns of rising air that allow for long runs. So Gene had sent me a sail-savvy aide. I hoped the man didn't have instructions to cuff me to the steering column and take my place in the harness. As tall, muscular, and tough looking as he was, he'd have a fight on his hands if he tried.

"If I do, it'll be pure luck. I'm counting on lee waves on the western slope of the mountain to give me enough altitude. As far as using a power plant, too much noise. I'd have to cut it before I got anywhere near the mesa, and then it would be too much added weight."

Clark shook his head. "Maybe it'll work. Sandia's a shade under ten five, and it's five-thousand-plus feet down to the valley."

"Yeah, but not to the West Mesa. That's seven hundred or so feet above the floor of the valley."

"More in some places. But you'll catch a lift when you approach the escarpment."

"Probably not as much of a lift as I want, though. The cliff's not on the windward side."

"It'll still give you a boost. You got a target picked out?"

For the first time I glanced through the dark night down at the city. Albuquerque looked twice its actual size. A carpet of twinkling lights blanketed the broad valley on both sides of the Rio Grande before crawling up the slope and halting abruptly at the base of the far escarpment. Everything beyond that was a huge black hole—the West Mesa.

Fifty years ago a large Eastern property development company acquired most of the area, graded huge grids of unnamed and unimproved streets, and started selling individual lots. Legal and practical problems soon collapsed the project. As a result the whole massive area remained virtually unoccupied.

The mesa had a grisly past. Bodies had a habit of turning up from time to time. Last year a woman walking her dog stumbled upon human remains. The police found a total of eleven young women, all thought to be prostitutes, in adjacent shallow graves. The discovery made national headlines.

To the south of the mesa, Interstate 40 stabbed the landscape with a luminous lance. I pointed to a cluster of lights on the far side of the valley.

"Initially I'm going to use the detention center as a target. Gene had the Open Space people put a homing device in La Boca Negra Park, and when I get within range, I'll zero in on that. My final destination is somewhere almost due north of the park."

"How will you operate from there? You're going to spot them with this night vision equipment?"

"That and the heat-imaging gear."

"It's top-of-the-line stuff. It'll paint a warm body clear as day."

"The special tape Gene put on the roof and hood of the Plymouth ought to make the car visible to me. The Santos are going to be somewhere out in front of that car, and I've got to disrupt their plans before they get close enough to discover I'm not the driver."

"It's a quarter till ten. We better get you hooked up and ready to go."

Clark handed over a ballistic vest and a ballistic baseball cap Gene had sent, figuring that was better protection than nothing in case of a firefight. Then he scoped out a downhill slope long enough and clear enough for a run to fill the flexible paraglider wing. While he was doing that, I assembled the glider. Finally I checked that the Ruger Gene had loaned me was firmly in place. Then we were ready. I activated my PTT—push-to-talk transceiver—with the switch strapped to one of my fingers.

"We're ready here," I said.

Gene responded immediately. "Okay. Charlie headed out five minutes ago. The timing on this thing's gonna be dicey, BJ."

"I know, but I'll do the best I can. Charlie's wearing my jacket?"

"Right. And Hazel scared up a hat for him. She also dyed his hair to match yours. You know, I think those two are working on something together."

I laughed, breaking the tension as he had intended. "That'll be one positive thing to come out of this mess."

"Roger. I've got teams at all four cardinal points. When you give the word, we'll move from the Rio Puerco side, come down from the Paradise Hills area, up from I-40, and climb that blessed escarpment on the east side. The environmental people gave us some grief on that last one because our guys will be stomping all over some thousand-year-old petroglyphs. Have you tested the night vision equipment?"

"Yeah, but it's not going to do me any good until I get to the West Mesa. The city lights will blind me until then."

"How about the heat-imaging gear?"

"Picked up Clark in the bushes and painted a coyote and a herd of mountain sheep about a hundred yards below us. Worked just fine."

"You sure you can still fly that contraption?"

"I better."

"That's reassuring. Have you tested your harness release and your reserve chute?"

"I'm not carrying a reserve parachute, and the harness release works fine."

"You're not carrying a chute?"

"Extra weight."

"So you're going to dead fall on Puerco in the dark without knowing how far you've gotta drop or whatever kind of ground's below you. Providing, of course, you make it that far in the first place."

"You've described the situation perfectly. Pessimistically but accurately. I have a flashlight for the final landing. I'm going to launch now."

"Good luck, and keep in touch."

"Constantly. Well, here I go."

Clark fed out the fabric of my wing as I raced down the slope and stepped out into space. The moment my foot left terra firma, I was aware of several things at once. My heart raced like a revving motor. A dizzying sense of falling and loss of control. And fear. Fear for Paul.

Chapter 33

My heart almost stopped as I plunged toward a stand of trees on a promontory below. Then the sail took hold and billowed properly. My right foot snagged the top branch of a fir, jerking me sideways and spilling some air. Before I had time to panic, a lee wave—an updraft caused by warmer ground air pushing up the face of the mountain—sent me soaring higher than I'd anticipated. I shifted my body and tugged on my wing tether until the distant glow of the detention center's lights was directly ahead of me.

The night was still and calm. Except for the darkness, it could have been 5:00 p.m., the ideal time for soaring from Sandia Peak. The heavy overcast was a plus and a minus. There was no moonlight, but the city lights lit the underbelly of the clouds, making the night seem unusually bright. Gloves and a visored helmet made the forty-degree temperature bearable. I'd have to remember to flex my extremities to keep from going numb.

My glide ratio was about seventeen to one, meaning I traveled seventeen meters forward for every meter of altitude lost. Good, but not good enough. Unable to search for thermals by seeking out favorable cloud formations, I sacrificed some forward propulsion to maneuver north and south in the blind hope of picking one up. As I was about to give it up as a poor gamble, a mild thermal grabbed the sail, giving me enough altitude to ease some of my concern and allow me a moment to linger on the glittering lights of the city far below me.

The radio jerked me back to the present. "BJ, dammit! Give me a report."

"Can't cuss over the airwaves, Gene. I'm airborne and just caught a thermal."

"The Plymouth's on Coors."

"Tell him to slow a bit. Need some recon time."

"We're pushing the ten o'clock deadline."

"Puerco knows we're on the way. He won't do anything rash at this point. You receiving me okay?"

"Hear you fine."

The reception on the little headset was good, and my visor provided some protection from the rushing wind, allowing Gene to understand me. That would be crucial when Puerco phoned, as he was bound to do when his patience ran out.

The paraglider sailed over the wide sandy banks of the Rio Grande and the parallel swaths of dark cottonwood bosque, their boundaries defined by a double-stranded necklace of sparkling streetlamps. The river gleamed dully as it flowed south through the valley. The vast starkness of the West Mesa loomed beyond.

Crumbled remnants of dormant volcanoes called the Five Sisters lay at the western edge of the Rio Grande Valley. Their last eruption about one hundred thousand years ago had been a cataclysmic event, sending untold tons of molten igneous matter pouring down the slopes toward the valley. When the monsters ran out of steam, the burning rock simply halted, leaving a fifty-foot wall of black lava hanging over the western landscape… the escarpment.

Even after a hundred millennia, the mesa, actually hardened lava thinly covered by sand and soil, was warmer than the terrain in the valley. Snow melted faster atop the mesa than along the river. This residual heat should provide me with a final lift to allow for reconnaissance.

As the massive void rushed toward me, I snapped on my night vision goggles and heat-imaging gear. The paraglider had lost more altitude than I'd expected, but moments before reaching the black wall of the escarpment, a minor thermal jerked me upward. I spilled air to keep from soaring too high and began searching the ground below me, grateful the paraglider let me sit upright in the harness rather than lie prone as in a hang glider.

When the signal from Boca Negra Park began registering, I turned the kite northward. There was no sign of Paul's old Plymouth, but the city's lights would blind me until Charlie neared the top of the escarpment. It was time to locate Puerco.

The heat sensors picked up a couple of images, probably foxes or coyotes. Then two prone forms on the southern edge of my target area glowed faintly on the heat-imaging screen. Vehicles parked nearby radiated heat from cooling motors. Gene acknowledged my whispered warning.

"Got it. I'll send in the Boca team."

Almost immediately, Puerco's stakeout team in the south came into focus. I informed Gene. It hadn't taken long to find the Saints covering Puerco's north and east flanks, and I eventually found the Saints guarding the west. Somewhere in the center of those four points, was the head Saint—and Paul.

Praying the glider had enough altitude, I circled the area again and corrected the course of the La Boca team. Gene's police squad—merely heat forms to me—moving in from the north seemed on course, and the assault team at the escarpment on the east side had already scaled the lava cliff and were bearing down on their targets. But the team coming in from Rio Puerco wasn't even on my screen yet.

Sailing out over the valley floor to try for another updraft from the escarpment earned me a small boost, but not much. Heading back for another look, I caught sight of several cars emerging from the glare of the streetlights below the base of the cliff as they tore up Unser toward the mesa. Three of the vehicles had flashing light bars. The second car in line would be Charlie in the Plymouth. Blinking against the temporary blindness caused by looking directly at the lights, I started seeking out the lion in his den, or rather the boar in the bushes—Puerco Arrullar.

His shimmering yellow-green image showed up in my goggles at the same moment my cell phone vibrated against my wrist. Puerco, standing on the mesa floor a hundred feet below me, was getting nervous. My story ready, I hugged the phone close to my mouth beneath the face guard and pressed the answer button as I sailed soundlessly over the bulk of what seemed to be a big Hummer parked near him.

"Where are you, motherfucker!" Puerco shouted. "You better not be fucking with me."

"I'm on Unser just coming up the grade to the top of the escarpment. There are three cop cars with me, so don't get nervous. They have instructions to turn around and leave as soon as my Plymouth's at the top."

"What's that noise?" the thug demanded. "How come I can hardly hear you?"

"I'm shouting as loud as I can. We had to break the driver's window to get the keys, and it's noisy as hell. Don't get nervous now, Puerco. Not when we're about to get this thing done."

"You got the money?"

"In the backseat like you instructed."

"You alone?"

"Except for my escort, which will depart immediately. I'm hanging up now. Make sure that bozo with the flashlight gives me the signal."

Worried about getting too near Puerco and the figure lying prone near him—Paul?—I veered to the south. That maneuver probably saved my life. My heat-imaging equipment picked up a third individual lying prone nearby. Puerco's personal backup. Zancón, probably.

A voice growled in my ear—Gene doing his whispering bit. "Targets on the south are out. East team got their two guys."

"Good." I twisted around to see if I could find what was happening to the north and the west. I watched the northern police team overpower their targets.

"North team's achieved targets, but I'm worried about the west, Gene. I can't visually locate our guys."

"Late getting started. Might have a problem there."

"Kick them in the ass. The Plymouth's on the mesa now. It's headed north to the target area. Charlie knows about the guy with the flashlight, right?"

"He's been warned, and he's well armed."

"God!" I moaned as turbulence rocked me unexpectedly. "I hope they don't shoot him as soon as they see him."

"Don't lose your cool, BJ. We talked this out. They'll want to see the money first. And then Puerco's gonna want to deal with you personally. Charlie knows how to handle it."

I described Puerco's location to my ex-partner and signed off the air. The turbulence had cost me some altitude. The kite was getting too low. I needed to find a landing place fast. That was the most dangerous part of the whole caper. My depth perception was virtually zero, especially when I lost contact with the heat sources painted by the imaging equipment. But I had to go in blind unless I wanted to drop right on top of the gangsters. I began to mentally prepare for a landing, praying it wouldn't be in the middle of a cactus or on a jagged boulder, which could seriously hamper my ability to take them out before they harmed Paul.

My blood froze and my plans changed with the most unwelcome sound imaginable. It started with a single gunshot. And then all hell broke loose. An astounding number of red dots peppered the night to the west. A pitched battle was taking place down there. Suddenly realizing how vulnerable I was hanging below a slip of fabric, my muscles spasmed. Oh, God, not now.

Activity on the ground below me steeled my nerves and pulled me back to the crisis at hand. A shimmering, luminous image stood staring off to the west. He turned and pointed at the figure lying prone beside him. Oh, God! Puerco was going to shoot Paul.

Then the second figure rose to stand beside Puerco. I forgot the rushing wind, the sinking kite. I forgot the lives at risk on the battlefield to the west. Gene had been right. Paul was a part of the whole scam. My heart turned to stone. Well, the fuckers weren't going to get away with it.

I turned the kite and prepared to come in behind the two men. Screw finding a landing place and sneaking up on them. I'd drop right on top of them. My angle was too steep; my speed, too fast. But there wasn't much I could do about it. Then the second figure broke away and raced to the third form I'd spotted moments before. I gave a sigh of relief when he dragged an obviously helpless man across the mesa floor. Paul! He *was* a captive.

I'd been worrying about coming in too fast; now I felt suspended helplessly in space above the three. The two standing images raised shimmering arms in unison. Jesus, they were going to kill Paul!

Then one of them lifted his head. Puerco had heard something— the flutter of my wing, the rush of wind. Tossing away my night vision goggles to avoid being blinded by the flash of a gunshot, I tore off my heavy gloves and hit the harness release without knowing precisely where I was.

Instead of landing atop Puerco and Zancón, I fell short, abruptly striking the ground. Surprised and off-balance, I scrambled to keep my feet but went over, striking my right kneecap on the sharp edge of a stone. I sucked wind to keep from making an audible sound. Totally blind in the absolute darkness, I heard the glider's canopy dragging in the dirt ahead of me. Suddenly there was the roar of a weapon, a muted flash, and then something caught fire. Puerco had taken the paraglider's wing full in the face; his gun went off, igniting the kite's sail.

I'd lost precious moments because of the distraction. Ignoring the crippling pain in my knee, I flopped onto my belly and brought up my Ruger, firing blindly in the general direction of the man I assumed was Zancón. He got off two shots before he went down.

I twisted on my side just as Puerco fought free of the glider's fabric. Yelling to draw his attention from Paul, I rolled quickly to the left. The gangbanger might be fat, but he was fast. Bullets tore up the ground where I had been lying a second before. Using his gun flashes as a target, I fired twice more, rolled again, and quickly inserted a fresh clip into the pistol. The flaming wing died; it was totally dark again. Had I hit Puerco?

A stone rattled in the darkness. He was alive—and working his way to his hostage. Frantic, I slithered like a snake in Paul's direction. But Puerco was headed the other way. The night vision equipment! He was going for my glider. If he got to it, Paul and I were both dead. When I tried to stand, my leg collapsed. As I fell to the ground, Puerco's salvo tore through the air directly over my head.

"Got you, you fucking queer!"

As if acting of its own volition, my handgun banged away until empty. Deafened, I almost didn't hear Puerco's scream. A heavy body crashed to the ground. Everything grew quiet. Even the battle to the west had fallen silent.

It felt like five minutes before my muscles would obey me. Where the hell was everyone? The world had gone silent. Or maybe I was deaf from all the gunshots. I clawed a small Maglite out of my jacket. Holding it at arm's length to the left, I switched it on.

Puerco sprawled motionless on his belly.

I swung the light around and located Zancón. He lay against the wall of the small arroyo where they had taken shelter, trying to staunch the flow of blood from a wound in his abdomen. His right shoulder didn't seem to be working right. I limped forward. Satisfied he was no longer a threat, I searched him and found a switchblade. Taking his weapons with me, I checked to make sure Puerco was dead and then made my painful way to Paul.

Trussed and blindfolded so tightly he couldn't move or make an intelligible sound, his painful gasps frightened me. I ripped off his gag and dug a rag out of his throat. In the excitement of the firefight, he'd almost swallowed the scrap of cloth stuffed in his mouth to silence him. In another minute or two, he would have suffocated. He took deep, shuddering breaths.

"Who... who's there? What happened? Where am I?" His voice wheezed through a raspy throat.

I laughed from relief and hugged him. "Damn. Trussed up like a Christmas goose, and you're still asking who-what-where questions." I carefully pulled off his blindfold. "It's me, Paul."

"Vince? Is that you? Be careful, Puerco—"

"Don't worry about him. He can't hurt you anymore."

"Zancón! He's here somewhere too."

"He won't bother you either. He won't bother anyone for a very long time."

Paul blinked against the glare of my flashlight, and then his eyes went wild at the sound of approaching vehicles.

"Don't worry. That's Gene and Charlie and about half the APD."

He sagged in relief. "Take me home, Vince. Please."

Epilogue

A PATROL car whisked Paul to UNM Medical Center to be checked out while Gene and I met with the team commanders in an APD conference room. A considerable amount of brass sat in on the debriefing.

Amazingly, although something like five hundred rounds had been expended earlier that night, there were relatively few casualties on either side. No one except Puerco had died, and Zancón suffered the most serious wounds. He would recover, hopefully to live out the rest of his life behind bars. Most of the rest of the Santos Morenos members were in custody too. The gang would probably never recover.

After the critique, which was declared a righteous operation, the Public Information types scurried off to feed data to the press, and the rest of us were free to go our own way. Gene had a blue-and-white drive me to the UNM emergency ward, where I found Charlie patiently sitting in the big waiting room. He'd driven over in the Plymouth after turning over the bags of cash to the police for safekeeping.

Paul came out shortly thereafter. Beyond a knot on the head, a few scrapes and bruises, and a sore throat from the gag he'd almost swallowed, he was unscathed. It remained to be seen if he suffered subtler, more durable injuries. But I was betting he was stronger than that. The doctor ordered him to take it easy for a few days, gave him a spray for his sore throat, and released him.

We delivered Charlie to his place before heading home.

The sun was over the horizon, and the neighborhood appeared to believe this was a day like any other by the time I pulled the Plymouth to the curb. The old place had never looked so good. Both of our fannies were dragging by the time we entered the house.

When I left last night, there had been half a dozen people in or around the house. Gene had done a good job of clearing the place out before we got there. I wondered how he'd handled Hazel.

"You need to get some rest," I suggested.

"We both do, but I don't think I could sleep if I went to bed."

"Delayed reaction."

"Damn, Vince, is this what you go through every day?"

I laughed. "My days are usually boring as hell."

He snorted. "Your house is firebombed. Your front porch and your neighbor's house are shot to pieces. A man you're waiting to meet gets sliced to death, and that doesn't mention this Emilio guy getting iced. Sounds pretty *boring* to me."

"And for the next couple of years, my existence will be dull, dull, dull."

A shaft of light caught in his black hair and shot sparks. "Don't feed me pablum, Vince."

"Not pablum, truth. Contrary to recent events, my life is very ordinary. Pretty much like the guy next door."

"God, platitudes, yet. From pap to platitudes in sixty seconds." He turned somber. "There's something I should have told you a long time ago."

"That Puerco was blood? Yes, I knew. And you tried to tell me that night at the C&W, but I interrupted you."

"Yeah, but I should have made you listen. And I should have fought them harder, talked sense into Puerco. Something!"

"You did what you were supposed to do—you survived. And right now the last thing you need is to load yourself up with guilt. Nothing would have changed if you had told me."

"You know what I was really afraid of? Crying like a fag! I was worried I'd break down and start begging for my life."

"But you didn't, did you?"

His deep brown eyes met mine, and a smile broke out on his face. "No, I didn't. I got mad instead. I cussed them until they finally put a gag on me."

We broke into laughter—more a release of pent-up tension than mirth.

"Anyway, it worked out just the way I planned it," I said when I could speak again.

His grin turned mischievous. "Yeah, but what if it had been raining or—"

"I'd have found a way, Paul. I'd have found a way."

I took his hand and slipped the silver ring I'd bought at the Zozobra burning over his finger. He looked blankly at it for a brief moment and then smiled.

Keep reading for this exclusive excerpt:

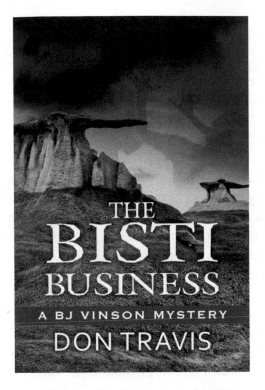

Although repulsed by his client, an overbearing, homophobic California wine mogul, Confidential Investigator BJ Vinson agrees to search for Anthony Alfano's missing son, Lando, and his traveling companion—strictly for the benefit of the young men. As BJ chases an orange Porsche Boxter all over New Mexico, he soon becomes aware he is not the only one looking for the distinctive car. Every time BJ finds a clue, someone has been there before him. He arrives in Taos just in time to see the car plunge into the 650 foot-deep Taos Gorge. Has he failed in his mission?

Lando's brother, Aggie, arrives to help with BJ's investigation, but BJ isn't sure he trusts Aggie's motives. He seems to hold power in his father's business and has a personal stake in his brother's fate that goes beyond familial bonds. Together, they follow the clues scattered across the vast Bisti/De-Na-Zin wilderness area and learn the bloodshed didn't end with the car crash. As they get closer to solving the mystery, BJ must decide whether finding Lando will rescue the young man, or place him directly in the path of those who want to harm him.

Coming Soon to
www.dsppublications.com

Prologue

Bisti/De-Na-Zin Wilderness, South of Farmington, New Mexico

A LOPSIDED moon daubed wispy tendrils of scattered clouds with pewter. Glittering pinpricks of muted light smeared the Milky Way while moonshine bleached the barren landscape silver. Sharp-edged shadows shrouded the feet of mute, grotesque gargoyles of clay and sandstone: hoodoos masquerading as monumental toadstools, spheroid stones aping gigantic dinosaur eggs, and eroded clay hills with folds like delicate lace drapery.

A great horned owl soared above the high desert floor, its keen eyes scouring the panorama below. The plumed predator dipped a wing and veered eastward, attracted by the dull metallic shine of a large foreign object. Quickly discerning it represented no culinary opportunity, the raptor flew in slow, ever-widening circles in search of something more promising.

The huge bird's flitting shadow startled two figures, interrupting their heated argument. Both glanced up quickly. Taking advantage of the moment, the larger man snaked a belt from his waist and slipped behind the other. He whipped the leather strap over his victim's head, driving him to the ground with a knee to the back. After a short, desperate struggle, the man sprawled in the cooling sand ceased to resist. The violent tremors in his extremities passed, and he lay still.

Panting from his exertions, the killer rose and began the hunt for a suitable crevice to hide the body. It wasn't difficult to find one in the unstable terrain of these remote badlands. Satisfied his cairn of loose stones and sandy soil blended well with the rest of this weird, otherworldly place, he turned and plodded toward his distant vehicle.

Chapter 1

Albuquerque, New Mexico

THE TELEPHONE jolted me out of my reverie. Hazel Harris, my secretary, aide, and surrogate mother, had left for the day, but the answering service could field the call—90 percent of my clients were attorneys, and there weren't many of them working this time of day. But when the phone shrieked a second time, I glanced at the unfamiliar long-distance number on the caller ID and caved in to curiosity.

"B. J. Vinson, Confidential Investigations."

"Who's speaking?"

"B. J. Vinson. What can I do for you?"

"What's this?" a gravelly voice demanded. "Some rinky-dink outfit where the boss answers his own phone?"

Curiosity has its limits. Without another word I dropped the receiver back into its cradle. It usually takes a while to recognize a problem client, but this obnoxious prick had done me a favor by convincing me of it within a couple of sentences.

I swiveled my chair around to return to what I had been doing, savoring the view from the north-facing window of my third-floor office in one of Albuquerque's historic buildings at Fifth and Copper. I often undertook this ritual before heading home. It was my favorite vista at my favorite hour in my least favorite time of year—about three-quarters of the way into evening on a muggy summer's day made uncomfortable by the lingering humidity of an earlier quick-moving thunderstorm. Fortunately a more hospitable autumn hovered just around the corner.

The phone intruded again. Determined to cut this guy off at the pass, I snatched up the receiver, but before I could say anything, a loud laugh threatened to burst my eardrum.

"Short fuse, huh? Okay, I can respect that. Look, I'm in Hawaii on business and lost track of the time difference. Sorry to call so late."

The bastard was pretty good at defusing things.

"Let's start over, shall we? I'm Anthony P. Alfano. I run Alfano Vineyards in Napa Valley. I've got a problem out there in New Mexico, and I think you're the guy who can help me. I got your name off the Internet. I like your website. It's a solid, professional layout."

He left me little recourse except to respond gracefully. "Thanks. I assume you checked me out with someone too." I exhaled and tried to ignore the feeling I was being manipulated by an expert. "Okay, what's the problem?"

"My son. He's missing. Probably nothing serious, but I need to locate him."

Orlando Selvanus Alfano—was this family Italian, or what?—twenty-one and a graduate student in history at UCLA, had left on July 22 for an extended vacation. He and his traveling companion, another student named Dana Norville, intended to explore the natural wonders of the great Southwest and sample the wares of the local vineyards. Even though they were three days late returning home, the vacationers were still registered at the Albuquerque Sheraton on Menaul and Louisiana across the street from Coronado Mall. Repeated phone messages left at the hotel and on Orlando's cell phone had gotten no response. The two were going to miss the first classes of the fall semester if they didn't return immediately.

"I take it the other student—this Dana—is his girlfriend."

Alfano's pregnant pause and terse answer raised my antennae. "It's Dana James Norville. One of those names that can go either way."

So that's the way it was. Alfano needed a gay PI to look for a gay son. "Does he? Go either way, I mean?"

His rage was palpable. "Only *one* way. The wrong way."

"And your son?"

Instead of the expected explosion, Alfano sighed heavily. "You have to understand something. Orlando's not queer. Hell, most of us jerked off with buddies when we were kids. We grew out of it, no harm done. Lando's just a slow developer. He hasn't come out of it yet, but he will."

"How about Norville?"

"That bastard's a dyed-in-the-wool pansy, and he's contaminating my son."

I bit my tongue at the sophomoric outburst. "For your information, Mr. Alfano, I'm pretty 'dyed-in-the-wool' myself. I think you need to call someone else."

"Now wait a minute." Anthony Alfano obviously was not accustomed to getting the brush-off. "I know all about you. And except for that… nonsense, you've got a good reputation. You can move in both the straight world and the gay world. You're the one I want. Find my son, Vinson, and send him home to his mother and me."

"It's *Mr.* Vinson." Might as well set the bigoted SOB straight right at the beginning.

"All right, *Mr.* Vinson, score one for you. Are you sure you're gay? You don't sound it."

"Does your son?"

"No, but—"

"But in your dreams he's not twisted, right? How about Norville? Am I looking for a flaming queen?"

"Of course not. Lando wouldn't hang out with someone like that. No, I've got to admit, looking at Dana Norville, you wouldn't suspect."

"Then how can you be certain?"

"I did a quick background check on Norville when the two of them started bumming around together, and the guy was clean. But when they… uh, got close, I took another look and found the man Norville had been shacking up with before he latched onto my son."

"Very well, Mr. Alfano, I'll look into the matter. I'll do it for Orlando and Dana, but you're going to be footing the bills."

He promised to have his secretary in California call Hazel tomorrow with the credit card information for my retainer and to provide anything else we requested. I asked him to e-mail color photos of the two men. If they were as close as he believed, there would be a few around somewhere. He also gave me his son's cell and pager numbers.

After hanging up I tapped my desk blotter with a gold and onyx letter opener fashioned into a miniature toledo blade. I sighed aloud. The Alfano case had all the hallmarks of developing into a nightmare. Working for attorneys was easier; they understood the process. Private individuals had a warped idea of what a PI did, which was nothing more or less than gathering information. But I was committed, so I might as well make the best of it.

I returned to the visual meditation of the landscape outside my window. As nature's glow dimmed, manmade lights came alive: amber lampposts, white fluorescents, flamboyant neons, yellow vehicle headlights reflecting off wet pavement, and far in the distance, a tiny spot moving slowly across the sky—one of the aerial trams hauling patrons up Sandia Peak's rugged western escarpment to the restaurant atop the mountain.

By leaning forward I caught the faint, rosy underbelly of a western cloudbank, the lingering legacy of a dead sunset. Was that what had drawn Orlando and Dana to the Land of Enchantment? Spectacular scenery and surreal sunsets? Or was it our rich heritage of Indian and Hispanic art? The two were history majors, and Albuquerque had a long history. It was approaching its three-hundredth birthday, while Santa Fe and many of the nearby Indian Pueblos had longer lifelines.

Beyond my line of sight, the city's original settlement lay to the west where one- and two-storied adobe shops—some ancient and some merely pretending to be—hearkened back to their Spanish colonial roots. Now known as Old Town, it was founded in 1706 by Governor Francisco Cuervo y Valdez as the Villa del Alburquerque—some say Ranchos del Alburquerque. In either case the Spanish colonial outpost was named in honor of New Spain's viceroy in Mexico City. The first *r* of the duke's name disappeared in 1880 with the coming of the railroad to New Town, located two miles east of Hispanic Old Town, a signal the Anglos had successfully wrested the heart, if not the soul, of the community from its founders.

It seemed as though a similar battle was being waged between Dana Norville and Anthony Alfano for the heart and soul of Orlando. Papa Alfano had given me cell phone *and* pager numbers for his son. He kept his pup on a short leash—or tried to. Not only that, but the old man had checked Norville out at the first signs of a budding friendship between the two.

I'd bet Alfano was accustomed to throwing his weight around, railroading or buying whomever he wanted, including his son. My instinctive dislike of the homophobic bully made me wonder how far he would go to "turn his son around." Maybe Orlando went on the run to get out from under the thumb of his tyrannical patriarch.

After spinning back to the desk, I went on the hunt for information over the Internet.

According to Dun & Bradstreet, the Alfano Vineyards' net worth was somewhere around $100 million. Although California is notoriously anal-retentive about releasing its criminal records, the Superior Court websites I searched revealed nothing on Alfano. That only meant he wasn't a known murderer, rapist, or kidnapper. He would have bought his way out of anything less than that.

Orlando, on the other hand, had a sheet in Los Angeles. From the limited information available, it looked to be nothing more than a couple of disturbing the peace charges. Norville's record was about the same, leading me to believe they had been activists in their early university days. Maybe they met while agitating for some cause or the other. Gay rights? Voting rights?

There was no answer at their room in the uptown Sheraton. Well, no surprise there. The call to the kid's cell phone went to a message center. I left a callback on the pager without much hope. Things are never that easy.

I had finished dictating instructions for the Alfano contract and was reaching to snap off my old-fashioned, green-shaded banker's lamp when the telephone rang again. Maybe I'd caught a break.

I hadn't, but the sound of Paul Barton's baritone sent my energy level soaring.

"You still at work?" he asked.

"Just finishing up. How about meeting somewhere for a late dinner?"

A deep chuckle. "Meet me at 5229 Post Oak Drive NW."

"You're home?"

"Yep. And I have a surprise for you."

"Let me guess—green chili stew and warm, buttered tortillas. Uh… what's for dessert?"

"I'll leave that to your imagination." He hung up in the middle of a wicked laugh.

DON TRAVIS is a man totally captivated by his adopted state of New Mexico. Each of his mystery novels features some region of the state as prominently as it does his protagonist, a gay ex-Marine, ex-cop turned confidential investigator. Don never made it to the Marines (three years in the Army was all he managed) and certainly didn't join the Albuquerque Police Department. He thought he was a paint artist for a while, but ditched that for writing a few years back. A loner, he fulfills his social needs by attending SouthwestWriters meetings and teaching a weekly writing class at an Albuquerque community center.

Facebook: Don Travis
Twitter: @dontravis3

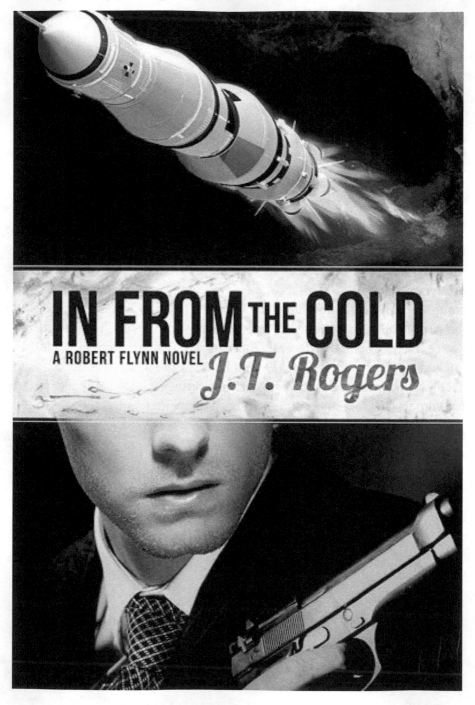

Mystery/Suspense from DSP Publications

IN FROM THE COLD

A ROBERT FLYNN NOVEL

J.T. Rogers

A Robert Flynn Novel

Robert Flynn abandoned a sterling military career when his best friend and fellow soldier, Wesley Pike, died under his command. More than a decade later, Flynn's quiet life is disturbed by the troubles of a fledgling CIA and Alexander Grant, a flashy agent with a lot to prove. As the space race between the United States and the Soviets heats up and the body count rises, the two men fight to find common ground. Grant knows Flynn believes in the cause, but all Flynn sees is the opportunity to fail someone like he failed Wes. An attack by a Soviet agent spurs Flynn to action and a reluctant association with the agency, and tilts Flynn's world on its axis with a shocking discovery: Wesley Pike may be alive and operating as a Soviet assassin.

With Grant to bankroll the operation, his superiors looking the other way, and Flynn's hard-earned peace officially forfeit, Flynn reunites his old team with the singular goal of finding Wes. But they get more than they bargained for—Wes is amnesiac and dangerous, brainwashed into becoming the perfect weapon. Flynn struggles to reach his friend, lead his team, and navigate his charged relationship with Grant—something neither of them expected and aren't sure how to parse—while coming to grips with his long-buried feelings for Wes.

www.dsppublications.com

Mystery/Suspense from DSP Publications

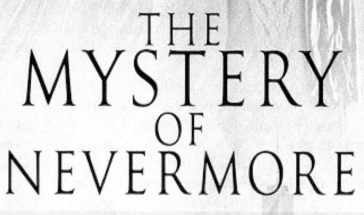

THE MYSTERY OF NEVERMORE

SNOW & WINTER: BOOK ONE

C.S. POE

Snow & Winter: Book One

It's Christmas, and all antique dealer Sebastian Snow wants is for his business to make money and to save his floundering relationship with closeted CSU detective, Neil Millett. When Snow's Antique Emporium is broken into and a heart is found under the floorboards, Sebastian can't let the mystery rest.

He soon finds himself caught up in murder investigations that echo the macabre stories of Edgar Allan Poe. To make matters worse, Sebastian's sleuthing is causing his relationship with Neil to crumble, while at the same time he's falling hard for the lead detective on the case, Calvin Winter. Sebastian and Calvin must work together to unravel the mystery behind the killings, despite the mounting danger and sexual tension, before Sebastian becomes the next victim.

In the end, Sebastian only wants to get out of this mess alive and live happily ever after with Calvin.

www.dsppublications.com

For more
great fiction
from

DSP PUBLICATIONS

⟞⟝

visit us online.
WWW.DSPPUBLICATIONS.COM